PK ROMANCE

3 2487 00246 8636

P9-BZN-263

STACKS

WITHDRAWN

FAMILY MAN

Also by Jayne Ann Krentz
in Thorndike Large Print ®

Perfect Partners

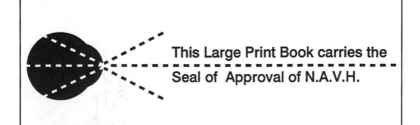

This Large Print Book carries the
Seal of Approval of N.A.V.H.

FAMILY MAN

JAYNE ANN KRENTZ

Thorndike Press • Thorndike, Maine

Library of Congress Cataloging in Publication Data:

Krentz, Jayne Ann.
  Family man / Jayne Ann Krentz.
    p. cm.
  ISBN 1-56054-604-2 (alk. paper : lg. print)
  1. Large type books. I. Title.
[PS3561.R44F3   1993]   92-35978
813'.54—dc20   CIP

This book is a work of fiction. Names, characters, places and incidents are either products of the author's imagination or are used fictitiously. Any resemblance to actual events or locales or persons, living or dead, is entirely coincidental.

Thorndike Large Print® Romance Series edition published in 1993 by arrangement with Pocket Books, a division of Simon & Schuster, Inc.

Cover photo by Thayer Smith.

The tree indicium is a trademark of Thorndike Press.

This book is printed on acid-free, high opacity paper. ∞

FAMILY
MAN

CHAPTER ONE

Technically speaking, Luke Gilchrist was not a bastard. But despite his legitimate heritage, he had been cast in the role thirty-six years ago on the day of his birth, and he had played the part to the hilt ever since.

Gilchrists were nothing if not dramatic about everything they did, Katy Wade reminded herself as she got out of her car. It would be easy to laugh at them if it were not for the fact that they could be so damn dangerous.

Katy resolutely picked up her briefcase and walked toward the front porch of the old, weather-beaten house. Luke Gilchrist lounged in the doorway, waiting for her the way a hawk waits for a mouse to emerge from its burrow. He was not alone. A massive black dog of indeterminate breed waited with him. The dog carried a large metal feeding dish clamped in its teeth.

Katy had never met Luke, but she had been surrounded by Gilchrists for years, and she knew the species well. She would have recognized this particular member of the family anywhere. As she had confided to her brother and her secretary, the Gilchrist clan reminded her of a coven of tall, elegant witches and warlocks.

It was not just the dominant family traits of jet-black hair, aristocratic features, and distinctive green eyes that had put the notion into Katy's head. It had more to do with the underlying aura of grimness she often sensed in them. It was a strange, rather depressing darkness that lay just below the surface.

As far as Katy was concerned, Gilchrists were, by nature, extremists. They were either ice cold or scalding hot. For them there was rarely any serene middle ground.

Gilchrists seethed. They brooded. They could easily become obsessed with getting their own way. They were capable of nursing grudges for years.

They were also intelligent, even brilliant, as Luke was reputed to be, but they had no interest in the lighter side of life. For them everything was passion or anguish, victory or defeat. Katy could not imagine a Gilchrist in a playful mood.

The only time Gilchrists appeared to experience an emotion that even vaguely

8

resembled happiness was when they were talking about money or revenge.

Katy had had occasion to give the matter a great deal of thought during the past few years, but she honestly did not know what caused the absence of light she sensed in the members of the Gilchrist family. Sometimes she thought it was a result of their ambitious natures. At other times she decided it was some weird genetic thing. Then there were occasions when she was convinced the family's problems stemmed simply from the years of iron-fisted rule it had endured under the clan's matriarch, Justine Gilchrist.

All Katy knew for certain was that she had been well treated by Justine, and she was deeply indebted to her. That did not mean, however, that Katy was not looking forward to escaping Gilchrist clutches at the earliest possible moment. That moment was, at long last, on the horizon. It was nearly within her reach. But first she had to persuade the clan's chief warlock to return to the bosom of his family.

Luke Gilchrist, although he did not know it, was Katy's ticket to freedom.

She eyed him cautiously as she approached the porch, aware of her growing sense of unease. It was ridiculous to feel this way, she thought. She was accustomed to dealing with Gilchrists. The trick was not to take them as seriously as they took themselves.

But for some reason this particular Gilchrist was having an unexpected effect on her senses. Perhaps it was simply because she needed him. Her own future was tied to his now.

Luke was typical of his clan in that he exhibited a predatory grace. Because she was well acquainted with the family legends surrounding him, Katy knew he was thirty-six years old, eight years her senior. There were already a few silver shards in the black depths of his hair.

The green ice in his eyes had probably been there since his birth.

To Katy, who stood a mere five feet, four inches, Gilchrists were annoyingly tall. And this one was the tallest specimen she had seen, six-one or -two at least. When she got closer he was definitely going to loom over her.

Katy hated being loomed over.

As she approached the steps she could not help but notice how Luke resembled the large black dog that hovered beside him. Both were powerfully muscled and cold-eyed. Of the two, Katy decided, she would rather face the dog in a dark alley. The animal appeared a trifle more reasonable than his master.

Katy glanced warily at the evil-eyed dog as she reached the bottom step. Then she looked up at the man who stood waiting in the shadowed doorway. This entire experience was getting downright creepy, she thought. Talk about atmosphere. But then, Gilchrists always went in for atmosphere.

The wind howling behind her was driving a storm in off the sea. The waves below the lonely, windswept bluff were already churning into white foam. The rain sweeping across the ocean would hit land any minute.

It had been a long drive from Dragon Bay on the Washington coast north of Seattle to this desolate section of Oregon. Nevertheless, Katy suddenly could not wait to get back into her car and scurry home. She did not care if she had to drive all night. She wanted this unpleasant expedition completed as soon as possible.

"I assume you're Luke Gilchrist," Katy stated. She had learned long ago to be assertive around Gilchrists. They tended to turn lesser mortals into road kill without even noticing the thump.

"I'm Gilchrist," Luke said. "Who the hell are you?"

"Katy Wade, your grandmother's personal assistant." Katy tightened her grip on her briefcase and tried not to notice the way his

11

dark voice ruffled her nerve endings. What was the matter with her? she wondered. Gilchrists never had this effect on her.

"Ah, Ms. Wade," Luke drawled softly. "I thought you might show up sooner or later."

"I've been trying to reach you for weeks, Mr. Gilchrist. I've left no less than twelve messages on your answering machine. I also sent four Express Mail letters and two telegrams. I know you received the letters and the telegrams. I have receipts showing that they were delivered. You signed for them."

"So?" Luke propped one sleek shoulder against the doorjamb and regarded her with the patented Gilchrist vampire stare.

Katy had to admit that Luke did the look better than anyone else in the family. She found his alarming green eyes far more disturbing than those of the rest of the clan.

There was something literally mesmerizing about his gaze. Katy had a sensation of vertigo, as if she were about to fall into pools of emerald fire. A curious thread of unfamiliar excitement began to uncoil within her.

Desperately she tried to focus on something besides his eyes and wound up examining his attire.

He was dressed in a snug-fitting black crew-neck sweater, black chinos, and low black boots. The clothes emphasized the natural elegance of his lean frame. All Gilchrists seemed to have an affinity for the color that best suited their difficult personalities. They all favored black.

And they all had nice white teeth.

"So, you have not given me the courtesy of a response, Mr. Gilchrist." Katy held tendrils of her wind-whipped red hair out of her eyes as she glowered up at him.

"I never respond to people who call on behalf of Justine Gilchrist or Gilchrist, Inc." His eyes raked her from the top of her red head to the toes of her very yellow high heels. "Nothing personal."

Katy felt herself blushing furiously under his intent examination. For an instant she was certain there was something disturbingly sensual about the way he was watching her. In the next breath she told herself it had to be her imagination. No Gilchrist would ever be attracted to her. She was definitely not their type.

And they certainly weren't hers.

At that moment the dog, which stood nearly thigh-high to its master and had a broad head that reminded Katy of a snake's, whined hungrily. The beast's lips curled around the bowl clamped in its teeth. Saliva dripped from its mouth.

Katy got hold of her scattered senses and

13

squared her shoulders. "Look, Mr. Gilchrist, would you mind if I came inside? It's starting to rain."

She started boldly up the steps, knowing that if she waited politely for an invitation, she would probably end up standing outside for the duration of the conversation. Gilchrists were quite capable of exercising a near-lethal charm on occasion, but they only did so when it suited them. Katy guessed Luke Gilchrist didn't consider her worth the effort.

Luke and his dog both hesitated as she strode toward them. Then with a shrug Luke stepped back into the hall.

"What the hell. You're here now, and you don't look like the type to leave without a struggle." Luke glanced down at the dog. "Out of the way, Zeke. Looks like the lady's coming inside."

Zeke gave Katy a glowering glance. He whined softly one last time, displaying enormous fangs. Then he reluctantly turned and padded down the hall. He vanished around the corner into what must have been the living room.

"Why does he carry that dish around like that?" Katy asked uneasily.

"Zeke never goes anywhere without his dish."

"I see. What type of dog is he?"

"Damned if I know. He wandered into the yard a couple of years ago and stayed. He's got most of the qualities I require in a housemate. He doesn't make a lot of noise, doesn't have to be entertained, and doesn't borrow my stuff."

"Yes, well, I shall try not to be overwhelmed by the gracious hospitality the two of you are extending." Katy sailed briskly through the door and set her leather briefcase down on the ancient linoleum floor. She started unfastening the buttons of her sunshine-yellow jacket.

She had worn a yellow silk blouse and a businesslike, pencil-slim green skirt for this interview. It had been impossible to guess precisely how to dress for a confrontation with Justine's mysterious grandson, but Katy had known enough about Gilchrists in general to wear her highest heels.

"You're wasting your time, you know," Luke said.

"I'll be the judge of that." She pointedly held out the bright yellow jacket.

Luke eyed the splash of sunshine in her hand with obvious distaste. He made no move to take it from her. "No reason to hang it up. You won't be here long. Toss it over a chair in the front room."

Katy gritted her teeth and folded her jacket

over her arm. She picked up her briefcase and followed her unwilling host down the hall. Luke Gilchrist was even more impossible than she had been led to believe.

Then again, what had she expected from a man who had not bothered to have any real contact with his grandmother, uncle, and cousins since the day he was born? His father, Thornton Gilchrist, had defied Justine to marry Luke's mother, Cleo, and the rest of the family had referred to Luke as "the Bastard" ever since his conception.

He certainly fit the title.

Luke had his back to her as he went down the hall, so Katy took the opportunity to examine him more thoroughly. The impression of height that she had had when she first saw him was slightly misleading. Maybe he was only five-eleven or possibly six feet, after all. No big deal, she told herself. Her seventeen-year-old brother, Matthew, was nearly that tall.

But there was a breadth to Luke's shoulders and a hard, lean quality about the rest of him that was worlds apart from Matt's youthful physique. It was the difference between boy and man, and that difference was spelled *power*.

Luke's sleek, flat-stomached body would have looked good on a young warrior, Katy

16

decided, but his eyes were those of an old sorcerer. She shivered for no apparent reason.

Behind Katy the front door shuddered as the Pacific storm struck in full force. By the time she followed Luke into the shabbily furnished living room the rain was sheeting down the windows. Zeke was sprawled on the floor near the fire. His bowl was lying next to him. He opened one eye when Katy appeared, then promptly closed it.

"Have a seat." Luke picked up a pile of *Wall Street Journal*s that had been stacked on an armchair. He tossed them down onto a coffee table that was already littered with recent issues of *Fortune, Barron's,* and a variety of small, independent financial newsletters.

"Thank you." Katy sat down cautiously, not wanting to raise the cloud of dust she feared was embedded in the threadbare cushions.

She glanced covertly around the room as she set down her briefcase. It was hard to believe Luke Gilchrist made money as easily as most people lost it. The room showed no sign of what she knew must have been a considerable income. He certainly didn't bother to spend any of it on his home.

Katy was shocked in spite of herself. She did her best to conceal it. Every Gilchrist

17

she had ever known had a taste for the finer things in life. Other than the black Jaguar she had seen in the drive, there was no evidence that Luke had inherited that particular family trait.

True, this house, which was perched on a bluff overlooking the raw Oregon coast, had a terrific view, but that was about all it had going for it. Luke had clearly not invested a dime toward refurbishing the aging structure.

The furniture appeared to be composed of leftovers from a garage sale. The drapes were floral in pattern, and faded. The flowers on them were no longer recognizable. The fabric must have been at least thirty years old. A seriously stained braided rug lay beneath the wobbly metal legs of the scarred coffee table.

"You've come this far," Luke said as he sprawled gracefully in the sagging armchair across from Katy. "Say what you have to say, and then you can leave."

Katy's mouth tightened. He was making her nervous, but she was not about to let him bully her. Not even Justine was allowed that privilege. "I suspect you have a very good idea of why I'm here, Mr. Gilchrist."

"Call me Luke. I'm sure as hell going to call you Katy." He smiled mockingly. "Zeke and I tend to be casual about that kind of thing."

Katy arched a brow and glanced meaningfully around the decrepit living room. "You're not big on formality, I take it."

"Unlike my grandmother," he agreed.

"What would you know about Justine Gilchrist's attitudes toward such matters?" Katy retorted. "You don't even know her."

"I met her once. She showed up at the funeral. That was enough. I have no interest in getting to know her any better."

Katy winced inwardly. The last thing she wanted to do was bring up old and painful memories for Luke. She knew his parents and his beautiful wife, Ariel, had all been killed in a plane crash three years before. They had been on their way to Los Angeles to rendezvous with Luke for the opening of the newest in the successful group of upscale restaurants Luke and his father had established in California.

The restaurants Luke and his father had created on the Gold Coast had been even more successful than the group owned by Luke's grandmother, Justine, in Seattle. There had never been direct competition between the two corporations because they had never gone toe-to-toe in the same cities. But the implicit rivalry had been there, and ev-

19

eryone in the family knew it. Thornton Gilchrist had set out to show Justine he did not need her company or her backing to be successful, and he had proved it. Luke had followed in his father's footsteps.

Luke had sold all of the restaurants he and his father had owned within months after the funeral, however. Rumor had it that he had made a fortune on the sales, even though he had literally dumped the restaurants onto a glutted market. No matter what he did, Luke made money.

He had never built another restaurant. These days he used his remarkable monetary skills to arrange financing for companies in all areas of the food and beverage business. He made it possible for new restaurants to open, chains to expand, companies to merge. From what Katy had been able to glean, Luke orchestrated the deals, took a sizable commission, and vanished from the scene. He had apparently lost all personal interest in the restaurant business, which had been in his family's blood for three generations.

Katy took a deep breath and forced herself to sound conciliatory. It was not easy. She was extremely annoyed with Luke Gilchrist. "You must know by now that your grandmother wishes to end the feud that has existed

20

between herself and your side of the family all these years."

Luke's gaze was expressionless. "There is no feud."

"How can you say that?"

He shrugged. "We don't have what you might call a close relationship, but there is no feud. A feud implies active, ongoing hostilities. I don't care enough about her or the rest of the family to bother doing battle with any of them."

Katy shivered again. It occurred to her that the Gilchrist clan should consider itself fortunate under the circumstances. If the Bastard had gone to war with them, they would have been in even worse shape today than they were already.

"Luke, I'm here to ask you to put the past aside," Katy said quietly. "Your family needs you."

Pain, cold and dark, flashed for an instant in Luke's eyes. Then it disappeared, sinking back into the pit where it had originated. "My family is dead."

Katy looked across the room at Zeke, who was asleep. "I understand your loss. My parents were both killed in a boating accident when I was nineteen. My brother and I are the only ones left in our family."

There was a short, taut silence.

"I'm sorry," Luke said finally. Some of the cold had evaporated from his voice. Again, there was silence. Then Luke said, "How the hell did you wind up working for my grandmother?"

"She was kind enough to give me a decent job when I needed one desperately."

"Is that so?" Luke eyed her with curiosity. "How desperate were you?"

Katy hesitated, sorting through her words. "When my parents were killed there was very little left except a small trust fund that had been set aside for my brother's college education. My father, we discovered, had been teetering on the edge of bankruptcy for two years before his death. After he died everything fell apart financially."

"So you were flat broke?"

"For all intents and purposes, yes. Matt was only eight, and I needed work fast in order to be able to keep him with me. I was only a sophomore in college at the time. I had no real skills to market."

"You're saying my grandmother offered you a job as her personal assistant out of the kindness of her heart? I find that a little hard to believe. Justine Gilchrist has never been known for her charitable nature."

"Well, it's true." Katy straightened determinedly. "And I've tried to repay her by being the best personal assistant she's ever had. Now, then, I'd like to get back to the matter at hand, if you don't mind."

"Save your breath. The answer is no."

"I don't think you entirely understand the situation," Katy said crisply.

"Sure I do. Gilchrist, Inc. is in trouble. My grandmother's health has been failing for the past couple of years. What is she now? Eighty-one? Eighty-two?"

"Eighty-two," Katy agreed stiffly.

"She's been running her own private kingdom for years, and she's finally losing her grip. She's got trouble with at least two of the restaurants. Gilchrist Gourmet, her new line of frozen entrées, has not acquired the market share it needs to survive. Her upper management people are getting restless because there's no heir apparent to take her place. They're starting to worry about their own futures, and the best ones are jumping ship."

Katy swallowed uncomfortably. Everything he had said was true. It was all supposed to be secret, too. "You're very well informed."

"I make my living with information. I use it the way other people use oxygen."

"I see. Well, as you seem to be aware of the financial picture, I won't go into details.

23

I would just like to point out that Gilchrist, Inc. is not simply another faceless corporation. It's a family business. *Your* family business. I should think you would feel some sense of loyalty."

Luke's smile was bleak. "Give me a break."

"All right, so you don't have any fondness for Justine." Katy searched quickly for another angle. "You must feel some sense of responsibility toward your relatives, regardless of the problems that existed between your grandmother and your father."

"I don't." Luke's black brows rose slightly. "Feel any sense of responsibility, that is."

"Good grief, how can you continue to be totally irrational about something that happened before you were even born? The disagreement was between your father and Justine, not you and her."

"It was a little more than a disagreement," Luke said dryly. "My grandmother cut my father out of her will and insulted my mother to her face. Justine labeled me a bastard before I was born and made it clear she did not consider me an heir, let alone a real member of the family. Which is fine with me, by the way. I don't need her money or her floundering restaurant business."

"That much is obvious," Katy said, struggling to keep a reasonable tone. "But that's not the point."

"My father didn't need her money, either," Luke continued as if she hadn't spoken. "He started from scratch after Justine disowned him. Took over the management of a small restaurant in California that was in trouble. He put it back on its feet and then bought it from the owner. After that, there was no stopping him. At the time of his death he and I owned seven of the finest restaurants in California."

"Luke, your grandmother respects your father's accomplishments. She also respects what you've done. Now she and the rest of the family need you. Surely you can find it in your heart to help them. There are a lot of innocent people involved here. How can you turn your back on them?"

"The same way my grandmother turned her back on my parents thirty-seven years ago."

Katy shut her eyes briefly and then lifted her lashes to give Luke a direct look. "No doubt about it. You're definitely Justine's grandson. That streak of pure bullheaded stubbornness obviously runs in the family just like eye color. Good heavens, I don't know why I'm even bothering to try to reason with you."

"You're bothering because Justine Gilchrist pays your salary, and when she says jump, you jump. How long do you intend to go on jumping through hoops for my grandmother, Katy?"

Katy sighed. "You're the last hoop. I hope to be resigning from my position with Gilchrist, Inc. in the near future."

Luke's eyes narrowed. "Finally had enough of working for the old bitch?"

"Do not ever again refer to your grandmother that way in my presence," Katy snapped. She was out of patience with his insufferable rudeness. "Is that quite clear?"

Luke smiled thoughtfully at the outraged reaction he had elicited. He lounged back in his chair and stacked his booted feet on the badly marred coffee table. "She's really got you under her thumb, hasn't she?"

"I told you, I'm grateful to her. As it happens, I've enjoyed working for her."

Luke's expression was derisive. "Come off it."

Katy flushed. "For the most part," she amended with compulsive honesty. "In any event, I assure you she's been extremely generous to me, and I've learned an enormous amount about business that I could not have learned in any other way."

"So why are you so eager to quit your job?"

"I'm leaving Gilchrist, Inc. because I'm ready to pursue my own business plans."

"What plans?" Luke asked with lazy interest.

Katy eyed him warily. She was uncertain how far off the subject she should allow him to drag her. Gilchrists could be devious. "I'm planning to open a small specialty take-out business."

"How quaint." Luke gave her his humorless smile. "I suppose you know the failure rate in the restaurant business."

"I'm aware that it's quite high."

"Something like three out of four go under within two years." Luke sounded almost cheerful for the first time.

Katy was getting close to the end of her patience. "As I'm not paying you a consulting fee, I would appreciate it if you would not give me any advice. If I ever want it, I'll ask for it. In the meantime, you may keep your professional opinions to yourself."

Luke narrowed his eyes. "Do you ever talk to Justine like that?"

"Justine rarely annoys me as much as you're annoying me." Katy rose from the chair and went to the window. Hands clasped behind her back, she stared out at the storm-swept sea and took a calming breath. "I want you to consider what's at stake here before you completely dismiss the notion of helping your family."

"Nothing is at stake. At least nothing that I particularly care about."

"How can you be so callous?" Katy whirled around. She noticed out of the corner of her eye that Zeke had lifted his head and was studying her intently. "Think about your aunt and uncle."

"Why?"

"For heaven's sake, your uncle Hayden is an artist. A very fine one, as it happens. But he has absolutely no talent for running a business like Gilchrist, Inc. He can't possibly step into Justine's shoes."

"I know."

"Maureen, his wife, runs a gallery. She knows art, but she doesn't know the food and beverage business. She can't take on Gilchrist either."

"I can see you're very involved in all this."

"And what about your cousins, Eden and Darren?" Katy continued desperately. "Your grandmother doesn't believe either one of them has the talent to take over the company. As a matter of fact, Eden went through a nasty divorce six months ago and is very depressed."

"Hire a shrink."

"She doesn't need a shrink, she needs the

support of her family," Katy retorted. "And I'm worried about your cousin Darren, too. He's been acting a little strange lately. I think there's something wrong, but he won't talk about it."

"Do you always get this worked up about things?"

"I've got a right to get worked up. I'm supposed to fix this whole mess, and I can't do it alone. This is your family. You should be the one fixing things." Arms crossed beneath her breasts, Katy began pacing the room. "Everything's falling apart. I've got to do something."

"Why don't you just quit your job? That sounds like the easiest way out of the situation," Luke said. He watched her stride up and down the room.

"I can't just quit. Not until I've done my level best to help Justine save Gilchrist, Inc. Don't you understand? I owe her."

"Just because she gave you a job?"

"*Yes.*"

"I've got news for you. Smart employees are not that loyal. Not in this day and age. Doesn't pay."

She turned her head to meet his eyes. "What would you know about loyalty?"

Luke's grim mouth tightened. "I don't need lectures on the subject from you, Katy Wade."

She bit her tongue. "This is getting us nowhere."

"I agree."

"All right. I won't waste any more time appealing to your obviously nonexistent sense of family responsibility. Let's try another approach. Couldn't you consider saving Gilchrist, Inc. a professional challenge?"

Luke's teeth flashed in a brief grin. "You're persistent. I'll give you that. What does it take to deflect you from your flight path?"

"You can't deflect me. I need you."

He arched a brow. "Is that a fact?"

Katy saw the gleam in his eyes, and she felt herself grow hot with embarrassment. What an idiotic slip of the tongue that had been. Being a Gilchrist, he had of course interpreted her words in the worst possible way.

"We all need you. Don't you understand?" Katy thought of the problems awaiting her back in Dragon Bay. She could not give up yet. "It's true we've got Fraser, thank God. I don't know what we'd do without him. But Fraser can't handle this thing alone. Justine won't give him the clout or the authority to run the company on his own."

"Who's Fraser?"

"What?" Katy scowled at him, distracted by the question. "Oh, Fraser. Fraser Stanfield. He's your grandmother's chief operations manager. He's been handling things at corporate headquarters for her ever since Justine began to withdraw from an active management role. Fraser has been terrific, but the bottom line, so far as your grandmother is concerned, is that he's not a Gilchrist."

"Is he as loyal as you are?"

"Well, very nearly. As I said, he's been wonderful. I try to help, but I'm Justine's personal assistant, not her executive assistant. I'm coordinating things as best I can for her, but I'm not a Gilchrist either. Only a Gilchrist can run the company as far as Justine's concerned. You've got to come home, Luke. That's all there is to it. It's your duty."

"I want no part of Gilchrist, Inc., and that's final. If you can't get that through your head, you're even more thick-skulled than you accused me of being," Luke said.

Katy stared at him in angry despair. He meant it, she realized. There was no way to reach him. He had made up his mind, and that was that.

He had a lot in common with his grandmother.

She halted directly in front of him and stood with her hands planted firmly on her hips. "You know something, Luke Gilchrist?

You should be ashamed of yourself."

"Spare me."

"No, I will not spare you. You deserve this, and you're going to get it." A growl from Zeke stopped her for a second. Katy glared at the dog and then switched her gaze back to Luke. "I don't care if you sic that monster on me. I'm going to have my say."

"Don't worry. I don't think Zeke is any match for you."

"Are you finding this amusing?" Katy demanded.

"Not particularly. But it's interesting. You have certainly livened up what might otherwise have been a rather dull afternoon."

"I'll just bet it would have been a dull afternoon," Katy shot back. "I'll bet all your afternoons are dull. Your mornings, too. I won't even get into the subject of your evenings."

"Just as well. They're not much more interesting than the mornings and the afternoons," Luke admitted dryly.

"You think this is one big joke, don't you? Well, I've got news for you, Luke Gilchrist, it's not a joke. A lot is at stake here. You have the chance to salvage everything your grandmother has spent her life building. Future generations of Gilchrists are depending upon you. You alone are in a position to keep a fine company in operation and thereby preserve your family's proud heritage."

"You're beginning to sound like a commercial," Luke said.

"I don't care how I sound. I'm trying to make you understand what you're giving up by refusing to do your duty. Just think of what you could accomplish. Justine Gilchrist has single-handedly created the Gilchrist restaurant dynasty in Seattle. As her grandson and logical heir, you can take her place. You're the only one of the bunch who can."

"I'm breathless."

"You're laughing."

"Maybe. A little. I take back what I said earlier. You're not just interesting, you are definitely amusing."

"The heck with it." Katy threw up her hands in disgust. "Everyone was right when they said there was no point trying to talk to you. I should have listened to them."

"True. But you don't take advice well, do you?"

"Gilchrists do not give advice, they give orders. But you're right. I'm tired of taking them." Katy strode back to the chair where she had been sitting. She snatched up her yellow jacket and briefcase and headed toward the hall without a backward glance.

"Damn," Luke muttered.

She heard his boots on the hardwood floor as he got up quickly to follow her to the door.

"I know you're not paying me for advice," Luke said behind her, "but I'm going to give you some anyway. When you resign from Gilchrist, Inc., get out of the business world entirely. You're too emotional for it."

"Me? Emotional? That's ridiculous coming from someone who can hold a grudge for thirty-six years. You may feel free to shove your advice where the sun doesn't shine, Mr. Gilchrist. I certainly am not interested in it." Katy wrenched open the front door and stepped out onto the porch.

Rain thundered on the porch roof and cascaded off the edge. There were already several puddles between the steps and her car. She was going to get drenched. A fitting end to a wasted day.

"It's pouring out there," Luke said behind her. "Hang on a second and I'll get an umbrella."

"Forget it. I don't want to hang around you or your vicious dog that long."

Katy stepped off the porch and was soaked instantly. Her hair turned into a sodden mass that clung to her neck and hung in front of her eyes.

She had been too angry even to think of putting on her jacket. The rain promptly rendered her yellow silk blouse virtually transparent. The thin fabric of her bra and lacy camisole were not proof against the torrent, either. She realized with deep chagrin that she probably looked half naked.

"Hell," Luke muttered as he followed her down the steps. "This is stupid. You'd better come back inside the house and get dried off before you leave."

Katy swung around to face him. She held her rain-streaked briefcase protectively in front of her so that he could not see the way her nipples were puckering against the wet fabric of her blouse. "I've told you once, and I'll tell you again. When I want your advice, I'll pay for it. Until then, kindly shut up."

"If that's the way you want it." Luke opened the car door for her and offered her a mocking bow. He was just as drenched as she was. His hair hung in wet clumps, and his black sweater was saturated.

There was no way to get into the car without putting aside the briefcase. Katy tossed it angrily onto the front seat. Then she hunched her shoulders and leaned forward in a vain effort to shield herself from Luke's gaze as she climbed behind the wheel. She fumbled quickly with the keys.

"Drive carefully." There was a distinctly sensual curve to Luke's mouth as his gaze went to the front of her blouse.

Katy felt an outrageous thrill shoot through her. This was crazy, she told herself. No man's gaze had ever affected her this way. He was casting some sort of spell on her.

She shoved wet hair out of her eyes and glared up at him. Suddenly the dam holding in all her frustrations burst. "I hope you enjoy your miserable existence up here on this godforsaken bluff. I hope you really love every single minute you spend brooding over your hoard of gold."

"Thanks."

"I hope you get a real kick out of knowing that when your family needed you, you turned your back on them the same way Justine turned her back on your father all those years ago."

"I'll do my best."

Katy was raging now. "I hope you enjoy your revenge, but I warn you, it's going to feel very cold in a few years. Your grandmother has already learned that lesson."

Luke's eyes suddenly glittered with something more dangerous than amusement.

Holding the car door open, he braced his fist on the roof and leaned down.

"Who the hell are you, anyway, Katy Wade, and why are you so concerned about my family's future? You must have done something real bad in a previous life to get yourself appointed guardian angel to the Gilchrist clan."

"I told you, I owe your grandmother. I always pay my debts."

"Just why did she give you that job when you were nineteen? And don't hand me that crap about doing it out of the kindness of her heart. I know too much about her to fall for it."

Katy turned the key violently in the ignition. The engine started with a shriek of protest. "She gave me the job because she's a woman with a strong sense of family pride and responsibility. She saw an opportunity to make up for what your father did to my mother, and she took it."

Luke went still. "What the devil are you talking about?"

"Haven't you figured it out? My mother was the woman your father stood up at the altar when he decided to elope with his secretary."

37

CHAPTER
TWO

Luke braced his hands on the porch railing and watched until Katy Wade's car vanished from sight. Then he swore softly, turned, and stalked back into the house to change his wet clothes.

Zeke, who had been smart enough not to go rushing out into the rain, was waiting at the far end of the hall. He gave Luke an inquiring look over the rim of his dish.

"I guess that answers the question about the lady who was leaving all those damn messages on the answering machine," Luke said to the dog. "I can now state with unequivocal certainty that Ms. Wade is a genuine holy terror. A true self-appointed Gilchrist guardian angel. Someone should have told her a long time ago that on good days Gilchrists eat angels for breakfast."

The first messages on the answering machine had caught Luke's attention because the warm, feminine voice had been infused with cheery charm. Luke had played them back a couple of times before erasing them. The nights could get long in his aerie by the sea. The sound of a woman's voice was not unwelcome.

By the time the twelfth message had been recorded, however, the charm had vanished. In its place was a feisty determination that had been just as interesting in its own way. The lady was obviously the sort who made a point of seeing a task through to completion. She would not give up until she had either reached her goal or been knocked out of the fight. That kind of gutsy fortitude could spell trouble, Luke knew, but he had to acknowledge a certain grudging respect for it.

Katy's letters and the telegrams had been equally fascinating. The first of them had been full of enthusiasm and vitality. They had projected a boundless optimism that had made Luke feel ancient and cynical.

She had tried almost everything to convince him to come to Dragon Bay. The one thing she had not done was whine. Luke liked that. He could not stand whiners.

Toward the end the letters had turned into fierce little lectures on the subject of family honor and responsibility. The last telegram had been no less than a ringing call to arms:

THINK OF FUTURE GENERATIONS STOP
DON'T BE AFRAID TO TAKE UP THE
CHALLENGE STOP YOU CAN DO IT STOP.

Luke had known when he received that one that the next step was probably going to be a personal visit from Katy Wade herself. He had found himself looking forward to it. He wanted to see if the lady matched her voice.

Now his curiosity was satisfied, he thought in disgust as he peeled off his soaked sweater. Katy Wade was everything he had suspected from her letters. She was a bright-eyed crusader who had, thanks to an unusual set of circumstances, assumed the thankless task of saving a bunch of Gilchrists.

She was young, probably only twenty-seven or twenty-eight at the most. Luke scowled. She was far too young and inexperienced to have the responsibility for saving Gilchrist, Inc. on her shoulders.

And she was a redhead.

Luke had not guessed that from her messages and letters, but somehow he was not surprised. He had never been fond of red hair. Still, he had to admit that the sunrise color of Katy's hair suited her. He had liked the way it curved in at her chin, framing her delicate features and emphasizing the deep

40

blue of her eyes.

Luke rather wistfully recalled a few other details he'd noted thanks to a wet silk blouse and a snug-fitting skirt. Katy had a neat, subtly curved body. A good body. Healthy. Strong. Vital. *Female.*

There was an oddly restrained, rather naïve sensuality about her that he had found unexpectedly disturbing.

More than disturbing. He had a feeling he was going to have trouble getting to sleep tonight because of Katy Wade. And she was not even his type.

No doubt about it, he had spent too many nights alone here during the past three years. Odd he had not realized it until today.

Luke ran his fingers through his hair to get rid of the excess moisture. Then he pulled a black cotton shirt out of the closet and shrugged into it.

She was not really pretty, he thought. He frowned as he went down the hall to his study. *Not compellingly beautiful the way Ariel had been.*

But somehow, what with all the feminine vitality Katy exuded, he hadn't particularly noticed the absence of classical perfection in her features.

Still, she was not like Ariel. And if he were ever to remarry, he would definitely want a woman like his first wife.

Exotic, witchy, mysterious Ariel with her long ebony hair and pale silken skin. Even now, three years after her death, she sometimes stole into his dreams, trying to seduce him once more.

Luke had been certain from the moment he first saw Ariel that she was his natural mate. The attraction had been mutual and instantaneous. They had had only eighteen months together before she was killed. During that time they had loved together and fought together in a torrid, simmering whirlwind of all-consuming passion.

It had come as a shock to Luke that in addition to love, lust, and possessiveness he had experienced an excruciating jealousy with Ariel. That emotion was unexpected because Luke had grown up with the example of his parents' marriage. Thornton and Cleo had been bonded for life, and each of them knew it. Each had trusted the other completely, and Luke had taken such intimate bonding between man and wife for granted. He had expected it in his own marriage.

But Ariel had almost seemed to enjoy tormenting him at times. It was as if his passionate jealousy aroused her. He did not believe she had ever actually been unfaithful during their short marriage, but she had made no secret of the fact that she delighted in the admiration of other men.

Deep down inside Luke sometimes wondered what would have happened if the marriage had lasted five, ten, or twenty years. No other woman had ever had the power to arouse the violent emotions in him that Ariel had. On the other hand, no other woman had ever been able to suck him into a vortex of desire the way Ariel had, either.

The memories of the nights spent with Ariel in his arms still haunted him.

Yes, he might remarry one of these days, he decided, but never a woman like Katy. He knew what he wanted and needed in a wife. He needed someone like Ariel, a woman whose dark passions matched his own.

The problem was that it was highly unlikely he would ever encounter another woman like Ariel.

Luke walked into his study and sat down at his desk. He gazed at the blank computer screen for a long moment but did not immediately reach out to switch on the machine.

Now that he had started thinking about what he required in a wife, he could not seem to stop. Katy Wade had done this to him, he decided grimly. Her presence in his house had somehow brought the old, bone-deep hungers to the surface.

"Shit," Luke muttered. It was going to be a long night.

Zeke padded into the study with his dish in his mouth. He dropped the metal bowl on the floor near Luke's chair and flopped down next to it. Luke reached out and idly rubbed the big dog behind his ears. Zeke rumbled with satisfaction.

When Zeke had first appeared in Luke's front yard the dog had been scrawny and desperate. It was obvious he had been abused, starved, and abandoned. The last thing Zeke had wanted was to be touched by a human being. But he had also been hungry. Very, very hungry.

Luke had understood and respected the courage it had taken for Zeke to approach the house. Zeke had not begged, but he seemed to have realized that he had reached the end of the line. The dog had just stood there shivering in the rain, waiting with an air of stoic challenge for whatever fate held in store.

Luke had found the old metal dish, filled it up with canned chili, and put it out in the yard. The chili had vanished within seconds, and Luke had filled the bowl a second time.

One thing had led to another, and a pattern was established. Zeke disappeared during the day and returned in the evenings for a bowl of chili. Six weeks after the dog's arrival a freezing rainstorm struck the high bluff. Luke had opened the front door and found Zeke huddled on the porch, the bowl in his mouth.

Luke stood back and held open the door. Zeke padded warily inside and found a place by the fire. He had been there ever since.

"You and I are definitely two of a kind, Zeke. We don't need lectures on family responsibility from a self-righteous little redhead."

Zeke looked up at him.

"Okay, *I* don't need lectures from her," Luke amended. "You can make your own decisions."

Zeke rumbled agreement and sprawled on the floor.

Luke pushed the distracting image of Katy Wade out of his mind and punched up the spreadsheet he had been working on that morning. He forced himself to concentrate on his latest consulting project. It was a routine task resembling countless other such projects he had undertaken in recent years. He should be able to finish off this job tonight or tomorrow morning at the latest, he thought.

And when he was finished he would write his report for the client and collect another hefty fee to add to the treasure Katy Wade had accused him of hoarding.

Luke eyed the screen full of numbers. Normally he entered the clean, clear world of computerized data with a sense of profound relief. He could lose himself in the universe of disembodied information that was always at his fingertips.

There was no pain in this world, no past and no future. When he was working he moved in an eternal present, correlating facts, aligning data, making decisions. For the past three years Luke had spent almost all of his waking time in this computer universe. He had learned to manipulate the information he found there the way a sorcerer manipulated the words in an incantation.

But today he could not seem to get into his work. He kept feeling as if he were crouched over a pile of gold instead of his keyboard.

So he made money at what he did. So what? Making money was second nature to him. It was like swimming or riding a bike. Once he had learned the trick of it, he never forgot it.

His mother had always claimed the talent was in his genes. She called it the Gilchrist curse and claimed it had descended from his grandmother to his father and then to Luke.

There was no denying that, as a team,

Luke and his father had been unbeatable. Together the banished Gilchrists had built a restaurant empire in California that had outstripped the Northwest-based Gilchrist, Inc.

And then, in one terrible instant three years ago, Luke's whole world had been shattered. The jet that had crashed on the Los Angeles runway had carried everything that had been important in his life. Ariel and his parents were gone in the blink of an eye.

Afterward there had not seemed much point in owning an empire.

But the habit of making money was hard to break. Luke had gone north to Oregon and found a place where he could retreat from the world and all he had lost. He sat alone in his house on the cliffs overlooking the sea, went into his computer, and made money. It gave him something to do with his days, which would otherwise have been intolerably bleak.

Unfortunately, it did not fill up the nights.

Two hours later Luke got up from the computer and went into the kitchen. Zeke picked up his dish and ambled along to watch Luke scrub a couple of baking potatoes, stab them with a fork, and put them into the oven.

Luke liked baked potatoes, which was for-

47

tunate, because his cooking skills were extremely limited. He could heat a can of soup, microwave frozen vegetables, scrub potatoes, and that was about it. Not particularly impressive accomplishments for a man whose family had been in the restaurant business for three generations.

But then, as his father had once explained, no Gilchrist ever cooked any more than was absolutely necessary. It was a family tradition.

The word "family" caused Luke's back teeth to clamp together. He closed the oven door, poured himself a glass of cabernet, and wondered if the official Gilchrist guardian angel could cook. He figured she probably could. She looked like the wholesome type who would be at home in the kitchen.

Luke smiled as he recalled the way Katy had clutched her briefcase in front of her as if it were a battle shield. No doubt about it, Ms. Wade was perfect personal assistant material: faithful, loyal, and devoted to the end.

Luke sipped his wine and contemplated Katy's future with moody fascination. She did not stand a chance of holding Gilchrist, Inc. together by herself. Not even with the help of Fraser Stanfield, whoever the hell he was.

Gilchrist, Inc. was a true family business in the old-fashioned sense of the term. If no other Gilchrist was smart enough or strong enough to step into Justine Gilchrist's shoes, the end was in sight. That was why the company's upper management was getting nervous. They knew damn well the five Seattle restaurants and Gilchrist Gourmet would have to be sold if Justine had indeed lost her grip.

Selling off the assets was the only reasonable course of action the guardian angel and her friend Stanfield could take. Luke wondered if Katy understood that.

Of course, even if she did, Justine Gilchrist would undoubtedly forbid the sale. Luke remembered his father's description of Justine: Boadicea in her knife-wheeled chariot ready to take on the Romans and anyone else who got in her way.

Justine Gilchrist had fought long and hard to build Gilchrist, Inc. And she was just as stubborn as Luke's father had been. She would never consent to selling the business to outsiders.

Which meant there was no good alternative available to Katy Wade.

Which meant disaster for the redoubtable Ms. Wade, because she clearly was not one who would quit.

Not that it was any concern of his, Luke decided. If Katy could not see the writing on the wall, that was her problem. Too bad she felt indebted to Justine Gilchrist. A smart personal assistant in Katy's position would abandon ship real fast at this point.

But something told Luke that Katy was the type to go down on the bridge.

She would go down fighting all the way, too.

He strolled back down the hall to the study. The computer was humming softly. The sound soothed Luke. He got rid of the calculations he had been doing for his client and punched up a familiar file.

He was not certain why he had started keeping tabs on Gilchrist, Inc. a few months ago. Curiosity or sheer boredom, probably. After he had started getting the messages from Katy Wade he had paid more attention to the information he had quietly been collecting.

Luke sat down and propped his heels on the desk. He leaned back, took a swallow of wine, and contemplated the facts displayed on the glowing screen.

He wondered how long it would take the angel and her friend Stanfield to figure out that the losses they were suffering at two of the restaurants were due to more than just a temporary downturn in the Northwest economy.

The pattern that was taking shape was an old and familiar one. Someone was systematically and cleverly bleeding cash out of Gilchrist's Grill and Gilchrist's of Bellevue.

Things looked and felt wrong at Gilchrist Gourmet, too, although the problems there did not fit a pattern yet. There were just *problems.* Far too many of them. The kind that crippled a business. If Gilchrist Gourmet kept sliding downhill the way it had been doing for the past six months, Justine would be lucky to sell it at a fraction of its original value.

No doubt about it, Katy Wade was going to need more than a pair of wings and a halo to save Gilchrist, Inc. She was going to need the devil's own luck.

CHAPTER THREE

Katy stood at the window of Justine Gilchrist's glass-walled living room and watched the fog roll silently in off the ocean. The gray mist crept inevitably closer, slowly but surely consuming the world. In another few minutes the beach below the window would disappear. Then the magnificent old mansion that was Justine's home would be lost in a gray void.

Normally Katy enjoyed the drama of incoming fog, but today it disturbed her. The relentless approach of the gray void made her think of the disaster that was threatening to overtake Gilchrist, Inc.

"You tried, Katy," Justine Gilchrist said. "It was good of you to do so, but the outcome is not entirely unexpected. It's obvious my grandson is just as proud and unforgiving as his father was."

Katy turned her head to look at the regal, silver-haired woman seated in the wingback chair. At eighty-two, Justine Gilchrist was still a striking member of the clan.

In spite of her recent problems her shrewd green eyes were young in her patrician face, and her figure was trim. Today she was wearing a black silk blouse and a black skirt. A simple strand of pearls graced the neckline of her blouse.

Lately an assortment of ailments had begun to plague Justine. None of them appeared to be imminently life-threatening, but during the past two years they had robbed her of the driving energy that had enabled her to build and guide Gilchrist, Inc. for nearly six decades.

"I'm sorry, Justine. I don't think I handled the interview with Luke very well. I'm afraid I lost my temper."

"Don't blame yourself." Justine smiled wearily. "You are so very open and forthright, my dear. Just like your grandfather, Richard. He always said exactly what he thought, too. You always knew where you stood with him. I have missed him these past few years. I owe him more than I can ever repay."

Katy thought wistfully of her loud, laughing, boisterous grandfather. Richard Quinnell had been a self-made man in every way.

Lacking a formal education, money, and family, he had come west to make his fortune.

He and his wife had opened a fish-and-chips restaurant on the Seattle waterfront and had prospered quickly. The Quinnells had been in a position to help the young Justine Gilchrist when she had been left widowed and alone in the world with her two small sons and her husband's failing waterfront café. The Quinnells had kept her afloat financially until Justine, working night and day, had managed to turn a profit.

The friendship between the Quinnells and Justine had endured over the years in spite of a friendly rivalry between the two growing restaurant chains. When Justine's son, Thornton, had asked Katy's mother, Deborah, to marry him, Justine had made no secret of her satisfaction. She had even broached the possibility of a merger between the two restaurant corporations. Richard Quinnell, who had recently lost his wife, agreed.

The marriage and the merger had been big news in Seattle's business community. The combined events had filled the papers, and the guest list for the wedding had been impressive.

When Thornton Gilchrist failed to show up at the church, Justine was deeply ashamed. The Quinnells and the Gilchrists had gone their separate ways after the debacle. Both businesses continued to thrive, but there was no more talk of a merger.

When Richard Quinnell had collapsed from a heart attack sixteen years ago, his West Coast chain of innovative fast food restaurants had been on the verge of going into the international market.

Unfortunately, Richard's successor, Katy's father, had not had Quinnell's magic touch when it came to running a business empire. Under Crawford Wade's control the Quinnell chain had floundered, eventually going bankrupt.

"I probably should have been more diplomatic with your grandson." Katy turned back to the scene outside the window. "But he really annoyed me, Justine."

"I can imagine."

Katy considered the approach she had taken with Luke, searching for flaws in her plans. It was true she had lost her temper with him, but he had deserved it.

"You wouldn't believe how he's living," she said. "He just sits there all alone in that awful old house and makes money day after day. He doesn't even seem to be enjoying it. The place needed painting, and the furniture was old and shabby. As far as I can tell, his only friend is a large, vicious-looking dog."

"Good Lord." Justine sounded genuinely

alarmed for the first time. "I do hope he isn't turning into another Howard Hughes. Did you notice if his hair and fingernails were getting overly long?"

Katy smiled wryly. "Don't worry. He hasn't flipped out completely, at least not as far as I could tell. He needed a haircut, but other than that he looked reasonably normal."

For a Gilchrist.

Hah. Who was she kidding? Katy asked herself silently. She had been fascinated by him. Another of those unsettling little chills of sensual awareness went down her spine at the memory of Luke's sorcerer's eyes and coiled grace. She was still having problems dealing with the realization that he had affected her so strongly.

For one thing, she simply did not understand her own reaction to him. Never in her wildest dreams would she have envisioned herself attracted to such a man. And she could not believe he had been attracted to her.

Rumors about his beautiful wife had circulated among the Washington State members of the Gilchrist family at the time of Luke's marriage. Katy had once seen a photograph of the pair in a trade magazine. Luke and Ariel had obviously been perfect for each other, a dark, brooding warlock and his exotic witch of a wife.

"So his inheritance means nothing to him after all." Justine rested her head against the back of the chair. "I must admit I had rather hoped to lure him to us with the promise that I would reinstate him in my will and turn complete control of Gilchrist, Inc. over to him."

Katy cleared her throat. "I did not exactly offer him Gilchrist, Inc., Justine. To be perfectly honest, I didn't tell him that you were willing to put him back in your will, either."

Justine's brows rose slightly. "But I thought that was the whole point of trying the personal approach, my dear. He has steadfastly refused to have anything to do with me, but when he agreed to see you, I was certain we had a foot in the door. He seemed prepared to listen to my proposal delivered through you."

"Well, he didn't exactly agree to see me, either," Katy admitted. "I know I gave you the impression that he had, but the truth was, I got so annoyed with him when he didn't bother to respond to my calls and letters that I just decided to get in the car and drive down to Oregon to confront him."

There was a pregnant pause. "I see," Justine finally murmured. "How did you locate him? All we had was a phone number and a post office box address. Did you hire a private detective?"

"No. I stopped in the town where he keeps the post office box and started asking questions. It wasn't that hard to find him." Not with the distinctive description she had been able to provide thanks to her knowledge of the Gilchrist clan. The attendant at the town's single gas station had been very helpful. *"Tall? Black hair? Looks sorta like one of them Wild West gunslingers? Sure, I know him. He works out at the gym sometimes. Does some kind of weird martial arts stuff, you know? He drives a honey of a black Jag."*

Justine nodded. "You are ever resourceful, my dear. May I ask why, once you were actually face to face with him, you failed to make him my offer?"

"Damn it, Justine, I just couldn't do it." Katy closed one hand into a small fist. "He doesn't deserve to have everything you've worked and fought for turned over to him just like that. He shouldn't come back because you're offering him Gilchrist, Inc. on a silver platter. He should come back because it's his duty to the family."

"You told him that?"

"Yes, I did." Katy raised her chin. "In no uncertain terms."

Justine sighed. "Well, I suppose I can understand why he didn't precisely jump at the offer."

Katy wrinkled her nose. "He's no fool. He must have known that if he came back, he could probably do so on his own terms. I just didn't feel like groveling. And I didn't want him to think you were willing to beg, plead, and bribe him to come back. I guess I messed up, Justine. I'm sorry."

"Don't be too hard on yourself. It is very likely that even if you had told him he was back in my will and that I was quite prepared to — er — grovel, he would still have turned you down."

"I know." Katy straightened her spine. "Justine, we have to talk about the future. We've tried everything we can to get Luke to assume his responsibilities. It's obvious he's not going to do so. Therefore, we must discuss alternatives. Fraser is getting anxious."

"If this is your unsubtle way of telling me we must talk about selling off Gilchrist Gourmet, as Stanfield suggests, you may as well save your breath, Katy." There was a familiar thread of steel in Justine's voice, one that had not been there in a while.

Katy swung around. "The company is facing disaster. You know that as well as I do. Only a Gilchrist has the clout to run things the way you've always run them. You've admitted yourself that you don't have the strength or the desire to continue at the helm."

"I'm tired, Katy."

"I know." Katy looked into Justine's once-fierce eyes and felt a rush of sympathy.

"I've left it too late, haven't I? I should have made arrangements for my successor years ago, but I kept putting it off. A part of me always hoped that Thornton would return."

"I understand, Justine."

"After he was killed I convinced myself that Luke would want to join his family. We're all he has left now. You'd think he'd want to be here with us. I deluded myself into believing it would all come right in the end. But it hasn't, has it?"

Katy stifled a small groan. The note of melodrama in Justine's voice was a familiar one. Gilchrists were good at melodrama. But in this case, Katy had to admit it was warranted. She knew better than anyone that Justine had long harbored the secret hope that Thornton and his family would rejoin the Seattle Gilchrists.

"It looks bad, Justine, but there are moves we can make that will enable us to salvage at least the net worth of the assets before we lose everything the way my father did when Quinnell Restaurants went under."

"I wish you were a Gilchrist," Justine muttered. "I could turn the company over to you."

Katy blinked in surprise. "Thank you, Justine. That's very flattering. But even if I were a member of the family, I couldn't take over Gilchrist, Inc. We both know I don't have the kind of mind-set it takes to run a corporation that size. I don't like that kind of management. I wouldn't be any good at it even if I wanted to do it, which I don't."

"Yes, you would. I think you could do just about anything you decided to do, Katy. But I understand how you feel. You have your own dreams to pursue, and you have every right to do so."

"I want a business of my own," Katy said softly. "Something that's all mine. Something I can run myself. I want to shape its destiny and watch it grow." *And I don't want to have to answer to Gilchrists for the rest of my life, which I most certainly would if I took over Gilchrist, Inc.,* Katy added silently.

Justine's expression was speculative for a moment before it faded back into one of grim resignation. Katy shook her head wryly. They both knew the topic of putting her in charge of Gilchrist, Inc. was moot. Justine would never turn the company over to anyone outside the family.

"I suppose if worse comes to worst, I'll have to consider Darren as a successor. But he simply is not ready for that kind of responsibility." Justine's mouth hardened. "In the meantime, I will never consent to selling off what I created from scratch with my own bare hands."

"All right. What about going public with a stock offering? We could raise capital that way. Hire outside management. Get in a good consulting firm. Just on a temporary basis."

Justine's eyes glittered. "*No.* This is my company. I am not about to turn it over to paid consultants with no sense of history and tradition. This is a family business, and it will stay a family business."

Katy stared helplessly at her employer. "I understand, Justine, but times have changed. You can't run it like a family business any longer. You haven't got a member of the family who is capable of taking your place. At least not yet. Maybe, as you say, your other grandson, Darren, will be able to do it in time. But I agree he's not quite ready."

"Sometimes I think Darren will never be ready to step into my shoes no matter how old he gets," Justine snapped.

"That's not entirely fair, Justine. You must admit he's doing very well managing the new restaurant on Lake Union."

"I'm still not certain I should have let you talk me into giving him that position," Justine grumbled.

"It will be a learning experience for him. Darren wants to be part of the business," Katy said gently.

"Oh, he's ambitious enough, I'll grant you that, but he hasn't got the flair to run an operation the size of Gilchrist." Her mouth twisted bitterly. "Hardly surprising, since his father didn't have it either. My own fault, I suppose. I was a fool to let Hayden dabble with those art lessons when he was a child."

The fact that Justine's second son, Hayden, had been drawn to the art world rather than the world of business had never set well with his mother. Justine had no respect for Hayden's talents, and she made no secret of it.

Unfortunately, in the past few years Justine had come to the conclusion that neither of Hayden's offspring, Darren nor Eden, had inherited her business genius either. Her lack of faith in her two youngest grandchildren had become an ongoing source of friction in the family.

"Justine, there isn't anyone else to take your place," Katy said, exasperated.

"Luke is fully capable of running Gilchrist."

"Well, he doesn't want the job," Katy reminded her gently. "So where does that leave us? There is no one else in the family who can handle it."

Justine gave her a grim smile. "We shall see. I want to think about this problem a bit longer before I make any drastic decisions. There must be a solution."

Katy drew herself up. "There are solutions, but none of them involves that arrogant, mule-headed grandson of yours. I'll be in my office. Let me know when you want to talk about the future."

The fog was at the glass walls of the living room now, shrouding the mansion. Katy walked out of Justine's private suite and into the main hall of the huge house.

She worked off some of her frustration by taking the stairs to the second floor two at a time. At the top of the staircase she turned and strode down the corridor of the mansion's south wing.

The main corporate headquarters of Gilchrist, Inc. were an hour's drive away in downtown Seattle. For the past ten years, however, Justine had ruled her empire from her castle overlooking Dragon Bay. She had until recently made frequent trips into the city, however, so that her management team was assured of close contact. Those visits, along with her fax machines, computers, and telephones, had made it possible for Justine to keep her thumb on the pulse of her kingdom.

But when Justine had begun to retreat from the day-to-day task of running the company, the geographical distance between Dragon Bay and downtown Seattle had seemed to grow. Katy had done her best to conceal Justine's gradual withdrawal from daily operations, but things had gotten to the shaky stage. She could no longer keep giving management excuses for Justine's failure to show her face at headquarters, nor could she continue to pen memos herself under Justine's name. Fraser Stanfield had helped her disguise the dire situation as long as possible, but the company had reached a crisis point.

Katy walked into her office. Her secretary, Liz Bartlett, looked up at her over the round rims of a pair of reading glasses. She put down the book she had been reading so that Katy saw the title: *Introduction to Short-term Cognitive Therapy.*

Two years ago, the day after Liz turned

forty, her husband had walked out on her. At Katy's urging she had begun taking evening classes at the local community college as a way to meet new people and develop new interests.

To everyone's surprise, including Katy's, Liz had become an enthusiastic professional student. She had sampled everything from Floral Design to Heating and Air Conditioning Systems Repair, and she loved to apply her newfound knowledge.

Katy had not really minded the three months she had spent in an office filled with ever-changing flower arrangements. But disaster had struck when the mansion's ancient furnace had broken down and Liz had insisted on repairing it free of charge. The inhabitants of the big house had been forced to rely on the mansion's fireplaces until a licensed electrician arrived to correct the wiring problem Liz had created.

Fortunately, after that debacle, Liz had concluded she was intellectually more suited to the liberal arts and had moved on to Creative Writing.

Most recently, she had started a course in psychology and had acquired just enough knowledge to be dangerous.

"There you are, Katy," Liz said. "How is Her Highness today?"

"Holding her own."

Liz shook her head sadly. "You know that woman is very close to being in a state of full-blown clinical depression, don't you?"

"She's just a little tired lately, that's all. Any calls?"

"Let's see." Liz picked up a stack of message slips and flipped through them. "Miss Anorexia Nervosa phoned. She wants you to call her ASAP."

Katy groaned. "Eden is not anorexic. She's lost some weight lately because of the trauma of the divorce, that's all."

"She's on the brink of a major eating disorder. Mark my words." Liz picked up another slip. "Maureen called about fifteen minutes ago. She wants a return call as soon as possible, too. A lot of repressed hostility in her tone, as usual."

"She's got a reason to feel hostile," Katy said patiently. "Justine isn't turning Gilchrist over to either of her kids. Any normal mother would be upset."

"There is no such thing as a normal Gilchrist."

"You have a point," Katy admitted. "Anything else?"

"Yep. We heard from the Great Sublimator."

"Hayden is an artist, Liz. I wish you would

stop referring to him as the Great Sublimator. He happens to be doing some of his best work these days."

"That's because he's sublimating the guilt and anger he feels toward his mother," Liz explained cheerfully. "If he wasn't working it all out in those glass sculptures of his, he'd be one sick man."

"As it is, he's one successful artist."

Liz pursed her lips. "You know, I'd like to see the whole family in counseling, including Darren. He's cute as hell, but I sense some anxiety in him due to his inability to prove himself to his grandmother."

Katy grinned in spite of her mood. "Nonsense. Gilchrists don't get anxious, they get mean. And you can forget family counseling. They'd eat the poor counselor alive. What they probably need is a witch doctor."

"I suppose so. Mr. Stanfield has arrived to give you the weekly report, by the way. He's in your office. I think he's getting restless."

"He wants a full briefing on yesterday's disaster. I guess I'd better let him know I blew it."

"What do you want to do about returning these calls?" Liz waved the slips in the air.

"I'll get around to it when I have a few minutes free."

"Gilchrists get hostile when their calls aren't returned in a timely fashion," Liz warned.

"I'll placate the coven when I get a chance." Katy pushed open the door of her inner office and went inside.

Fraser Stanfield was propped against the edge of her desk. He was reading the morning paper, a cup of coffee beside him on the polished wooden surface. He looked up when the door opened.

He took one glance at Katy's flushed cheeks and compressed mouth and smiled wryly. "I take it the big trip south to confront the errant grandson was not a roaring success."

Fraser was a good-looking, likable man in his late thirties. He was also a natural clothes-horse. Everything he put on looked terrific on his athletic frame. His light brown hair had a casual windblown style that gave him the appearance of having just stepped in from a walk on the beach. His dark eyes were warm and friendly and sincere, and his teeth were white beneath his mustache. Put him in a leather bomber jacket and he could have modeled for an armed forces recruitment poster.

"No, it was not," Katy said. She grabbed the coffeepot off the burner and poured herself a cup. Then she went around behind her desk and threw herself into the chair. "For the record, Luke Gilchrist is a cold-blooded, heartless, unfeeling, arrogant rat. The man is pond scum. A snake. Lower than a snake. He is a cruel, callous, stubborn, impossible *bastard*."

"In other words, he didn't fall all over himself when you got down on your knees and pleaded for him to return to the bosom of his family, get reinstated in Justine's will, and take complete control of Gilchrist, Inc. forever, huh? Amazing. The man must be blind."

"Well, I didn't exactly put it to him like that."

Fraser grinned. "That figures. I'll bet you went down there and lectured him on his duties and responsibilities, didn't you? Katy, when are you going to learn you can catch more flies with honey than you can with vinegar?"

"I don't think honey would work with a Gilchrist. They tend to go for blood, and I didn't feel like offering up a ritual sacrifice."

"That's beside the point." Fraser put down the newspaper and moved away from the desk. He shoved his hands into his pockets and went to stand at the window. "The point is, you need him."

"We all need him." Katy leaned back in

her chair and gazed gloomily at the stack of folders on her desk. She was supposed to summarize the various reports and give them to Justine. But why should she bother? she wondered. Justine hardly even glanced at them anymore. "But he isn't coming home, so we're going to have to find an alternative."

"There is no alternative," Fraser said quietly. "Not unless you can get Justine to agree to start selling off the assets. Gilchrist Gourmet has got to go first. It's starting to flounder."

"I know. I'll keep working on it."

Fraser rubbed the back of his neck in a gesture of defeat. "Why not give up and pack it in?"

"I can't. Not yet."

"Eventually we're both going to have to cut our losses with Gilchrist. You know that as well as I do. You want out anyway. You can't keep your personal plans on hold forever."

Katy glanced at his handsome profile and smiled. Fraser had been with Gilchrist, Inc. for the past five years, but she had not gotten to know him well until recently. After Justine had appointed him as her operations manager, Katy had been brought into increasingly frequent contact with Fraser. She was starting to think of him as a friend, and she knew

Justine was relying on him to hold things together at headquarters.

But Fraser was intelligent and ambitious. He had his own future to think of, just as she did. He had responsibility at Gilchrist, Inc., but no real power, and he knew it. Unless things changed, he would have to move on.

"I know, Fraser. But I'm not ready to walk out on Justine just yet. She needs me."

"And you feel you owe her."

"I do owe her."

"Katy, your sense of loyalty does you credit, but it's not realistic."

The intercom buzzed before Katy could respond.

"Katy, Her Highness wants to see you immediately," Liz informed her.

"I was just with her."

"I know. Something's come up." Liz paused for effect. "It seems Luke Gilchrist has arrived unexpectedly."

"*What?*" Coffee slopped over the edge of Katy's cup as she straightened abruptly in her chair. "Are you certain?"

"That's what the housekeeper said a minute ago when she called. Of course, she made it sound like the arrival of one of the Four Horsemen of the Apocalypse, but you know Mrs. Igorson."

"I don't believe it. He's here." Katy released the intercom button and leapt to her feet. "Fraser, we're saved. The stubborn son of a gun came through after all. Everything's going to be all right."

Fraser eyed her. "You really think so?"

"Of course. You heard Liz. Luke Gilchrist is right here in the house. If he's here, it can only be for one reason. He's decided to come home and assume his responsibilities. I've got to get downstairs right away. I'll give you a full report when I get back. I knew he'd do it. I just knew it."

"What do you mean, you knew it? I thought this guy was pond scum." Fraser made a face. "Lower than a snake. Callous and cruel."

"Obviously he's educable." Katy was at the door. She whipped it open and hurried into the outer office. "Hold my calls, Liz. I'll be back in a little while."

"Got it." Liz gave her a strange look. "You really think everything is going to be all right now that the Bastard is here?"

"Everything's going to be perfect," Katy said over her shoulder as she sailed out the door. "And we'd better stop calling him the Bastard."

"Going to be a tough habit to break. I'm a sucker for tradition," Liz called after her.

Katy raced along the south wing corridor

and dashed down the stairs. She was panting for breath by the time she knocked on the door of Justine's private suite.

Mrs. Igorson responded to the knock. A woman of indeterminate years and dour countenance, the housekeeper was built along stout and sturdy lines. She had worked for Justine for nearly two decades.

Katy privately thought Mrs. Igorson was perfectly suited to work in the Gilchrist household. There was something appropriately forbidding about her. It was all Katy could do to resist addressing the poor woman as "Igor."

"About time you got here," Mrs. Igorson muttered. "The Bastard is with her now. I don't like this. I don't like it one bit. I know Mrs. Gilchrist wanted him here, but I have a feeling he's going to be nothing but trouble."

"You've got it backward, Mrs. Igorson. We've already got trouble. The Bastard — I mean Mr. Gilchrist — is going to fix it. By the way, as he is going to be the boss around here, we should probably stop referring to him as the Bastard."

"I'm not so sure about that. If you want my opinion, he looks like a real mean son of a bitch."

"Gilchrists often come across that way. You

74

should know that." Katy stepped into the hall with a reassuring smile. "He's probably just a little tense. This must be a very emotional occasion for him, after all."

"I wouldn't put money on it. Those two didn't exactly throw themselves into each other's arms when he walked through the door."

"Well, what did you expect? This is a traumatic moment for them both."

Katy went briskly down the tiled hall. She was feeling triumphant's — euphoric, in fact. The crisis had been resolved. She would soon be a free woman. She could bow gracefully out of the picture, secure in the knowledge that Gilchrist, Inc. was in good hands.

Katy could hardly wait to tell her brother the good news. *Free at last.*

Wearing a wide smile, Katy swung around the corner into Justine's glass-walled living room. She was prepared to be gracious to the Bastard. After all, he had seen the light and come home to do his duty to the family. She had won, and she could afford to be magnanimous in victory.

The tension in the beautiful, formal living room hit her like a wall of solid ice. Katy nearly stumbled in shock. She hesitated in the entrance and took in the scene in a single glance.

Justine was still seated in her wingback chair. She appeared as regally composed as ever, but her eyes betrayed a deep unease. There was a stiffness about her that immediately put Katy on full alert.

Katy turned to Luke. The fine hairs on the nape of her neck stirred.

He was standing in front of the bank of windows, a dark figure in his black sweater, black jeans, and low black boots. His gaze was on the fog-shrouded landscape. She knew he was aware of her presence, but he did not turn around.

He stood in what appeared to be a relaxed stance, but Katy sensed the casualness was superficial. He looked coiled and ready to strike.

"Katy, my dear." Justine was clearly relieved to see her. "I'm so glad you're here. My grandson has made a momentous decision."

In spite of the ominous atmosphere in the room, Katy decided to accentuate the positive. After all, Luke was here; that was the main thing.

She turned up the voltage on her smile and laid on all the graciousness she could muster. "I'm delighted to see you made the right decision, Mr. Gilchrist. I know you won't regret it."

Luke turned slowly to face her. His emerald eyes glittered unnervingly. "My decision has not been finalized. I've just explained to Justine that I will take on the job of salvaging Gilchrist, Inc. only under certain conditions."

Katy's stomach clenched, but she managed to keep her smile pinned firmly in place. "What conditions?"

Justine shifted slightly in her chair. "Luke says he does not wish to be reinstated in my will. Nor does he want control of Gilchrist on a permanent basis. He says, however, he will attempt to pull us out of our immediate problems for a fee."

"A fee?" Katy was stunned. She glared at Luke. "Money? You mean you're going to treat your family just as you would any other client?"

"Not quite," Luke said softly. "My fee in this case will be considerably higher than it would be for an average client."

"How much higher?" Katy demanded.

"If I succeed, I want the Pacific Rim restaurant."

Katy blinked, confused. "What on earth are you talking about?"

Luke shrugged. "You heard me."

Realization dawned. Katy's mouth fell open. "You want the Pacific Rim as your *fee?*"

"Yes."

Katy threw Justine a horrified glance. She was certain she was missing something in the equation. But Justine just smiled wearily.

"I'm afraid he means it," Justine said quietly.

"But that's outrageous." Katy's gaze swung back to Luke. "That's the most successful restaurant in the entire group. The jewel in the crown. The flagship of the line. It made more money last year than Gilchrist's Grill and Gilchrist's of Bellevue combined."

"I'm aware of that." Luke's smile was ice cold.

"Well, you can't have it," Katy said stoutly.

Justine held up a hand. "That's enough, Katy. I have already agreed to Luke's price."

"Justine, you can't just turn that restaurant over to him. It's not right."

"I had intended to turn over the entire group to him," Justine reminded her, "together with Gilchrist Gourmet."

"Yes, but that was when you thought he would join the company on a permanent basis and assume his full responsibilities to the family." Katy waved a hand toward Luke in disgust. "He's obviously only going to act as a paid consultant. Gilchrist, Inc. will be nothing more than a client as far as he's concerned. He just said so, for heaven's sake."

"I will take what I can get," Justine said bluntly.

Katy crossed the room in three quick strides and crouched beside Justine's chair. She took the old woman's elegant, long-fingered hand in hers and squeezed fiercely. The three-carat solitaire diamond in Justine's ring bit into Katy's palm. "I won't let you grovel and plead with him, Justine. I will not let you humble yourself like this. He has no right to set such outrageous terms."

Luke smiled dangerously. "Better save the noble outrage, Katy. You've only heard my first condition. There's another."

Katy scowled furiously at him. "What's your second condition?"

"I want you as my personal assistant. You'll work for me instead of Justine."

Katy recoiled in shock. "Out of the question."

Luke shrugged. "I'm going to need someone who can provide continuity and act as a liaison with both management and the family. You're perfect for the job."

"How do you know?" Katy retorted.

"Justine assures me you know almost as much about the inner workings of Gilchrist, Inc. as she does. She also says you have an intuitive understanding of most of the people who work at the management level. On top of that, you're practically a member of the family. I'm going to need that kind of inside knowledge."

Katy staggered to her feet, dazed. In her mind's eye she saw all her private plans going up in smoke once more. She had been so close, she thought. Almost free. She swallowed, trying to find her voice. "Justine, are you just going to hand me over to him like this?"

Justine's brows rose. "It's not an unreasonable request, my dear. But the choice is yours. I won't insist."

"Think about it," Luke advised, his gaze amused. "Take your time. I have some details to discuss with Justine. I'll stop by your office in an hour or so and get your decision then."

Katy eyed him warily. She knew Justine was agreeing to Luke's conditions because she hoped that once on board at Gilchrist, Inc. he could be persuaded to stay. It was a possibility, Katy conceded. A remote one, but still a possibility. After all, he was here at last, which was a major step forward.

Katy thought quickly. Persuading Luke to stay and take on the job of saving Gilchrist, Inc. was her best hope of early escape.

"There's no need to wait for my decision," she said coolly. "I'll stay on with the company."

It was Luke's turn to smile slowly in triumph. "Excellent."

"For a limited period of time," Katy added calmly.

Luke quirked a brow. "How limited?"

Katy took a stab in the dark. "Three months."

Luke considered that. "I don't know if I'll have Gilchrist under control in three months. The job may take longer. No, I'm afraid I can't accept any limitations on your commitment. I need to know I can count on you for as long as it's necessary to do so."

"All right, four months," Katy said quickly.

"Nine."

"Six."

"Done," Luke said a little too easily.

Katy gritted her teeth. She was sure he would have settled for less if she had bargained more cautiously. "You certainly live up to your reputation, Mr. Gilchrist."

"Call me Luke. After all, we're going to be working closely together. Tell me, Katy, do you always make major career decisions without taking time to think them through?"

Katy felt her face growing warm. "That was hardly a major decision. It was blackmail. If you'll excuse me, I have work to do."

Without waiting for a reply Katy swung around on her heel and walked swiftly out of the room.

Mrs. Igorson was waiting in the hall. The housekeeper gave her a knowing look. "Lives up to his nickname, don't he?"

"Yes, he does," Katy muttered.

Bastard.

Then her natural optimism set in and Katy brightened. Six months was not all that bad, she consoled herself. It was not great, but she could survive it. She could spend the time researching locations and recipes for the small take-out business she intended to open.

At least now she had a definite release date.

Katy could hardly wait to mark her calendar so that she could start counting down the days to freedom.

CHAPTER
FOUR

A charged silence filled the living room after the door closed behind Katy. Luke was aware of a curious sense of satisfaction. It wasn't easy winning battles with guardian angels. Virtue always had an unfair advantage.

He almost smiled as he listened intently to the sound of Katy's footsteps retreating into the distance. He had her now. She was all his for the next six months. It was a heady thought, even though he was not at all certain just what he would do with her.

"You upset her," Justine said after a moment.

"Did I?"

"Yes. She's normally very calm. Quite unflappable. She's also extraordinarily cheerful most of the time." Justine frowned thoughtfully as she picked up her cup of tea. "I've often wondered how she does it. It doesn't seem quite natural somehow. Nevertheless, she's rather a delight to have around, actually."

"Is that why you've kept her? Because she amuses you?"

Justine did not take offense. "On the contrary, I believe it is she who finds us Gilchrists amusing. When she's not exasperated with us, that is. She needed a job. I gave her one. It's been a mutually beneficial arrangement. I don't know what I would have done without her, especially these past two years."

"I know she's Richard Quinnell's granddaughter." Luke moved back to the window.

"Yes. She's Richard's granddaughter. The resemblance is unmistakable. She got that brilliant red hair and those deep blue eyes from him. Her mother looked just like her at that age."

Luke frowned. "Justine . . ."

"I'll never forget that day at the church when we all finally realized your father was not going to show up. Most brides would have collapsed in humiliation. Deborah Quinnell was so very brave about it all. She and her father insisted that everyone attend the reception. Richard said that as long as he'd paid for the food, someone was going to damn well eat it."

"Justine, let's get something straight. If this new association of ours is going to have a chance of working, there will have to be some ground rules. Number one is that we don't talk about the past. You and I are on opposite sides in that old war, and unless you want to refight it, I suggest you don't mention it."

Justine's mouth thinned. "I'm sure you're right. A very logical decision. But you can't blame me for wanting you to understand that there were two sides in the feud between your father and the rest of us. We were the ones who had to face the Quinnells that day at the church."

"And you were the one who called off the merger between Quinnell and Gilchrist right after the wedding. You had made a deal, and you backed out of it."

Justine's expression was suddenly stark. "I had to call it off. Without the marriage there was no real link except that of business between the two families. Who knew what would happen when Richard's daughter married someone else, as she eventually did? I couldn't risk having everything I'd worked for eventually falling into the hands of outsiders. Surely you can understand that."

"Yeah, I understand," Luke said. Because he did. If he had been in Justine's shoes, he would have called off the merger, too. It was a sobering thought. He did not like the idea of empathizing with Justine in any way. His loyalties lay elsewhere.

"Your father ruined everything when he ran off with your mother," Justine snapped, her voice growing stronger as she sensed a small victory.

Luke smiled wryly. "Given that I wouldn't be here if he hadn't fallen in love with her, I'm sure you can understand that I have a slightly different view of the situation. Look, Justine, there are always two sides to a story. But in my case there's no question about which side I'm on. Don't waste your time trying to influence me with propaganda for the other side."

Justine almost smiled. "Katy has frequently pointed out to me that we Gilchrists tend to see things in overly simplistic terms — black and white. She claims we have a problem with the gray areas of life."

"I don't have a problem with them."

Justine nodded. "Because you don't even see them. I know. I've been that way most of my life." She paused. "Katy sees them, you know."

"People who deal in shades of gray get bogged down in sentiment and indecisiveness."

"Oh, my," Justine murmured. "It's going to be interesting watching you and Katy interact."

Luke shrugged. "Katy and I will get along

just fine so long as she remembers I'm the boss. In the meantime, you and I don't talk about the past. Agreed?"

"Agreed." Justine put down her teacup. "I'm too grateful to have you here at last to risk arguing with you. I must say, however, that I find it ironic that it's Richard Quinnell's granddaughter who has achieved the impossible by getting you here."

Luke narrowed his eyes. "You think I'm here because of Katy?"

"Aren't you?"

Damned if he was going to admit anything to the old witch. The truth was, he was not altogether sure why he had come to Dragon Bay. "I'm here because the Pacific Rim restaurant is a ripe plum. As a businessman, I can't bring myself to pass up such easy pickings." It was partially true. He certainly intended to take the restaurant when this was over.

"Katy Wade is a ripe plum, too," Justine said quietly. "I think you should know that she's been living an almost cloistered existence for the past several years."

Luke smiled grimly. "That figures. It goes with the wings and halo."

"It's because of her brother," Justine said coolly. "The fact that she comes with a teenager as part of the package has put off most males. Her social life has been far too limited for a young woman of her age."

Luke studied the fog. "My social life has been a little limited lately, too. Just what the hell are you trying to say, Justine?"

"Her brother will graduate from high school in another month. Then he'll be off to college, and Katy will be on her own for the first time in her life. She has a right to make up for some of what she's missed out on during the past few years, and I believe she intends to do so."

Luke hesitated. "She said something about business plans she wants to pursue."

"Yes. She yearns to open her own small business. A rather naïve dream, I admit. I am, however, encouraging her to sample some of the other aspects of the freedom she has hungered for in recent years."

Luke arched one brow. "You think she should rush out and have a few passionate affairs?"

Justine inclined her head. "Don't be crude. Perhaps one or two interesting relationships, yes. I would like her to experience some genuine passion in her life. She is, after all, an attractive young woman. I fear, however, that because she has had to postpone so much for so long, she is rather more vulnerable than other, more experienced young women are at her age. I do not want her hurt."

Luke looked at Justine. "Are you warning me off, by any chance?"

"Yes, I suppose I am." Justine's gaze was unreadable. "There was a man a year ago. Nate Atwood. He was dating Katy when he met Eden. He dropped Katy to marry my granddaughter."

"Atwood is the name of the man Eden divorced six months ago?"

"Yes." Justine pursed her lips in fierce disapproval. "I fear he used Katy to get close to the family. His real goal was Eden. He wanted to marry a Gilchrist, you see. Thought he could worm his way into a position of control at Gilchrist, Inc. He is no longer a problem, but I do not want to see Katy hurt again."

"I'll keep that in mind. Now, if you'll excuse me, I'm going to go upstairs and start letting everyone know who's running Gilchrist, Inc. these days."

Justine sat forward with sudden urgency. "Luke."

"Yes?"

"I am not entirely certain why you have come here. But I want you to know I am grateful."

"Maybe you'd better wait and see how it all works out before you decide whether or not to be grateful."

Justine eyed him closely. "I think it is you who isn't certain how it's going to work out. By the way, you will be needing a place to live. Have you given the matter any thought?"

"If you're about to offer me a room here in the mansion, forget it. I'll find myself something."

"There are several cottages along the cliffs not far from here. Katy and her brother live in one. I'm sure you can rent one if you like."

Luke considered the suggestion, aware that he was being pulled more deeply into some invisible web. On the other hand, he needed a place to live until he had sorted out Gilchrist, Inc. And he wanted to be near Katy. "All right."

He walked out of the room, ignoring the tight-lipped housekeeper. He let himself out of Justine's private suite. In the hall he took the stairs to the second floor and strode down the south wing corridor to a door that stood open.

The woman at the desk looked up quickly from a book she was reading when he appeared in the doorway. The nameplate in front of her read Liz Bartlett.

"May I help you?" She peered at him

through a pair of oversized glasses.

"I'm looking for Katy Wade," Luke said.

Liz's eyes widened behind her glasses as she put down her book. "Yes, sir. You must be Mr. Gilchrist. I'll let her know you're here. She's with Mr. Stanfield." She reached for the intercom.

"Never mind," Luke said. "I'll announce myself."

"But Mr. Gilchrist — "

"It's all right. She works for me now."

He went to the inner door and opened it without knocking. Katy was standing next to a man at the window. The two were huddled in an obviously intense conversation.

The pair sprang apart with guilty haste as the door opened. Katy spun around and glowered at Luke. The man narrowed his eyes briefly and then smiled and stuck out his hand.

"Luke Gilchrist? Welcome to Gilchrist, Inc. I'm Fraser Stanfield, your operations manager."

Luke shook hands briefly. He found himself wondering if this man was one of those who were waiting in line for Katy to be free of her responsibilities to her brother. "Stanfield, you're just the man I want to talk to this afternoon. I'm going to set up an office here in the mansion."

"Justine's old office is available next door," Katy volunteered.

Luke nodded, still watching Stanfield. "Be there at two with a summary status report on the restaurants and on Gilchrist Gourmet."

Fraser's smile faded slightly. "Yes, sir."

"I'll be going into headquarters on a regular basis. Several times a week to start. Set up an office there for me, too, will you?"

"Sure. No problem."

"Fine." Luke turned to Katy. "I'm going back to Oregon tomorrow to pick up a few things. I'll drive back to Seattle in the afternoon and spend the night there. I'll want to meet with everyone at the restaurants and at Gilchrist Gourmet during the afternoon, evening, and the following morning. Have Liz make arrangements for me at a downtown hotel for tomorrow night, will you?"

Katy nodded quickly. She looked relieved. "Certainly."

Luke turned to leave and then paused. "By the way, I'll need someone to look after my dog while I'm gone. I thought I might leave him with you."

Katy's eyes flickered with alarm. "Your dog? With me? I don't think your dog likes me."

"I'm sure the two of you will get along

just fine." Luke nodded to Fraser and walked out of the office.

The next morning Katy sat across from her brother at the kitchen table and watched as Matt guzzled freshly squeezed orange juice and downed vast quantities of the homemade muesli cereal Katy had prepared.

Matt was a bottomless pit these days, she thought, smiling to herself. She spent an incredible amount of time throwing food at him and watching it disappear. But it was all worth it. He had turned into a fine young man. The morning sunlight gleamed on his bright red hair, and she noticed again the increasing breadth of his shoulders.

Her little brother was growing up quickly, she realized. It would be strange not having him around the place next year.

"What do you mean, Gilchrist's going to leave his dog with us?" Matthew spread jam on his third slice of toast. Katy had baked the bread the previous evening.

"Just what I said. He's leaving today to tour the restaurants and Gilchrist Gourmet. He wants to introduce himself to management and the employees. Apparently he feels he can't take the monster with him, so he's leaving it with us."

"And you want me to be in charge of

feeding and walking it, huh?"

"Right. Do we have a deal?"

Matt munched toast. "You'll owe me one."

"I'm aware of that."

"Okay. Deal."

Katy sat back in her chair. "That's a relief. They should be here in a few minutes. Luke said he was going to drop the beast off on his way out of town. I hope he brings a sturdy chain we can use to tie the creature up outside in the yard."

"So you really think this guy can save Gilchrist?"

Katy made a face. "I think that if anyone can do it, he can."

Matt poured more orange juice into the glass. "You don't like him, do you?"

"I think he's going to be difficult to have around," Katy said dryly. "Like all Gil-christs."

"Cheer up. He'll probably spend a lot of time in Seattle."

"I'm counting on it," Katy murmured.

A knock on the front door of the cottage came just as Katy was adding milk to her own muesli.

"I'll get it," Matt said. He got to his feet and went into the front room of the small cottage to open the door.

Katy heard the rumble of voices and the

unmistakable sound of dog claws on the old wood floor. A few seconds later Luke and Zeke appeared in the kitchen doorway. Luke had a huge sack of dry dog food under one arm. Zeke had his bowl in his mouth.

Zeke was not on a leash, Katy noted with disapproval. And there was no heavy chain anywhere in evidence. She glowered at the dog. Zeke glowered back and dropped his bowl in the middle of the kitchen floor. He stood protectively over it. Luke put the sack of dog food down beside him.

Luke was dressed in a black sweater and black jeans. It was obvious that, like the rest of the family, he was going to stick to black. But Katy had to admit he looked good in it. The color underlined all that lean masculine grace and power.

Luke caught her studying him, and his mouth curved faintly. His sorcerer's eyes gleamed green in the morning light. Katy's fingers trembled slightly as she reached for her orange juice. She was not going to let him make her nervous, she promised herself.

"Good morning." Luke glanced meaningfully at the coffeepot as Zeke made a royal tour of the tiny kitchen. "Mind if I have a cup? I've got a long drive ahead."

"Help yourself," Katy said, not bothering to get to her feet.

"Thank you," Luke murmured as he rummaged in a cupboard for a mug. "I see you are by nature a gracious hostess."

She smiled blandly. "It's more hospitality than I got when I dropped in on you down in Oregon."

"What are you complaining about?" Luke asked as he poured coffee for himself. "You got to walk back out again in one piece, didn't you?"

"I'm supposed to be grateful?"

"Yes."

"Excuse me." Matt's eyes flickered from his sister's face to Luke's as he leaned down to pat Zeke. "Katy says I'm elected to feed your dog. How much does he eat?"

"So she delegated that job, did she? I wondered how she'd get out of it." Luke sipped his coffee. "Fill his bowl to the top twice a day. If he starts chewing on the furniture, you might want to give him a little extra food. Let him run on the beach in the mornings and evenings, and he'll take care of himself the rest of the time."

Matt nodded. "Got it."

Luke lounged against the counter and watched Matt intently. "I appreciate this."

"Sure." Matt gave Zeke one last pat and straightened. "Well, I'd better get going or I'll be late for school. See you later."

"Good-bye," Katy said. "Good luck on that math exam."

"Thanks." Matt hoisted his books. "Oh, yeah, I almost forgot. Can I borrow your car tonight? Some of the guys are going to a show in town."

Katy froze. Lately Matt was requesting the car more and more often and staying out until all hours. It was getting difficult to control his actions. He was a good kid, Katy reminded herself, and Dragon Bay was a small town, but she could not help but worry.

"The last time you went to a show with your friends, you didn't get in until two in the morning, Matt."

"I told you, we were just messing around at Jeff's place."

"It turned out that Jeff's folks were out of town that weekend." Katy was acutely conscious of Luke listening to the exchange. "They had not given Jeff permission to have friends over."

Matt gave her a disgusted look. "Stop worrying, Katy. How much trouble can anyone get into in this dumb burg? Besides, I'm almost eighteen. I'm not a kid anymore."

Katy steeled herself. These small skirmishes with Matt were becoming increasingly unpleasant. She wished Luke was not a spectator this morning. Things were difficult enough as it was. "Matt, you can take the car, but I want you home by ten. It's a school night."

"Ah, come on, Katy, everyone else has a midnight curfew on school nights."

Katy felt herself turning red under Luke's watchful eyes. "Please don't argue, Matt," she said tightly. "We agreed a long time ago that ten o'clock was curfew on school nights. What about your homework?"

"I'll get it done during study hall."

Katy flicked an embarrassed glance at Luke and then frowned at her brother. "We'll talk about it this afternoon when you get home."

Matt rolled his eyes. "Come on, Katy, you're not my mother. I'll see you later." He started for the door.

"Hang on a second," Luke said quietly.

Matt hesitated. "Yeah?"

"You have a part-time job?"

"Sure. All the guys do. Me and some of the others work at the new fast food place on Bay Street."

Luke nodded. "I know it. You want to hang onto that job?"

"Well, sure." Matt was becoming increasingly bewildered. "It pays for my gas and stuff."

"Then be in by ten on school nights. Got it?"

"Huh?" Matt stared at him.

"You heard me," Luke said. "I agree with your sister. Ten is late enough on school nights. Hell, you probably shouldn't be going out at all during the week."

"Are you crazy?" Matt started to turn red with anger.

"My mental health is not your problem. Your problem is that as long as your sister works for me I've got a vested interest in her peace of mind. I don't want her attention distracted from her job during the day. That means I don't want her worrying about what you're up to at night."

"Who the hell do you think you are?" Matt demanded. "You can't get me fired."

Luke smiled. "Don't kid yourself. I can get you canned in a minute if I decide to do it. Your friends, too, for that matter. All I have to do is have a little talk with the owner of that fast food franchise on Bay Street. He'll see things my way."

"Why would he do what you tell him to do?" Matt challenged.

"I helped him arrange the financing on that restaurant and the two others he owns. Let's just say he's very grateful to me. If you want to keep the job, be in by ten."

Matt looked stunned. "I don't believe this." He turned to Katy. "Are you going to let him issue orders like that? This is our house."

Katy was too busy reeling from the shock of Luke's interference to find her voice. "Uh . . ."

"Take off, Matt," Luke ordered easily. "I'll see you when I get back. Thanks again for looking after Zeke."

"Jesus Christ," Matt growled. He was clearly struggling to control his anger in deference to the fact that Luke was Katy's employer.

"Don't swear in front of your sister."

Matt gave him one last furious glare and then slammed out of the cottage.

Katy sat fuming at the table until the front door closed behind her brother. Then she leapt to her feet. "Don't you *ever* interfere like that between my brother and me again, do you understand? Our problems have nothing to do with you!"

Luke regarded her with unreadable eyes. "I don't think you know much about seventeen-year-old boys."

"And you do?" she raged.

"More than you do. I was one once."

"Is that right?"

"Right. The thing to remember about seventeen-year-old boys is that you have to use the carrot-and-stick approach. And you always start with the stick."

"This is my brother we're talking about.

I've been raising him by myself since he was eight years old, and I don't need any help from you."

"Simmer down, Katy. Your little brother is on the verge of becoming a full-grown man. He's going through some tough times right now."

"I'm well aware of the problems of peer group pressure and the desire to be independent that young men face at this age. Liz gave me a book to read on the subject."

"Sometimes books overcomplicate matters. Seventeen-year-old boys need things real simple and straightforward. I just made things easy for your brother."

"Easy?" Katy nearly choked on her fury. "How can you say you made them easy?"

"Put yourself in his place. How can he look his friends in the eye and admit he has to be home by ten because his sister says so? He'll sound like a wimp. No way he can avoid it. Much easier to tell them that the bastard his sister works for will get his ass fired if he doesn't get in on time. The guys will respect that."

Katy sank back down into her chair. Luke had a point. "This male thing is very difficult at times."

"Only because you're a female trying to figure it out."

"All the same, you shouldn't have interfered. It was none of your business."

"Everything around here is my business," Luke said. "If you don't like it, that's too bad. You're the one who brought me here to the bosom of my family, remember?"

"How was I to know you'd act like this?"

"You should have guessed from all of the signs and rumors that I wasn't going to be Mr. Nice Guy." Luke put his coffee cup down on the counter and glanced at his watch.

Katy gave him a fulminating look. "You shouldn't have handled it that way."

"What way?"

"Making it sound as though you had the power to make the owner of that fast food franchise repay a business favor."

Luke shrugged, showing no particular concern. "I do have the power to do it."

Katy gritted her teeth. "Don't you understand? It sets a very poor example."

Luke looked surprised. "A poor example of what?"

"Of proper business ethics and procedures," Katy snapped, totally out of patience. "I don't want Matt to think such methods of getting your own way are acceptable or appropriate."

Luke poured himself a second cup of coffee. "They work. That's the bottom line in the business world. I'm surprised you've been able to work for Gilchrist, Inc. for this long without figuring that out."

"I'm well aware that some people are willing to stoop to such methods," Katy said, "but I will not have Matt exposed to the notion that they are the right methods."

"Matt needed a face-saving way of telling the guys he has to be in by ten. I gave it to him. That's all there is to it. Do you always get things this twisted up?"

"I'm not twisting them up. I'm trying to explain something very important to you."

"Right." He glanced at his watch. "Unfortunately, I've got to get going. I'm afraid we'll have to finish this fascinating discussion on modern business ethics some other time."

Katy sighed. "It's obvious you haven't had the responsibility of raising a teenager. I suppose you meant well."

"Don't be too sure of that. Meaning well is not one of my top priorities in life."

"Why did you get involved, then?" she demanded.

"For the sake of efficiency. Like I told your brother, I need your full attention in the office. I don't want you worrying about your family problems."

Katy tapped her irritation out against the edge of the cereal bowl with her spoon. "I've been worrying about my brother and managing to do my job at the same time for a long time now. It's not nearly as distracting as worrying about *your* family."

"Yeah, well, the job has suffered. Gilchrist, Inc. is in a hell of a mess."

Katy flushed furiously. "That's not my fault, damn it. I've been trying my best. Once your grandmother started letting go of the reins there was nothing anyone could do. Besides, I'm a personal assistant. My job was to coordinate things for her, not run her company."

"Uh-huh." Luke didn't sound convinced.

Katy bit her lip. "Are you saying things are in worse shape than I realized, or are you just being deliberately obtuse?"

"I'm saying we've got some real problems." Luke leaned down to stroke Zeke. "I'll know more about them when I get back from Seattle."

Katy dropped her spoon in alarm. "What do you mean? What's going on?"

"Not all of the losses Gilchrist has suffered lately are due to the state of the economy and lack of leadership at the top. I think that in the case of two of the restaurants and Gilchrist Gourmet, someone at the management level has helped dig the holes they're in."

Katy was horrified. She leapt out of the chair. "Are you saying Gilchrist has been the victim of embezzlement or something?"

"Or something. I'm not certain just what is going on yet."

"Good grief." Katy stared at him. "Who would do a thing like that?"

Luke gave her a mildly disgusted look. "Katy, I've got a news flash for you. There are a whole lot of people out there in the real world who leave their wings and halos at home when they go to work."

"Yes, I know. I'm not naïve. But Gilchrist, Inc. is not that large a company. If someone has been deliberately sabotaging the firm, it's probably someone I know personally." Katy felt a little ill at that thought. "A friend."

"Probably." Luke straightened away from the counter and put down his cup. "Could even be a member of the family."

"Good grief." Katy sat down again. "You don't mean that."

"I told you, I don't know enough yet to say who's behind it. But the possibilities definitely include members of the family."

"It's outrageous even to suggest that family members might want to hurt the firm. That's the last thing they would do. Good Lord, I'm a more likely candidate than one of the family."

Luke smiled briefly. "For the record, you're the last person I'd suspect."

For some reason Katy felt warmed by that comment. She felt herself blush with pleasure. "I suppose I should be grateful you have some respect for my years of loyalty to Justine and the company," she said gruffly.

"The hell with your years of loyalty. You don't exactly have a poker face, Katy. You're as easy to read as a newspaper. Everything you're feeling is right there in your eyes. If you were involved in something shady, I'd know it."

The warmth she had been feeling turned to ice. "You make me sound like a five-year-old kid who couldn't organize a candy heist."

"I think you could organize it," Luke said thoughtfully. "You've got the brains to do it. I just don't think you could lie about it later."

His condescending attitude was really beginning to annoy Katy. "You don't know me as well as you think you do."

That possibility did not appear to worry Luke. "We'll see. Don't mention this little matter to anyone until I get back. Not even Justine. I've got a few more questions I want answered before I make any general announcements." He glanced once more at his watch. "I'd better get moving."

"So go. Nobody's stopping you."

"You're really pissed, aren't you?"

"Yes, I am, as a matter of fact."

Luke nodded. "Right. Well, I apologize. Didn't mean to insult you by telling you I think you're basically honest. Hell. And you think men are complicated." He walked to the door. "Zeke, stay here, boy. They've got food."

Zeke whined and sat down in the middle of the kitchen floor next to his bowl. His bushy tail thumped heavily as he watched Luke prepare to depart.

Luke stopped in front of Katy. He caught her chin on the edge of his hand and tilted her face upward. "Whether you know it or not, we've made a bargain, Katy."

"A bargain?" Katy stilled. Her pulse was suddenly racing. Some part of her was afraid that if she moved she might fall off a cliff and sink into the bottomless green pools of his eyes.

Luke smiled whimsically. "I'll explain it to you later. In the meantime, take care of my dog." He bent his head and brushed his mouth lightly, possessively across Katy's startled lips.

Then he was gone.

Katy sat where she was for a long moment. She took several deep breaths to calm her disordered senses. When she thought she had herself under control again she turned to eye Zeke.

"I don't want any trouble out of you," Katy said firmly.

Zeke focused intently on her half-full bowl of cereal.

"What do I have to do? Bribe you?" Katy got up and dumped the remainder of her breakfast into the dog's bowl. "There. Take the food right out of my mouth. See if I care. I'm just the hired help around here."

Zeke downed the cereal and milk in one large gulp. Then he sprawled in the middle of the floor next to his bowl and promptly went to sleep.

Katy hesitated, wondering if she should try to tie the dog up outside before she left for work at the mansion. Zeke did not appear inclined to move, so she abandoned the notion.

She cleared the table and filled Zeke's bowl with dog food. Then she checked herself in the mirror. The long-sleeved green dress she was wearing fell softly to midcalf. The wide belt accented her narrow waist. She ran a brush through her hair one more time, hitched the strap of her leather bag up over one shoulder, and went out the front door of the cottage.

A brisk breeze made Katy's hair snap as she walked along the cliffs toward Justine's big house. She watched the morning light on the calm sea, aware once again of just how fortunate she was that Justine had offered her the job of personal assistant all those years ago. Not only had it provided financial security, it had also given Katy the opportunity to raise Matt in a small, quiet, safe town rather than the city.

Dragon Bay was only an hour out of Seattle, but it might as well have been on a different planet. The town was large enough and trendy enough to provide the amenities of life, such as supermarkets that carried fresh basil. But it was small enough to have a low crime rate, good schools, and a sense of security. It had been a good place to raise Matt.

One more reason why she was indebted to Justine, Katy thought.

It was a short trip to the mansion, no more than a ten-minute walk. The route took her past the cottage she knew Luke would be renting. She realized that when he was home he would be able to see her kitchen window from his kitchen window. She would have to remember to pull the blinds in the morning.

Katy spent most of the ten minutes between

her cottage and the mansion mulling over what Luke had told her. The possibility that someone she knew and trusted might have been deliberately sabotaging Gilchrist, Inc. was hard to swallow.

She recalled Liz talking about the basic paranoid personality profile. Katy wondered now if paranoia might be Luke's problem. Surely only a paranoid person would look for suspects among the members of his own family.

That's all she needed, Katy thought with a grimace. The notion of spending the next six months working for a paranoid boss was not pleasant to contemplate.

But the most unsettling thing of all was the fact that she had been kissed by a sorcerer.

Katy heard her own car in the drive at five minutes to ten that night. With a small sigh of relief she turned off the food processor. Matt was home. Regardless of his tactics, she felt a wave of gratitude toward Luke. This was one night when she would not have to worry about where Matt was or whom he was with.

She spooned the batch of parsley and green olive pesto she had just made into a plastic jar. She stuck it in the refrigerator and went to stand in the kitchen doorway. She realized she was tense as she waited for Matt to come into the cottage. He would probably be in a surly mood because of what Luke had done that morning.

Zeke had carried his bowl into the living room earlier and was stretched out beside it. The dog rolled leisurely to his feet as the door opened and Matt ambled into the room.

"I'm home," Matt called, sounding surprisingly cheerful. "Hey, how you doin', Zeke, old buddy?" He leaned down to pat the dog. Then he glanced at Katy. "Maybe I'd better take him outside for a few minutes."

"That would probably be a good idea," Katy said cautiously. "How was the film?"

"It was okay. Nothing special. Come on, Zeke. Let's go, pal." Matt opened the door again. Zeke scooped up his dish and bounded out into the chilly night.

"Matt?"

"Yeah?"

"I appreciate the fact that you got home on time tonight."

Matt shrugged. "It's not like I had a lot of choice. Your new boss is one tough son of a — "

"*Matt.*"

Matt grinned. "Well, he is. I think you're right. If anyone can save the Gilchrists, it's

111

probably him. See you in a few minutes."

Dog and boy vanished into the night.

It occurred to Katy as she went back into the kitchen that Matt's voice had held genuine respect, not sullenness or anger. She relaxed and told herself the incident was merely an example of one of those mysterious male bonding rituals she had heard about.

She went over to where her notebook lay open on the counter and made a few entries. This latest pesto recipe showed genuine promise. The thick, zesty sauce would be especially good over buckwheat pasta, Katy decided. If it passed the taste test tomorrow, she would definitely include it in her lineup of specialty pestos destined for her gourmet take-out establishment.

Her plans for Pesto Presto were still on hold, but only for six more months. She would soon be free. Her brother would be safely off to college, and her commitment to Justine would be fulfilled.

And there would be no stopping Katy Wade. She would be her own boss at last, captain of her fate, in command of her own destiny.

Freedom.

The word was like nectar on her tongue.

CHAPTER FIVE

Katy reached the pool wall, turned smoothly beneath the water, and launched herself back toward the opposite end. She swam hard, working off the tensions of the day.

Luke had returned this morning looking grim and preoccupied. He had gone straight to his new office next to Katy's and had immediately begun issuing orders. Katy and Liz had skipped lunch to plow through the enormous pile of work he was generating.

Liz had begun to worry that the new boss was a compulsive overachiever. Katy had assured her it was more likely that Luke simply enjoyed giving orders. It was a typical Gilchrist trait.

There would be another few hours of work tonight, but not the kind Katy could do in her office. A royal command had been issued from Justine's suite. Mrs. Gilchrist was entertaining the family in her quarters. All family members and Katy were expected to attend.

Katy did not enjoy such gatherings. There was no getting around the fact that she was definitely not family. Far too often she found herself playing the role of peacemaker among the temperamental Gilchrists.

She soared through the water, reveling in the sensation of freedom it provided. The glass-enclosed pool room was attached to the back of Justine's mansion. It had been a conservatory until Justine had ordered the blue-tiled pool installed. Many of the exotic hothouse plants still thrived in the humid atmosphere.

Justine swam punctually at seven o'clock every morning. The pool was empty for the rest of the day until Katy arrived at five for her own swim. This was definitely one of the perks of working for Justine Gilchrist, she thought as she slipped through the water. She did not know what she would do without the release of her afternoon swim.

There were days when, feeling the pressures of a life that seemed to be permanently on hold, Katy tore through the water at five o'clock. On such days she would swim until she was exhausted, churning the water into a white froth as she swam up and down the length of the pool. When she was finished she would climb out and stand on legs that trembled from exertion while she dried herself.

Today was not one of those days, she reflected. Today all she needed was the sense of exhilaration the water provided.

That realization struck her like a bolt of lightning. A surge of relief poured through hcr. She could relax a little, even if she was going to be working for a slave driver during the next six months. The burden of saving Gilchrist, Inc. had finally been lifted from her shoulders. The responsibility had been safely handed over to the Bastard.

Katy reached the end of the pool, planted both hands on the tiled edge, and hauled herself upward in a cascade of water. As soon as she saw who was standing in front of her she nearly dropped back beneath the surface.

Maureen Gilchrist, Justine's formidable daughter-in-law, loomed straight ahead. She was backed up by her husband, Luke's uncle Hayden, and her two offspring, Eden and Darren.

Maureen smiled determinedly as Katy surged up out of the water. "There you are, Katy. We just arrived. We've been looking for you. Mrs. Igorson said she thought you might be in here."

Luke's aunt was not a Gilchrist by blood, but she certainly fit right into the clan in terms of looks and personality. Gilchrist men were apparently all attracted to tall, dark-haired women with thoroughbred bones. Maureen also shared the family preference for black.

On Maureen a basic black surplice dinner dress turned into a dramatic gown with the aid of a heavy crystal and jet necklace. Her discreetly tinted dark hair was styled in a short, sophisticated cut.

"Hello, Maureen. Hayden." Katy smiled politely at Luke's cousins, Eden and Darren. "Good to see you all again."

"Not much choice," Hayden said darkly. He was a typical Gilchrist, tall and aristocratic, even at sixty. He had thickened a bit around the midsection, but the added weight only made him more imposing. It certainly did not detract from the impact of his brilliant green eyes and patrician features.

Hayden did not fit Katy's private image of a successful artist. But then, it would probably be impossible for any Gilchrist to look bohemian. Their innate sense of drama prohibited such sartorial disasters as baggy, paint-stained pants and untrimmed beards. In the well-cut black jacket and trousers Hayden wore tonight he could have passed for the chairman of the board of a major corporation or an elegant Old World vampire.

"Mother has summoned the family, as I'm sure you're well aware," Hayden continued.

The edge of his cultivated voice betrayed a hint of his lifelong resentment of Justine. Her failure to applaud his talents had eaten at him for years. No amount of success in the world of art had compensated.

"I understand we're here to welcome back the prodigal grandson," Hayden added. "Finally agreed to take on the job of saving our asses, has he?"

"That's the theory." Katy picked up her towel and began drying herself. As usual, she felt puny surrounded by a bunch of Gilchrists. They towered over her, sleek, dark, and predatory.

Darren — lean, black-haired, and green-eyed like the rest of his family — lounged with insouciant ease in a poolside chair. He was dressed in a fashionable charcoal-gray jacket and slacks that suited his aristocratic good looks.

Darren was currently managing Gilchrist's on Lake Union, the newest restaurant in the group. The popular, upscale establishment was doing well under his management. Darren was showing a flair for the job, and he knew it. He was bitter about the fact that Justine had not acknowledged his budding talents and rewarded him by making him her successor.

He was only twenty-seven, but there was already a dash of bitterness, perhaps even desperation, in his eyes.

Darren smiled at Katy with languid charm as he watched her dry the water off her legs. His eyes moved over her bright blue one-piece racing suit and lingered at the points where the snug fabric was cut high at her thighs. She hastily wrapped the towel around herself. There was nothing more than idle male interest in Darren's gaze, but Katy felt uncomfortable under the scrutiny.

"How's it going, Katy? What's it like working for the Bastard?" Darren asked with suspicious blandness.

For no good reason other than her natural instinct to defend anyone under attack, Katy leapt to Luke's defense. "It's going rather well, to be honest. I can feel a change in the organization already. I think Gilchrist, Inc. is in good hands."

"It had better be," Eden muttered. "There's a fortune at stake." At thirty, she was three years older than her brother, but the age difference was indiscernible. As in Justine's case, Eden's blue-blooded features and lean, elegant body would guarantee her an appearance of agelessness until the day she died.

She was wearing a simple black silk sheath and a silver choker. Her black hair curved just above her shoulders in a vampish style straight out of classic *film noir*. It emphasized the blood-red lipstick on her fine mouth and her long crimson nails.

Eden had inherited at least some of Justine's talent for numbers. She worked as the supervisor of the payroll and accounting department at Gilchrist, Inc.

Remembering Liz's armchair diagnosis, Katy took a second glance at Eden's slender frame. No, she was not anorexic, Katy decided in relief, but there was no doubt Eden had lost some weight. Since her divorce six months ago a strange haunted look had appeared in her eyes.

Another generation of dissatisfied Gilchrists, Katy thought as she covertly studied the coven. The emotional darkness in them must have been hereditary, too.

The genetic explanation did not account for the darkness in Maureen, Katy reminded herself. But then, as she had told Liz, there was explanation enough for Maureen's resentment. Katy knew Maureen had tried hard to be the perfect daughter-in-law, but in the end her husband's talents had been ridiculed and her offspring had been overlooked by Justine.

"I take it Grandmother still refuses to consider selling off any of the company assets," Eden said, looking annoyed.

"She won't hear of it." Katy peeled off her swimming cap and shook out her hair.

"She's turned into a fool in her old age," Maureen declared. "We're going to have to unload the two troubled restaurants, at least. We can't go on taking the sort of losses we took last year. Did you tell her that?"

"I suggested she think of selling them, yes," Katy replied, even-toned.

"But you failed to convince her," Maureen muttered. "Do you think the Bastard can talk her into it?"

"I don't know if he's even going to try," Katy said. "I have no idea what Luke's plans are yet. So far I think he's just been gathering information and letting people know there's new blood at the helm. He's only been here a couple of days."

Darren's smile was cynical. "That should be long enough to see that only three out of the five restaurants are really doing well and Gilchrist Gourmet is sliding downhill fast."

Katy looked up quickly, wondering if Darren knew that Luke intended to snaffle the Pacific Rim as his fee for saving Gilchrist, Inc. Apparently not, she decided as she examined his face. Far be it from her to make the announcement. Justine could handle that. Or Luke himself. He certainly was not shy about his intentions.

"If you'll excuse me, I've got to change for dinner," Katy murmured. "You're staying the night, I assume?"

Hayden nodded. "We've been assigned our usual rooms upstairs." His eyes narrowed. "I'm not sure I like this business of bringing Luke into the family like this. It's a risk. He's an unknown quantity."

"Oh, I wouldn't say that." Katy smiled. "He has a lot in common with the rest of you. I think there's reason to be hopeful that Gilchrist, Inc. will survive. Whatever else you can say about Luke, he does seem to know what he's doing when it comes to the food and beverage business."

"What I'd like to know," Eden said coolly, "is why did the Bastard finally decide to join us?"

"Maybe he just felt it was time to explore his roots," Katy suggested brightly.

"Sure." Darren chuckled grimly. "The guy walks into our lives after all this time because he's suddenly developed a deep longing for family ties. If you believe that, I've got another bridge I can sell you."

"I should think it's obvious he's here because Justine offered him the position of head of Gilchrist, Inc.," Maureen announced. "Why that woman refuses to see that she has plenty of talent to pick from on this side of the family defeats me. Damn it, we're the ones who've been loyal to her all these years."

Eden's crimson mouth twisted. "She tried to get Luke to take over Gilchrist after his wife and parents were killed three years ago. He's known all along he could show up on her doorstep and take over at any time. Why did he decide to do it now, when Gilchrist, Inc. is in the worst shape it's ever been in?"

"Good question," Darren muttered. "Why now? If he'd been smart, he would have joined the company years ago, when everything was still rosy."

The coven turned accusing emerald eyes on Katy, as if expecting her to come up with a suitable explanation. She smiled quickly and started backing toward the exit. "Like I said, I've got to change."

"Revenge," Hayden said in portentous tones.

Katy cleared her throat uneasily. "I beg your pardon?"

"That's why he's here." Hayden nodded to himself. He gazed into the still pool water as if he could foretell the future in its depths. "My brother Thornton never forgave Justine for failing to accept his choice of a wife. Thornton passed that anger down to Luke. And now Luke sees a chance to avenge his parents. He's here to burn Gilchrist, Inc. at the stake."

An unfortunate choice of words in this family, Katy thought. "Gilchrist was starting to totter all by itself," she pointed out hastily.

"But it probably would have survived," Maureen said slowly. Her gaze rested on her husband. "Oh, we might have lost a couple of the restaurants and had to scale back plans for Gilchrist Gourmet, but we would most likely have made it. Justine would have seen sense in the end. She's not stupid."

"You're right." Eden eyed her mother thoughtfully. "Luke knows we're in deep water, but we can still swim. He probably realized that if he wanted to ensure that the company goes under, he has to be here to give it a shove."

"It's revenge, all right," Darren muttered. "That's the only logical explanation. Damn. Justine is going to hand him enough rope to hang the whole family."

Katy was startled at the rapidity with which they were all jumping to the same conclusion. "Now hold on just a second. I'm sure Justine

123

knows what she's doing. She would never have invited him here if she thought there was any real danger he might deliberately crush the company. You know how much Gilchrist, Inc. means to her."

"We also know how badly she wants to mend fences," Hayden said. "Her desire to do that may have blinded her to certain realities."

"I don't think that's the case," Katy said firmly.

"No offense, Katy, but your problem is that you always tend to look on the bright side," Eden said. "You can be extremely naïve."

"You would know," Katy murmured with a rare flash of irritation.

Eden blinked, obviously surprised by the cut from the normally serene Katy. Then her gaze narrowed. "My God, you're not going to fling Nate Atwood in my face, are you? When are you going to figure out that I did you a favor by marrying him? Be grateful he didn't marry you instead."

"I am," Katy said. But that didn't mean she had to forget her own humiliation. Katy knew Nate would have been all wrong for her, but that knowledge did not lessen the sense of having been used.

"Forget it," Darren said quietly. "We'll

all find out soon enough what Luke has planned." He smiled at Katy. "See you in Justine's suite at seven."

Katy nodded and hurried through the conservatory jungle toward the door. It was always a relief to be able to escape from a gaggle of Gilchrists.

On the way back to the cottage she recalled Hayden's remark about Luke burning Gilchrist, Inc. at the stake. Perhaps she would wear her flame-retardant underwear tonight.

The knock on the cottage door came just as Katy finished struggling with the zipper of her turquoise dress. She frowned at her image in the mirror, afraid she knew who the caller was.

"I'll get it," Matt called from the kitchen where he was studying at the table.

"Thanks."

Katy held her breath as she brushed a swath of hair back behind one ear and anchored it with a gold clip. A moment later she heard a familiar deep voice in the living room.

"Evening, Matt," Luke said easily. "Tell your sister I stopped by to pick her up, will you? I decided I didn't feel like walking into that roomful of sharks alone."

"I don't blame you." Matt chuckled. "Katy

says a bunch of Gilchrists surrounding her always makes her kind of nervous."

"Yeah?"

"But she calls them a coven of witches and warlocks, not a school of sharks."

"*Matt,*" Katy yelled from the bedroom, "shut up."

"The boss is here, Katy," Matt called back. "He says he's going to be your date for the evening."

Katy groaned as she watched her cheeks turn pink in the mirror. Trust a teenager to treat what was essentially a business function as a date. She stepped into a pair of very high heels and walked reluctantly out into the front room.

She was not surprised to find Luke looking dangerously elegant in a black dinner jacket, black trousers, and a snowy white shirt. His midnight hair gleamed in the light, and his green eyes held cool speculation. He gave her an approving glance.

"Very nice." Luke held her coat for her. "Don't forget your wings and halo. You may need them tonight to make a quick getaway from the coven."

"I've been handling Gilchrists for years. It doesn't take wings or a halo. It takes a whip and a chair."

"Suit yourself. Don't say you weren't

126

warned." Luke gave Matt a man-to-man look. "Don't worry about your sister. I'll bring her home when it's all over."

"Sure. Right." Matt grinned at Katy. "Don't stay out past curfew. Remember you have work tomorrow."

Katy made a face. "Don't worry. I won't be staying any later than absolutely necessary. I only wish I had a ten o'clock curfew. It would be a great excuse to leave at a reasonable hour."

"Always nice to go out with a woman who's looking forward to the evening ahead," Luke remarked dryly. "Come on, let's get this over with." He took Katy's arm and guided her out the door.

"You didn't have to pick me up," Katy said as he opened the door of his black Jaguar for her. "I don't mind walking. It's perfectly safe around here."

"I wasn't worrying about your safety. It's my own I was thinking of. Like I told Matt, I'm the one who wanted an escort this evening."

She slanted him a curious glance as he got in behind the wheel. "I can't believe you're afraid of your own relatives."

"I'm not afraid of them. I'm just not looking forward to spending an evening surrounded by a pack of witches and warlocks."

Katy was acutely embarrassed. "Matt should never have repeated that remark. It was a gross exaggeration. A silly joke. I certainly never meant to imply — "

"Forget it. I told you once you don't lie well. Katy, I want your honest opinion on something. Which member of the coven do you think might have reason to embezzle from Gilchrist, Inc.?"

Katy stared at him in stunned amazement. Then she scowled. "Are you still on about that?"

"More so than ever." Luke eased the Jaguar onto the road and turned toward the nearby lights of the big house. "There's something going on."

"Forget it, Luke. No one in your family would do anything like that."

"My gut instinct tells me that what's been going on is inside work. If I can't clean it up quietly in the next month or so, I'll launch a full-scale security investigation at Gilchrist, Inc."

"Oh, my God." Katy studied his profile. "How are you going to try to clean it up quietly?"

"With an outside computer investigator. Someone I've gotten to know during the past three years. He makes a living doing this kind of thing. I'd do the investigation

128

myself if I had the time, but I'm too busy putting out brush fires all over Gilchrist, Inc. these days. I can't bury myself in a computer long enough to find the culprit."

"Well, I refuse to believe it's someone in the family, or even in upper management. And I hope you'll keep quiet about your lack of faith in your relatives," Katy said forcefully. "If the other Gilchrists find out you suspect one of them of this kind of thing, they're going to be hurt and angry."

"So what?"

Katy raised her eyes toward the heavens in exasperation. "So you're supposed to be acting as the head of the coven — I mean the clan — now. You should try to get along with the others. Show them you aren't the enemy. Luke, this is your *family*."

"You're too damn sentimental for your own good, Katy."

"I'd rather err on the side of family sentiment than turn into a callous, cold-blooded, unfeeling brute."

"Is that what you think I am?"

Katy hesitated. "I think it's what you try to be," she said gently. "After what happened three years ago you probably think it's safer to be that way. Luke, I know what you went through. I know what it feels like."

"Is that right?"

"Don't mock me. Don't you think I know what a temptation it is to just pull back from everything? I couldn't do that because I had Matt to care for. But you have family members counting on you, too. It's time you came out of your shell and started acting like a man with family responsibilities. You're a Gilchrist, Luke, and there are other Gilchrists depending on you."

His expression was chillingly amused. "Why would I want to be responsible for a bunch of witches and warlocks?"

"Because you're one of them."

"No. I'm not one of them. I'm the family bastard, remember?"

"You make it difficult to forget," Katy said tightly.

Luke was quiet for a moment. "I wonder if Justine will have told the others that I intend to take the Pacific Rim as my fee for saving the collective Gilchrist ass."

"I have no idea."

Justine had indeed told the others. The hostility that greeted Katy and Luke when they walked into the suite was palpable.

Hayden and Maureen got right to the point as Mrs. Igorson served sherry.

"You've got a hell of a nerve, Luke," Hayden growled. "I wonder what your father would have said."

"My father would never have come back to do the job for you," Luke said. "You know that as well as I do."

"You have no business taking the most successful restaurant as a fee," Maureen declared, outraged. "This is a family business."

"So Katy keeps reminding me." Luke swirled the sherry in his glass and went to stand alone at the window.

He remained there, aloof and isolated, as the family members attacked. Justine, looking surprisingly strong and regal in a black and silver dinner dress, watched speculatively as one by one the others registered their protests.

"It's not fair," Eden said passionately. "It's wrong. You don't deserve to be taken back like this in the first place, and you certainly have no right to act like an outside paid consultant."

"If you don't like it, hire yourself another consultant." Luke sipped his sherry and gazed out into the gathering shadows.

"This is all some kind of revenge for what happened to your parents thirty-seven years ago, isn't it?" Darren narrowed his eyes. "Why don't you admit it?"

Katy could stand it no longer. "For heaven's sake, stop it, all of you," she said crisply. "Luke has agreed to save Gilchrist, Inc. Give him a chance."

The Gilchrists turned on her en masse, eyes glittering.

"From what Grandmother has told us," Eden said, "he's only here because you persuaded him to come back. Were you the one who offered him the Pacific Rim as a fee for services rendered?"

Katy's fingers tightened around the stem of her sherry glass, but she kept her voice calm. "No, I did not. No one offered it to him. He simply announced he was going to take it as his fee. It was part of the deal he made with Justine."

Maureen frowned. "Just where do you fit into all this anyway, Katy? I must say, you're certainly moving in the inner circles these days. I thought you were supposed to be Justine's personal assistant, but lately you've been acting more like a member of the family."

Luke spoke coldly from the window. His voice sliced like a sword through the grumbling and muttering of the others. "That's enough, Maureen. And that goes for the rest of you, too. Your claws are showing."

Hayden frowned. "What are you talking about?"

"I'm warning you that Katy is not fair

game. She no longer works for Justine. She is now my personal assistant. That makes her my responsibility, and she answers to no one but me. Is that clear?"

The others — including Katy — stared at him in shock. It dawned on Katy that no one had thought it necessary to come to her rescue in years. She was the one who generally did the rescuing.

"But she's always worked for Grandmother," Darren finally muttered. "Ever since she joined the company."

"Well, now she works for me." Luke's voice was dangerously soft. "That was also part of the deal I made with Justine."

Silence gripped the room. Katy was aware of the speculation in the eyes of Eden and her mother. She had the feeling the two women were leaping to more conclusions.

"I believe we're ready to sit down to dinner," Justine said. She rose from her chair with an odd air of subtle triumph and accepted Hayden's arm. "Shall we adjourn to the dining room?"

No one argued.

It was not the most pleasant evening Katy had passed in Gilchrist company. In fact, she decided, it probably ranked as one of the worst evenings of recent memory.

The family alternately attacked, retreated,

regrouped and charged — again and again. Luke sat impassively through the siege and didn't give an inch of ground. He looked bored most of the time.

Katy grew increasingly depressed until the meal finally came to a conclusion with thin wedges of cheese and a lemon mousse.

She cheered up slightly, however, when the others gathered in the living room for demitasse. Escape was at hand. As soon as the coffee was finished she would be able to leave.

Darren smiled at her with what might have been sympathy as the others fell into desultory conversation about the future of Gilchrist, Inc. He carried his gold-edged cup and saucer over to where she sat.

"You look like you could use a break." Darren nodded toward the French doors. "What do you say we go out onto the balcony for a few minutes and get some fresh air?"

"All right." Katy had always gotten along reasonably well with Darren and was grateful to him now for making a friendly gesture. She put down her cup and got to her feet.

Luke looked up from something he was saying to Hayden as Katy followed Darren out onto the balcony. She could feel his eyes watching her until she stepped out of sight through the glass-paned doors. The shiver of awareness that went through her was not caused entirely by the chilled evening air. She sensed that Luke was not pleased by her exit.

"Whew." Darren made a show of mopping his brow. "Talk about dropping a bombshell on the family. Trust Justine to pull it off. I have to admit I never thought she'd get him here. Dad told me that when Uncle Thornton eloped with his secretary all those years ago, Grandmother said she never wanted to see Thornton, his floozy, or their son as long as she lived. Uncle Thornton is reputed to have said that was fine with him."

Katy gripped the teak railing. "Justine must have been in a rage. I know she was terribly humiliated."

"Did your mother ever forgive the Gilchrists?"

Katy smiled. "Eventually. She was quite happy with my father. They had a good marriage. Unfortunately, Dad was not the businessman my grandfather was."

"Just as my father hasn't got the genius for business that Justine has. Damn it, I wish Justine wouldn't assume that the talent has dried up on our side of the family just because my father didn't inherit it. Talent sometimes skips generations." Darren's hand clamped around the railing. "All I want her

135

to do is give me a chance."

"I know, Darren. I'm sorry. I've tried to talk to her about it, but she's convinced herself that Luke is the only one who can take her place. That's all she's been able to think about lately."

"Bastard. Walks right in through the front door and plucks the ripest fruit from the tree. I can't believe it. How could Justine agree to turn the most successful restaurant over to him as a fee? We don't need him that badly."

"Justine thinks you do."

"Shit." Darren looked down at her with sudden intensity. "Look, Katy, I need to talk to you."

"You are talking to me."

"In private. I've got to discuss something important with you. I can't do it here with the others in the next room. When can I see you?"

"Anytime, I guess. I'll be in my office tomorrow at eight."

Darren shook his head quickly. "No, not in your office. I'll come by your place late tomorrow afternoon."

Katy hesitated and then shrugged. "All right."

"Thanks, Katy." He leaned down to kiss her lightly on the cheek. "I appreciate it.

You've always been a good friend of the family."

There was no sound behind her, but Katy sensed a familiar presence standing in the open French doors. She turned her head and saw Luke standing there. The lights of the living room blazed behind him, throwing his face into impenetrable shadow.

"Are you ready to leave?" Luke's voice was expressionless.

"Yes." Katy stepped forward in relief. "I'll get my coat from Mrs. Igorson. Good night, Darren. See you tomorrow."

"Right," Darren said softly.

Luke glanced at Darren and then followed Katy back into the living room.

"I'm going to take Katy home," Luke said to his grandmother.

"Of course." Justine nodded at Katy. "It was a pleasure to have you with us, my dear. Say hello to young Matt for me."

"I will. Good night, Justine." Katy gave her a quick little peck on the cheek. She bade the others good night and moved to take her coat from Mrs. Igorson.

"Can't blame you for skipping out early," Mrs. Igorson grumbled. "Just wish I could leave, too. It's not going to be what you'd call real cheerful around here after you two take off."

137

"I hadn't noticed it being real cheerful around here up until now," Katy said dryly. "But then, I don't suppose Gilchrists would know what to do with a lot of cheerfulness. See you later, Mrs. Igorson."

Luke took Katy's arm and led her out into the night. He said nothing as they got into the Jaguar and started back toward the cliff cottages.

"Well, that was certainly the fun and entertaining event I expected it to be." Katy leaned her head back against the seat.

"Yeah, it was everything I expected, too." Luke gazed straight ahead into the night as he drove. The light over the front door of his cottage was visible in the distance. "Come in and have a nightcap with me."

Katy felt a tingle of uneasy excitement go through her. "Is that an order from boss to humble employee, or are you asking me politely?"

"I'm asking politely. Of course, if you refuse, I'll probably make it an order. I feel like some company while I unwind. It's been a long day and an even longer evening."

"You've got Zeke for company."

"Zeke is terrific in a lot of ways, but he's not much of a conversationalist." Luke parked the car in the drive of his small cottage.

"That's what you want tonight? Conversation?"

He removed the key from the ignition and turned to look at her. "What else would I want?"

Kitty winced. "Darned if I know. Sure, I'll come in for a nightcap. But I can't stay long. Matt will be expecting me."

"I know."

Luke got out of the car and walked her to the front door. Zeke was sprawled on the rug in the front room. His bowl was beside him. He twitched an ear and opened one eye when Luke turned on a lamp, but he didn't bother to move.

"Terrific watchdog," Katy observed.

"Zeke knows when to get excited and when not to bother. I'm going to start a fire. It's cold in here." Luke took Katy's coat and shrugged out of his black jacket. He loosened his tie and unbuttoned his collar as he moved to the fireplace. "The brandy's in the kitchen," he said as he went down on one knee and reached for kindling.

Katy decided that was a hint. "Check."

She went into the kitchen and started opening cupboard doors until she found a bottle with an impressive French label. Gilchrists, even apparently nonindulgent Luke, showed good taste in this sort of thing. She poured

139

the brandy into two glasses and carried them back out into the front room.

Luke already had a brisk fire going. When he turned toward her she saw the crisp, curling black hair in the opening of his shirt. Her hand trembled slightly when she set down the drinks.

"Thanks." Luke uncoiled smoothly from the hearth and crossed the room to pick up one of the glasses.

"Okay, what do you want to talk about?" Katy forced herself to ask lightly as she sat down on the sofa. The full, flared skirts of her bright blue dress flowed over her legs.

"Hell, I don't care. Anything. Pick a subject." He sank down beside her, sprawled back against the cushions, and stretched his legs out in front of him.

Katy was startled by the unexpected air of weariness about him. She frowned in concern. "Are you all right?"

"I'm fine." He gazed into the flames. "I guess I'm just not accustomed to the happy warmth of family gatherings."

Katy forgot about her nervousness in a rush of sympathy. This could not be easy for him, in spite of the cold, arrogant air he was affecting. "It's going to take a while for your family to get used to you, too.

140

They don't seem to trust you for some reason."

Luke's mouth curved faintly. "Nobody ever called Gilchrists stupid."

"You didn't exactly go out of your way to reassure them about your intentions," Katy reminded him gently.

"Why bother? My intentions aren't all that honorable in the first place. I really am going to take the Pacific Rim, you know."

Katy sat stiffly on the edge of the sofa. "Maybe you'll change your mind."

"Damn, but I love wide-eyed optimists. They say the cutest things."

"Doesn't it get a little tough playing the Bastard all the time?"

"The part comes naturally to me."

"I see." Katy crossed her legs and then quickly uncrossed them. She tucked one foot behind the other and pressed her knees tightly together.

"Relax," Luke ordered quietly. "I'm not going to jump you."

"I didn't think you were."

"Talk to me."

"What about?" Katy could feel dampness under her arms. "Last quarter's earnings?"

"Tell me about your big plans for the future." Luke closed his eyes and rested his head on the cushion. "What are you going to do when you finally escape my clutches?"

Katy hesitated. "I told you. Open Pesto Presto, my specialty take-out restaurant."

Luke's lashes lifted slightly. "Why don't you just stay with Gilchrist, Inc. if you like the restaurant business? You'd probably make more money. You can lose a bundle in your own business."

"To be perfectly blunt, I've been taking orders from Gilchrists for years, and I'm tired of it. I want to be my own boss." Katy watched the flames leap on the hearth and thought about all her dreams. "I want to be free. I want to make my own decisions. I want to create my own future."

"One way or another, you've been tied down for a long time, haven't you?"

"I love my brother more than anything else in this world. And Justine's offer of a job when I was nineteen was a godsend. Don't get me wrong, I'm not complaining. But now Matt is ready to go off on his own. In a couple of months he'll be able to activate his trust fund. It'll see him through college. And Justine finally has you to look after her precious Gilchrist, Inc."

"So you figure you're free to fly off into the wild blue yonder?"

"I'll be able to spread my wings and take a few risks, yes." Katy smiled to herself and relaxed back against the sofa. Thinking about her future always made her feel better. She took a sip of brandy and savored the warmth. "I know just what I want in my little restaurant."

"Tell me about it."

She was surprised by his interest, but more than willing to sink into her favorite daydream. "It will be first class all the way. Good location with an upscale, adventurous clientele. Maybe Bellevue or Edmonds or downtown Seattle. I'll feature my own line of frozen and fresh pesto sauces and a full range of pasta."

"Pasta, huh?"

"Pasta is the perfect modern food. It's good for you, and it's fast. All you have to do is boil it for a few minutes and put some sauce over the top. Pesto Presto will provide everything a person needs for a gourmet meal."

"No kidding."

"I'll offer all sorts of little extras," Katy explained. "Oriental pastas made from buckwheat. Whole wheat pasta. Flavored pastas. And each of my private label pestos will be freshly made on the premises. Maybe I'll even make the pasta on site."

"You're going to run this place all by yourself?"

"I'll have to hire some staff, naturally."

"Naturally. But you're still going to be damn busy. You won't have much time for a social life. Justine says you haven't had much of one for the past few years. She figures you're ready to spread your wings in that department, too."

He had not even opened his eyes to look at her, but Katy realized his question had made her palms damp. What was the matter with her? She was turning into a nervous wreck. She put the brandy glass down quickly. "I'd be interested in a slightly more exciting social life," she admitted cautiously. "If the right man came along, that is."

"The right man? Have you got a profile on this guy?"

"Everyone has an image of what he or she wants in a mate."

"Describe your perfect mate."

She gave Luke an uncertain glance, but his eyes were still closed. She noticed that his lashes were inky black and quite thick, and that the firelight was creating deep shadows beneath his aristocratic cheekbones.

"Well," she said slowly, "I guess my ideal man would be someone open and warm and gentle. Someone I could trust. Someone who's capable of commitment. But most importantly, someone who can cook."

"*Cook?*" Luke's lashes shot up. "You want a man who can cook?"

"Certainly. There are bound to be times when he'll have to help out in the kitchen at Pesto Presto."

"Hell." Luke looked annoyed. "You don't ask for much, do you? You haven't said anything about this perfect man's abilities in bed. Or don't you care about that side of things, so long as he's sweet-natured and handy in the kitchen?"

"You started this conversation." Katy glowered at him. "Now you're deliberately trying to embarrass me."

Luke leaned over her, forcing her deeper into the cushions. His shadowed gaze was brilliant with sensual threat. "You know what I think?"

"What?" She was breathless. Her pulse had kicked into high gear, and a deep heat was pooling in her lower body. She looked up into Luke's face and was transfixed. *Sorcerer's eyes,* she thought.

"I think you've put sex a little too far down on your list."

"Is that right?"

"Damn right. I think that if you have to choose between a man who can cook and one who can make love properly, you'd better pick the guy who can make love."

145

"Why? I can always buy my perfect chef a book on sex. Any man with enough brains to be a good cook is certainly smart enough to learn how to make love properly."

"That's what you think. I've got news for you. Cooking is a skill any idiot can learn. Making love to a self-appointed guardian angel, on the other hand, takes real talent."

He was going to kiss her. Katy bit her lower lip. "I don't think you should do this, Luke."

Just before Luke's mouth came down on hers, he replied, "When I want advice, angel, I'll ask for it."

CHAPTER
SIX

Luke thought he was going to drown in the crystal-clear blue pools of Katy's eyes. She was watching him with a cautious feminine curiosity that made him feel as if he were being weighed and measured on some invisible scale. The sensation bothered him. He wanted her, and he wanted her to want him. Badly.

He leaned into her, savoring the anticipation that was flowing like lava through his veins. He realized he had been contemplating this moment from the instant he had decided to come to Dragon Bay. The only factor that had been in doubt was the timing.

Seeing Katy out on the balcony with Darren earlier had settled the matter, Luke told himself. If she wanted to get involved with a Gilchrist, she could damn well get involved with him, not his cousin.

The glaring fact that Katy was definitely not his type no longer seemed important.

She was soft, he thought. Soft and sweet

and vulnerable. He curved his hand around the nape of her neck, enjoying the silken feel of her skin. Her scent slowly filled him, sinking deeply into his awareness. He could feel the enticing thrust of her breasts against his chest and the curve of her hip pressed into his thigh. His body was already tight and hard with arousal. He took her mouth hungrily as he lowered himself along the length of her.

For a moment nothing happened. Nothing at all.

Luke was so consumed by the rising tide of his own desire that it took him several heartbeats to become aware that Katy was not responding to him. The knowledge stunned him when it finally worked its way into his brain. She was not fighting him, but she was not exactly melting, either.

He was chagrined to realize that she was just lying against the cushions. Her body was stiff, her mouth primly closed. He wondered irritably if she was waiting for some grand revelation from on high before she deigned to surrender to the human emotion of passion.

A terrible sense of impending disaster welled up in Luke. He could not believe he was this aroused by someone who did not want him as much as he wanted her. Surely this kind of powerful, driving need had to be mutual.

Luke took Katy's earlobe between his teeth. She tensed as if she actually expected him to bite her.

Frustration washed through him. What the hell did she want from him? he wondered. It had occurred to him that she might challenge him in this arena, just as she challenged him in other areas of their relationship. He had been prepared to deal with a variety of reactions — but not a lack of reaction.

He was certain she had been aware of him on this fundamental level right from the start. All his masculine instincts had assured him she was as conscious of the electrical charge that crackled in the atmosphere around them as he was.

Luke lifted his head, dazed. He could not believe she was not caught up in the currents of sexual tension flowing between them. He did not want to believe it.

Deliberately he crushed Katy into the cushions. He bent his knee, forcing his leg up alongside her hip. The movement pushed her turquoise skirts up above her knees. A new wave of excitement roared through him when he felt her nylon-clad thigh next to his leg. Katy's lips moved against his for the first time.

"Luke? I really don't think this is a good idea."

"Damn it, is that all you can say?"

"Well, it's not as if you're my type, and I'm certainly not yours. And given the fact that we have to work together for the next six months, I think it would be best if we avoided this sort of entanglement, don't you?"

With a husky groan Luke sealed her mouth shut with his own. He thereby effectively cut off her protest, but he accomplished little else. He slid his hand up over her hip, letting his fingers climb higher until they rested just beneath the enticing weight of her breast.

Katy flinched, but she did not throw her arms around him and beg him to take her. To his shock, Luke could not even tell if the tiny tremor that went through her was desire or disgust.

"I don't believe this," he muttered hoarsely.

"What?"

"I don't believe you're not even a little bit curious about what it would be like between us."

Katy touched his rigid jaw with gentle fingertips. "I didn't say I wasn't curious, just that I don't think it's a very good idea to find out."

The gossamer feel of her fingers on his

face sent sharp talons of desire through him. He sought for answers. "You're afraid of me, aren't you?"

"No. Just cautious, the way I always am around Gilchrists."

"Christ, don't lump me in with the rest of the coven. I'm not like them."

She smiled faintly. "You don't think so?"

"No, damn it. Katy, stop fighting this and kiss me."

"Why?"

He gazed down at her, astounded. "Why? Because you're going to like it, that's why."

"What about you?"

"I'm going to like it, too. A lot. Kiss me, honey. Put your arms around me and let me show you how it'll be between us."

She touched the tip of her tongue to the corner of her mouth. Her eyes searched his intently. "If I do, will you promise me that you won't be angry when I tell you to stop?"

Relief soared in him as he sensed victory. His mouth curved with newfound indulgence. Everything was going to be all right now. "Word of honor."

"All right." Katy slipped her arms around his shoulders.

A hot surge of pleasure ripped through him. Luke gathered her close, one arm under her head, the other around her waist.

"That's better," he muttered. "Much better."

He took her mouth again, this time with every intention of gaining admittance to the inner sanctum.

Her lips trembled uncertainly and then parted beneath his deliberately gentle assault. Euphoria raced through Luke. When Katy's hands tightened around his shoulders and she whimpered softly, he felt as if he had been handed the keys to the citadel.

He realized his hands were shaking. The strangeness of the experience nearly unnerved him.

Luke plunged inside her mouth, tasting, teasing, drinking in the essence of her. He felt her shiver in his arms, but she did not pull away. He edged his knee more deeply upward, lodging it between her thighs. He sensed the sultry heat that emanated from between her legs.

She wanted him. Thank God. He had not been wrong on that score after all. She was wary of him, that was the problem. He could overcome her fears easily enough. If she needed time, he would give her time. Hell, when it came to this kind of thing he had the patience of a saint.

Luke stroked her slowly, letting his hand glide over her breast. He could feel the hard tip of her nipple and gloried in the knowledge that she was at last beginning to respond.

He found the zipper of her turquoise dress and lowered it slowly. His fingers traced the curve of her spine all the way down to the small of her back. She felt so good, he thought. So sleek and smooth and soft. He touched her lightly in the small hollow at the top of her buttocks. He felt deeply rewarded when another tremor of desire rippled through her.

A hungry need was clawing at his insides now, but Luke clamped a steel chain around his own sense of urgency. It had been a long time since he had wanted anything or anyone as much as he wanted this woman, but he could wait a while longer. He wanted to be certain Katy was as caught up in the whirlwind as he was. He needed to know she was experiencing the same shattering excitement.

There was no rush. They had all night.

Katy made a small, exquisitely alluring little sound as her fingers tightened on him. Luke felt the tentative upward surge of her hips. She was melting at last. All hot honey and liquid fire. In another few minutes she would be his.

Luke cradled Katy's buttocks in the palm of his hand, remembering what Justine had said about her cloistered life-style. He promised himself he would move slowly and carefully from here on in, even if it drove him crazy. Seducing angels was new to him.

"Luke?"

He did not hear her at first. Luke was so involved in trying to decide if it was too soon to strip off the turquoise dress that he did not realize Katy had spoken.

"I think that's enough," Katy said tremulously.

"Huh?" He curved his hand around her thigh, squeezing gently. He loved the soft, resilient feel of her.

"I said that's enough. I have to go home, Luke."

He finally realized she had her hands splayed against his chest. She was pushing at him. Dazed with the white-hot need that was threatening to char his insides, Luke raised his head. He looked down at her through narrowed eyes. Her mouth was swollen from his kisses, and her cheeks were flushed.

"You want to go home?" he asked in disbelief.

"It's very late. My brother will be wondering where I am."

"You can't leave now."

She bit her lip. "You promised me you

would stop when I asked you to stop."

"I know, but — "

"But you didn't think I'd ask, did you?" Katy's mouth twisted ruefully. "Typical Gilchrist attitude."

"Katy, I'm warning you, if you don't stop telling me I'm like every other Gilchrist you've ever met, I'm going to lose my temper."

"What will you do? Fire me?"

He scowled at her. "You'd like that, wouldn't you?"

"It would certainly simplify things from my point of view."

"Don't get your hopes up."

She sighed. "I won't. Please, Luke, I really must be going."

He stifled an oath and released her. He took a deep breath as his body protested violently. "Go ahead, angel. Run while you can."

"There's no call to get surly. You started this." She sat up quickly, struggling with her zipper. "I told you it wasn't a good idea."

"There's nothing wrong with the idea." He took charge of the zipper, yanking it up. Hell, he thought. She wasn't playing a game, she really was going to walk out. "You're just scared, that's the problem."

"Can you blame me for being cautious?" She fumbled with her shoes. "I am not interested in having an affair with you, Luke."

"Why not? Because I can't cook?"

"Among other things." Katy stood up quickly.

Luke sprawled back against the cushions, one leg drawn up, his hands behind his head. He eyed her broodingly. She looked flushed and warm and aroused. And he wanted her. He decided to try a different tactic.

"Katy," he said in a soft, coaxing tone, "let's talk about this."

"Stop looking at me like that." She picked up her purse. "We both know you're not really interested in me, Luke. You're annoyed with me because I talked you into coming here to help your family. You're feeling resentful and angry because I made you accept your responsibilities to the other Gilchrists. You decided to get even tonight by asserting yourself over me in a sexual way."

He blinked in amazement at her idiotic logic. "Bullshit."

"It's true, and you know it." She smiled wearily. "I can understand your reaction. Seducing me probably seems like a way of paying me back for interfering in your life. But I don't want to be seduced for that reason, Luke. You'll have to get your vengeance by bullying me in the office, just like all the other Gilchrists do. Now, if you'll excuse me, I've got to be on my way."

She turned and headed for the door. Luke experienced a few seconds of some indefinable panic. He came up off the sofa in a swift rush. He was right behind her when her hand closed around the doorknob.

He put his palm flat against the door and held it shut as she started to open it. "I'll take you home."

"I can walk that far by myself."

"I said I'll take you home, goddammit. I told your brother I'd take care of you tonight, and I intend to do just that." Luke turned and grabbed a black windbreaker out of the closet. Then he pulled her coat off the hanger.

"Thank you," Katy said quietly as he helped her into the coat with short, brusque movements.

He swung her around and caught her face between his palms. She stared up at him with troubled eyes. "You're going to regret this, Katy Wade."

"Why? Because you're going to make life hell for me at work? I can handle Gilchrists. I've been doing it for years."

"What happens between us at work has nothing to do with this," he ground out. "The reason you're going to regret walking out of here tonight is because you're going to spend the rest of your life wondering what it would have been like between us."

She blinked, and then, to Luke's amazement, she seemed to relax. "Good heavens, Luke, where on earth did you get that idea?" Her mouth curved softly. She reached up to pat his cheek gently. "I already know what it would have been like to go to bed with you."

"You think so?" he demanded, goaded.

"Of course. I've got a very good imagination, and I'm sure it would have been quite exciting. Hot, seething, and tempestuous. I would expect nothing less of a Gilchrist."

He set his teeth but decided to ignore the fact that she was still generalizing about Gilchrists. "So what the hell is wrong with hot, seething, and tempestuous?"

"Nothing, if you're the type. I'm not, and we both know it."

"Hell, maybe you could learn to be the type," he growled. "Maybe I could teach you." The image that came into his head at that thought made his whole body clench with desire.

"No." Her eyes were clear and solemn. "I'm not going to learn it from you."

"Why not?"

"The last thing I want to do is get involved

with you, Luke." She opened the door.

Luke did not try to stop her this time. He glanced back at Zeke. "Come on, boy. You might as well come with us."

Zeke picked up his bowl and followed Luke and Katy out into the night.

The chilled night air hit Luke like a dash of cold water. He began to think more clearly. His body calmed somewhat. It was all right, he told himself. He had six months ahead of him. Six months in which to convince Katy that she wanted him as much as he wanted her.

He did not bother to break the silence that hung between Katy and himself during the short walk to her cottage. When they reached her front door he stood waiting patiently until she had it unlocked. The lights were on in the living room, but the rest of the house was in darkness. Matt had apparently gone to bed.

Katy smiled apologetically as she stepped over the threshold and started to close the door in Luke's face. "I'm sorry if I misled you in any way. I realize I shouldn't have let you kiss me. If you feel that what happened back at your cottage was my fault, then I can only say I regret it very much. I realize Gilchrists tend to get very intense about everything."

Luke planted a hand against the door frame and leaned close. He wanted to be certain she could see the anger in his eyes. "Let's get something clear here, Katy Wade. What happened back at my cottage was my fault. I take full responsibility for it. I started it, and one of these days I will damn well finish it. Now go to bed and think about that before you fall asleep."

"But Luke — "

"And stop assuming that I'm just like every other Gilchrist you've ever known." He reached out, caught hold of the doorknob, and yanked the door shut before she could react.

Zeke looked up at him inquiringly.

Luke raked his fingers through his hair. He glanced up at the starry sky. The moon was full tonight. It cast a broad swath of silver on the sea.

"Come on, boy. Let's go down to the beach. I need a long walk."

Zeke bounded forward, heading toward the path that led from the top of the bluff to the rocky beach below. The chilly breeze whipped at Luke's windbreaker as he followed the dog down to the water's edge.

Luke strode swiftly along the coarse, moonlit sand for a long while. He focused on letting the brisk, tangy air drive the remnants of passion out of his system.

When he finally came to a halt at the far end of the beach he had himself firmly back under control. His mind had calmed to the point where he could think clearly and coldly again.

He had been asking himself why he had come here to Dragon Bay ever since he had made the decision. He had tried telling himself he was after the Pacific Rim restaurant. He had played with the idea of vengeance against the rest of the clan. He had wondered if perhaps it was sheer boredom that had driven him to accept the challenge of saving Gilchrist, Inc.

Now Luke realized with grim self-awareness that he finally had the real answer to his question.

He was here because of Katy.

The following morning Katy walked into the office and put a small plastic container down on Liz's desk. Liz leaned forward expectantly as Katy opened the container and reached for a knife. She dipped the knife into the pesto and spread the green paste onto a cracker.

"Okay, tell me what you think," Katy said as she handed the cracker to Liz. "I want your honest opinion."

Liz took the cracker, popped it into her mouth, and munched thoughtfully. "Good. Very good."

Katy frowned. "Are you sure?"

"No. I can't be absolutely positive with just one bite. Better let me have another sample."

Katy spread pesto on another cracker. "This one is made with basil and spinach. I've been experimenting with the amount of pine nuts to use in it."

Liz bit into the next cracker and grinned. "I think you've got another winner here, Katy."

"You really like it?"

"It's terrific," Liz assured her. "Mind if I just help myself to the rest?"

Before Katy could respond there was a soft sound from the office doorway. The hair on the back of her neck stirred in primal reaction. She knew who stood there even before he spoke. He had been on her mind all night, hovering at the edge of her dreams like a dark, dangerous, all-too-exciting phantom. He was the last thing she had thought about before she fell asleep and the first thing that had popped into her head this morning when she opened her eyes.

The Bastard was haunting her.

"Don't you think you need more than one

opinion before you reach any conclusions in this consumer survey?" Luke asked.

Katy forced herself to remain outwardly calm as she glanced over her shoulder. Luke stood there, one shoulder propped against the doorjamb. He was dressed in his customary black. This morning it was a pullover and black trousers. There was no sign of a jacket or tie. Apparently he didn't plan to drive into Seattle this morning.

"Would you care for a taste?" Katy asked politely.

His sorcerer's eyes gleamed. "Yes."

She clutched the knife handle tightly as she obediently spread pesto on another cracker. "Spinach and basil. I'm still experimenting with it."

Luke straightened and came forward to take the cracker from her fingers. His eyes never left hers as he took the offering. His teeth flashed for an instant as he put the whole cracker into his mouth. He chewed reflectively for a long moment. "Not bad," he finally pronounced.

Katy wrinkled her nose. "I can do without the faint praise. If you don't like it, just say so."

He smiled slowly, a smile of pure sensual menace. His eyes drifted over her with deliberate intent and then came to rest on her mouth. "Like I said. Not bad. A little bland. Needs some snap."

"Snap?" She eyed him cautiously. She was beginning to realize he was not talking about her pesto. The heat rose in her cheeks.

"Yeah. Snap. You know, something to spice it up. Pesto ought to have a little zest. I sense some shyness here. An element of uncertainty. A certain lack of experience, no doubt."

"Is that right?" Katy lifted her chin proudly.

"A really good pesto has a natural intensity. The goal is to unleash the underlying passion of the herbs. Know what I mean?"

Katy glowered at him. "I believe so, yes."

"Don't worry. There's nothing wrong with this particular pesto that can't be fixed with a little experimentation and practice."

"I'll keep that in mind," Katy said through her teeth.

Luke nodded, satisfied. "Good." He took the knife out of her hand and spread another cracker with pesto. "Don't worry. You'll get the hang of it."

He handed the knife back to Katy, popped the cracker in his mouth, and walked out of the office.

"Whew." Liz wiped imaginary sweat off her brow. "What was that all about?"

"The man obviously thinks he's an authority on pesto." Katy clamped the lid down on the plastic container.

"Don't give me that," Liz murmured. "He was not talking about pesto."

"Of course he was." Katy stalked toward her own office. "You know how Gilchrists are. They get intense about everything, including food."

"I suppose it's only natural." Liz frowned thoughtfully. "They are in the restaurant business, after all."

Katy closed the door quickly and threw herself down into her chair. She swung around and sat staring out the window for a long, contemplative moment. If the next six months were going to be like this, she was going to be in big trouble.

She had realized from the start that Luke was feeling hostile and resentful toward her. She had been fully aware that he blamed her for forcing him to meet his obligations. She had known he was not happy with his decision to come to Dragon Bay and that she provided a focus for his dissatisfaction. But she had told herself she could handle all that.

Unfortunately, after what had happened last night she had to face a new element in the equation. She was very much afraid that she had somehow become a challenge to Luke.

Gilchrists could become obsessive about getting their own way, especially when someone told them they could not have something they wanted. It was in the blood.

Handling a Gilchrist who had decided to pursue a particular goal was difficult under the best of circumstances. In this instance, however, things were going to be far more tricky. After last night Katy knew she could no longer deny that she was attracted to Luke.

He must never guess how much willpower it had taken to walk out of his cottage.

The realization of just how vulnerable she was shook her to the core.

Luke was dangerous. She had known that from the first moment she saw him. She would have to be extremely careful during the next six months if she wanted to escape the sorcerer unscathed.

The sound of an expensive engine in the drive late that afternoon reminded Katy that Darren had said he would be dropping by to talk to her. She looked up from the cookbook she was studying.

"Sounds like Darren's new Porsche," Matt said from the kitchen table. He closed his textbook with a snap. "What's he doing here?"

"He wants to talk to me about something," Katy said.

"Yeah? What?" Matt got up and went to the window. "The only time that guy talks to you is when he wants something."

"That's not true, Matt."

"The last time he stopped by to see you he wanted you to talk Justine into giving him a trial run as head of Gilchrist, Inc., remember? Man, that is some kind of car. Don't suppose he'd let me try it out."

"I'd say you have two chances, fat and slim. That car is Darren's prize possession." Katy put the cookbook aside. "Let him in, will you, Matt?"

"Sure." Matt obligingly opened the door.

Darren stood on the step. He was dressed in a black leather jacket and black slacks that went nicely with the black Porsche. He smiled at Matt.

"Hello, Matt. Haven't seen you in a while. How's it going?"

"Okay." Matt looked past him to where the Porsche stood parked in the drive. "Nice car."

"Thanks." Darren handed him the keys. "Want to try it out?"

Matt's eyes widened in disbelief. "Are you kidding?"

"No. Why don't you take a run into town? Grab a burger or something while I talk to your sister. Go on, take off."

"Hey, that's great. Thanks. I'll take good care of it." Matt was out the door in a flash.

Katy watched uneasily through the window as her brother reverently opened the Porsche door and eased himself into the cockpit. "I really don't know if this is a good idea, Darren. He hasn't had any experience with cars like that one."

"A car's a car. I've seen Matt drive. He'll be fine. Don't worry about him." Darren closed the door. "Mind if I sit down?"

"No, of course not." Distracted by the sound of the Porsche engine, Katy waved vaguely toward a chair. When the black car started slowly out of the drive she sighed and turned away from the window to confront her guest.

Darren's finely etched mouth curved in the devastating Gilchrist smile. "I appreciate this, Katy."

"No problem. I'll fix us some tea."

"That sounds great." He got up quickly and followed her into the kitchen.

"What did you want to talk to me about?" Katy asked as she filled the teakettle and set it on the stove.

"It's a little complicated." Darren's smile disappeared. Its absence only served to underline the hint of grim bitterness in his eyes. "I'm in trouble, Katy. Big trouble. And you're the only one who can help me."

Katy took the announcement with the grain of salt she applied to all such dramatic Gilchrist statements. "I'll be glad to do what I can, Darren, you know that. What kind of trouble are we talking about this time?"

"The kind that adds up to one hundred and fifty thousand dollars."

"*What?*" Katy nearly dropped the mug she was in the process of taking down from the cupboard. "Darren, is this some kind of joke?"

"I wish it were." Darren shoved his hands into his pockets and looked down at the toes of his shoes. When he raised his eyes to meet hers his expression was bleak. "I owe some people some money."

"A hundred and fifty thousand dollars?"

"Yeah."

"Oh, my God. Darren, what have you been doing? Have you gotten hooked on gambling?"

"No. It was a partnership deal. Real estate. It had the potential to go big, Katy. Real big. If it had worked, I could have proven to Justine that I have a talent for business."

Katy winced. "I see. What happened?"

"The partnership folded because it couldn't get a financing commitment. The developer who set it up, Milo Nyle, told my broker that some of the early purchasers who bought on spec are going to sue if we don't come up with the cash to pay them off. My share is a hundred and fifty grand."

"Oh, my God."

"I need a loan, Katy. Fast. Nyle claims we're all going to be left hanging out to dry if we don't pay up. We could go to jail."

"Jail." Katy stared at him. "Darren, I don't have that kind of money. You know that."

"Yeah. But you could get it," Darren suggested.

"How on earth am I supposed to get a hundred and fifty thousand dollars? Rob a bank?"

Darren's mouth twisted. "Not quite. I've got a plan."

"I don't think I want to hear this." Katy poured boiling water into the teapot. "Go ahead. Tell me your plan."

"It's real simple. You ask Justine for a start-up loan for Pesto Presto. You know she'll help you."

"I do not want to take money from your grandmother," Katy said tightly. "In fact, that is the last thing I want to do. I'm trying to get free of Gilchrists."

"Katy, the money's not for you, it's for me. You get the loan from Justine and turn the money over to me. I'll use it to pay off the investors. Then I'll pay you back."

"It won't work."

"Yes, it will. I won't be able to pay it back all at once, of course," Darren said, "but I can manage it eventually. I'll find a way." He hesitated and then added wistfully, "I suppose the Porsche will have to go."

"Oh, certainly," Katy said grimly. "The Porsche will most definitely have to go. Darren, this is never going to work. You're going to have to approach your grandmother yourself."

Darren slammed a hand against the side of the wall. "Christ, I can't do that, and you know it. It will confirm everything she already believes about my lack of business ability."

"Then talk to Luke."

Darren looked at her in amazement. "Are you crazy? Go to Luke and ask for a hundred and fifty grand to bail myself out of trouble? He'd laugh in my face."

"I'm not so sure about that."

"I am. Katy, you've got to help me. I can't go to anyone in the family. Justine

171

will be furious. My parents will believe she's been right about me all along if I tell them what's happened. And as for Luke, the Bastard probably wouldn't care if I wound up in jail. I'm depending on you, Katy."

CHAPTER
SEVEN

Luke spotted the black Porsche as he walked out of the Dragon Bay Super Food Mart with a week's supply of dog food. Darren's car was parked on Bay Street in front of a fast food restaurant, the place where Matt and several of his friends held part-time jobs. The bright yellow and green logo on the roof was familiar.

Luke scowled at the sight of the Porsche, surprised that Darren had driven all the way to Dragon Bay for a burger and fries. Then he recalled the tail end of the conversation he had overheard on Justine's balcony last night. Darren was in town because he wanted to talk to Katy.

Luke tossed the sack of dog food into the trunk of the Jag. He wondered if Darren's idea of treating Katy was to take her out for a cheap meal.

He closed the lid of the trunk, pocketed his keys, and started across the street. When he reached the corner he saw the door of the restaurant open. Matt, grinning widely, emerged with a couple of friends in tow.

As Luke watched, Matt tossed a set of keys into the air and sauntered toward the Porsche. After one last lingering look at the car his friends reluctantly headed off in the opposite direction.

Luke reached the Porsche at the same time Matt did. Matt glanced up in surprise.

"Hi, Mr. Gilchrist. What are you doing here?"

"Buying dog food. This is Darren's car, isn't it?"

"Yeah. He wanted to talk to Katy, so he let me take it for a spin." Matt shrugged. "Probably wanted me out of the way, but what the heck? It may be the only chance I'll ever have to get behind the wheel of a car like this."

"Darren's with Katy now?"

"Yeah. At the cottage. I guess I'd better get his car back to him before he starts wondering what happened to it."

"No rush. I'll explain things to Darren if he wants to know why you were delayed. Let's go back inside. I'll buy you a coffee or soda or whatever you want to drink."

Matt hesitated. "Why?"

Luke grinned. "I see you've got your sister's natural caution."

"She always says to be wary of Gilchrists bearing gifts."

Luke shook his head with mock regret. "I can't imagine why she's got such a negative attitude toward the Gilchrist family. Come on, let's go inside and get something to drink."

"All right."

Five minutes later Luke slid into a booth opposite Matt and eyed the boy with a thoughtful glance. "What is Darren discussing with your sister?"

"Who knows?" Matt jiggled the ice in his cola. "Maybe he wants her to talk to Justine about something for him again."

Luke considered that possibility. "What kind of things does Darren have her talk to Justine about?"

"A while back he wanted Katy to convince Justine to let him manage Gilchrist's on Lake Union."

"Katy was obviously successful," Luke observed. "He's managing it."

"Sure. Katy can usually convince Justine to do things. But not always. She couldn't get Justine to give Darren a shot at running Gilchrist, Inc."

"Justine can be stubborn."

"Yeah. Maybe Darren wants Katy to try again. You'd think he'd give up now that you're on the scene, though. But Katy says Gilchrists can be real persistent when they want something. She says they get obsessive."

Luke swore softly. "Your sister seems to have made herself an authority on Gilchrists."

"Uh-huh. Had to, I guess." Matt's brow furrowed. "I'll be glad when she's finally free of them. I've tied her down long enough. As soon as I'm in college she'll be able to dump the Gilchrist job and get on with her life." He glanced up, abashed as he suddenly realized what he had said. "No offense."

Luke smiled grimly. "Don't worry. I don't understand how she's been able to work for Justine Gilchrist as long as she has."

"Liz says it's because Katy's adaptable and nonconfrontational."

"What does Katy say?"

Matt shrugged. "Katy says the job's not that bad. Says there are worse jobs. I think she's kind of fond of Justine, if you want to know the truth. She says the rest of the Gilchrists are okay in their way."

"But you don't like them?"

Matt flushed. "I didn't say that. It's just that they try to push Katy around sometimes. Maureen and Hayden are always giving her orders. Darren tries to charm her in order to get what he wants, and Eden . . ."

"What about Eden?"

Matt's young eyes hardened. "There was a guy hanging around Katy about a year ago. I didn't like him very much, but Katy did. I think she was in love with him."

Luke stilled. "Nate Atwood?"

"Uh-huh. Eden came along, and the jerk took one look at her and fell like a ton of bricks. They got married a couple of weeks after Katy introduced them. Justine was really pissed."

"Son of a bitch," Luke said quietly.

"Yeah," Matt said. "He was. But Katy didn't know that right away. See, the problem is, Katy hasn't had a lot of experience, if you know what I mean. She's twenty-eight and all, but she doesn't know as much about guys as you'd think she would at her age. She's been too busy taking care of me and holding down a job, I guess."

After stewing about it all night Luke decided to try the blunt approach the next morning. He walked past Liz and straight toward the inner door of Katy's office shortly after nine o'clock. Liz glared at him through her glasses, but they both knew she couldn't get to the intercom in time to warn Katy that Luke was on his way.

Luke opened the door silently and found Katy propped on the edge of the desk. She had a folder in one hand, but she was not studying its contents. Instead she was gazing thoughtfully out over the gray sea. She was wearing a green silk blouse and a bright gold skirt. There was a splashy gold scarf around her throat. Her red hair glowed with dark fire in the morning light. Luke decided she looked like a bouquet of spring flowers.

"What did my cousin want from you yesterday?" he demanded as he closed the office door.

Katy almost fell off the desk in surprise and whirled around to face him. "Good grief, you startled me. I'd appreciate it if you wouldn't sneak up on me like that."

"Sorry." He walked over to her coffeepot and helped himself to a cup. He'd noticed Katy's coffee always tasted better than anyone else's. "Next time I'll knock. What did he want?"

Her mouth tightened with disapproval. "It was a personal visit. Nothing to do with business."

"Your brother says Darren usually wants something from you when he drops by for one of his little chats. What did he want this time?"

"He just wanted to talk. Is that so strange? Darren and I have known each other for years. It was no big deal."

Luke eyed her consideringly and decided she was not going to tell him a damn thing this morning. So much for the straightforward approach. "If you say so. Be ready to leave for Seattle after lunch. Pack a bag. We'll be spending the night."

She stared at him. "Now hold on just one minute."

"Separate rooms," Luke said blandly. "This is business. You're my personal assistant, remember? I want you along. You'll be sitting in on most of the meetings. I'll want your intuitive analysis of management's input afterward. You know those people better than I do."

He could tell from the distinctly wary expression in her eyes that she did not believe him. Too bad.

He could hardly tell her he intended to take her out to dinner, wine and dine her, and hopefully charm her into his bed. If he told her that, she'd get really upset.

At precisely one o'clock that afternoon Katy zipped her garment bag closed and carried it out into the living room along with her small bag. Matt was waiting along with Luke and Zeke. Zeke glared at her over the rim of the metal dish clamped in his mouth.

"Are you sure you're going to be all right

alone?" Katy asked Matt for the hundredth time.

"Geez, Katy. How many times do I have to tell you me and Zeke'll be fine? Don't worry."

"I'll call this evening," Katy said.

"It's Friday," Matt reminded her patiently. "I'll be working this evening until nine."

"Oh, yes, that's right. Promise me you'll come straight home after work."

"I promise."

"And drive carefully," Katy added.

Luke took the garment bag from her hand. "Don't worry about him, Katy. He'll be fine. He's seventeen, remember?"

Matt threw Luke a grateful glance. "Yeah, don't worry about me."

"Okay, okay, I get the point." Katy hugged him quickly. "I'll be back tomorrow afternoon."

"Right." Matt followed them to the door. "Have a good time."

Katy grimaced. "This is a business trip."

Luke smiled wryly as he tossed her bags into the trunk of the Jag. "That doesn't mean you can't enjoy yourself, Katy."

"Yes, it does." She slid into the passenger seat of the Jag and waved at Matt and Zeke.

Luke said nothing as he guided the car out of the drive and onto the road toward

180

Dragon Bay. A few minutes later they were through the small town. Luke took the freeway that headed south toward Seattle. The sky was heavy, and a light misty rain was falling.

"I take it you haven't left Matt alone very often," Luke said, breaking the long silence.

"No. I know I have to get used to the idea that he's almost an adult, but it isn't easy. I worry about him."

"He worries about you, too."

Katy glanced at Luke in surprise. "He does?"

"He thinks he's to blame for tying you down all these years."

"That's nonsense."

"No, it's not. It's the truth, and he knows it. He's afraid that because of your responsibilities toward him, you haven't had enough experience in the real world."

"Is that right?"

"He's worried you aren't sophisticated enough to be able to tell the sons of bitches from the good guys."

"I'm sure I'll figure it out," Katy said. "I've always been a fast learner."

The corporate offices of Gilchrist, Inc. occupied one floor of a sleek high rise in downtown Seattle. The view through the bank of tinted windows on the twentieth floor was spectacular. The city hummed with the energy that only a Pacific Rim port could ignite.

Elliott Bay, slate gray beneath a leaden sky, was dotted with monster ships. Small worlds of their own, the tankers and freighters bore the logos of shipping companies scattered all over Asia and the Pacific. In the distance the snow-capped Olympics were almost lost in the mist that seemed to cover the world.

"Why did Luke bring you with him today?" Eden asked. "What's going on, Katy? What's he up to?"

Katy turned away from the splendid view and looked at Luke's cousin. Eden lounged elegantly behind her desk, her body betraying a subtle tension. She was wearing a crisp black suit that emphasized her slenderness and highlighted the stark red of her mouth and nails. Her green eyes were sharp and anxious.

"I'm supposed to give him my analysis of the people in the various meetings he's holding with management today." Katy shrugged. "What can I tell you? I'm a glorified secretary."

Eden drummed her nails on the polished surface of her desk. "But what is he up to?"

Katy thought of the computer investigation Luke had launched but said nothing. Luke had specifically told her not to tell anyone, and she was supposed to be working for him now. Like it or not, her business loyalty was to the Bastard.

"I'm not sure," Katy said cautiously. "Right now he's gathering data. That's all I can tell you."

"He's got something planned. I can feel it." Eden stared accusingly at Katy. "You've got to let us know what's going on, Katy. There's too much at stake here."

"As far as I know, he's doing exactly what he told Justine he would do. He's trying to save the company."

"Dad says we can't trust him, and I agree." Eden gazed into the glowing screen of the computer on her desk as if she could divine the future there. "He makes me nervous."

"I think Luke makes everyone nervous. Look, Eden, I really don't know what else to tell you. Justine wanted him. She's got him. All the rest of us can do is hope for the best." Katy glanced at her watch. "I've got to run. Luke's called another meeting in the boardroom in five minutes. I'm supposed to attend."

"Katy, wait." Eden leaned forward, her expression intense. "You will warn us if you find out Luke is planning anything that will hurt the family, won't you? You owe us that much."

Katy hesitated. "I'll warn Justine," she agreed quietly. "I owe her that much. I don't really owe the rest of you anything, do I?"

Eden's eyes narrowed. "What is that supposed to mean?"

"Just what it sounds like. I've always worked for Justine, not the rest of you."

"No," Eden whispered. "It's more than that. A lot more. You've never forgiven me for marrying Nate, have you? Why don't you admit it?"

"Nate has nothing to do with it."

"I don't believe you." Eden rose and went to stand at the window. She gazed moodily out at the gray skies. "You don't know how lucky you were that he ditched you for me. In fact, the way I look at it, you owe me for having saved you the experience of marriage to Nate Atwood."

Katy studied Eden's striking profile. "I know."

"The man was a user."

"Yes."

"He didn't love me. He never loved me. He used me," Eden hissed.

"I know." *And he used me to get to you,* Katy thought. "But you're free of him now.

Thank God Justine had her lawyers handle the divorce proceedings. She protected you."

"You think so?"

Katy frowned, not fully understanding the bitter tone in Eden's voice. "Perhaps not emotionally. No one could protect you in that way. But financially, yes. Nate didn't get much. Just a token amount."

Eden closed her eyes briefly. "God, what a bastard he was." She opened her eyes. "And now we've got another bastard to deal with."

"Life's tough, isn't it?" Luke said from the doorway. He glanced at Katy. "You ready? The meeting starts in two minutes."

"I'm ready." Katy gave Eden a last uneasy glance and followed Luke out into the hall.

Luke slanted Katy a speculative look as he paced beside her down the hall to the boardroom. "What was that all about?"

"Her divorce."

"Cheerful topic."

"Not particularly," Katy murmured. "Gilchrists are rarely — "

"Don't say it. You know, Katy, sometimes I get a little tired of your generalizing about Gilchrists."

"Fair enough." Katy brightened. Something about sparring with Luke seemed to perk up her spirits. "Sometimes I get a little tired of Gilchrists, too."

Fraser Stanfield was standing with a small cluster of management-level people when Luke and Katy walked into the room. He nodded at Luke and smiled at Katy. He came forward to hold a chair for her.

"What are you doing in town?" he asked under cover of the murmur of conversation.

"Beats me. I'm told I'm here to advise."

"I can believe it. You're good at that. Staying the night?"

"Yes, as a matter of fact, I am."

"Great." Fraser grinned. "How about dinner?"

Katy was startled. Fraser had never before suggested anything resembling a date, but after what they had been through together during the past few months she certainly had no objection. "Sounds great."

"I'll meet you in the lobby of your hotel at seven," Fraser said. "Don't worry. We won't go to a Gilchrist restaurant."

Katy laughed. Out of the corner of her eye she saw Luke turn his head at the sound. His gaze flicked toward Fraser and then rested for a moment on Katy. He did not look pleased.

She realized with a jolt of intuition that he had planned to take her to dinner himself. A thwarted Gilchrist was a dangerous Gilchrist.

On the other hand, she knew she'd narrowly escaped a situation that would have been fraught with sensual menace. She was no good at dealing with sensually menacing situations. She was not the type.

So why wasn't she feeling relieved? Katy wondered.

"What the devil is he up to?" Fraser asked later that evening.

Katy looked up from her menu. It occurred to her that she was being pumped yet again for inside information on Luke's intentions. So much for a pleasant, relaxing dinner date. All day long people had been cornering her to ask what she thought the Bastard planned to do about the Gilchrist situation. With an inner sigh of regret she realized that Fraser was no different.

She supposed she shouldn't be too hard on him. Fraser had his own future to worry about. On the other hand, she still worked for Luke and had to remain loyal to him.

"I don't know," Katy said, and she went back to studying her menu.

"No hints?"

"None."

Fraser smiled. "Hey, come on, Katy, this is me, Fraser. Your old buddy, remember? We've been in the Gilchrist trenches together for the past six months. You can tell me what's going on. I've got a career here that

I'm trying to maintain."

Katy reluctantly put down the menu. "I know. I'm sorry, but the truth is, there isn't anything I can tell you at this point. Luke seems to be gathering data. I know he's concerned about the declining situation at Gilchrist Gourmet, and he's looking at the two restaurants that are in trouble. But I don't know what he's going to do."

"If he's got half the business sense everyone credits him with, he'll sell off Gilchrist Gourmet."

"Maybe."

"Gilchrists have always been in the restaurant business," Fraser said forcefully. "They should stick with what they know. They ought to get out of the frozen entrée market. They don't understand it."

"Gilchrist Gourmet was doing very well at this time last year."

"That was last year." Fraser picked up his wineglass and swirled the contents with an impatient movement. "Today it's headed down the tubes. Gilchrist has to realize he's got no choice but to sell it off."

"If it has to be sold, I'm sure he'll sell it," Katy said equably. "But if anyone can save it, he can."

Fraser eyed her. "You've got a lot of faith in the Bastard."

"The man may not be a gentleman and a scholar, but he's good at what he does."

"In other words, he knows how to make money?"

Katy smiled ruefully. "From all accounts, yes."

Fraser put down his wineglass and touched her hand with intimate urgency. "Katy, I meant what I said earlier. I've got a lot on the line right now, career-wise. Can I count on you to keep me informed of any moves the Bastard makes?"

"I'll do what I can," she said quietly. "Would you mind very much if we ate dinner now? I'm starving."

Fraser seemed reluctant to get off the subject. His gaze flickered, and then he managed a smile. "You bet. Try the salmon. They do a good job with it here. You know, I've talked to Eden a couple of times."

"Have you?"

"Trouble is, she doesn't know what's going on either. And I'm not sure she'd tell me if she did. Hell, she's family, and I'm just the hired help. In any event, I think she's got other things on her mind right now."

The offhand remark about Eden caught Katy's attention. "What makes you say that?"

"Saw her with her ex-husband this week." Fraser spoke casually as he opened his menu.

"Maybe they're planning a grand reconciliation." He chuckled wryly. "Justine is going to have a fit if that happens, isn't she? She was so damn relieved when the divorce was final."

Katy was shocked. "Eden and Nate? You saw them together? Are you certain?"

Fraser glanced up. "They were getting into a cab together outside one of the restaurants. I had just finished talking to the manager and was on my way out. Looked like Atwood had been waiting for her."

Katy recalled the bitterness in Eden's voice that morning. *He used me.* "That's hard to believe."

"You know Gilchrists. They like lots of drama. Having an affair with her ex might appeal to Eden. Kind of kinky. You know something, Katy?"

"What?" Katy tried to imagine why Eden would rekindle the flames of passion with Nate Atwood. As far as Katy knew, Eden hated the man now. But she'd always heard hate was the flip side of love.

"I'm really glad to know I've got you on my side," Fraser said deliberately. "When it comes to dealing with Gilchrists, friends have to stick together. And we're friends, aren't we, Katy?"

"Yes," Katy said quietly. "I think I'll skip

the salmon and try the pasta in pesto sauce. I want to see if it's any better than my own."

Katy unlocked the door of her hotel room an hour later, relieved that she had managed to shed Fraser downstairs in the lobby. For a few minutes there she thought she had detected a businesslike speculation in his eyes that had angered her.

It occurred to her that Fraser might try to seduce her in order to ensure that she kept him informed of events inside the head office of Gilchrist.

Did everyone think she was an unsophisticated little fool? she wondered wearily as she opened the door. If she wanted to get herself seduced, she would prefer a man who was driven by some emotion other than concern about his career.

Luke, for example.

The thought staggered her. She must be crazy even to consider the idea. But at least with Luke a woman would know that there was some passion involved. Gilchrists were nothing if not passionate.

With Fraser, Katy thought, a seduction would be strictly business.

Not that she was interested in getting herself seduced by anyone, she assured herself as she started to close the door.

She was groping for the light switch when she sensed the other presence in the room. Her hand froze.

"At least you had the sense to come back to the room alone." Luke's voice was dark, gritty and dangerous in the shadows.

Katy sucked in her breath. She snapped on the wall switch and stood glowering furiously at Luke.

He did not notice her expression. He was sprawled in the chair near the window, gazing out over the city. His booted heels were propped on the sill. Ice clinked in the glass in his hand. One glance at the small refrigerator in the corner showed that he had been into the room's small liquor supply.

"My God, you nearly scared me to death." Katy realized her pulse was racing and her insides felt tight. Her whole body had gone into the fight-or-flight mode even though her brain had already recorded the fact that there was no immediate threat of attack. "What are you doing here?"

Luke did not turn around. "Did you accept the date with Stanfield to make me jealous?"

Katy was flabbergasted. "Good grief, no. Of course not. Are you crazy? Why would I want to make you jealous?"

"How should I know? All I know is that

it's a tactic women use."

"Some women, maybe. Not all women." Katy pulled her scattered senses together. Finding Luke here in her room was like falling down the rabbit hole. Nothing seemed quite real.

"It worked," Luke said quietly. "I was jealous." He took a swallow from the whiskey in his glass. "Christ, that's one emotion I really hate. Spent most of my marriage being jealous."

"Luke — "

"When Ariel walked into a room every man looked at her and wanted her. Instantly. She knew it. She loved to see my reaction. Said it made for good sex later."

Katy perched cautiously on the edge of the bed. Her fingers were trembling. Luke had still not turned around, so she could not see his face. But she heard the razor's edge of the old, buried anguish in his voice. She had a sudden desire to comfort him but did not know how.

"I'm sorry, Luke."

"No reason to be." Ice clinked again in his glass. "She was a beautiful woman. She couldn't help it."

"No, of course not." But Ariel should not have enjoyed Luke's jealousy, Katy thought. She should not have used it to provoke him to passion. The man had enough passion in him as it was. So much passion.

"She always made up for it later. In bed."

Katy clenched her hands together in her lap. "I see. It didn't bother you, then? You didn't really mind feeling jealous because you knew she would make up for it in bed?"

"I hated it." The words were a soft, savage snarl. "The only thing that made it bearable was that I knew she loved me. She was only playing games. But I got to hate the games. She never seemed to understand that."

Katy searched for something to say. "Luke, I didn't set out to make you jealous tonight. You and I do not have a relationship, so there is no reason for either of us to feel jealousy or any other strong emotion toward each other."

"Is that right?"

"For the record," Katy continued determinedly, "I would just like to say that I would never try to make someone I cared for jealous. It would be the last thing I would do. It seems cruel."

"Not very exciting?"

"No. Just cruel."

"I agree with you," Luke said. "It is cruel." He swallowed the remainder of his whiskey. "For the record, I hereby state that I would never deliberately set out to make someone

I cared for jealous."

She believed him. Katy smiled tremulously. "Well, I suppose that takes care of that."

"We don't have a relationship, but we have just sworn not to try to make each other jealous. Nothing like getting the fine print out of the way first, I guess." Luke set his glass down on the table.

He unstacked his booted feet from the windowsill and got up out of the chair. He turned to face Katy for the first time. His hooded gaze held hers with mesmerizing intensity.

"Luke?" Katy stilled, aware of him at every level on which it was possible for a woman to be aware of a man. She rose slowly from the edge of the bed as he came toward her.

"I know I'm not your type." He came to a halt directly in front of her. "You've made it clear I'm not the man of your dreams. But I want you very much. If you come to me, even for a little while, I swear I won't play games with you. Whatever we have between us will be completely honest. Is that enough for you?"

Katy realized she was holding her breath. A sweet, hot flame was scorching through her. The feeling was unlike anything she had ever experienced. She was breathless and anxious and exhilarated at the same time.

She was not a creature of great passions, she reminded herself desperately. But she could not ignore this shattering sensation. It occurred to her that she might never know this feeling with another man. If she did not seize the opportunity, she would spend the rest of her life wondering what she had missed.

And she had already missed so many things in life.

Katy made her decision.

"Yes," she said. "It's enough."

CHAPTER
EIGHT

Luke smiled at her. It was a slow, haunting smile that barely touched his mouth but turned his eyes into emeralds. It was a sorcerer's smile; a smile that conjured secrets she could only imagine; a smile that promised he would share the magic with her. Breathless in the face of her own daring, Katy looked up into his brilliant eyes and wondered what she had done.

But it was too late to retreat, even if she had wanted to do so. Her whole being was already committed. Her soul was committed. She felt alive in a way she never had before, and she knew she was not going to back away from this fire, come what may. For once she was going to let passion rule, just like any Gilchrist.

"Something amusing you?" Luke circled the nape of her neck with one hand. His thumb traced the line of her throat as if it were a vein of gold.

"No." Katy shivered at his touch. "Yes."

"Tell me." He brushed his mouth lightly, persuasively across hers.

"I was just thinking that I may have spent too many years surrounded by Gilchrists. I'm beginning to act like one."

"Do me a favor."

"What's that?"

"I would appreciate it very much if tonight, just for once, you would avoid the generalizations. I'm the one who is going to make love to you. The rest of the Gilchrists have nothing to do with this."

She flushed. "I see your point. It's not exactly a group activity, is it?"

"No. It's just you and me." His fingers moved slightly on her throat, pushing aside the curve of her red hair. He leaned close again and kissed the place directly behind her right ear.

Katy was amazed at how incredibly sensitive that particular spot was. She took a deep breath and touched Luke's jaw. He turned his head and kissed the vulnerable skin on the inside of her wrist. Katy's fingers trembled.

Luke smiled his sorcerer's smile again when he felt the tremor go through her.

"You want me tonight, don't you?" he asked softly.

"Yes."

"That's how it's supposed to be. Not like it was last time on my sofa."

"Last time I wasn't sure I wanted to get involved."

"But tonight you're sure you do want to get involved?" His eyes gleamed.

"No. But I'm going to do it anyway." Katy smiled and lifted her arms to circle his neck.

Luke laughed softly as he scooped her up into his arms. Taken by surprise, Katy instinctively clutched at his shoulders. He carried her as though she were weightless.

"Where are we going?" Katy asked anxiously as he started toward the door with her in his arms.

"Not far." He stopped in front of the wall switch. "Turn out the light."

Katy glanced up at him and then obediently flipped the switch. The room was plunged into darkness, and the sultry intimacy of the moment was intensified a hundredfold. She was acutely aware of her body's reaction to being cradled in Luke's arms. Katy was no longer certain she could have stood on her own two feet if she had been forced to do so.

She closed her eyes, luxuriating in Luke's strength as he carried her back across the room. She was certain he was going to put her down on the bed. She could already picture the next few minutes in her mind. He would lower himself down beside her and take her into his arms. She prayed he would not move too quickly, the way he had the other night. She needed time to adjust to this kind of passion. It was so new to her.

Katy clung to Luke tightly as she sensed the shadows spinning around her. In a second she would feel the bed beneath her back. *Please, not too fast,* she whispered silently. *I'm not like you. I'm not the type to explode into passion at a single touch. I need a little time. I think.*

But it was not the bed she felt when the world stopped shifting around her. It was Luke's hard, muscled thigh under hers. She opened her eyes and saw the rain-drenched lights of the city spread out before her like so many diamonds in the night. She realized that instead of setting her on the bed Luke had sat down in the chair in front of the window. His arms were warm and strong around her.

"I'll try to get it right this time," Luke said, as if he had somehow read her mind.

He bent his head and took her mouth, kissing her with a slow, inviting passion that took Katy's breath away. She felt herself sinking into warm quicksand. Her lips parted beneath his gently persuasive mouth.

Luke made a soft, hoarse sound that told Katy of his desire and set her senses vibrating. Deep inside her something responded to the masculine need in him. She leaned into him and kissed him back with growing eagerness.

When he opened his own mouth and invited her inside she hesitated. Then curiosity overcame her. She tasted him cautiously until she discovered an exciting heat that seemed to emanate from the core of his body. It hinted at a smoldering fire she longed to touch. She curled closer, silently asking for more.

Luke groaned softly, deeply. His hand tightened tenderly on the nape of her neck and then his fingers slipped beneath the collar of her dress. Katy felt the coolness on her back as he lowered the zipper, but it was the warmth of his fingers gliding down her spine that jangled every nerve ending in her body. She tensed instinctively.

"Relax, honey. I'm not going to rush you this time." Luke raised his head slightly to look down at her. "We've got all night."

Katy smiled tremulously. She could feel the hardness of his body beneath her thighs, and she knew he was fully aroused. But she also sensed the discipline he was exerting over himself. It was there in every line of his body, from the set of his jaw to the corded muscles of his shoulders. She touched the side of his face with a sense of wonder.

"I knew you were a passionate man," she whispered, "but I hadn't realized you were in complete control of that passion." She had never known a Gilchrist who was in control of his passions. They always seemed at the mercy of them.

"Passion without control is the most destructive force on the face of the earth," Luke said. "I had to learn how to tame the fire a long time ago."

"And passion that is under control?"

Luke smiled his mysterious smile. "The most creative force in the universe. Tamed fire."

"I've never known a man who has tamed fire." Katy slid her hand down the column of his throat to the open collar of his black shirt. "You're unique, Luke Gilchrist."

"No. You're the one who is unique." His hand moved in her hair. "Definitely one of a kind. The fire is in you, too. Sweet and hot and waiting to be discovered."

Katy was fascinated. The notion that this man who fairly seethed with passion could see that emotion in her was incredibly seductive. She had never, ever thought of herself in that light. "How do you know it's within me?"

"I can see it," he said. "And hear it. And feel it. It was in your eyes when you told me I had a duty to save Gilchrist, Inc. It was in your voice when you ordered Justine not to grovel to me. It vibrates in you when you talk about your plans for the future. Honey, you're a regular volcano."

"No. I don't think so." Katy splayed her fingers against his chest. She loved the feel of the crisp, curling black hair she found beneath his shirt. "But I'm glad you think you can see a few flames inside me."

"The fire is there, all right," Luke said against her mouth. "You and I are going to go up in flames together."

"Then what?" she asked quietly. The part of her that always had one eye on the future could not be completely banished, not even for one night.

"Then I'm going to tame it for a while." Luke's hand stole around her to cup her breast. "But only for a short time. Half the fun of playing with fire is watching it burn wild and free."

Katy took a grip on her resolve and ruthlessly crushed all thought of the future. For once in her life she would live only in the present. She wrapped her arms around Luke's neck and hugged him fiercely.

"Sweet and hot," Luke whispered. He touched her nipple through the lacy fabric of her bra. His fingers moved lightly, coaxing forth her response.

Katy moved restlessly beneath the caress. She realized she wanted more. She fumbled with the buttons of Luke's shirt, opening it all the way to his waist. Then she reached inside to touch him the same way he was touching her.

Luke shuddered in response. His mouth closed over hers for a long, searing moment, and his hand was warm and strong on her breast.

Katy felt the quicksand tugging at her, pulling her deeper and deeper until she could not move without being aware of its over-powering embrace. She realized she did not want to be free now. She twisted against Luke, seeking more of his fire.

He responded by moving his palm up over her leg and under the hem of her skirt. He did not pause. His hand slipped along the inside of her thigh, gliding lightly over her silken pantyhose straight to the heart of her own fire. His fingers closed gently around her.

Katy cried out softly as a deep tremor shook her.

"You're already wet," Luke said, sounding pleased and satisfied and awed all at the same time. "Hot and wet. I can feel you right through your panties and these damn pantyhose." He squeezed gently.

"*Luke.*" Katy was having difficulty breathing.

"Relax. I told you there was no rush."

"I can't relax. Luke, I feel so strange."

"You feel beautiful." He released her long enough to slide his hand beneath the waistband of her underwear.

He eased the pantyhose and her panties down over her hips and off her bare feet in one slow, sensuous movement that was a caress in itself. Katy clung to him when his hand returned to the damp, hot place between her thighs.

She buried her face against his shoulder when Luke tested her gently with one finger.

"Tight," he said in her ear. "Tight but ready." He eased his finger back out of the snug passage and used her own moisture to lubricate her small, swelling button of desire.

He repeated the action slowly and deliberately, easing his finger into her and then teasing the small nubbin of female flesh. He did it again.

And again.

The delicious torment seemed to go on forever.

A desperate hunger gripped Katy. She felt ready to explode. She dug her nails into Luke's back. She kissed him frantically, her lips moving feverishly over his mouth, his throat, his chest.

"Now?" Luke asked softly.

"Oh, God, yes. *Yes.*"

"You're sure?"

She bit down on his lower lip, punishing him gently. "Yes. Now. Do it."

"All right, honey. If that's what you want."

She was vaguely aware that Luke was unfastening his black jeans. She heard the rasp of his zipper and felt his hand move as he made himself ready for her. There was a soft ripping sound in the darkness as he opened the small foil packet with his teeth.

Katy waited eagerly for him to pick her up and carry her over to the bed. But he made no effort to get up out of the chair. Instead he lifted her slightly and turned her so that she was gazing straight down at him. He put his hands on her thighs and urged her legs apart so that she straddled him.

"What are you doing?" Katy asked, too dazed with desire to understand.

Luke's eyes glittered in the shadows. "Taming fire."

He lowered her slowly. Katy gasped when she realized what he intended. So much for the bed. He was going to make love to her right there in the chair. A *chair*, for heaven's sake. She could not believe it. This was what came of consorting with sorcerers, she thought.

She felt Luke's broad shaft brush against her, probing gently. She braced herself with her hands on his shoulders. "So big," she whispered, startled at the size of him.

Luke gave a short, husky laugh. "Don't worry, sweetheart. We're going to fit together perfectly."

He began to ease himself into her, letting her set the pace. Katy gripped his shoulders tightly and held her breath as she sank down slowly.

He *was* big. She felt him opening her, stretching her, making a place for himself in the very heart of her. Her body clenched in reaction. Luke forced himself slowly, gently past the tightness. Katy felt him climb higher and higher within her until she was full.

"Feel the fire, sweetheart," Luke said against her throat. "Let it burn."

He gripped her hips and urged her into a passionate rhythm. With a soft exclamation of wonder and surrender Katy gave herself up to the surging pattern. Her body took control. She wrapped herself around Luke, riding him as though he were a magnificent wild stallion.

When the flames swept through her she did not recognize them for what they were. It was the first time she had ever experienced them. Stunned at the power of her own body, uncertain of what to expect next, she whispered Luke's name like a mantra.

"That's what the fire feels like," Luke said. His hands tightened on her hips. "Don't be afraid of it. You were born to walk in fire."

With a tiny, muffled shriek of surprise Katy shuddered in the throes of her first climax. A thrilling euphoria raced through her as her whole body sang the song of release. Somewhere in the shimmering darkness she heard Luke's guttural sound of masculine satisfaction. She felt his fingers close around her buttocks with urgency. And then a heavy shudder racked him.

He was hers, she thought triumphantly. For this moment in time he belonged to her just as surely as she belonged to him.

And then she was spiraling downward into a dreamy state that obliterated the earlier instant of infinite awareness.

She barely noticed when Luke eventually lifted her in his arms and carried her over to the bed. When he came down beside her

208

she reached for him, burrowing into his warmth. His arms closed protectively around her, and she slept.

A long while later Luke lay propped against the pillows, one arm around Katy, the other folded behind his head. He gazed out at the rain-drenched neon night and did what he had learned to do exceedingly well during the past three years. He concentrated on the present.

But the present was different now. He was no longer alone in it. The present meant Katy.

He had not felt this good in a long time, Luke realized. Hell, he had never felt quite like this. Not even with his beautiful witch of a wife. Sex had been terrific with Ariel, but there had never been this sense of peace afterward. There had never been this feeling of completeness. It occurred to Luke that with Ariel he had always been hanging on the brink of uncertainty. Life had been exciting but wearing.

With Katy there would be moments like this one, moments of peace and tranquillity. Serenity and calm without having to be alone. It was a novel thought.

The present definitely meant Katy.

It also meant problems.

His mind drifted freely for a time, touching briefly on many things. He reran the meeting he had held that afternoon with the management team of Gilchrist Gourmet. Then he moved on to his most recent conversation with the computer investigator he had hired to ferret out the embezzler.

For a time Luke's mind hummed softly like any good computer. Automatically, almost effortlessly, he compiled data in his head, analyzed it, processed it, searched for patterns.

Then his thoughts shifted again. He frowned in the darkness.

"Is something wrong, Luke?" Katy's voice was soft and slurred with sleep. She did not open her eyes.

"No. I was just thinking."

"About what?"

"A lot of things."

"You're thinking about the company, aren't you?" she accused softly.

He smiled faintly. "How did you know?"

"Lucky guess." She touched him reassuringly. "It's going to be all right, Luke. You'll put Gilchrist, Inc. back on track." She snuggled closer and yawned. "I have complete confidence in you."

"Is that so?"

"Umm-hmm."

"What would you say if I told you I didn't

give a damn what happens to Gilchrist, Inc. in the long run?"

"I wouldn't believe you," she mumbled. "You're a Gilchrist. You took on the job because you're a part of the family, and you'll do your best to save the company for the family."

"You'd better understand something, Katy. I didn't take on the job because of family loyalty. I took it on because of you."

"*Me?*" She opened her eyes at that. The glow of the night filtering in through the window revealed her expression of confusion. "What on earth are you talking about?"

"You heard me." He looked down at her, willing her to understand. "I'm here because of you."

"I don't believe it." No one had ever done anything like that for her in her entire life. She was not the type of woman for whom men did such things.

"Believe it," he advised softly. "I didn't understand it myself at first, but I realized the truth soon enough. I wanted you. A part of me knew I wouldn't stand a chance of getting you unless I agreed to take over the company. So I made the bargain."

Her mouth opened in astonishment. She closed it quickly. "A bargain? Is that how you see it?"

"We have a deal. It lasts for six months."

Katy gasped. Clutching the sheet, she levered herself upright and curled her legs under her, tailor fashion. "This is crazy. I don't understand. Are you telling me that when you forced me to agree to stay on for six months you were making some sort of bargain with me to be your lover?"

"Right the first time." Luke studied her with lazy hunger. He realized it gave him a deep satisfaction to know that she had experienced her first climax in his arms.

He had not needed Justine's comments on the subject to know that Katy's experience with sex had been extremely limited. He had guessed the truth of that the first time he touched her that night in his cottage. Her startled surprise tonight when she had shuddered in his arms had confirmed it.

Luke savored the knowledge that he was the man who was going to spend the next six months introducing Katy to her own passions. His body began to harden again at the thought.

Katy was glaring at him, but the expression did not affect the sexy picture she made. Her hair was in soft, tangled disarray, and the sheet she held so tightly to her breasts was barely covering the most interesting points.

"Luke, this is utterly outrageous. You can't mean it. People don't do things like that. Not for me, at any rate."

"Like what?" Luke reached and twisted his fingers lightly in her hair. He loved the texture of it. It was like silk.

"They don't take on monumental tasks like saving Gilchrist, Inc. simply to get a chance to have a six-month affair with a woman they barely know," Katy sputtered.

Luke smiled. "But that's exactly what I did."

"I don't believe it," she stated again. "I'm not the sort of female who inspires that sort of reaction in a man. Especially a man like you."

"You don't know your own power, lady."

Her eyes narrowed with speculation. "What if I hadn't let you seduce me so easily? What if I had managed to resist you for the entire six months? What would you have done?"

"Suffered mightily." Luke used his grip on her hair to tug her down across his chest. She felt warm and soft against his hardness. The scent of her created a new wave of gathering excitement in him.

She lay gazing up at him, wide-eyed. "Is this whole thing just a source of amusement for you? A challenge you accepted on a whim?"

His hand tightened briefly in her hair. He

moved, rolling her onto her back. Then he sprawled on top of her. "Believe me, I am not amused by the problems of Gilchrist, Inc. Nor am I amused by Justine and the others. I wouldn't have gotten involved with them after successfully avoiding them for all these years just because I felt I had to respond to a challenge."

"Then why?"

"I told you. I wanted you." He kissed her slowly and deeply. When he lifted his head he was fully aroused. "And I still do."

She touched her tongue to her lower lip. "For the next six months?"

"Yes."

"That's not very long," she whispered.

"It is for me." He did not know how to explain to her that after three years of an eternal present, six months sounded like forever. It was as far into the future as he could see.

But he knew how to tell her of his desire for her.

Luke stroked Katy from breast to thigh, reveling in her firm curves and smooth, satiny skin. He edged between her legs and moved his hand down over her soft stomach to find the tightly curled hair that concealed her humid secrets.

"Luke?"

"Hush, love," he muttered against her breast. "I don't want to talk about the future. I want to concentrate on the present."

A long time later Katy stirred and turned on her side. She was not accustomed to sharing a bed with another human being. She noticed that Luke took up a great deal of it.

She resettled herself and felt his arm close warmly around her again. It was quite pleasant to sleep with Luke. Rather comforting, in fact.

She did not really believe he had taken over Gilchrist, Inc. on account of her, but she would worry about that later. Tonight she was too pleasantly exhausted to lie awake fretting about it. She yawned and started to drift back down into sleep.

"Katy?"

"Hmm?"

"What did Darren want from you?"

She was too sleepy to pay much attention to the question. She answered automatically, without stopping to think. "A loan."

"How much?"

Katy blinked, roused back to partial wakefulness by the sharpness of the question. Sensing trouble, she tried to stall. Unfortunately, her brain was still clogged with sleep.

"Well, uh, a certain amount."

"How much?"

"A hundred and fifty thousand," she heard herself say.

"A hundred and fifty thousand dollars?" Luke sat up abruptly. "He wanted you to loan him a hundred and fifty grand? Christ, I'll kill that son of a bitch."

Katy belatedly realized she had unleashed a whirlwind when she was in no condition to contain it. "Now, Luke, calm down."

"Calm down?" Luke tossed aside the covers and surged to his feet. Seemingly unconscious of his own nakedness, he began pacing the room. "That bastard asks you for a hundred and fifty grand, and I'm supposed to calm down? I'm going to break every bone in his body. How the hell did he expect you to come up with that kind of money in the first place?"

Katy sighed. This would have been a lot easier to deal with over breakfast, but she knew Luke was not going to let go of the issue now. She sat up slowly against the pillows, holding the sheet over her breasts. "He knows I don't have that kind of money. He had a plan."

"Yeah, I'll just bet he did." Luke stopped pacing and came to a halt beside the bed. "What kind of plan? He wanted you to go

216

to Justine, didn't he?"

She sighed at how swiftly he had leapt to the correct conclusion. "He wanted me to ask Justine for a start-up loan for Pesto Presto."

"And once you got the money from her you were supposed to turn it over to him. Shit. I'll throttle the bastard."

Katy winced. Luke had certainly grasped the essential facts of the situation very quickly. She was not surprised. The man was good when it came to money. Very good. "That's about the size of it."

"Why does Darren need a hundred and fifty grand?" Luke demanded.

Katy bit her lip. "Well, I think he's in some sort of trouble."

"What kind of trouble?"

"I'm not sure. Something to do with a real estate development partnership that's gone sour. The purchasers are apparently clamoring for their money. The man who organized the deal says Darren will go to jail if he doesn't come up with the hundred and fifty."

Luke chewed silently on that for a few seconds. "So why didn't Darren go to Justine himself?"

"Don't be ridiculous. He couldn't possibly go to Justine. He's in this mess because he was trying to prove himself to her. The last thing he can do is go to her or his parents. They'll all think he's a complete failure."

"He's a goddamned idiot, that's what he is. He's also a damned fool if he thinks he's going to get away with using you like this."

"Now, Luke — "

"Just what in hell did you think you were going to do to bail him out of this mess?"

"Well, I came up with a plan. Sort of."

"Sort of." Luke rammed his fingers through his hair. "I don't believe this. All right, give it to me straight. What did you plan to do? Ask Justine for the loan?"

"No, of course not. I knew that would never work."

Luke slanted her a speculative glance as he resumed his restless pacing. "Why the hell not? She'd probably have given you the money."

"Yes, she probably would have. But I could never lie to Justine like that, not even to protect her from finding out that Darren had gotten into trouble."

"Yeah, you're the loyal type, aren't you?" Luke said. "And you think you owe her. So what did you plan to do?"

Katy decided there was no point putting off the inevitable. She had intended to do this after she'd had time to think about it some more, and she had certainly intended to do it at a more opportune moment. But she was trapped now.

"I planned to turn the whole problem over to you," Katy explained.

Luke came to an abrupt halt. He swung around to confront her. "Me? You were going to come to me about this mess?"

"Yes. Darren is your cousin. This is a Gilchrist family problem. For the next six months you're responsible for Gilchrist problems."

"The hell I am. I'm responsible for putting Gilchrist, Inc. back on its feet," Luke roared. "I am not responsible for solving all Gilchrist family problems. There's a difference."

"No, there isn't," Katy said calmly. "Gilchrist, Inc. is the family, and the family is Gilchrist, Inc. You are now head of the family. The way I see it, Darren's problem is your problem."

"Christ. You want to know how I'll solve Cousin Darren's problem? I'll let the idiot go to jail. That's how I'll solve it."

Katy smiled. "You're angry because Darren came to me for the money, aren't you?"

"Angry? I'd like to tear his head off his shoulders and use it for a bowling ball."

"That's a bit extreme, don't you think?"

"No. It's not extreme. It's only the beginning." Luke leaned over the bed, planting his hands on either side of her. "No one uses you and gets away with it."

Katy touched his clenched jaw. "Luke, he was desperate. Can't you find it in your heart to understand what it's been like for him? Justine wouldn't even consider him as a successor. She wouldn't give him a chance. He only wanted to prove himself in the business world."

"He proved he's an ass. And no, to answer your question, I can't dredge up one single drop of understanding for the jerk."

"Well, you're going to have to do something to help him," Katy said.

"Give me one good reason."

"I told him you would."

CHAPTER NINE

If she had been any other woman, Luke thought — any other female on the face of the earth — he would have sworn he had been deliberately manipulated. But it was hard to blame a guardian angel for doing what came naturally.

Besides, there was no getting around the fact that he had seduced Katy, not the opposite. Under the circumstances it would have been a little difficult to accuse her of employing her feminine wiles with the goal of manipulating him.

The situation he was in was of his own making. Luke swore under his breath. He had to admit that even if he had known last night where it was all going to lead, he would still have taken Katy to bed.

Damn, but it had been good. He was getting hard just thinking about it. Even allowing for the fact that he had been without a woman for a long time, it had been an incredible experience. Unlike anything he had ever known. She had made him feel so alive. He had felt so damn good afterward. At least until she had dropped her bombshell.

Christ. He still could not believe he was doing this.

Luke, dressed in his customary uniform of black jeans and a black pullover, lounged against the lobby wall of the downtown athletic club and smoldered silently while he waited for his quarry.

The club was located near the Pike Place Market. Its upscale clientele arrived in business suits and changed into brightly colored sweats that carried designer labels.

Outside on the street a long string of vans and trailers occupied a row of prime parking spaces. Luke idly noticed that the vehicles were all white and unmarked. Another film company was shooting on location in Seattle.

The vans contained portable dressing rooms and lighting and sound equipment. Cables, folding chairs, and large black boxes sat on the sidewalk. There was even a catering truck parked nearby, although the crew was shooting scenes on streets that contained some of the city's best restaurants. One of the establishments being thus immortalized on film was the Pacific Rim.

Luke frowned thoughtfully at the sight of the restaurant, his mind switching briefly to what he had learned in yesterday's series of meetings.

"Luke, what are you doing here?"

At the sound of Darren's startled, wary voice Luke groaned silently. He unfolded his arms and straightened away from the wall. "I want to talk to you."

"Yeah. Sure. What about?" Darren had obviously just finished working out. His hair was still damp from his shower. He was dressed for work in close-fitting black slacks and a black shirt and tie. He carried a black jacket over his arm.

"Not here." Luke started toward the glass doors at the front of the lobby. "Let's go someplace quiet."

He pushed open the doors and went out onto the sidewalk. Darren followed, his expression one of caution.

"Is this about business?" Darren asked as he reluctantly fell into step alongside Luke.

"You could say that." Luke turned at the corner and walked a few paces uphill to get out of the busiest section of the market. Halfway up the block he turned again and started down a quiet brick-lined alley. The noise and bustle faded.

"Come on, what the hell is this all about?" Darren demanded.

"I had a long talk with Katy this morning."

"Shit." Darren was silent for a few seconds. "She told you?"

"She said you were involved in a real estate scam."

"Goddammit, that's not true," Darren flared. "It wasn't a scam. It was a legitimate partnership deal that went sour, that's all. I just need a little cash to help pay off the initial purchasers."

"A hundred and fifty grand?"

"Jesus, Luke, that's not much. Not when you're talking real estate deals. You know that."

"But it's more than you have on hand."

"Well, hell. How many people have that kind of money sitting in the bank?" Darren muttered.

"Katy doesn't, that's for damn sure." Luke halted and turned to confront Darren. "You had no business even approaching her about this."

Darren stopped. "It wasn't like I was asking her for the cash. Didn't she explain?"

"You wanted her to lie to Justine in order to get it."

"Christ, I could hardly go to the old witch myself. She'd have had my head. Katy understands the situation. She knows what Justine is like."

"You tried to use Katy to get what you

wanted," Luke said.

Darren shrugged. "Katy can deal with Justine. At least sometimes."

"Is that so? How often have you asked Katy to get money for you?"

"This is the first time I've ever asked her to help me come up with cash," Darren muttered. "I was desperate. Don't you understand?"

"Yeah, I understand," Luke said softly. "You got into a bind, so you turned to the Gilchrist guardian angel for a little help."

Darren's mouth kicked up at the corner. "Guardian angel, huh? I guess that does sort of describe Katy, doesn't it?"

It was Darren's smile that did it. Luke moved.

He slammed Darren up against the brick wall and pinned him there. Then he leaned in close. "One thing you've got to watch out for in a situation like this, cousin. Before you decide to use someone like Katy, you'd better damn sure find out who's guarding the guardian angel."

"What the hell?" Darren stared at him, eyes stunned, mouth open in shock. "Are you crazy?"

"Not crazy. Just real irritated."

"Damn you, you think you can just walk in the front door and take over Gilchrist,

Inc., don't you? You think you can have the whole company, just because Justine decided she wanted to end the feud. Well, I've got news for you: You're not going to get away with it. One way or another, we're going to find a way to stop you."

"Not a chance." Luke smiled. "I've got the guardian angel on my side."

"You think this is some kind of joke? Let go of me, you goddamned bastard." Darren lashed out with his foot in a well-trained kick.

Luke barely had time to avoid the blow. He spun away from it, using his grip on Darren's shoulder to jerk his cousin off balance.

Darren staggered, caught himself, and aimed another savage kick at Luke's midsection. Luke sidestepped it and went in low before Darren could regain his balance.

He used the edge of his hand and with a short series of blows sent Darren crumpling against the alley wall.

Darren sank slowly to his knees, gasping for breath.

Luke took a step forward but stopped abruptly when he realized he and Darren no longer had the alley to themselves. He glanced over his shoulder and saw a middle-aged couple standing in the entrance. Their faces showed the shock that had frozen them in place.

"Run, Ethel," the man finally managed in a midwestern accent. His eyes locked on Luke's face. He grabbed the woman's arm and took an unsteady step back toward the safety of the street. "For God's sake, run. Find a policeman."

Luke stared at the couple as his mind produced an image of what the tourists were seeing. Two men dressed in black locked in violent hand-to-hand combat in an alley. Luke smiled reassuringly.

"It's okay. Take it easy." Luke took a couple of steps away from Darren and flashed another grin at the horrified tourists. "We're with the film crew. He's the star. I'm his stuntman. Just running through a couple of routines." He glanced down at Darren. "Isn't that right?"

Darren stared up at him in amazement. Then he looked at the couple and grimaced. "Yeah. Right."

The woman brightened immediately. "Really? And you're the star?" She plunged a hand into her bulging purse and withdrew a pen and a small notebook. Then she freed herself from her husband's grasp and trotted forward. "Can I have your autograph?"

★ ★ ★

"Film crew? Was that the best you could do?" Darren glowered at Luke as he poured beer into a glass. The busy lunchtime crowd in the small restaurant created a hum of conversation that made it possible to talk without being overheard.

"Sorry. It was the only thing I could come up with at the time. What are you complaining about? I made you the star, didn't I?"

"Big deal. You weren't the one who had to invent a name to sign in that lady's little notebook. I could barely think straight, let alone dream up a fake name."

"What did you put down?" Luke asked.

Darren made a face. "Luke Darren."

"Not bad. Sounds Hollywood." Luke leaned back in his chair and eyed his cousin. "Where the hell did you learn the karate?"

"I've been studying it for a couple of years. I was just coming out of a class at the club when you found me." Darren winced as he picked up the glass. He put it down again and gingerly touched his rib cage. "Something tells me you've been studying it longer than I have."

"I've got a few years on you," Luke pointed out.

"Right. More time to get sneaky and mean." There was grudging admiration in

Darren's voice. "I didn't recognize some of that stuff you used on me. How long have you been studying?"

"Since I was a kid. I got into a fight once when I was in my teens. The fight turned into a brawl, and a bunch of us got hauled off to the police station. Dad came down to get me. Instead of yelling at me he took me straight to the nearest martial arts academy and signed me up for lessons."

Darren nodded in understanding. "Wanted you to learn how to take care of yourself properly, huh?"

Luke smiled faintly. "Not exactly. He said a Gilchrist needs to learn how to avoid trouble in the first place. He figured the martial arts training would teach me self-discipline and self-control."

"No shit." Darren grimaced. "Guess it didn't work."

"Sure it did. I left your head on your shoulders, didn't I? If I hadn't been exerting so much discipline and self-control, I would have ripped it off."

"Jesus. You're really pissed that I went to Katy about the money, aren't you?"

"Yeah. Really pissed."

"I tried everything else I could think of first," Darren muttered. "But the broker says the guy who put the deal together is really putting on the pressure. Says we've got to come up with the cash or we'll all wind up in jail. What the hell was I supposed to do?"

Luke wrapped his hand around the cold glass of beer. "It's time you learned something, cousin."

"What?"

"If you're going to go around getting yourself into messes like this one, you'd better damn well learn how to clean 'em up. Don't rely on a guardian angel."

Darren scowled at him. "How am I supposed to clean up this mess?"

"You don't use karate to defend yourself in the business world," Luke said. "You use information. Tell me about this real estate partnership."

Darren hesitated. "Why?"

"Because you are apparently ass-deep in alligators. To prevent future annoying incidents such as this one, I am going to teach you how to drain the swamp."

Katy gazed into the glowing bowl, lost in the brilliant, swirling color that had been captured in the glass. Graceful and elegant, the bowl stood nearly three feet high. It shimmered with light.

This particular piece was one of the most

beautiful Hayden had ever done, Katy thought. It sat in isolated splendor on a plain white pedestal in the center of the gallery. There were several other spectacular pieces arranged discreetly on other white pedestals in the white-on-white room.

Maureen knew how to display Hayden's work to its best advantage.

Katy walked over to another pedestal to examine a red and gold glass vase. At the back of the room Maureen, dressed in a black silk jumpsuit that made a striking statement in the white room, talked softly to a young couple.

In the end, the couple decided on a small amber and green bowl. Maureen smiled with satisfaction as she entered purchase information into the computer behind the white-tiled counter. She waited until her clients were out the door before she bore down on Katy.

"Thank God you got my message," Maureen said without any preamble. "I was afraid you might already have left town."

Katy glanced at her watch. "Luke is picking me up at the hotel in an hour. What's wrong, Maureen?"

"I want to talk to you about Eden." Maureen's mouth tightened ominously. "I am extremely worried about her. I was going to call you, but when I found out you were in town on business I decided I would discuss the problem today."

"I saw Eden yesterday in her office. She looks a little tense, but otherwise she seems all right."

"She is not all right," Maureen snapped. "There is something very wrong, and she won't tell me what it is. But I think I know. Something she let slip to Darren makes me think she may be seeing that awful Nate Atwood again."

Katy frowned, remembering what Fraser had said about seeing Eden get into a cab with Nate. "That doesn't make any sense, Maureen. Why would she get involved with Nate after everything she's been through?"

"God knows. You know how much she wanted him a year ago."

Katy smiled wryly. "Believe me, I haven't forgotten."

Maureen peered at her. "Good Lord. You're not still upset about that unfortunate business, are you?"

"No, Maureen. I'm not upset."

"I should think not. You must be reasonable, my dear. Eden thought she was in love."

"And that says it all, doesn't it? Nothing gets in the way of a Gilchrist who has her heart set on something."

Maureen drew herself up. "If you ask me, Eden is quite right. You were the lucky one. It was my daughter who suffered. That dreadful man married her solely because she was a Gilchrist."

"It does appear that was a factor," Katy agreed dryly.

"He thought that by marrying her he could get his hands on a chunk of the company. He used my daughter."

"Yes, I think that's a fair assessment of the situation." Katy tilted her head and gazed thoughtfully at Maureen. "But Eden knows that as well as anyone. She said something just yesterday about the way Nate used her. There's no reason to think she would take him back."

"But she's apparently seeing him again."

"You don't know that for certain."

Maureen shook her head. "Something is going on. I know it is."

"Even if it is, what do you expect me to do about it?"

"I want you to stop Nate Atwood from whatever it is he has in mind."

Katy stared at her. "Stop him? Me? How on earth am I supposed to do that?"

"It's quite simple. A man like that understands only one thing. Money. I want you to go to him and offer him a large sum of money to stay away from my daughter."

Stunned, Katy stepped back swiftly and collided with a white pedestal. The green and orange bowl on top swayed precariously and started to topple.

Maureen shrieked in dismay. Her hand went to her throat. "Catch it before it falls."

Katy whirled around and stretched out her hands. The bowl fell straight into her arms. She breathed a sigh of relief and set it carefully back on the pedestal. "Sorry about that."

"My God, that's one of Hayden's finest pieces. Be careful, Katy. I've got a five-thousand-dollar price on that bowl."

"Five thousand? Maybe you could just offer Nate a few of these bowls instead of cash."

Maureen nodded seriously. "It's a possibility. The thing is, I don't know how much it will take to make him go away. He is a very greedy man, and he got virtually nothing out of Gilchrist at the time of the divorce."

"Thanks to Justine's lawyers. Maureen, if you think there's a real problem with Nate, why don't you go to Justine and tell her?"

Maureen's eyes widened. "Are you mad? She would be furious with all of us if she thought Atwood was still a problem. She hasn't forgiven Eden for marrying him in the first place."

Katy sighed. "I know."

Maureen closed her eyes in brief anguish. "Nor has she let Hayden and me forget that she blames us for not putting a stop to the relationship before it led to marriage. That old witch will probably never forgive or forget."

"Typical Gilchrist," Katy said with a poor attempt at a smile.

"This is not funny, Katy. I am scared to death of what might happen if Nate Atwood gets his hooks back in my daughter. It would be the final straw as far as Justine is concerned. She might disown all of us."

"Oh, come now, Maureen, she's not going to disown ninety percent of her family."

"Why not? She doesn't need any of us now that she has her precious bastard grandson. She's made it clear she would rather have him than us anyway."

"It's the prodigal son syndrome. Luke was the one she didn't have, so she focused on him. But that doesn't mean she wants to disown the rest of you."

Maureen gave a soft, despairing exclamation. "She'd do it if she got sufficiently angry, Katy. She's disowned family before. She'd do it again."

Katy frowned. "Are we talking about what happened when she kicked Luke's parents out of the fold?"

"Yes. You weren't even born. But I had just gotten engaged to Hayden. I was there that day at the wedding when Luke's father failed to show. I saw how angry Justine was. I have never seen such rage, not even in another Gilchrist."

Katy bit her lip. "I guess it must have been a dreadful scene."

"Just as dreadful as the scene she made a month later when Thornton brought Cleo to the mansion. He wanted to introduce her to Justine and the rest of us." Maureen lowered herself onto the small white bench near the wall. Her fingers shook, and her face was strained.

Katy sat down slowly beside her. "It must have been terrible for everyone."

"Cleo was the one I truly felt sorry for, if you want to know the truth," Maureen said quietly. "That poor woman couldn't have known what she was getting into. I shall never forget the way she just stood there as Justine turned on her. Justine called her the most terrible names. Told her no child of hers would ever be acknowledged as a Gilchrist heir."

"What did Cleo say?"

Maureen shook her head. "She stood there so bravely while Justine pronounced sentence. When it was over she looked at Justine and said she felt sorry for her. And then she said the Gilchrists were their own worst enemies. Thornton took her by the hand and led her out of the living room. We never saw either of them again."

"How very sad." But a typically dramatic Gilchrist moment, Katy thought.

Maureen stared straight ahead at a wide bowl that glowed pink and green in the light. "I learned my lesson that day. I knew then that Justine would not forgive a daughter-in-law who transgressed. I vowed to myself that I would never give her cause to turn on me the way she turned on Cleo."

Katy looked at Maureen's set profile. "I know this is none of my business, but why did you even go through with the marriage to Hayden? Why would you want to marry a Gilchrist after seeing what happened that day?"

"I loved Hayden, and I saw the genius in him. I knew I couldn't walk away and abandon him to that old battle-ax. Justine would have tried to crush the talent in him, tried to force him to take his brother Thornton's place."

"So you married him to protect him from Justine?"

"I loved him. I married him so that he could grow and develop as an artist. He

would have hated running Gilchrist, Inc."
Tears glittered in Maureen's eyes.

"Yes," Katy agreed softly, knowing it was
the truth. Without stopping to think about
it she reached over and put her arm around
Maureen.

"You have no idea what it's been like
trying to shield Hayden and at the same
time placate Justine all these years. I was
so certain that once I produced grandchildren
she would be pleased with me. I thought
she would focus her attention on them. It
worked for a while. I think she was even
starting to view Darren as a successor."

"Then Thornton and his wife died in that
crash, and everything changed," Katy concluded softly. She patted Maureen's shoulder.

"Suddenly nothing would do but to get
Luke to take over the reins." Maureen sighed.
"That bastard. After all these years, Cleo
has had her revenge hasn't she? Her son is
now at the helm of Gilchrist, Inc. And I'm
still struggling to protect my family from
Justine."

Katy sat silently for a long while, thinking
it over. "Are you absolutely certain Eden is
involved with Nate Atwood?"

"No." Maureen removed a hankie from
her pocket and blew her nose. "Not absolutely
certain."

"See if you can find out for sure," Katy said gently. "Call me when you're positive. I'll see what I can do."

Maureen blinked away her tears and smiled tremulously. "Thank you, Katy. I knew I could count on you. You're always so helpful at times likc this. You won't say a word about this to anyone, will you?"

"No, of course not."

Katy waited until Luke had the black Jaguar heading north toward Dragon Bay that afternoon before she tried to talk to him. One glance at his grim profile had already warned her that he was not in the best of moods. But she was accustomed to Gilchrist moods.

"How did your meeting with Darren go?" she asked anxiously as the Jag merged seamlessly into the heavy traffic on the interstate.

"Cousin Darren and I came to what is often termed a meeting of the minds."

"Oh, good. I'm so glad, Luke." Katy relaxed in the seat. "I was very concerned. He meant well, you know. He was only trying to prove himself."

"Uh-huh."

Katy glanced at him. "So what exactly is the plan?"

"He's still working on it."

Katy frowned. "But you're helping him, aren't you?"

Luke's brows rose as he pulled out to pass a truck. "Let's just say I'm pointing him in the right direction. He's going to have to do the work."

"I don't understand."

"He's in this mess because he got suckered by an expert named Milo Nyle. It has all the earmarks of a scam designed to set up naïve fools like Darren who think they know how to wheel and deal in the business world."

"How does it work?"

"Nyle sets up a real estate partnership deal that's too good to be true. Very little money required up front. Huge profits when it's finished. Folks like Darren fall for it and then get told the partnership has folded. They're told that, as partners, they're liable."

Katy pushed her hair back behind her ear. "Then they're told they have to come up with cash to pay off innocent people who actually purchased the properties or risk going to jail?"

"Right. The kicker is there aren't any innocent purchasers. There was no development project. Just Nyle. He collects what he can from the various partners and vanishes. Goes somewhere else and sets up shop."

"Good grief." Katy was shocked. "And

poor Darren fell for the scam?"

"Yeah."

"But how did you find out it was all a con?"

"I did a little research. The kind of basic investigation Darren should have done when Nyle first approached him through the broker. Nyle's partnership deal is a complete fraud. It's all built on smoke and mirrors. Darren is safe."

"He must be terribly relieved to hear that."

"He doesn't know it yet," Luke said succinctly.

"You haven't told him? Luke, how could you do that to him? You know how worried he is."

"It won't hurt him to do a little more worrying. I told him how to go about finding out what he needs to know to save his ass. He'll discover that he's in the clear in a few days if he goes after the information I told him he'd need. In the meantime, maybe he'll learn something."

Katy mulled that over for a couple of minutes. The fact that Darren was safe was wonderful news. The fact that he did not yet know it seemed cruel. Perhaps she should call him tonight and tell him the whole truth.

"Don't even think about it, Katy."

"Think about what?"

241

"I can read you like a book. You are not going to call Darren and tell him what I just told you. He's going to learn this lesson the hard way. The Gilchrist guardian angel is going to stay out of it."

"But Luke — "

"Forget it. That's an order, Katy. You asked me to help. You got my help. Now you're stuck with it. If you don't like the way I solve problems, that's just too damn bad."

"I'll remember your approach the next time I have a problem," she grumbled.

Luke grinned suddenly. "You do that."

She did not like his smile. Too many teeth. She decided to change the topic. "Did yesterday's round of meetings give you any new information?"

"Not really. I'm convinced the problems we're having in the restaurants and in Gilchrist Gourmet are due to criminal actions, not bad luck or even bad management."

"Oh, dear. So you're continuing with the investigation?"

"Yes."

Katy hesitated. "You still think someone in the family might be behind the problems, don't you?"

"Let's just say I'm not ruling anyone out."

"But Luke, the only members of the family

who work in the business are Darren and Eden. They wouldn't do anything like this."

"I'm not so sure about that. But you're wrong when you say they're the only suspects in the family. Maureen and Hayden have been connected to Gilchrist, Inc. for decades. They don't work directly for the company, but they've had access to vital information for years. And in this day of computers, anyone who knows what he's doing can cause trouble."

"But why would any of them want to cause trouble?"

"How about a nice little motive like revenge? It may have escaped your notice, angel, but not everyone in the family thinks Justine is a saint."

Katy winced, remembering Maureen's frustrated anger and fear of Justine. She also recalled the computer in Maureen's gallery. "I suppose you're right."

"Of course I'm right. When it comes to business, I'm always right. Now let's talk about something that's a hell of a lot more interesting than Darren and the rest of the family."

"What's that?"

"Us."

A delicate thrill went through Katy. She had been trying hard not to think about their relationship. At the same time she had known that sooner or later she would have to confront it. The knowledge had filled her with an edgy anticipation. "What about us?"

"I just want to be real clear here. I don't want any misunderstandings. We're together now, Katy. You and me."

The intensity in him was radiating outward, drawing her into his force field. Katy found herself struggling to balance desire with common sense. "I don't think you're going to like having an affair with me," she warned gently.

He threw her a quick, annoyed glance. "Why the hell not?"

"Because I can't just abandon myself to passion the way a Gilchrist would expect," she explained.

"Don't worry about the passion part. You were doing just fine last night."

She blushed and concentrated on the car ahead. "That's not what I mean. Luke, I can't just fling myself into a scorching affair. I'm raising a seventeen-year-old boy, remember? I have to set an example."

"For all intents and purposes he's a man, Katy. And you're an adult. You don't have to explain your private life to him."

"Don't you understand? I'm not used to this kind of private life. I don't want Matt walking in on us some morning. You can't stay the night with me at my place. I won't stay the night with you at your cottage."

"In other words, we have to sneak around?"

"We have to be discreet," she said. "Very discreet."

"Damn it, Katy, I'm too old to play games."

She lifted her chin, aware that her lower lip was trembling. She had known this would never work. "I told you that you wouldn't like having an affair with me. I'll understand, of course, if you would prefer to call the whole thing off right now."

"Not a chance."

"Luke, it might be best if we did. Last night was very special for me. You must know that. But the truth is, you and I are very different. We have nothing in common. Things are bound to end eventually. You said six months was the limit."

"Look, Katy — "

"To be honest, I would rather end it all now than have you turn surly whenever you don't get what you want."

To Katy's astonishment, Luke gave her a slow, enigmatic smile that rattled her nerves all the way to her toes. "If that's all you're worrying about, forget it. I'll handle the passionate side of things. I won't turn surly just because you can't spend the night in my bed."

She slanted him a wary glance. "What's that supposed to mean?"

"It means that if you want to sneak around, I'll sneak around. For a while."

CHAPTER TEN

Two mornings later Liz stuck her head around the door of Katy's office. "Psst. This is it. Justine just sent for him. He's going downstairs in a few minutes to give her a full report."

Katy leapt to her feet. "Thanks, Liz."

Liz grinned. "Hey, no problem. Now that I'm handling his calls as well as yours I'm a regular gold mine of information. A vital cog in the corporate wheel. An indispensable asset. A valuable and loyal employee who is willing to give her all to her boss."

"If you're fishing for a raise," Katy said as she went through the door, "save the sales pitch for Mr. Gilchrist. He's the one in charge of that kind of thing now."

"True, but I've been analyzing him, and I've come to the conclusion he's putty in your hands. So put in a good word for me, will you?"

Katy halted in astonishment at the outer door. "You've come to the conclusion he's what?"

"You heard me." Liz picked up a book that was lying on her desk and opened it. "You know how to handle him, just like you do the rest of the members of the coven."

Katy felt herself turning a brilliant shade of red. She peered at the title of Liz's book. *Return to the Jungle: The Psychology of Male/Female Sexual Dynamics in the Modern World.* "What on earth is that about?"

"Take a guess. We're studying human sexual response in my psych class this week. You know, it says in here that even though modern psychology has created a lot of new theories about sexual behavior, the truth is that men are still motivated by a bunch of really primitive hormones and instincts."

"Oh, for heaven's sake, Liz."

Liz flipped to a page in the middle of the book. "Listen to this, and I quote: 'A male in pursuit of a female is fundamentally an animal.'"

"Tell me something every woman doesn't already know."

" 'Having selected his chosen mate, he will concentrate on her. He will cut her out of the herd, perform courtship rituals to get her attention, and fight off other males who attempt to get close to her.' " Liz snapped the book shut and shivered. "Sends chills down your spine, doesn't it?"

Katy clutched at the edge of the door. "Yes, it does. I'll be glad when you move on to something that involves rats in mazes."

"Actually, I think we're going to cover sociopathic behavior and other forms of deviancy next. Do you know what a sociopath is?"

"I've heard the term. Someone without a conscience."

"You know, I wouldn't be surprised if your old friend Nate Atwood fits the clinical definition of a sociopath." Liz assumed her best professorial manner. "Charming, intelligent, and absolutely no conscience at all. As cold-blooded as a reptile."

Katy was about to agree, but something made her hesitate. "No, I don't think so. Nate was not cold-blooded. He had his own agenda and it was important to him, but I don't think he wanted to hurt me."

"You always look for the best in people, that's your problem." Liz shook her head. "Poor Eden. Her life with that man must have been awful. You were lucky you escaped his clutches."

"So everyone keeps telling me," Katy muttered. "Excuse me. I've got to talk to Luke." She hurried out into the corridor and knocked on Luke's office door.

"Come in," Luke called.

Pushing open the door, Katy stepped inside. She stood with her hands behind her on the knob. Luke looked up from the file that was open on his desk. His eyes gleamed at the sight of her.

Katy suddenly felt very warm. No doubt about it, that was an extremely primitive look. He had not made love to her since they had returned from Seattle three days ago, but he was definitely looking at her as if she belonged to him.

Good Lord, Katy thought, he had promised to be discreet, but at this rate everyone was going to know they had started an affair. That was the trouble in dealing with Gilchrists. There was nothing subtle about them.

"What's wrong, Katy?"

"Liz says you're going downstairs to give Justine a report."

"In a few minutes. She's asked for regular reports, and I figure she's entitled to one occasionally. She does own Gilchrist, Inc., if you'll recall."

Katy released the doorknob and rushed over to the desk. "Luke, I don't want you to say anything yet about your suspicions."

He lounged back in his chair and eyed her consideringly. "No?"

"No. Wait until you've completed the investigation and know for certain who's to blame for the trouble at the restaurants and at Gilchrist Gourmet. There's no reason to make her think someone in the family may be behind the problems. After all, you may be wrong."

"Not likely."

Katy glowered at him. "Don't be so damn arrogant. I happen to think you are wrong. Until we find out for sure what's going on, I don't want you alarming Justine. She'll go crazy if she thinks there's a traitor in the family."

"What do you suggest I do?"

"I don't know." Katy made a vague gesture with her hand. "Yes, I do know. Gloss over the problems for now. Tell her you're getting them under control."

"Lie to her?" Luke's brows rose. "Tsk, tsk, Katy. That doesn't sound like the angel I know."

"There's no need to lie exactly. Just tell her you're still collecting data. Which is the truth." Katy leaned forward and planted her hands on the desk. "There's something else. I want you to promise me you won't mention Darren's little problem either. It will upset her, and there's no telling what she might do."

Luke contemplated her instructions for a moment. "Let me see if I've got this straight.

I'm not supposed to tell her that I think someone in the family is embezzling from the company."

"Right."

"And I'm supposed to avoid mentioning Darren's situation."

Katy nodded quickly, relieved that he understood. "Right."

"Anything else you want me to keep quiet about?" Luke asked politely.

Katy frowned in thought. "I think that covers it."

"Okay. I'll follow orders."

She brightened with relief. "You will?"

"If you make it worth my while."

"What?" She straightened in outrage.

"Give me a good reason to keep my mouth shut about embezzlement, the fraud, and the extremely poor judgment of a certain member of the family, and I'll do it," Luke said.

Katy glowered at him suspiciously. "What sort of reason do you want?"

"Not having your high standards, I'm susceptible to a good bribe. Invite me out on a date," Luke said.

Katy blushed. "A date. Yes, well, I've already explained that it's going to be extremely inconvenient to conduct an affair with me."

"Correction, you said it was going to be

extremely difficult to find opportunities to make love to you. I'll worry about that problem. Right now I'm just fishing for a dinner date."

"Oh."

"Is that all you can say?"

Katy hid a smile. "No, I was somewhat surprised, that's all. I can't quite see you on a normal dinner date."

"What do you think I do for nourishment?"

Katy's eyes widened innocently. "Drink blood?"

Luke started to get out of his chair.

Katy warded him off with both hands. "Just a joke. Okay. Come over for dinner tonight. I'll try out one of my new pesto sauce recipes on you."

"You've got a deal. My silence on certain matters when I talk to Justine in exchange for dinner tonight. Sounds fair to me."

Katy hesitated. "You do realize my brother will be there? We won't be alone. You'll have to go home around ten. Alone."

Luke got to his feet and came around the desk. "I told you, I'll worry about organizing our sex life." He brushed his mouth lightly across hers. "You just worry about fixing dinner."

He walked out of the office before Katy could think of a suitable response.

After he was gone she stood lost in thought for several minutes. She realized she didn't know what to expect next from Luke. It was true she had not had any experience with affairs, but she'd had plenty of experience with the passionate Gilchrist family. They were nothing if not predictable in that they were ruled by their passions. She had been certain that once Luke decided he wanted her, it would be extremely difficult to control him.

And what he wanted from her, apparently, was sex.

But to her surprise, Luke had not pushed for sex since they had returned from Seattle. In fact, this was the first indication he had given her that he was still planning on pursuing her. She felt confused and curiously disoriented.

A Gilchrist who could discipline his own passion was an anomaly.

A sorcerer.

It occurred to Katy that such a Gilchrist might be infinitely more dangerous than an ordinary Gilchrist.

Katy went back to her office and sat stewing at her desk. She would have given a great deal to know exactly what Luke was reporting to his grandmother.

Having wrung from him the promise to

keep silent about his suspicions and about Darren's predicament, she did not think he would betray her. She trusted him that far. But she also knew that Justine would expect some definite answers to her questions about the state of the company and Luke's plans to save it. Justine could be very persistent. But then Luke could be extremely unhelpful when he chose.

Forty minutes later Katy heard footsteps in the hall outside the office. Luke was back. She heard the outer door open and close and realized he must have stopped by to tell her he had followed instructions. She summoned up an approving smile.

There was a single peremptory knock on the inner door before it opened to reveal a grinning Darren.

"Hi there, Katy. Luke's not in his office, so I thought I'd drop in to see you while I wait."

"Of course. Sit down, Darren. What are you doing here?"

"I drove up here to fill Luke in on the situation with Milo Nyle." Darren dropped lightly into a chair. He was looking happier than he had in a long while. "Damn, I still can't believe the Bastard was right about Nyle. But he was. The guy's as phony as a three-dollar bill. Man, did I get suckered.

But it won't happen again."

"You don't have to come up with the hundred and fifty thousand dollars?"

"Hell, no." Darren shoved his hands into his pockets and stuck his legs out in front of him. "I don't owe him a damn thing. There are no innocent purchasers left hanging because there was no development project."

"Thank goodness," Katy said.

"Yeah, it was all on paper. Luke said that when I had the information I needed we'd contact the authorities. But he also said Nyle will probably have disappeared by the time the authorities make their move. Guys like Nyle operate for years without getting caught. He's probably in a different state by now. The broker Nyle used as a go-between seems innocent. He was just trying to structure what he thought was an honest deal."

"Darren, I can't tell you how relieved I am to hear you're in the clear."

"You think *you're* relieved? Believe me, it's nothing compared to how I feel. When I'm not feeling like a total idiot, that is."

"You're not an idiot, Darren. Anyone can get taken in by a good con artist."

"I'll bet Luke wouldn't get taken in by one. The man knows what he's doing."

Katy raised her brows at the tone of respect in Darren's voice. "Yes, he seems reasonably intelligent," she admitted dryly.

"Intelligent, hell. The Bastard's a damn genius. I'll tell you one thing, I sure learned something from this mess." Darren's mouth curved ruefully. "Of course, I could have done without lesson number one. But I guess I deserved that, too."

Katy looked at him curiously. "What was lesson number one?"

"That was the one where Luke dragged me into an alley at Pike Place Market and beat the shit out of me."

Katy was dumbstruck. "He did *what?*"

"He was kind of pissed that I had approached you to help me get the money," Darren explained cheerfully. Then his smile faded as he took in the expression on her face. "Hey, it's okay, Katy. Luke had a point."

Katy shot to her feet. "I don't believe this. Luke never told me that he attacked you."

"Take it easy," Darren said soothingly. "He didn't do any permanent damage."

"But he beat you up because of me. I'm the one who asked him to help you, and instead he assaulted you."

"Hell, I'm sorry I even mentioned it. I didn't mean to get you upset. I figured he'd probably told you about it." Darren broke off at the sound of footsteps in the hall. "That must be Luke. I'll let him know I'm here."

Katy squared her shoulders and marched around the edge of the desk. "You will wait right here in my office. I want to talk to him first."

Darren's eyes widened as he realized her intention. "Hold on a second. I don't want you getting any more involved in this. What happened in that alley was between me and Luke."

"It was not just between you and Luke. I am also involved. I asked Luke to help you out of that mess."

"He did." Darren scrambled to his feet and hurried after her. "Katy, wait . . ."

But Katy was already out of her office. She sailed straight past a curious Liz and stepped into the hall. Luke's office door stood open. He was standing at his desk, examining a fax that had just arrived on his machine.

"I want to talk to you, Luke."

He looked up, taking in her militant expression in a single glance. "What's with the flaming sword this time, angel?"

"Don't call me angel." Katy started to slam his office door, but she was forestalled by Darren's foot, which was firmly lodged in the opening.

"Sorry about this, Luke," Darren said over the top of Katy's head. "She's a little upset. I didn't realize she didn't know about our scene in the alley."

Comprehension dawned in Luke's eyes. He tossed aside the fax, leaned back against the edge of the desk, and folded his arms. "It's all right, Darren. I'll handle this. Close the door, will you? I want to talk to Katy alone for a while. You can wait in her office."

Darren looked doubtful. "You're sure?"

Luke nodded. "I'm sure. Go on, get out of here."

"Right. I'll be next door." Darren grinned. "I've got a lot to tell you about Milo Nyle."

"Somehow that doesn't surprise me. Take off."

"I'm out of here." Darren closed the door firmly.

"First," Katy announced in ringing tones as she faced Luke with her hands on her hips, "I want some answers and an explanation, Luke Gilchrist. Is it true that you assaulted Darren?"

"Is that what he said?"

"His exact words were that you beat the you-know-what out of him."

"Shit?"

"Yes," Katy shot back. "Exactly. Luke,

259

that is utterly appalling. How could you do such a thing?"

"It wasn't easy. Darren's had some fairly decent karate training. He can handle himself, I'll say that much for him."

"That's not what I mean, and you know it," Katy said through her teeth. "I asked you to help him."

"I did."

"After you beat him up?" she demanded incredulously.

"We had to get that part out of the way first," Luke explained gently.

Katy threw up her hands in a gesture of complete frustration. "Luke, that is no way to handle things." She started to pace back and forth across the small office. "What kind of an example does that set?"

"One he'll remember, with any luck."

"Violence is never a proper approach to problem solving."

"Think of it as aggressive intervention." Luke watched her as she stalked past him. "Calm down, Katy. The matter has been resolved. Darren appears to be satisfied with the way things turned out, so there's no call for you to be upset."

"Why did you beat him up?" Katy demanded.

"Because he tried to use you."

Katy stopped short, taken off guard by the smoldering green flames in his eyes. "Are you saying you engaged in a brawl with him because he asked me to help him out of a jam?"

"No." Luke's expression hardened briefly. "I did it because he put you in a completely untenable position. In effect he asked you to lie for him. He had no right to do that. And now he understands that. He won't do it again."

Katy stared at him. "I don't know what to say. You make me very nervous, Luke."

"I did what you asked me to do," he reminded her softly.

"Yes, but I didn't realize how you would go about doing it." She shot him a grim look. "This raises some serious issues. What am I going to do with you?"

"You could try thanking me," he said, his expression suspiciously bland.

"For what?"

"For saving Darren's ass."

Katy was torn. Luke was right. He had saved Darren from a very unpleasant situation. More to the point, he had taught his cousin how to avoid similar situations in the future. And Darren seemed content with the way things had turned out.

Katy dropped into the nearest chair and

glowered at Luke. "I suppose you meant well."

"I told you once before that do-gooding is not a major objective in my life. I did what you asked me to do. No more, no less."

"But you did it in your own way," she said, disgruntled. "You know, having you around is like having a genie in a bottle. I get my wishes fulfilled, but nothing ever turns out quite as I had envisioned."

Luke laughed softly. "That's the way it goes sometimes." He unfolded his arms and moved away from the desk.

Katy watched as he crossed the room and locked the door. "What are you doing?"

"I'm in the mood to fulfill a few wishes of my own." He walked toward her and came to a halt in front of her chair.

Katy looked up at him through her lashes, not trusting the expression on his face. Her insides were turning to liquid under the impact of that molten emerald gaze. "Luke, what's going on? What are you doing?"

"I told you. A little wish fulfillment." He leaned down without any warning and scooped her up out of the chair.

Katy uttered a soft screech. "Luke, stop it." She was acutely aware of the presence of Liz and Darren just next door. "Put me down. What on earth do you think you're doing?"

"Think of this as an exercise in management creativity." He sat Katy down on the edge of the desk and slid his hands up under the hem of her skirt. His fingers clamped firmly around her knees.

Katy gasped as Luke spread her thighs wide and stepped between them. She grabbed his shoulders to brace herself as she realized what he was going to do. "Luke, stop. You can't do this. Not here. Not now. Good grief."

"Don't worry, angel. I'll handle everything."

"That's what you said when you agreed to help Darren," Katy hissed. "Luke, really, we can't do it like this. This is an office, for heaven's sake. There are two people right next door. Justine is downstairs. What about Mrs. Igorson? Or one of the day maids?"

"I don't plan to invite them to watch." He bent his head and took her earlobe between his teeth. One of his hands moved up the inside of her thigh until he touched the crotch of her pantyhose. His finger started to move in a gentle rhythm.

Katy sucked in her breath and instinctively tried to close her legs, but Luke's strong thighs were in the way. Katy felt his teeth on her ear and thought she was going to melt. Part of her did.

"Oh, no," Katy wailed softly as she felt her panties dampen. "This is terrible. What am I going to do for the rest of the day? I don't keep spare underwear here at the office. For goodness' sake, Luke."

"One of these days, angel, you're going to learn that I don't do anything for goodness' sake." Luke's fingers slipped inside the waistband of her pantyhose and panties. He wrapped one arm around Katy's waist and lifted her slightly off the desk. Then he peeled the underwear down over her hips in a single swift movement.

"Oh, my God," Katy breathed. She nearly collapsed when she felt Luke's hand on her softness. He was touching her the way he had the other night in the hotel room, the way she had been fantasizing about ever since. This was ridiculous. She was turning into a quivering mass of gelatin.

"You know what I like best about making love to you, angel?" Luke stroked her slowly, parting her with his fingers, opening her. "You couldn't hide your response to me if you tried."

"This is insane."

"Just the opposite. This is going to save my sanity. I've been going crazy for the

264

past three days plotting how and when to make love to you."

Still bracing herself with her hands on Luke's shoulders, Katy glanced down just as Luke unzipped his black jeans. His heavy, fully aroused manhood thrust outward from the nest of black hair. Impulsively she reached down to curl her fingers gently around him.

"Yes," Luke muttered thickly. "Like that. Damn, that feels good."

He pushed himself forward, deeper into her palm. Katy forgot about where she was and who was next door. Luke's fingers continued to move on her, drawing forth the wet heat, stoking the flames until she was half mad with desire.

"Luke," she whispered urgently.

"I know, angel, I know." His voice was hoarse with his passion.

But still he made her wait.

And wait.

Then, when she was digging her nails into him and biting her lip to keep from crying out, he made himself ready. He eased himself slowly and deeply into her snug passage.

Katy's hands trembled as she wrapped herself around him. She felt him retreat slightly and then plunge back into her with a long, sure movement.

"Luke, I don't . . . I can't . . . oh,

Luke." She felt the delicious twisting sensation build swiftly inside her. She knew where it was going to lead this time, and the knowledge alone was almost enough to send her over the edge.

"That's it, angel. I'm going to do this a little harder now. Hold on tight." He pushed into her with a controlled force that was unbelievably erotic.

"Oh, God, Luke."

"Just a little deeper. I want to get a little farther inside. Come on, sweetheart. Open wider for me. Yes, that's it. You're so tight. So sweet and hot and tight."

"Luke, I can't stand it any longer."

"Then go up in flames for me, angel." He reached between her parted thighs, found the point where his body joined hers, and touched the magic place.

The small convulsions shattered Katy into a million glittering pieces. She clung to Luke. He was the only solid thing in her universe. She parted her lips to cry out her pleasure. Luke instantly clamped his mouth tightly down over hers, swallowing the soft sounds of her passion.

Katy felt him shudder and surge forward into her one last time. His barely stifled groan of satisfaction reverberated deep in his chest.

For a few minutes there was complete silence in the room. Katy finally took several deep breaths in an effort to regain her composure. She was vaguely aware of Luke moving slightly away from her. She heard him zip his jeans.

She felt him reach around her for something on the desk, but she couldn't bring herself to open her eyes.

Then she felt him tuck a tissue between her thighs. She flinched, embarrassed. Blushing, she made a hasty grab for the tissue. "I'll do that."

Luke's smile held a wealth of masculine satisfaction. "It's all right, angel. I don't mind taking care of you."

Katy groaned. "This has got to be the most outrageous thing that has ever happened to me."

"I'll take that as a compliment."

"You're impossible, Luke Gilchrist." Katy fumbled with her clothing. "I cannot believe we just did this. What if Liz and Darren overheard us?"

"If either of them did, I trust they'll have enough sense not to mention it to you."

"That's not the point." Katy jumped down off the desk, staggered, and nearly collapsed. Luke caught her arm to steady her. He was still smiling that very masculine smile.

"Take it easy, honey."

She frowned at him, then reached down to pick up her pantyhose and panties. She realized at once the underwear was still damp. She was still damp, too, in spite of the tissue. "Oh, dear. I can't put these back on."

"It's your decision, but Liz is bound to notice if you're not wearing your pantyhose when you go back to your office."

"Oh, dear."

"Don't worry, angel, they'll dry. Eventually."

She frowned at him. "Easy for you to say. You're not the one who has to sit around in damp underwear for the rest of the day."

Luke grinned. "Tell you what. I'll empty out one of my desk drawers. You can use it to store a spare set for this sort of occasion."

Katy decided that if she hadn't been feeling so soft and warm and happy, she would have strangled him. The man clearly had no shame.

"We are not going to make a habit of this, Luke Gilchrist," Katy announced as she stepped into her panties and tugged on her pantyhose.

"All right," he said equably. His eyes followed her every movement with lazy possessiveness. "Next time I'll think of something to use besides the desk. Although I thought it worked just fine myself."

Katy felt herself responding to the expression in his sorcerer's eyes. "I think I had better get out of here."

"Don't forget that I'll be over for dinner tonight."

"Believe me, I'm not likely to forget." Katy straightened her skirt and fled toward the door.

"Right." Luke walked around behind his desk and sat down. He picked up a gold pen and smiled. "Tell Darren I'll talk to him now."

Katy paused in the act of unlocking the door. She glanced anxiously around the office. "Do you think he'll know that we, uh, did something in here?"

Luke shrugged. "Like I said, as long as he refrains from commenting on the subject, I don't really care."

"Well, I do," Katy muttered. "You Gilchrists are entirely too blasé about this sort of thing. You thrive on passion and drama. No sense of decorum whatsoever."

"Relax, Katy. If cousin Darren dares to make any tasteless remarks, I'll tear off one of his arms and beat him over the head with it."

Katy gave up. There was no reasoning with Luke. She went out the door and down the corridor to the nearest bathroom. When she emerged she felt much better. In control. Her hair was neatly brushed and her clothes looked presentable.

She had been right about one thing, however. Her damp panties took forever to dry.

CHAPTER ELEVEN

The following morning Katy sat with Justine in her suite drinking tea in front of the floor-to-ceiling windows. The good news as far as Katy was concerned was that the older woman no longer seemed withdrawn and depressed the way she had before Luke's arrival. She looked much more like herself this morning. She was wearing a crisp black shirtwaist dress that gave her a jaunty air, and her expression was resolute.

The bad news was that Justine was annoyed.

The problem in dealing with Gilchrists was that one did not always like what one got when their moods altered any better than what one had before. On the other hand, Katy told herself philosophically, she was accustomed to dealing with Justine's anger. It did not alarm her the way the older woman's depressed spirits had.

"Yesterday I asked Luke for a simple, straightforward report on the status of my company. That was all." Justine's teacup clinked loudly when she set it down in its saucer. "What I got was some nonsense about collecting data. It sounds to me as though he's accomplished absolutely nothing since his arrival."

Katy winced. She was the one who had asked Luke not to tell his grandmother any of the real news about Gilchrist, Inc. She searched for something bright and reassuring to say. "He seems to be having a very positive impact on management."

"I do not care what sort of impact he's having on management. That report he delivered to me was an insult. Who does he think I am? I won't be treated as if I'm feebleminded. I want results."

"I'm sure he'll get them, Justine."

"I wish I could be as certain as you are." Justine sat brooding silently on that for a moment. "Katy, I must ask you something. I want your honest opinion."

"Of course, Justine." Katy mentally crossed her fingers behind her back.

"I know that initially you weren't in favor of my efforts to persuade Luke to join the family. Do you still feel I made a mistake?"

Katy was startled by the hint of uncertainty she sensed in Justine. "No," she admitted cautiously. "I don't think it was a mistake.

I think Luke knows what he's doing and that he's quite capable of saving Gilchrist, Inc."

"If he wants to save it," Justine said grimly. "I'm beginning to wonder if he does."

Katy was surprised. "What do you mean?"

"I mean I am not at all certain he came back to help us. After that ridiculous report I got yesterday I have to wonder if perhaps Hayden and Maureen were right when they claimed he had returned to destroy the company."

"Justine, I'm sure that's not the case. If Luke was a bit vague in his report, it was only because he's still gathering information. He's a great believer in having all the pertinent information he can get before he acts. He seems to organize everything with a computer."

"I don't know, Katy. I just don't know." Justine leaned her head back in her chair and watched the fog roll in off the sea. "All my life I've been so sure of myself. I've always tried to do what was best for the company and for the family. But lately I've begun to realize I made a lot of mistakes along the way."

"Everyone does, Justine," Katy said quietly.

"It is entirely possible that Luke came

here to destroy Gilchrist, Inc. I convinced myself that once he was here he would want to become a part of the company and a part of the family. But I may have been wrong."

Katy chose her words carefully. "I don't know if he will want to become a permanent part of the company, but I don't believe he will deliberately destroy it, either."

"Why shouldn't he want to destroy it?" Justine's mouth curved sadly. "Why should he develop any affection for me? No one else in the family ever has."

Katy stared at her. "Justine, how can you say that?"

"It's true, Katy. You know it. Oh, they all tolerate me because I've held the purse strings all these years. They come to dinner when I demand it. They show up on my birthday and dutifully bring me gifts. But the truth is none of them really cares for me, and I've often felt that Maureen may actually hate me."

"She doesn't hate you," Katy said calmly. "She's afraid of you."

Justine scowled. "Afraid of me? How idiotic of her. Maureen always did lack backbone. What does she think I'll do to her?"

Katy sipped her tea. "I don't think she's afraid of what you'll do to her, but of what you'll do to her family."

"That's utter rubbish."

"No, it isn't," Katy said firmly. "You made a lasting impression on her thirty-seven years ago when you condemned Luke's mother out of hand and banished your son. Maureen has spent the past thirty-seven years trying to make certain you don't do the same thing to Hayden and your other grandchildren because of her. It's been a heavy responsibility for her to carry all these years."

Justine paled. "My God. Are you serious?"

"Yes. And if you ask me, she's had good cause to be concerned. You have not always been the most diplomatic or understanding sort of mother-in-law."

"Because I never approved of Hayden's obsession with glass?" Justine scoffed furiously. "What was I supposed to do when I realized he preferred to waste himself on his art rather than assume his responsibilities?"

"Accept his decision," Katy suggested mildly. "It's his life. He has a right to do what he wants with it. You did what you wanted with yours."

"What makes you think that?" Justine demanded, her eyes fierce. "I'll tell you something, Katy. Something I've never told another soul. I never wanted the responsibility of running Gilchrist, Inc. But when my husband died I was twenty-four years old and alone, except for two young sons to support. The only thing my husband left us was one shabby little waterfront restaurant that was losing more money each month it stayed open."

"Justine, please. You don't have to explain this to me. I know the story." Katy put down her cup and saucer and went over to kneel beside Justine's chair. She put her arms around the older woman's rigid shoulders.

"I worked night and day to make that damned restaurant pay," Justine whispered. "I had to take care of my boys. I had to find a way to make certain they never went hungry. I would never have survived that first year if your grandfather and grandmother hadn't taken pity on me."

"I know, Justine. They wanted to help you. You deserved their help. You were a hardworking young mother trying to make your own way in the world. Granddad respected that. He always respected hard work."

Justine's eyes were on the gray horizon. "They gave me advice. Sent customers to me. Told my suppliers to keep making deliveries even when I couldn't pay the bills. Then they paid those suppliers to make certain I got what I needed. Everything Gilchrist, Inc. is today I owe to your grandparents,

Katy. They kept me in business that first year until I could turn a small profit."

Katy smiled to herself. It was typical of a Gilchrist to overdramatize everything, including gratitude. "I think that's going a bit too far, Justine. Gilchrist, Inc. is what it is today because you worked darn hard to make it that way. My grandparents may have helped keep you afloat that first year, but you did all the rest."

"I owed them more than I could ever repay," Justine said as if she had not heard Katy. "I tried. God knows I tried. But it all fell apart when Thornton ran off with his secretary."

Katy stilled. "Are you telling me that you engineered the romance between my mother and your son as a way of repaying my family?"

"It was the least I could do," Justine said wistfully. "It would have been a good move for all concerned. It would have meant the merging of the two restaurant chains. It would have created an empire that would have doubled the wealth of both families. It would have united the Quinnells and the Gilchrists. It seemed fitting."

"Good grief," Katy whispered. Gilchrists never did anything by half measures, she reflected.

"I don't know where it's all going to end," Justine said. "Things have not worked out as I had planned them. And now that Luke is here they may not work out at all."

"The thing about Luke," Katy said gently, "is that he does things in his own way. We're just going to have to wait and see what happens."

"I don't like this feeling of being out of control of the situation," Justine muttered.

"If you wanted someone you could control in charge of Gilchrist, Inc., you should never have picked Luke for the job," Katy said. "Trying to control him is like trying to ride the tiger."

"In other words, it's a dangerous ride, but if we try to get off now, we'll all get eaten?"

"I'm afraid so," Katy admitted.

That evening Luke and Zeke arrived at Katy's cottage promptly at six-thirty. Luke glanced down at the dog as he raised his hand to knock. "You'd better behave yourself if you want this cushy setup to continue. No more swiping leftover pesto off the kitchen counter."

Zeke, bowl clamped between his jaws, looked up at Luke with as much feigned innocence as it was possible for such a large predator to manage.

Luke decided it was useless to lecture a dog. The night before, when Luke had first had dinner at Katy's, Zeke had developed a taste for pesto. Matt had slipped him some off his plate, and Zeke was in dog heaven. He had become a pesto junkie. When no one was looking he had sneaked into the kitchen after dinner and dragged the container of leftover pesto off the counter. By the time everyone realized what had happened he had downed the lot.

Once Zeke decided he wanted something it was virtually impossible to stop him.

He and Zeke had a few things in common, Luke reflected as he rapped on the cottage door.

The door swung inward with an ominous creaking sound reminiscent of an old grade-B horror film. Matt lurched into the opening, one shoulder hunched above the other, his eyes listing off to the right.

"Welcome, master," Matt cackled. "Welcome to the House of Green Slime. Dinner is almost ready. Only the fattest green things are being slaughtered for your gustatory pleasure. Even now they are being prepared. Listen to their screams. A cheerful sound, is it not?"

A whirring sound came from the kitchen.

Luke smiled faintly. "I take it we're going to be the victims of another pesto experiment tonight?"

"Yes, master. Katy says only the best for you and your pet demon." Matt grinned as he patted Zeke on the head.

Zeke tolerated the greeting for a moment, and then he trotted through the doorway and headed straight for the kitchen.

"Heck, it makes a change from baked potatoes," Luke said. He walked into the cottage. "I figure the worst that can happen is we'll all turn green."

For some reason Matt found that uproarious.

Luke followed Zeke into the kitchen and found his dog sitting beside his bowl in the middle of the floor. Zeke's eyes tracked Katy relentlessly as she carried a pile of green leaves from the sink to the food processor.

Katy, dressed in jeans and a salmon-colored sweater and wearing a checkered apron, flashed Luke a smile of welcome. "Hi. You're right on time."

"Zeke insisted. He didn't want us to be late."

Katy made a face at Zeke. "If you think I'm going to fix an extra batch of this for you, think again, Zeke."

Zeke drooled.

"Better give him some," Luke advised as he opened a cupboard door and took down two wineglasses. "Otherwise he'll probably help himself the way he did last night."

"I've got news for him. He's not going to get a second chance to pull a stunt like that last one. Tonight all the leftovers are going straight into the refrigerator." Katy dumped leaves into the food processor.

"I don't know if you're going to be able to save your pesto," Luke said as he poured two glasses of wine. "Zeke has had a taste of it now, and he's hooked."

Zeke whined hungrily.

"Are you trying to tell me it's like his having gotten a taste of blood?" Katy glared at the dog. "You should have fed him before you brought him over here."

"I did. But Zeke always has room for pesto."

"Well, he's not getting any of this." Katy switched on the food processor, effectively drowning out any response.

Luke smiled with satisfaction as he leaned back against the counter. Katy looked good in an apron, he decided. This was only the second dinner invitation he had managed to coax out of her, but he fully intended to make such invitations routine.

She was a hell of a good cook.

In addition, Luke had discovered last night that he liked being here with Katy and her brother. It had made him realize just how lonely his life had been for the past three years.

Although he had never considered himself a home-and-hearth sort of man, he found he enjoyed the cozy warmth of Katy's kitchen. He liked leaning against the counter and drinking wine while he watched Katy bustle around the small room. He liked joking with Matt. He even liked eating Katy's experimental pesto and pasta combinations.

The only thing Luke did not like was having to go back to his own cottage at ten. But the weekend was coming, he reminded himself optimistically. Matt would be staying out until midnight on Friday and Saturday.

Luke had big plans for Friday and Saturday.

"I wanted to talk to you about something," Katy said as she switched off the machine.

"I'm listening."

"I had a long talk with Justine this morning. She was annoyed."

"So what else is new?"

Katy threw him a quelling glance. "The thing is, she was not happy with that report you gave her on the condition of Gilchrist, Inc. She felt she didn't get any real information."

Luke raised his brows. "She didn't. You wouldn't let me give her any of the good stuff, remember?"

Katy's mouth tightened primly. "I asked you not to tell her about Darren or about your suspicion that someone is embezzling from the company."

"Right. The good stuff."

"What did you tell her?"

"Not much. Just said I was working on gathering information."

Katy spooned Parmesan cheese into the bowl of the food processor. "Couldn't you have been a little more diplomatic? More tactful?"

"Why?"

"Luke, she's your grandmother. And for better or worse, she does own the company."

"In case you haven't realized it yet, Katy, I don't feel any overwhelming urge to be diplomatic or tactful when dealing with Justine. *She* sure as hell doesn't go out of her way to exercise either of those qualities. Why should she expect me to do it?"

Katy scowled at him. "You and I both know you could have come up with something that sounded as though you were making real progress in saving Gilchrist, Inc."

"Maybe. But I didn't feel like it."

"For heaven's sake, Luke, she's starting

to wonder if you're here to destroy the company instead of to save it. I think she's getting nervous about your intentions."

"It'll give her something to think about," Luke observed.

Katy gave a soft, thoroughly frustrated exclamation. Spoon in hand, she marched over to stand directly in front of him. "Luke Gilchrist, I have had enough of this. I want you to behave yourself, do you understand? The next time you report to Justine you will be tactful and diplomatic. Is that clear?"

Luke smiled at the picture she made. The admonishing fire in her eyes was a clear challenge. If they had been alone, he would have stripped off her checkered apron and her jeans and made love to her on the kitchen table.

"I hear you, angel," Luke said softly. "What would you like me to tell Justine? That my hacker friend has traced the restaurant embezzlement problems to a computer located in the Gilchrist corporate offices?"

Katy stared at him. "Oh, no. Are you certain?"

"Yes."

"This is terrible," she said, sounding dazed. "I was hoping — "

"What? That there was no embezzlement going on? That the problems in the two restaurants were simple bookkeeping errors?"

"Frankly, yes," she admitted.

"The Pollyanna approach to business has never been a very successful one," Luke chided.

She bit her lip. "You still don't know who's doing the embezzling."

"No, but it won't take long to find out now."

"Luke," she said urgently, "if you do discover that it's someone in the family, I want you to talk to me first."

"Forget it," Luke said. "I'll handle the problem."

"Given your lack of tactfulness, I don't think that's such a good idea," Katy said grimly.

"Sorry, that's the way it's going to be."

"Luke, listen to me. This is very important."

Matt appeared in the kitchen doorway. His gaze went to his sister's irate face and then settled on Luke. "What's going on in here? Are you two arguing or something?"

"No," Luke said calmly. "Your sister was just giving me a lecture on how to run Gilchrist, Inc. I told her I was going to do things my way. She was trying to get me to do things her way."

Matt visibly relaxed. "She can be kind of persistent."

"I've noticed," Luke said.

"You get used to it," Matt explained.

Luke took another sip of his wine and smiled. "I know. Don't worry, I can handle her."

Katy drew herself up. "That's enough out of both of you. If either of you wants to eat dinner tonight, you will both refrain from discussing me in the third person. I'll give the whole batch of pesto to Zeke if I hear one more word."

Zeke's tail thumped eagerly on the kitchen floor.

"Hey, I can take a hint," Luke said.

"Me, too," Matt agreed quickly.

Katy studied both of them with narrowed eyes and then nodded once, apparently satisfied. "That's better. You can both make yourselves useful. Set the table."

Luke quickly opened the nearest drawer and grabbed a handful of knives and forks.

"I'll get the plates," Matt said, lunging toward the cupboard.

"That's better," Katy said with satisfaction. "I like to see men active in the kitchen. They always look at home there."

Zeke sat in the middle of the floor and licked his chops.

An hour later Luke finished his second helping of Japanese-style soba noodles and pesto sauce. He leaned back in his chair and grinned at Matt. "The sacrifice of all the little screaming green things was worth it."

Matt laughed. "Yeah, not bad."

Katy glanced suspiciously from one to the other. "What is this about a sacrifice?"

"Nothing," Matt assured her.

Katy smiled hopefully. "You really liked it?"

"It was great," Luke said. "What did you use in the pesto sauce this time?"

Katy glowed. She warmed to her topic immediately. "Fresh parsley and tarragon leaves. And the usual Parmesan cheese, pine nuts, and olive oil, of course. You don't think there was too much tarragon in it?"

"Definitely not," Luke said. "Another winner."

"Good." Katy got to her feet and started to clear the table. "I think I've finally got this particular recipe down just the way I want it. I'll add it to my file of Pesto Presto recipes."

"Is that all you think about these days?" Luke asked softly. "Pesto Presto?"

It was Matt who answered. "Yeah, take it from me, that's about all she thinks about all right. You should see some of the things I've had to eat. I'll tell you one thing, the guy who marries Katy had better be as interested in cooking as she is, or he won't stand a chance with her."

Katy flushed. Her gaze slid away from Luke's as she hurried into the kitchen.

Matt looked at Luke. "Hey, you want to give me some more chess lessons?"

"Sure," Luke said, his eyes following Katy as she whipped out of sight around the corner.

"I'd better warn you, I've been practicing."

A resounding crash from the kitchen interrupted Luke's reply. The jarring noise was followed by Katy's unmistakable shriek of dismay.

"You miserable, sneaky, conniving monster," Katy yelled. "One of these days you're going to go too far. Do you hear me?"

Luke walked to the kitchen door and glanced around the corner. Zeke was gulping down the leftover pesto. Katy was glowering at the dog, helpless to salvage the remains.

"How did he get hold of the container?" Luke asked with mild interest.

Katy raised her wrathful eyes to his. "I made the mistake of offering him a small bite. I was trying to be kind. I leaned down to put a spoonful into his bowl — just a spoonful, mind you — and the next thing

I knew he had snatched the entire container out of my hand. This dog of yours is a disgrace."

Luke shrugged. "What can I say? He likes your cooking."

Matt peered into the kitchen. "Look at it this way, Katy. Now you know for sure the stuff is good. A dog wouldn't lie about a thing like that."

At ten o'clock that evening Luke made his last move on the chess board and reluctantly got to his feet. He looked at Katy, who was sprawled on the couch with a cookbook. "Guess I'd better be on my way."

She put down her cookbook and stood up quickly. Her eyes searched his. "Yes. Well, thanks for sampling the new pesto sauce. I'll see you in the morning."

Luke gazed at her, all too aware of the sensual hunger gnawing at his gut. "Right. See you in the morning." He leaned down and kissed her right on her soft, unsuspecting mouth.

He heard her tiny gasp and saw her glance quickly at Matt. Did she really think he was going to pretend there was nothing between them just because her brother happened to be in the room? Luke wondered. He was willing to honor her wishes to be discreet, but Katy might as well learn that he had no intention of hiding their relationship.

Before she could recover, Luke was halfway to the door. "Come on, Zeke. Time to go home."

Zeke rolled to his feet, picked up his dish, and trotted to the door.

Matt stood up suddenly, his gaze shifting from Katy's flushed face to Luke's. "I'll walk with you partway," he said. "I feel like some exercise."

Luke held open the door. He had a hunch he knew what was coming. "All right."

Katy came to the door. Her cheeks were bright with warm color, and her eyes were anxious. Luke gently closed the door in her face.

Matt was silent for a long moment as they walked toward Luke's cottage. Luke said nothing, giving the boy time to gather his thoughts.

"I've been wondering if you and Katy are like — well, you know — interested in each other," Matt finally said.

"Yes," Luke said calmly. "We are."

There was a short, tense pause. "No offense, but you aren't exactly her type. Know what I mean?"

"No."

Matt did not seem to know quite how to

handle that roadblock. "Well, it's just that she thinks Gilchrists are sort of difficult."

"Your sister can be as difficult as any Gilchrist."

Matt digested that and tried a new tack. "Look, I don't want her to get hurt again, okay? It was bad enough when that Atwood jerk dumped her to marry Eden. It wasn't that I thought Atwood was good for Katy. He wasn't. I never did like him. But Eden didn't even say she was sorry or anything."

"You're trying to tell me that you don't trust anyone with the last name of Gilchrist?"

Matt hesitated. "I didn't mean that exactly."

Luke came to a halt and turned to face Matt in the cold moonlight. He could see the earnest concern in the younger man's expression, and he understood. "It's all right, Matt. I'll take care of her."

Matt studied him closely for a long moment. Whatever he saw in Luke's face apparently satisfied him. "Okay. I just wanted to be sure, you know? I mean, she's my sister."

"I know. Good night, Matt."

"Good night."

Luke turned and walked on toward the lights of his cottage. Zeke paced beside him to the front door. Luke let himself inside and went to stand at the window overlooking the darkened ocean.

He knew that he had just given Matt a promise and a guarantee. Promises and guarantees were commitments that extended into the future.

The future. Once again he was being wrenched out of the safe, comfortable present and forced to look ahead.

He realized as he gazed out into the night that although he still did not have a clear vision of his own future, he knew now that Katy Wade was very much a part of it.

She alone gave it whatever form or substance it held for him.

CHAPTER TWELVE

The phone rang just as Katy was getting ready to leave the cottage to walk to the mansion. She glanced outside, noticed it was raining, and grabbed the receiver and an umbrella at the same time.

"Katy?" Maureen's voice sounded heavy with undertones of doom and despair.

"What's wrong, Maureen?" Katy put down the umbrella. Something told her this was not going to be a quick call.

"I've discovered for certain that Eden is seeing Nate Atwood again."

"Oh, no. How did you find out?"

"A client saw her with him. She asked me if they were reconciling. Katy, you have to do something. Justine will never tolerate this. And we both know he'll only hurt Eden again. You have got to stop him."

Katy sank slowly down onto the arm of the sofa. She massaged her temple, trying to think quickly. Gilchrists frequently went off half-cocked. It was time to slow down and sort this out. "Have you talked to Eden?"

"No. I can't confront her with this. You know how she is. She'll be furious if I try to interfere."

Maureen was right about that, Katy reflected. Gilchrists frequently got annoyed when people tried to get in their way. "I think you should ask her what's going on before you do anything drastic, Maureen."

"I know my daughter better than you do," Maureen snapped. "Katy, I want that man out of her life once and for all. You introduced him to the family. A great deal of this is your fault."

"My fault?"

"Go and see him. Find out what he's after. I'm sure it's money. Find out how much he wants."

"Maureen, I can't offer him a blank check. He'll bleed you dry. You know that."

"Find out how much he wants to get out of my daughter's life. I'll find the money somewhere." Maureen hung up the phone.

Katy gazed at the humming receiver and then slowly replaced it in its cradle. The last thing she wanted to do was talk to Nate Atwood. The man was a snake.

Eden knew that. It was Eden who had wanted the divorce. And she was too proud to take him back. She was a Gilchrist, after all. She knew all there was to know about pride.

So what was going on here? Katy wondered. She sat on the arm of the sofa a moment, swinging one foot as she contemplated the situation. Then she picked up the phone again and dialed her own number up at the mansion. Liz answered on the first ring.

"Gilchrist, Inc."

"Liz? It's Katy. I'm not coming into the office today. I'm going to take some personal time off. I've got some things to do in town."

"What things?" Liz asked with her usual forthright approach.

"A dentist appointment. Some shopping. Small stuff. I'll see you in the morning."

"If you say so. Are you all right, Katy? I think I detect some anxiety in your voice."

"I'm fine, Liz. I'll call you this afternoon and pick up my messages. What is Luke's schedule today?"

"He went into Seattle this morning. He's got meetings most of the day. He'll be back this afternoon. Want me to give him a message?"

"No, that's all right. There's nothing urgent I need to tell him." Katy hung up the phone, frowning in thought. If Luke was in Seattle, she dared not meet Eden at corporate headquarters. There was too great a possibility she would run into Luke. He would start asking questions, one thing would lead to another, and matters would get complicated.

Katy glanced at the clock and decided Eden would not have left for her office yet. She dialed her home number.

"Yes?" Eden's voice was naturally sultry, even on the phone.

"Eden, this is Katy. I have to talk to you. I can be in Seattle in an hour. I want you to meet me at one of the espresso bars near Westlake Mall."

"What's this all about?" Eden demanded. "Have you got some information about what Luke is going to do? What is it? What's happening?"

It occurred to Katy that keeping Eden in suspense might be the most efficient way of getting her to agree to the meeting. "I'll explain everything when I see you. One hour." She named the espresso bar and hung up.

"What the hell do you mean, Katy's not in the office?" Luke gripped the telephone receiver with one hand and flipped through a file with the other. "Where is she?"

"She said she had some errands to run," Liz explained. "She's going to pick up her messages later this afternoon."

"Have her call me here in Seattle as soon as she checks in."

"Yes, sir."

Luke tossed the phone back into its cradle. He paused to read an entry in the file, and then he closed the folder. He looked up at the young man sitting across from him.

Roger Danvers was thin, wiry, and agitated. He was constantly in motion. He fiddled with his earlobes, tapped his feet, and drummed his fingers. It made Luke nervous just to look at him. But Danvers was the best there was at what he did.

"You're sure about this?" Luke asked softly.

"I'm sure about which access code is being used to get into the restaurants' accounts and skim money out of them," Danvers said. "And we both know who that access code is assigned to. It's possible someone other than that person got hold of it and used it to embezzle the funds."

"But you don't think it's very likely?"

Danvers twitched. "No. Access code security is fairly good here at Gilchrist. The skimming is done during regular working hours and on weekends when that person has been known to put in some extra time. It's not happening at midnight."

"So no one is sneaking in after hours to use the computer," Luke concluded. "All right, Danvers. You've done your job. I don't like the answers, but that's not your fault. Thanks."

"Sure. You want me to keep working on the Gilchrist Gourmet situation?" Danvers tugged at his earlobe as he got to his feet.

"Yes."

"You got it."

Luke waited until the door had closed behind Danvers. Then he looked down at the report that had been left behind.

"Damn."

Katy was not going to like this. Luke knew before he even dropped the bombshell on her that she was going to try to talk him out of doing what had to be done. The guardian angel was too soft when it came to this kind of thing. He had better have his ammunition ready. He was going to have to justify the actions he intended to take. He knew Katy was going to put up a fight.

"Damn."

Katy was definitely complicating his life. Luke scowled at the telephone. Where the hell was she today, anyway? he wondered.

Katy, wearing the slender, long-sleeved, mint-green dress she'd put on for work that morning, sat perched on a high stool behind the counter at the espresso bar. She idly stirred a latte as she waited for Eden.

The watermelon and black coffeehouse was crowded with downtown shoppers and business people taking their morning break in true Seattle style. The espresso machine was shrieking in agony. It hissed and roared as it produced an endless stream of lattes and espressos and a host of other interesting coffee concoctions that formed the lifeblood of Seattle's lively coffee culture. In Seattle even hardware stores and gas stations featured espresso machines for their customers.

Katy took her first sip just as Eden walked through the front door. One did not have to be a trained Gilchrist observer to know that something was very wrong.

Eden appeared every inch a Gilchrist this morning, from the toes of her gleaming black high heels to the wide lapels of her black suit. Her ebony hair was sleek and glossy, and her mouth and nails were crimson. She walked with the familiar Gilchrist stride, arrogant and regal, but there was a haunted look in her green eyes. Katy knew that whatever stress Eden had been under since the divorce had gotten much worse.

Eden saw her at the counter and walked straight toward her. She sat down on the neighboring stool, ignoring the interested gazes that followed her. "This had better be important, Katy. I'm extremely busy today."

"Are you seeing Nate Atwood again?" Katy asked bluntly.

Eden flinched. "Who told you that?"

"I believe Fraser Stanfield mentioned it first," Katy said. "Apparently he saw you getting into a cab with Nate. But the real clincher was one of your mother's clients who mentioned seeing you and Nate together. Maureen came unglued, as I'm sure you can imagine."

Eden sat frozen on the stool. "Mother knows?"

Katy took another swallow of her latte. "Uh-huh. That's why I'm here."

"Stay out of this, Katy. It has nothing to do with you." Eden's fingers trembled on the strap of her black leather shoulder bag.

"Eden, we both know Nate Atwood is poison. Why are you getting involved with him again? You just got free of the rat."

Eden's jaw tightened. "It's none of your business, Katy. Just stay out of it."

"I can't believe you'd take him back," Katy said slowly.

"I'm not taking him back."

"Then why are you seeing him?"

"I'm not seeing him," Eden bit out. "Not the way you mean. I am not in a relationship with him. There. Does that satisfy you?"

"No. If you're not involved in a relationship with him, then something else is going on. Is he forcing you to see him?"

"Damn it, Katy, will you please stay out of this?"

"What is he doing to you?" Katy searched Eden's face. "Is he putting some kind of pressure on you? We all know he was dissatisfied with what he got out of the divorce. Does he want more money?"

Eden's stricken expression was all the answer Katy needed.

"Good Lord," Katy muttered. "I should have guessed. Maureen wants me to try to buy him off. How much does he want?"

"You don't understand," Eden said desperately. "It's not that simple. Every time I give him money he tells me it will be the last time. But he keeps coming back for more."

"But why are you giving it to him?" Katy demanded. "Justine's lawyers took care of Atwood. Eden, what's going on?"

Eden closed her eyes in an expression of soul-wrenching agony. "He's blackmailing me."

"Oh, my God." Katy was floored. She

groped for the next question. "How? What could he possibly have on you that would make you vulnerable?"

"It's not me. It's Mother. He knows something about her. Something that happened a long time ago. Something that would enrage Justine. I can't tell Mother. She doesn't know that I know. She would be devastated if she thought anyone in the family knew."

"And terrified that Justine might find out?"

Eden nodded sadly. "Yes. You know how desperately Mother has tried to please Justine over the years."

"For the sake of her family," Katy whispered, remembering the conversation she had had with Maureen in the gallery. "She's tried to protect all of you from Justine."

"I realize that." Eden's fingers tightened on her purse strap. "And now I have to protect her from Justine."

Katy was silent for a few minutes, thinking. "What does Nate have on her?"

Eden hesitated and then gave a tiny shrug as if realizing that the damage was already done. "It all happened years ago. Back in New York. Before Mom and Dad were even married. There was a question of fraud."

"Fraud?"

"Fraud or forgery or something," Eden said impatiently. "I don't know the whole story. Nate hasn't told me everything. I don't think he knows either. But he has some old press clippings." Eden's eyes blurred with crystal tears.

"Go on," Katy urged gently.

"Long ago, when my mother was very young, she was convicted of selling forged art. Nate has threatened to send the clippings to Justine."

"Unless you continue to pay him off?"

"Yes." Eden opened her purse and withdrew a black linen handkerchief. She dabbed at her eyes with it and dropped it back into the bag. "I'm going mad, Katy. I can't get rid of him. No matter how much I give him, he won't go away."

"I've heard that blackmailers rarely do go away. And we both know Nate would have no compunction about bleeding someone dry."

"Oh, God, it's true."

Katy patted her on the shoulder. "It's all right, Eden. We'll find a way to deal with this. Tell me something. Where have you been getting the money to pay him off?"

Eden's eyes shimmered. "I withdrew what was left in my own bank account months ago. I couldn't go to anyone. So I did what I had to do."

Katy stared at her. "Please don't tell me

you're the one who's been skimming the restaurant accounts."

"How did you know about that?"

"Never mind. Are you the one behind the embezzlement?"

Eden sighed deeply. "I had no choice. I fully intend to repay the money as soon as I get rid of Nate."

"There are two major flaws in that plan," Katy said. "The first is that you're never going to get rid of Nate by paying him off. The second is that you're working on borrowed time. Luke knows what's going on at the restaurants. He's tracking down the person responsible even as we speak."

"He knows?" Eden looked terror-stricken. "But he can't know. I've been very careful."

"You may have been careful, but Luke is clever. He'll find out you're the one behind the embezzlement. It's just a matter of time."

"He'll go straight to Justine. She'll be furious." Eden's fingers were shaking. "There's no telling what she'll do. She'll turn on all of us. Mother and Dad, Darren, all of us. My God, what have I done?"

Katy forced herself to think through the tangled web of impending disaster. "All right, we'll take this one step at a time."

"There is no first step," Eden whispered. "We're standing on a precipice."

In spite of everything, Katy could not restrain a small smile. "We?"

"You've got to help me, Katy. I'm at the end of my rope."

"All right. First we'll do the obvious. We'll go see Nate and tell him that if he doesn't get out of your life and stay out, there will be hell to pay."

Eden frowned. "But we don't have anything we can use to threaten him."

"Yes, we do." Katy put down her empty latte cup and hitched the strap of her yellow purse higher on her shoulder. She thought of Luke closing in on the embezzler. "Let's go. We don't have a lot of time."

Katy knew she had gotten over any lingering feelings she'd had for Nate Atwood a long time ago. Nevertheless, she was tense at the thought of having to see him again.

She had seen almost nothing of him during his marriage to Eden. Most of her memories of him went back to the time when she herself had been dating him.

On the surface Nate had been everything she thought she had wanted in a man. To her he had shown a sunny, open personality. His sense of humor had been quick and lively. He had been interested in her long-range plans to open a small take-out restaurant.

He had befriended Matt. The fact that he was good looking, with chiseled features, hazel eyes, and sandy brown hair was a pleasant bonus.

But looking back on the whole thing, Katy knew that something in her had sensed the wrongness in Nate Atwood almost from the start. He was too good to be true, and deep down she had known it. It was why she had never gone to bed with him.

During those exciting weeks with Nate she had found herself constantly testing the waters, unconsciously searching for the flaw.

She had discovered it the evening she had walked in on Nate and Eden wrapped in each other's arms in a poolside lounge chair at the mansion. Later she realized the damning scene had been orchestrated for her. Neither Nate nor Eden had wanted to tell her what was going on, so they had simply arranged for her to find out for herself. Everyone knew Katy swam nearly every day after work.

When she had recovered from the shock of the discovery Katy had experienced an even greater surprise. She had watched Nate Atwood change personalities before her eyes. He was no longer the easygoing, friendly man she had known. Instead, like some clever chameleon, he turned himself into a mysterious, exotic lover for Eden.

He hinted at a past that included work for the CIA. He dropped the names of famous gangsters and politicians. He arranged for Eden to awake in a bed strewn with fresh blood-red roses. He gave her a string of black pearls. He quarreled with her in front of a crowd when he found her dancing with another man.

The quarrel had ended passionately when he had swept Eden off the dance floor and into a waiting limousine. Eden told Katy later that he had made love to her in the back of the limo while the chauffeur drove aimlessly around the city.

Eden had been enthralled right up to the point at which she had eloped with Nate. Shortly after the wedding, however, the realization that she had made a mistake had started to show in her eyes. If there was one thing a Gilchrist understood, it was passion, and Eden had eventually recognized that Nate's passion for her was not based on love. She had confided to Katy that she planned to get a divorce. Katy, recognizing the potential danger in Nate, had gone to Justine to get the best possible legal protection for Eden. It had paid off.

Until now.

"I thought Nate had an office in Seattle,"

Katy said as Eden drove her black BMW onto the Mercer Island Bridge.

"He moved it to Bellevue after the divorce," Eden said bitterly. "I wish he had moved it to the other side of the world. Katy, tell me how you think you can threaten him. I'm going crazy with worry. I can't eat and I can't sleep."

"I'm going to threaten him with Luke," Katy explained.

"Luke?" Eden was horrified. "You can't bring Luke into this."

"With any luck I won't have to bring him into it," Katy said wearily. She gazed out the windows at the wind-ruffled waters of Lake Washington. "I'm hoping that the threat alone will be sufficient."

Eden shook her head. "I don't think anything is going to work. Oh, God, Katy, what have I done? How could I ever have thought I was in love with Nate?"

"Beats me," Katy said dryly. "But you were sure you were at the time."

Eden gave her a piteous sidelong glance. "I was so wrong about him."

"Hey, don't keep beating yourself over the head because of it. I liked him a lot in the beginning, too."

The offices of Atwood Investments were in a gleaming new high rise in Bellevue.

Eden parked the BMW in the garage. Katy could see how anxious she was when she took the keys out of the ignition. The jangling sound disturbed Katy. It made her realize how tightly strung her own nerves were.

"How much have you given him to date?" Katy asked as they got into the elevator.

"I don't even want to think about it. Thousands. I am absolutely desperate, Katy."

They got out of the elevator and walked down the hall to Nate's office.

"What will we do if he's not here?" Eden asked.

"We'll wait for him."

Katy opened the office door and walked inside. Eden trailed after her. A young woman with an amazingly well-developed chest looked up inquiringly.

"May I help you?" Then the secretary saw Eden. Bright color flamed in her cheeks. Her eyes started to narrow. "Oh, hello, Miss Gilchrist."

"Hello, Cynthia. Please tell your boss that I want to see him."

"I'm afraid Mr. Atwood is busy at the moment," Cynthia said with great satisfaction.

"I'm sure he's not too busy to see us," Katy said. She walked straight past Cynthia's desk and opened the door of the inner office. Eden followed.

Nate was on the phone, one well-shod foot propped on his desk. He reclined in a swivel chair, his attention on the view of Lake Washington outside his window. He glanced around in obvious annoyance as Katy and Eden entered the room. His expression turned cold as he realized who his visitors were, but his voice was laced with warm camaraderie as he concluded his conversation.

"Look, Mike, I'm going to have to run. Something's come up. I'll catch you later. Think about the deal. It's solid. You'll make a killing." Nate hung up the phone and leisurely sat forward. "Well, well, well. To what do I owe the honor of this visit, ladies?"

Katy looked at him and wondered what she had ever seen in him. "I think you know the answer to that, Nate. Your little blackmailing scheme ends now. Today. This minute. Furthermore, you will repay the money you have taken from Eden."

Nate studied her for a long, chilling moment. His eyes were filled with scorn. "You always were a little on the naïve side." Then he turned to Eden. "I warned you not to talk about our arrangement," he said in a silky voice. "You've made me very angry, Eden. It's going to cost you."

Eden did not move. "It has to stop, Nate. I simply can't get any more money for you."

"You can get it. And you will. You're a Gilchrist. You owe me. By rights I should have a chunk of the company. Since you managed to keep me from getting my share at the time of the divorce, I'll get it any way I can."

Eden shuddered. "You've taken enough. More than enough. I can't give you any more."

"You will. One way or another you will. We both know I'll send those clippings about your mother to your grandmother. I've got nothing to lose."

Katy took a step forward. "You're wrong," she said quietly. "You have a great deal to lose. I'm here to warn you that if you don't stop the blackmail right now and repay the money you've wrung out of Eden, you will be very sorry."

"No shit." Nate chuckled. "How are you going to make me sorry, Katy? Go to that old witch, Justine? Not a chance. You know what she'll do to Eden and her family if she finds out about her daughter-in-law's previous career as a dealer in forged art. She'll disown the whole bunch."

"That's not true," Katy said firmly.

Nate grinned. "Come on. Who are you

trying to kid? I was a member of the family for a year. I know what Justine Gilchrist is like. I know exactly what she'll do if she finds out about Maureen. Stay out of this. It's between Eden and me. The Gilchrists owe me, and they're going to pay."

Katy steeled herself. She was going to have to make the counterthreat sound good or it would not stand a chance of working. "You may not be aware of it, Nate, but Justine no longer runs Gilchrist, Inc. Her grandson Luke is in charge. If you don't stop the blackmail, I'll go straight to him."

Nate's smile never wavered. The look in his ice-blue eyes was derisive. "The Bastard? Don't make me laugh. I know all about Luke Gilchrist. The man has a reputation. He's hard as nails, and he won't give a damn about Eden or her mother. He'll let them all sink. No, you won't run to him."

"Don't be too sure of that," Katy said swiftly.

"Jesus. How stupid do you think I am?" Nate asked. "I know about Luke Gilchrist, remember? I was family. I know what Justine did to his parents."

"That's got nothing to do with this," Katy said.

"The hell it doesn't." Nate leaned back in his chair. He smiled slowly. "I don't deal in restaurants specifically, but I know real estate in general, and I know the major players in the Northwest financial community. Word travels in the investment world, and Gilchrist is well known. He doesn't need Gilchrist, Inc. There's only one reason he'd take it over. He wants revenge for what happened to his parents."

Out of the corner of her eye Katy saw Eden start to cry. She concentrated on Nate. "You're wrong."

"The hell I am. I know his history, and I know Gilchrists. Luke Gilchrist is either going to destroy the company outright to punish Justine and everyone else in the family or to take it over completely and cut them all off. My personal guess is that he'll crush the business and leave the family with the remains. I have to admit it won't break my heart. But I intend to get a little more money out of it before it goes under."

"Not another dime, Nate," Katy said softly. "Luke will stop you. He won't allow you to blackmail a member of the family." Katy glanced at Eden. "Let's go."

"Go on, get out of here," Nate muttered. He waited until Eden had walked into the outer office. "Katy?"

Surprised by something in his voice, Katy turned back. "What is it?"

"You're wasting your time trying to save them all. Let them go to hell. They deserve it."

"I can't do that. I owe Justine. You know that."

"You don't owe her a damn thing. Dump the Gilchrists and get on with your life."

"Since when did you start caring about what I did with my life?" Katy asked. She walked out the door before Nate could answer.

Eden said nothing until they were both in the elevator.

"It didn't work," Eden said, gazing straight ahead at the closed doors.

"No."

"I knew it wouldn't. What are we going to do now?"

"We have no choice," Katy said grimly. "Nate called my bluff. That means I have to make good on the threat."

Eden looked even more horrified than she had earlier. "Go to Luke? Ask him for help? You can't do that."

"I don't have any choice. Stop worrying, Eden. Luke isn't going to be thrilled when he finds out what's going on, but he'll take care of the problem for you."

"No, he won't," Eden said in a voice dazed with shock. "He'll use it to get his revenge.

314

My God, I've ruined everything. Mother and Dad will suffer for my mistakes. And poor Darren. There's no telling what Justine will do to him. She'll probably fire him."

Katy had had enough drama for the day. "You've got to have a little faith in family ties, Eden."

"Family ties? Are you nuts? We're talking about the Gilchrist family."

"You've got a point."

Her next move would have to be made with great care, Katy reflected. She needed time to think.

She needed a good swim.

CHAPTER THIRTEEN

At ten o'clock that evening Katy resorted to the one form of stress release that she had come to depend upon during the past few years. She decided to take a swim in the mansion pool. She had not gotten back from Seattle until quite late. Instead of going directly home she had gone to the Dragon Bay Library to sit and think for a while.

It was Friday night. Her brother would not be home until twelve. She had the entire evening to herself, and thus far she had spent it pondering the right approach to take with Luke.

He was going to explode when she told him about Eden's situation. Being a Gilchrist, the explosion would not be a wimpy little sputter and shower of sparks. Luke would undoubtedly reach critical mass the instant she tried to explain.

She noticed there were no lights on in his cottage as she walked past on her way up to the mansion. Just as well. She wasn't ready to face him quite yet.

Katy did not bother to turn on the lights in the old conservatory as she let herself in with her key. The eerie blue glow of the underwater illumination was all she needed. She made her way through the jungle of palms and ferns. When she reached the pool she dropped her towel and robe on a lounge chair and slipped into the water.

She launched herself toward the far end of the pool with a sense of relief. As always, there was a blessed feeling of freedom to be found in the water. She stroked strongly and cleanly through the rippling blue world and forced herself to think about what she would say to Luke.

It was true he had come through in Darren's case, but that was a much simpler sort of disaster. Darren had been the victim of a con. Blackmail and deliberate embezzlement, on the other hand, constituted a slightly more difficult problem. Katy understood that. But it was, nevertheless, a family problem.

She had to make Luke understand that the matter had to be dealt with tactfully. Eden had certainly never intended to hurt Gilchrist, Inc. or the family. She had been trying to protect people. There had to be a way to make Luke see that.

She would approach him delicately, she

317

decided. Diplomatically. She would use sweet reason and logic.

Katy reached the far end of the pool and executed an underwater turn that sent her soaring back toward the opposite end. She could feel her tension lessening already. There was nothing like a swim to relieve stress and make her feel free for at least a little while. She should have come here earlier, she thought.

She reached the pool wall and paused to take a deep breath. A dark figure moved in the shadows near a palm. Katy went still.

"Where the hell have you been all day?" Luke asked in a soft, dangerous voice.

Katy's diplomatic intentions went up in smoke at the clear note of challenge in his words. She was under enough pressure as it was. She had been stressed out all day. She did not need any more Gilchrist nonsense tonight.

"I took the day off," Katy said. Then she ducked back under the water and shot off toward the other end of the pool. When she ran out of room she turned and made her way back at a leisurely pace.

Luke was still standing in the shadows, waiting with a predator's patience.

"I want to talk to you," he said.

"Maybe later, when I've finished my

swim." Katy gripped the curving edge of the tile rim and prepared to launch herself back out of range. She could feel the smoldering anger in him. It was coming at her in waves.

This was definitely not an opportune time to bring up the latest Gilchrist family problems, she concluded.

"I said I want to talk to you. Now." Luke took a couple of steps forward and sat down on the end of a lounge chair. The blue glow of the underwater lights revealed the fiercely elegant lines of his face. His eyes were gleaming with grim intent.

"Luke, can't this wait until morning? It's late."

He ignored that. "Where were you all day? Why didn't you pick up your messages?"

"I was busy. By the time I got home this evening it was too late to deal with any messages. I decided I'd wait until morning."

"Where did you go today?"

"For heaven's sake, Luke, that's my business. Just because you and I are involved in some ways doesn't give you the right to grill me every time I go off on my own."

"Involved? Is that what you call it? Lady, not only are we sleeping together — "

"We've only done it a couple of times," Katy interrupted. "That hardly constitutes a strong, enduring relationship."

"Not only are we sleeping together," Luke repeated through clenched teeth, "but you happen to work for me. That gives me the right to ask where you've been all day."

"No, it does not." Katy swam over to the edge of the pool and hauled herself upward onto the tile. "You are obviously spoiling for a fight tonight, and I am not in the mood to participate in any more Gilchrist dramatics today, thank you very much."

"What's that supposed to mean?" Luke got to his feet and started toward her.

"Nothing. Just a comment." Katy grabbed her robe and quickly belted it around herself. She glanced around hurriedly for her shoes. They were under the lounge chair. She knew she would not be able to get them on in time to make a run for it.

Luke came to a halt and stood looming over her. "I want some answers, Katy."

"Well, you're not going to get them. Not tonight, at any rate." She ripped off her bathing cap and shook out her hair. "I don't care what you feel like."

"Is that right? Well, you'd damn well better change your mind, because you're not going home until we have a long talk."

Katy ran a hand through her hair. "I said I don't feel like talking to you tonight."

"Too bad. I left three messages with Liz today. You didn't respond to any of them."

Katy lifted her chin. "Now you know how it feels not to get a response when you want one. Remember all those messages I left on your answering machine when I was trying to get you to assume your responsibilities? Remember those Express Mail letters I sent? Remember the telegrams? I didn't get a single damn answer from you."

"We are not talking ancient history here. We are talking about today."

"Tough. I don't feel like discussing it. And if you don't stop badgering me, I am going to lose my temper."

"Is that supposed to terrorize me? I've got news for you, Katy, watching a little guardian angel lose her temper is a lot like watching a sparkler on the Fourth of July. Amusing, but not exactly a real threat."

That did it. Katy had had enough of Gilchrists for one day. Maybe she'd just had enough of Gilchrists, period. Something inside her snapped. She raised her hands, took one step forward, and shoved hard against Luke's chest.

She caught him totally off guard. The pool's unearthly glow revealed the astonishment on his face as he toppled backward into the water.

Katy watched, equally astonished at her

own aggressiveness. Luke landed in the deep end of the pool with a magnificent splash and promptly sank below the surface.

Appalled at what she had done, Katy hurried to the edge of the pool and peered down through the water. Surely Luke could swim. Everyone learned to swim these days. She gnawed anxiously on her lower lip as she watched him uncoil underwater.

A couple of seconds later Luke shot to the surface. His excellent white teeth flashed in a wicked grin. "Damn. We'll make a Gilchrist out of you yet."

He stroked toward the edge of the pool and planted both hands on the tiled rim. Katy stepped back quickly as he surged upward and all the way out of the water. He got to his feet and started toward her. His black jacket and slacks dripped water, and his shoes made squishing sounds. There was a cheerful menace in his expression.

Katy gasped in alarm. She turned and fled toward the exit.

Luke caught her before she had taken more than a few steps. He was laughing softly as he swung her up into his arms.

"Put me down," Katy demanded imperiously.

"You started this." He carried her back toward the pool.

"I did not. Luke, what are you doing?" Katy realized he was not going to halt at the edge of the water. "Stop. No, don't. Please. For heaven's sake."

She thought he was going to throw her into the pool. Instead he stepped off the edge with her in his arms. Together they hit the water, splashed heavily, and sank.

Luke kept one arm around Katy's waist as they surfaced. She pushed wet hair out of her face with one hand and looked up to find him watching her with sensual intent. Her eyes widened.

"Luke, stop looking at me like that." She flailed about in the water, trying to free herself from his grasp. "I know what you're thinking."

"Do you?"

"I most certainly do, and we can't. Not here, for goodness' sake."

Luke tightened his arm around her and brought her back against his chest. He tugged her toward shallower water and stopped when he could stand. Then he put his mouth very close to her ear. "Your brother won't be home until midnight. We have this place to ourselves. No one ever comes in here at night. Justine and Mrs. Igorson are both in bed by now."

"I know, but that doesn't mean we can

do that sort of thing here, of all places."

"You don't think so?" He peeled off her robe and smiled slowly when he saw the outline of her nipples thrusting against the slick fabric of her racing suit. He stroked one small, firm bud.

All the heat and energy generated by their argument was swiftly converting itself into desire. Katy had never experienced this sort of transformation. To be spitting mad one minute and sensually aroused the next was a dizzying sensation. She looked up at Luke, wide-eyed with wonder and uncertainty.

"Are you still angry?" she asked.

He kissed her deeply, thoroughly, and then raised his head. "What do you think?"

She licked her lips. "How can you change so quickly?"

He chuckled. "I wasn't all that furious to begin with. Just annoyed because I wasn't able to get hold of you all day. You're the one who set a match to the fireworks."

"That's right. Blame me," she grumbled.

"Don't worry. I will." His hands slid up from her waist to cup her breasts. "And I'll thank you, too."

Katy shivered at his touch the way she always did. Her body seemed to be poised on the edge of surrender whenever Luke took her into his arms like this. The raw sensual and physical power in him was tantalizing enough to disturb Katy's senses. But she knew now that the discipline and control he exerted over that power was her true undoing.

For her, the process of taming fire would always be a matter of magic, and Luke was the sorcerer who knew the spell.

Katy wrapped her arms around his neck and did not protest as he stripped the snug suit down her body. A moment later she floated naked in the water, her sense of freedom a hundred times more delicious than it had ever been before.

A deep warmth spread through her. She smiled tremulously up at Luke and started to ease his suit jacket off his shoulders.

He paid no attention as his expensive coat floated away. The full force of his unwavering gaze was on Katy as she unbuttoned his black shirt.

When she had his shirt off Katy spread her fingers against his smoothly muscled chest. A sweet, hot longing gripped her. She floated against him, letting her breasts glide over his bare chest.

"You burn even in water, angel." Luke drew her against his thighs. Holding her in position, he wrapped her legs around his waist. Then he cupped her buttocks, bent his head, and took one of her nipples between his teeth.

Katy moaned softly as she felt his fingers slip into her. She held his head between her palms and kissed him with gathering urgency.

He eased his fingers more deeply into her, stroking gently. Katy cried out, a small sound of feminine excitement that seemed to captivate him.

"That's it, angel." Luke kissed her arched throat. "Let me watch you fly."

She tried to pull herself back from the brink. "But you're not ready. You've still got your pants on."

"It's all right. I'll do my flying later."

"But Luke . . ."

It was too late. His fingers moved on her again, and then Katy took off. Into a thousand shimmering pieces. Freedom had never been so sweet.

When it was over she started to slip gently down under the water.

"Hey, you're not going anywhere." Luke chuckled as he put his hands around her waist and lifted her back up against his chest. "Now that we've got a few of the preliminaries out of the way, we're going to talk."

"If this was a setup, I'm going to strangle you." Katy glowered at him. "I don't want you getting the idea you can manipulate me with sex."

"Cut me some slack, honey. I need every break I can get. Wrestling with an angel is hard work." Luke started toward the pool steps, floating Katy along beside him.

"I'm serious, Luke. Sex is no way to solve problems."

"Looks to me like it works just fine."

Katy was trying to think of a response to that when a harsh gasp from the shadows stopped her. An instant later the conservatory lights came on, blinding her for a few seconds.

"What on earth is going on down here?" Mrs. Igorson demanded in thundering tones.

"Hell," Luke muttered. He moved in front of Katy, blocking the housekeeper's view of her.

In spite of Katy's embarrassed shock, the sight of the housekeeper's stricken expression had a strange effect. To her horror, Katy had to stifle a giggle.

"Turn off the lights and go back to bed, Mrs. Igorson," Luke ordered calmly. "This doesn't concern you."

"You should be ashamed of yourselves. Just look at the two of you. You're half undressed, and Katy isn't wearing her swimsuit."

"You're very observant, Mrs. Igorson. I

suggest you turn off the damned lights and get out of here." Luke started up the steps.

Mrs. Igorson shrieked and snapped off the lights. "I can't believe this."

"Was there something you wanted, Mrs. Igorson?" Katy asked.

"Yes. Yes, there is. Your brother's on the phone. He says it's very important."

"Matt?" The last of Katy's embarrassment vanished. "What's wrong? Is he all right?"

"I assume so," Mrs. Igorson snapped. "He's on the phone, after all, and he sounds fine. He couldn't reach either you or Mr. Gilchrist at your cottages, so he tried here. He asked me to see if you were swimming by any chance. Who would have dreamed that you and Mr. Gilchrist would both be in the pool, and you stark naked?"

"Mrs. Igorson," Luke said coldly, "if you have any sense, you will go back to bed right now and forget you ever came down here. In the morning you can pretend the whole thing was a dream."

"Maybe I'll do just that." Mrs. Igorson sniffed. "You can take the call on the extension. I'm leaving."

"Good idea," Luke said. He took Katy's hand and tugged her out of the water as the door slammed shut behind Mrs. Igorson.

"I hope nothing's wrong." Katy grabbed

a towel off a lounge chair and wrapped it around herself. "There are more towels in that cabinet," she said over her shoulder to Luke as she snatched up the phone.

"Matt? Is that you?"

"Yeah."

"Matt, are you all right?"

"I'm fine. Sort of."

"Sort of?" Katy clutched the phone. She watched Luke shed the last of his wet clothes, take a terry-cloth robe out of the cabinet, and belt it around himself. He was listening to her as she talked to Matt, a dark frown on his face.

"I told you I was going to a dance down at Waterfront Park, remember?" Matt said hesitantly.

"I remember. Matt, what happened? Tell me."

"You're not going to like this, Katy. There was a fight."

"Oh, my God. A fight? Are you hurt?"

"Not too bad."

"Not too bad? How bad? Matt, how badly are you hurt?"

"Just a few bruises. I'm okay, Katy, honest. Some guys from out of town tried to crash the dance. A couple of them were giving some of the girls a hard time, you know?"

"Are you certain you're all right?"

"Yeah. The cops showed up and broke up the fight. The thing is, they hauled a bunch of us down to the station. I'm sort of in jail."

"Jail?" Katy went limp. Unable to stand, she dropped down onto the nearest chair. *"Jail?"*

"They said we're not exactly under arrest, but none of us can leave until a parent comes and gets us."

"My God."

"I told them I don't have any parents. They said an adult has to pick me up."

"Oh, my God." Katy stared up at Luke, who was standing in front of her.

Luke reached down and took the phone out of her hand. "Matt?" he said calmly. "This is Luke. What's going on?" He listened intently for a few minutes. "Right. Okay, I understand. I'll be there in a little while. Let me speak to one of the cops."

Katy stood up slowly as Luke spoke briefly to a policeman. She was recovering from her initial shock. It dawned on her that Luke seemed to be taking charge. Something within her rebelled at that.

Luke hung up the phone and turned to her. "Take it easy, Katy. This is no big deal."

"Are you out of your mind? Matt got into

330

a brawl. He's been arrested."

"Matt's fine, and he's not under arrest. The cops are just trying to throw a scare into the kids they picked up tonight. I'll go down to the station and get Matt for you."

"No. I'll go down and get him. He's my brother."

Luke caught her chin on the edge of his hand and tilted her face upward. "Listen to me, honey. This is men's business. I'll handle it."

"What an idiotic thing to say," Katy sputtered, outraged. "This is my brother we're talking about, and he's in trouble."

"Do you know anything about handling a young male who's in this kind of trouble?"

"No, but I'll soon learn, won't I?"

"Take it from me, he needs a man, not his sister. You know as well as I do that if you go down there, you're going to get emotional. Hell, you'll probably start crying. Believe me, that's the last thing Matt needs right now."

She knew he probably had a point, but Katy was too distraught to accept his edict without a struggle. "How do you know so damn much about this kind of thing? Just what do you think you're going to do?"

"I'm going to do exactly what my father did the night I wound up in jail."

Katy's mouth dropped open. She closed it swiftly. "I won't let you beat him up, do you hear me? You are not going to touch him. I won't allow it."

Luke's mouth twisted. "For Christ's sake, Katy, I'm not going to hurt him. Use your common sense. Beating up a kid is not exactly a logical way of teaching him how to avoid getting into a fight."

"You beat up your cousin," she reminded him.

"That was a different matter altogether," Luke explained patiently. "I wasn't trying to teach him how to avoid a fight. I was teaching him another kind of lesson."

"Are you actually trying to tell me that violence is a permissible approach in some instances and not in others?" Katy asked incredulously.

Luke considered that briefly. "Yeah, I guess that about sums it up."

"Excuse me," Katy said in scathing tones. "I had no idea there were so many fine nuances to this masculine mystique thing."

"Well, there are. And since you're a woman, I don't expect you to understand them all, so you will leave your brother to me tonight. Understood?"

"Luke, I'll go crazy worrying about what's happening."

He smiled reassuringly. "There's no reason to worry about your brother. He's going to be fine. If you want to make yourself crazy, start worrying about how you're going to deal with Mrs. Igorson the next time you see her."

"Oh, Lord," Katy whispered.

"Maybe you should fish your swimsuit out of the pool. Wouldn't want it to clog the drain. Think what the pool man would think when he found it in the morning."

"Oh, Lord," Katy said again.

Matt wore an expression of wary, sullen defiance when Luke walked through the door of the police station. The sight of him brought back memories. Luke recalled the night he had sat waiting in jail for his father to come and collect him. A lot of weird thoughts went through a guy's head at a time like that.

Matt was not in a cell. He was sitting on a bench with a handful of other equally sullen young males. He leaned back against the wall, holding himself proudly aloof from the furor that was going on around him.

Several anxious-looking mothers were fluttering around the room. Some were tight-lipped with anger, others were in tears. A few were already berating their offspring, and one or two were screaming at the two young cops who appeared to be in charge.

Luke noticed that there were very few fathers on the scene. That annoyed him. A boy needed a man at a time like this. Where the hell were all the fathers? He supposed it was a stupid question given the current divorce rate.

If it was his kid who was waiting here, Luke told himself, he would be damn sure he was the one who came and got him.

On the heels of that realization came another. He would not mind having a son of his own. Or a daughter. Christ, he was thirty-six years old, and he had not yet begun a family. He had always planned on having kids someday. Where had the years gone? Luke wondered. It was as if he had been caught in some sort of limbo since Ariel's death.

Matt glanced toward the door at that moment. His eyes met Luke's. Relief flared in his gaze for an instant, and then the expression of sullen wariness descended again. Luke understood. A man had to hang onto his pride at all costs.

Luke nodded at one of the young cops, whose eyes looked far older than his years. As Luke crossed the room to speak to him the officer detached himself from a crying mother. He seemed relieved to be able to deal with another male for a few minutes. Luke introduced himself.

"How serious is this?" Luke asked quietly.

"Not as bad as it looks, although you wouldn't know it from the way the mothers are reacting." The officer spoke just as softly. "No guns or knives. Just a bunch of small-town kids looking for trouble. I've seen a lot worse. I used to work in Seattle. Came up here to get away from the hard-core stuff."

"All right to take the Wade kid home?"

"Go ahead. We've already done our best to shake 'em up a bit and throw a scare into 'em. The Wade kid's okay. He tried to play hero when one of the gate-crashers hassled a couple of the girls."

Luke nodded. "I'll take it from here."

The officer smiled quizzically. "Your son?"

"No. His father's dead. All he's got left is a sister. I'm a friend of the family."

The officer eyed him thoughtfully and then nodded. "He's all yours."

Matt stood up uncertainly as Luke crossed the room and came to a halt in front of him.

"Hi." Matt's eyes slid away. "Where's Katy?"

"Going bonkers back at the cottage," Luke

answered easily. "I figured you didn't need her coming down here and going bonkers in front of a crowd."

Matt blinked and raised his eyes to meet Luke's. "Yeah. Thanks."

"No problem. What do you say we get out of here?" He examined the darkening bruise under Matt's left eye. "You okay?"

Matt flushed. "Yeah, I'm okay. Let's go."

They walked out into the night together and got into the Jag. There was a long silence in the car as Luke drove through town and turned onto the road that led back toward the Gilchrist mansion.

"Is Katy real upset?" Matt asked finally.

"She's a woman," Luke said. "Of course she's upset."

Matt sank back into a state of deep gloom for another minute or two. "You going to yell at me?"

"No."

"You going to get me fired from my job?"

"No. It doesn't sound like you did anything wrong, Matt. You got into a situation, and you did the best you could. These things happen."

"One of the assholes was hitting on a girl I know. She's kind of shy. I could tell she was scared of him."

"I see."

"I didn't exactly start it, you know. Things just sort of blew up out of nowhere. One minute I'm telling this turkey to leave Jenny alone, and the next the whole damn place was in an uproar."

"That's the thing about that kind of fighting. It has a way of exploding into a major scene before you know what's happened."

"I guess."

"One of the things a man has to learn is how to pick and choose his battles."

"I didn't exactly choose this one," Matt muttered.

"Another thing a man has to learn is how to avoid a fight that isn't going to be worth the effort or serve a purpose."

"I couldn't avoid this one," Matt said. The sullenness had crept back into his tone.

"And when he does get into a fight," Luke continued calmly, "he has to know how to limit the damage as much as possible. He gets in and finishes the job quickly. Above all, he stays in control of the situation and of himself."

"Yeah?" Matt scowled in the shadows, half intrigued and half defiant. "How's he supposed to do that?"

"He trains for it, just like anything else."

"How am I going to train myself to control situations like the one I was in tonight?"

"The same way I did," Luke said. "The local gym probably has a martial arts instructor. Tomorrow morning we'll go talk to him. If he looks like he knows what he's doing, we'll sign you up for classes. If he doesn't look any good, I'll give you some instruction myself."

"Yeah?"

"Yeah," Luke said. "Sound okay?"

"Holy shit," Matt breathed. "Katy's gonna blow her stack when she hears this."

"Why?"

"She doesn't approve of violence."

"Don't worry. I'll handle Katy."

CHAPTER
FOURTEEN

Luke stood at the kitchen window and watched Katy make her way down the cliff path to the beach. She was dressed for an early morning walk in a pair of faded jeans that fit her sweetly curved rear like a glove. She wore a bright yellow sweater to ward off the chill of the cloudy morning, and a slouchy white twill hat was pulled down low over her fiery hair.

Luke contemplated the pleasant view of Katy's derriere until it disappeared from sight. Then he collected his black windbreaker from the hall closet and summoned Zeke.

"Come on, boy, we're going for a walk."

Zeke dutifully picked up his bowl and padded out of the cottage behind Luke.

The morning air held the promise of rain later in the day. The clouds were gathering out over the sea. Luke made his way down the cliff path, Zeke at his heels.

A few minutes later he and the dog were

on the rocky, uneven beach. The retreat of the morning tide had left a number of interesting little pools in the gray sand. Zeke paused at the first one and dropped his dish to nose around the rocks.

Luke kept moving, his eyes on Katy's vivid yellow sweater and tight jeans. He caught up with her halfway down the beach, aware that she had not yet realized he had joined her.

"You and I have some unfinished business," Luke said as he fell into step beside her.

Startled, Katy came to a halt and whirled to face him. Her smile was tentative. "I didn't see you."

"I know." He was hungry for the taste of her. He bent his head and took her mouth in a kiss that was far too brief. He deliberately broke it off before he lost control of it. He had other objectives this morning, he reminded himself.

Katy touched his arm. "I want to thank you for what you did last night. I probably would have handled Matt all wrong."

"I doubt it."

"No, I mean it." Her brows drew together in a small, regretful frown. "It's hard to know what to do in a situation like that. There have been so many times when I wasn't sure what to do."

"Katy, you've done a fine job with Matt."

She sighed. "Sometimes he seems like an alien creature to me."

"He's a male." Luke smiled. "Men and women often feel like alien beings to each other."

"I suppose so. Looking back, there have been so many times when I wish I had done things differently. There were times when he needed a man's guidance, and I had to fumble through as best I could. Now he's almost a man himself, and I can feel him getting ready to leave."

"It's time, Katy."

"I know it's time, but I'm scared for him. When something like last night happens I realize that there are so many things I haven't been able to teach him. So many things I didn't know myself."

Luke cupped her face in his hands. "Honey, listen to me. You can't possibly teach him everything. He wouldn't listen if you tried. Some things he needs to learn on his own. That's life."

"I know, but — "

"He's a good kid. You've done a fine job. Matt is going to be okay."

"I hope so," she whispered. She stepped closer and leaned her head against Luke's shoulder. "I hope I haven't messed up too much along the line."

Luke wrapped his arms around her. "You haven't messed up at all. Stop fretting, Katy. Guardian angels sometimes have to stand back and let their charges practice flying on their own. Matt took a short trial flight last night, and things got a little bumpy. But there was no harm done."

"Thanks again for going down to the station to pick him up." Katy lifted her head. "I did what you said. I didn't fuss. I just let him go straight off to bed. He said the two of you had already talked."

"Right. We talked."

"How did you know what to say?" Katy asked. "You don't have kids."

"I just said to Matt the things my dad said to me once when I got into a similar jam." Luke kept his arm around her shoulders as he turned and started walking along the beach. "Now about our unfinished business."

Katy slanted him a wary glance. "You weren't the only one who had something to say last night, you know. I wanted to talk to you about a certain matter that came up yesterday."

"All right," Luke said. "You go first."

"Promise you won't lose your temper?"

"What makes you think there's a risk I might lose it?" he countered.

"Well, it concerns the financial problems we've been having at two of the restaurants."

"Hell." Luke had an ominous feeling he knew what was coming. "That just happens to be the topic of conversation I wanted to cover."

Katy looked up at him with an even more anxious expression. "I know who's doing the skimming."

"So do I. My dear cousin Eden."

Katy's eyes widened. "You know about poor Eden?"

"Poor Eden is not so poor these days. She's managed to embezzle a hefty amount from the family coffers. I knew it was someone in the family. It felt like an insider. I was sure of it."

"You were right," Katy said. "But there were extenuating circumstances, and once you hear them I know you'll understand. She's going to need a little help, Luke."

"Help?" The ominous sensation was a lot stronger. Luke narrowed his eyes as he looked down at Katy's earnest face. He read his future there as clearly as if she were a book. "Oh, no, you don't, angel."

"Now Luke, I just want you to listen to the whole story."

"No. Absolutely not. I am not listening to a damn thing. You're not going to sucker me this time. That thieving little witch is guilty of stealing a large chunk of change, and I am not interested in hearing about mitigating circumstances."

"This is a very serious situation."

"Damn right it is. And I'm going to treat it that way. You brought me here to clean up the financial mess at Gilchrist, Inc. I told you I would do it, and I will. My way."

"But Luke, this is a family matter," Katy said.

"The hell it is. This is a matter of embezzlement."

"Not exactly. You see — "

"Katy, I don't want to listen to this."

"Luke, she's being blackmailed."

"Shit." Luke closed his eyes briefly in frustration. He knew he was going to lose this one. He could feel it coming.

Katy came to a halt again. Her expression was serious as she gazed up at him from beneath the brim of her white hat. Red hair curled softly against her cheek. "It's a long story, Luke. I heard it all yesterday."

"That's where you were all day? Listening to Eden's sob story?"

"Don't sound so skeptical. You haven't even heard it yet."

"I don't have to hear it to know that she's deliberately dragged you into this mess."

Luke shoved his hands into the pockets of his windbreaker and scowled. "Okay. Give it to me in short, easy sentences."

"Her ex-husband is blackmailing her with information he has about Maureen."

Luke's stomach clenched. "Atwood's involved in this?"

Katy nodded quickly. "He's found some old newspaper clippings that apparently state Maureen was convicted of selling forged art years ago in New York. He's threatened to turn them over to Justine if Eden doesn't continue to pay him off."

"Jesus."

"He thinks he got a bad deal at the time of the divorce. But I don't think he's just after the money. I think it's revenge he wants."

Luke studied her in silence for a minute while he absorbed that. "Eden told you this?"

"Yes."

"She probably knows I'm closing in on her," Luke said thoughtfully. "She's come up with this story to get you on her side before the mountain comes crashing down on top of her."

"It's true, Luke. All of it."

Luke's mouth twisted. "Yeah? How do you know it's true? What proof did she offer?"

"We went to see Nate. He admitted the whole thing."

Luke was stunned. When he recovered from the shock, rage poured through him. He jerked his hands out of his pockets and clamped them around Katy's shoulders. "You went to see him? By yourself?"

Katy bit her lip. "No. Eden was with me."

Luke gripped her fiercely. "I don't believe it. No, scratch that. I do believe it. Katy, are you out of your mind? What the hell got into you?" He gave her a small shake. "What did you think you were going to accomplish?"

"I wanted to try to scare him off."

"Scare him off?" It was all Luke could do to keep himself under control. A terrible fear was gnawing at his guts. "How the hell did you think you were going to manage that?"

Katy drew a deep breath. "I told him I would go to you for help if he didn't stop the blackmail and repay what he had taken."

"Me?" Luke felt his jaw drop. He closed his mouth with a snap. "You threatened him with me?"

"Well, yes. I figured it was the strongest threat I had. The thing is, Luke, he didn't believe me. He didn't think I would tell

346

you what was going on."

"Yeah? What made him think that?" Luke demanded. For some reason he was annoyed all over again.

"He assumes he knows all about the Gilchrist family and how it works because he was married to Eden for a while. And he does know some stuff. He knows how hard Justine can be. He knows what she did to your parents, for example."

"And he's convinced Eden she'd banish Maureen and Hayden and their offspring if she found out about Maureen's past?"

"Yes." Katy smiled at him with relief in her eyes. "I'm so glad you understand, Luke. I knew you would. Now we've got to figure out how to handle this. I think the best policy would be to keep it quiet."

"You think so, huh?" He wanted to turn Katy over his knee and paddle her for being so naïve. *She had gone to see Atwood.* He still could not bring himself to accept that fact.

Katy frowned intently. "I'm not saying Justine would cut off that whole side of the family if she found out about Maureen's past, but there is a risk she'd do something drastic. The news would certainly upset her. Maureen would be panic-stricken. I don't know how Hayden would handle the situation. No, I think we had better keep a lid on this."

"What's this 'we' stuff?" Luke muttered. At least she had come to him about it, he consoled himself grimly. At least she trusted him enough to bring him into the situation. He supposed he ought to be grateful for small favors.

"I think we should try to contain it," Katy said. "It may blow up. If it does, we'll just have to deal with Justine. But it would be best if we took care of things before it got that far. You know your family, Luke. If the story of Eden being blackmailed gets out, we'll have another Mount St. Helens explosion on our hands."

"I've got a news flash for you, Katy," Luke said. "You're standing on the rim of a much bigger volcano."

She gave him a curious glance. "What are you talking about?"

"I'm talking about the way I intend to explode after I decide what to do about Atwood." He wrapped his palm around the nape of her neck and steered her back toward the cliff path.

"You're going to handle this, aren't you? I knew you would. I told Eden everything was going to be all right."

"Uh-huh."

"Thank you, Luke. You don't know how

much I appreciate this. I was sure you would help, but frankly, I was expecting more of an argument."

"I'm saving the good stuff for later," he assured her. He whistled to Zeke, who bounded forward, dish in his jaws.

"What are you going to do first?" Katy asked.

"The first thing I'm going to do is take Matt down to the local gym and sign him up for a karate class."

"*Karate.*" Katy dug her heels into the sand. "What on earth are you talking about?"

"Matt's going to get some training in the martial arts this summer. If he likes it, he'll continue with it next fall when he goes off to college. I'm betting he'll take to it like a duck to water."

"Hold it right there, Luke. You can't do something like this without my permission. And I'm not at all certain I want Matt exposed to that sort of influence. Teaching someone hand-to-hand combat techniques is bound to promote a negative, violent approach to problem solving."

Luke looked at her. "Katy, you can't take the warrior out of the man. All you can do is teach the man to control that side of himself."

She flushed. "I don't want to take away

that side of his nature. I understand it's important."

He smiled. "You should understand. You've got a real streak of Amazon in you, honey. Don't worry about the karate. It'll teach him discipline and control."

"I wish I could be sure of that."

"Trust me on this one. Look what training in the martial arts has done for me."

She nearly choked on a muttered exclamation. "All right — what exactly has it done for you?"

"Hell, at this very minute I'm exercising more self-discipline and self-control than you can possibly imagine."

She blinked owlishly. "Oh." She hesitated. "Are you really angry because I've asked you to help Eden?"

"There's only one thing you could have done that would have made me angrier."

"What's that?"

"Not come to me with the problem."

Katy gave him a tentative grin. "I get it. It was a sort of damned if I do, damned if I don't situation for me, is that it? That's okay. I get into situations like this a lot when I deal with Gilchrists."

"Katy, take some advice. Don't start with the Gilchrist generalizations. I am not in the mood for them."

★ ★ ★

Luke spent half an hour talking to the martial arts instructor at the Dragon Bay Athletic Club. When he was finished he was satisfied that Matt was in good hands.

The instructor taught self-defense from a philosophical perspective that emphasized self-control and the kind of discipline a man needed to survive successfully in the world.

Luke stood at the back of the room and watched for a few minutes as Matt settled into his first class. As the *sensei* walked to the front of the crowd of restless, energetic, unruly young men they froze into positions of respect. The quiet inner power their instructor radiated clearly fascinated them. They all wanted to imitate it. Matt was just as eager as the rest.

Matt was in the right place.

Luke left the club and walked out to where he had parked the Jag. When he had kids of his own he was definitely going to sign them up for instruction in the martial arts.

He realized as he turned the key in the ignition that this was the second time in the past twenty-four hours that he had contemplated having children of his own.

Katy was doing this to him, Luke thought as he drove out of Dragon Bay and headed toward Seattle. She was forcing him to become aware of his own future once more.

Luke leaned on Eden's doorbell until she answered it. Her expression was one of irritation when she opened the door, but it turned to one of defiance when she saw who stood in the hall.

"Luke."

"Right. You going to let me in so that we can discuss your little problem like civilized people, or shall I just turn the whole thing over to the cops?"

Eden's mouth tightened. "I told Katy this would never work."

"Yeah? Well, I told her I'd take care of things, so one way or another I'm going to do it. Would you mind if we had this conversation someplace other than the hall?"

"You might as well come in." Eden stood aside.

Luke stepped into the sleek red, black, and gold apartment. The decor gave him a sense of déjà vu. Ariel had used the same style and colors in the interior design of their home.

Luke examined a tall black and gold vase on a black lacquer table as he sank down into a black leather chair near the windows. He thought of how much Ariel would have liked it.

He stilled at the thought, waiting tensely for a reaction from deep inside himself.

Nothing happened.

Luke realized with a sense of relief that his surroundings were not sending a jolt of old pain through him.

Somewhere along the line during the past three years he had recovered from the loss of his wife. He wondered when that had happened and why he had not noticed the change in himself. Probably because he had been trapped in limbo.

"I suppose Katy told you the whole sordid story." Eden dropped gracefully down onto the black leather sofa.

"You're being blackmailed by your ex?"

Eden leaned her head back against the cushion and watched him from beneath lowered lashes. "That about sums it up."

Luke shook his head in disgust. "Stupid, Eden. Real stupid."

"What was I supposed to do?" she flared. "Go to Justine?"

Luke considered that. "A possibility."

"Not a possibility at all. She would have turned on Mother. You know that I couldn't let her do it. Mom has spent her whole life trying to protect the rest of us from Justine. I had to do what I could to protect Mom when this happened."

"You must have known it was all going to fall apart eventually. You couldn't keep skimming that kind of cash without being found out," Luke said.

"I kept hoping after each payment that Nate would be satisfied."

"You know what they say about black-mailers. They're never satisfied. You have to pay them off forever."

"Nate is not exactly a typical blackmailer," Eden muttered. "He's angry because of the divorce and he wants revenge. I thought that after a while he'd be satisfied and go away."

Luke stuck his legs out in front of him and studied the toes of his black running shoes. "Does Hayden know about any of this?"

"Of course not," Eden snapped. "Dad spends most of his time in his own private world. You know how it is with artists. Mom protects him as much as she can from un-pleasant realities. Besides, what could he have done?"

Luke ignored that. "What about Darren? Did you tell him about the blackmail?"

"No. There was nothing he could have done either. It was my problem, not his."

"Until you told Katy what was going on. And then it became her problem, didn't it?"

Eden's eyes slid away. She stared at the view of Elliott Bay out her window. "She came to see me because Mother told her I was getting involved with Nate again. Katy couldn't believe it. Once I started talking it all came out. I've been a nervous wreck. I had to talk to someone."

"So you just naturally spilled your guts to the Gilchrist guardian angel. You knew she'd help you, didn't you?"

"I sure as hell didn't know she was planning to run straight to you," Eden said coldly.

"Ah, but she didn't run straight to me," Luke reminded her softly. "She went to Atwood first to see if she could frighten him off. That's what really annoys me in this whole idiotic mess."

Eden's gaze slid back to his. "Why?"

"Because Atwood is slime. I don't want her having to deal with slime."

"Is that right? Well, in case you didn't know it, she used to date Nate Atwood. She thought she was falling in love with the man. Who knows what would have happened if I hadn't come along? She might have wound up married to him herself."

Luke smiled slowly. "I'm aware of that. And that, my dear cousin, is the only reason I agreed to help you get out of this mess."

Eden scowled. "What do you mean?"

355

"The way I look at it, you're probably the main reason Atwood didn't try to con Katy into marriage. He wanted a Gilchrist, not an angel. I owe you for that. So I'm going to repay you by getting rid of Atwood."

Eden looked baffled. "I don't understand. Are you telling me you're interested in Katy?"

"Yes."

"But *Katy?* Luke, she's not your type at all."

"I know. She told me that right at the start. Don't worry about it. It's not your problem. Let's get down to the main business here."

"What business?" Eden asked cautiously.

"I want to know everything you know about Atwood. The way he runs his operations, where he goes for his financing, the kinds of deals he favors. Everything. When you've told me what you know I'll use a computer to get the rest."

"What are you going to do?"

Luke shrugged. "First I'm going to gather information. It's what I do best. When I've got enough, I'll crush him."

Eden stared at him. "You're serious, aren't you?"

"Uh-huh."

Eden sat forward. There was a spark of hope in her eyes. "Can you really do it?"

"One way or another."

Eden hesitated, watching him closely. "Why?"

"I told you why."

"You're going to save my neck because of Katy?"

"She's the main reason," Luke admitted. "But there's another reason."

"What?"

"As much as I hate to admit it, I understand how you got yourself into this situation. You're a Gilchrist. As Katy keeps telling me, we Gilchrists tend to do things with a certain melodramatic flair."

In the end it was not particularly difficult. A little digging, a little probing, a little intuition, and it all came together.

Monday afternoon Luke sat in his Seattle office and studied the screenful of data he had compiled. He had all he needed to control Atwood.

The next step was informing Atwood of that fact.

Luke picked up the phone and dialed the office of Atwood Investments. A throaty voice on the other end of the line assured him that Mr. Atwood was in.

"Would you care to speak to him?"

"Not right now," Luke said. He hung up

without giving the secretary his name. Then he got to his feet and went down to the garage to retrieve the Jag.

Half an hour later he was in Bellevue. He took the elevator to the twelfth floor, got out, and walked down the hall to a door that had Atwood Investments inscribed on it.

Luke eyed the sign with acute distaste. The thought of Katy coming here to confront Atwood angered him all over again. The Gilchrist guardian angel needed her wings clipped. She took far too many chances.

Luke opened the door of the office. A young blonde in a low-cut dress looked up and smiled brightly.

"May I help you?"

"Atwood in?"

"Yes, sir. If you'll give me your name, I'll let him know you're here."

"Never mind. He'll figure out who I am soon enough." Luke crossed the office and opened the inner door.

"Sir, wait! You can't just barge in there like that."

"Watch me." Luke went into the office and closed the door behind him.

The man who had to be Nate Atwood sat hunched over the phone, talking into it in a smooth, mellow, utterly convincing voice.

Atwood was obviously a born salesman.

"To be real honest, Mel, the deal's been locked up tight since last week. The rest of the investors don't want to share this kind of potential with anyone else. You can understand their position. But I managed to save a couple of slots for my best customers. If you're interested, I'll . . . Hang on a second, Mel." Atwood looked up at Luke, scowling. He put his hand over the receiver. "Be with you in a few minutes. Check in with my secretary out front."

"I already did that," Luke said. He walked over to the nearest chair and sat down. "It wasn't a very edifying conversation."

Atwood glared at him. "Look, if you don't mind, I'm trying to conduct business here."

"But I do mind. I don't like the way you do business." Luke opened his briefcase and took out a file. He tossed it onto Atwood's desk. "The name's Gilchrist. Luke Gilchrist. I believe Katy Wade told you I'd be around if you didn't cut out the blackmail. You didn't agree to stop, so here I am."

"Gilchrist? Shit, are you crazy? You can't come in here like this and start making threats." Anger boiled to life in Atwood's eyes.

"I'm not making a threat. I never make threats. Anything I say you can take as a solemn promise. And I promise you I've pulled the plug on the financing you've arranged for the Crystal Harbor deal you're putting together right now. Tell Mel it's dead."

CHAPTER FIFTEEN

The lines around Atwood's mouth went white with tension. He never took his eyes off Luke as he spoke quickly into the phone. "Mel, something's come up. I'll get back to you. Sure. This afternoon. Don't worry. You'll get a piece of the action."

Atwood slammed down the phone. "All right, Gilchrist. What the hell is this all about? Talk fast, or I'll call the cops and have you tossed out of here."

"I told you what it's all about. The financing package for the Crystal Harbor development project just died an early death. I killed it with a couple of phone calls to your backers."

Atwood's hands clenched around the arms of his chair. "You can't do that."

"It's done. Take a look at what's in that file if you don't believe me. Your financial backers have been told that your little empire is built on bad paper, Atwood. Phony financial statements, false earnings reports,

361

questionable credit references."

"That's not true."

Luke smiled. "Unfortunately for you, whether it's true or not is beside the point. The data in that file make you look bad. I know because I put it together myself. I estimate it will take you months to clean up the misunderstandings and mistakes. And in the meantime, the Crystal Harbor project is dead."

Atwood snapped the file open and scanned the contents. When he was through he looked dazed. "You can't do this. This is a pack of lies."

"Not quite." Luke got to his feet and went to stand at the window. "That's the sweet part, Atwood. There are no lies in that report on your financial situation. I merely pointed out to your backers that you've been skating on thin ice for the past three or four years. The bad times started right after the High Ridge Springs project went sour, didn't they?"

"What do you know about High Ridge Springs?"

"Enough. Your backers there were in danger of taking heavy losses. You were desperate. So you phonied up some credit reports in order to get more loans. It worked. You salvaged High Ridge Springs. After that it

362

got easier to use fake paper, didn't it?"

"Goddammit, that's not true. I only did it the one time, and it saved a lot of people a great deal of money."

"Are you a betting man, Atwood? I am. And I'm willing to gamble that the report I put together is going to cause your backers to check out your true financial situation. Even if you're white as snow, it will take months to prove it."

"You can't do this to me, Gilchrist."

"It's done." Luke turned away from the window and looked at him. "Consider yourself lucky. You know what the sentence is for blackmail?"

"You can't prove I ever tried to blackmail anyone, you son of a bitch."

"We're even. You can't prove I put together that report on your financial picture. But your backers won't care where the information came from. They'll just be grateful they got it in time to cut their losses." Luke started for the door. "In the future, stay away from my family."

Atwood leapt to his feet behind the desk. "I don't believe this. What the hell do you care about the other Gilchrists? Everyone knows you're only back for revenge."

Luke paused at the door and looked back. "Everyone?"

"Don't forget I was married to your bitch of a cousin. I know a little family history." Atwood's eyes slitted. "There's something else going on here."

"Don't waste any time trying to figure it out," Luke advised. "You've got enough trouble as it is." He opened the door.

"Christ, it's Katy, isn't it? Hell, it all fits now. You don't give a damn about Eden or her family. You're doing this on account of Katy."

Luke started through the door.

"What do you want with her?" Atwood snarled. "Katy's hardly your type."

"Yeah? Well, she wasn't your type either, was she? You used her to get to Eden."

"At least I didn't sleep with Katy before I moved on," Atwood said softly. "Something tells me you're not being quite so noble. I'll bet you're screwing her. What does that make you? You know damn well you're not going to marry her. Gilchrists go for the more dramatic type."

Luke turned around, closed the door, and walked back toward Atwood. "You know something, Atwood? You're getting to be a real pain in the ass. By the way, I almost forgot. I want a check on my desk by the end of the week for the total amount you squeezed out of Eden. If it's not there, I'll do a lot more than kill one deal. I'll rip your entire house of cards to shreds."

Atwood lost what was left of his self-control at that point and launched himself at Luke. Luke stepped aside. He reached out, caught hold of Atwood's shoulder, and added momentum and spin to Nate's lunge. Then he stuck out his left foot.

Atwood yelled as he tripped over Luke's foot and fetched up against the office wall. The framed picture of a successful Atwood development that was hanging there shuddered, fell off its hook, and landed on Atwood's head. The glass shattered and dropped out of the frame, forming a sparkling ring around the stunned Atwood.

Luke looked down at his victim. "Katy keeps telling me I have to find nonviolent problem-solving techniques. I guess I'm a slow learner."

He walked out of the office past the nervous-looking secretary and went down the hall to the elevator.

His mission had been accomplished, he told himself. So why did he have an uneasy feeling that something was very wrong?

Even as he asked the question Luke knew the answer. Katy was right. Atwood did not need money. The amount he had pried out of Eden during the past few months was no more than what he could have made in a couple of successful real estate deals. Furthermore, Atwood had only been married to Eden for three short months, and he had never really loved her. He had only married her to get his hands on Gilchrist, Inc.

Any normal businessman would have seen the unsuccessful attempt to get a controlling interest in the company as just another deal that had not worked out.

But Atwood was enraged. His reaction to the loss was out of proportion to the situation.

Atwood's actions did not make sense. The only other logical explanation was that he had a screw loose. But nothing in the research Luke had done indicated the man was crazy.

There had to be more to this than was apparent. The infuriated look in Atwood's eyes had indicated there was something very personal about the assault on Gilchrist. Something that went far beyond the annoyance of a man who had lost a cold-blooded business gamble.

Luke got into the Jag and sat quietly behind the wheel for a moment. He decided he would do a little more probing on the subject of Nate Atwood.

Later that evening Luke sprawled on the sofa in Katy's cottage and brooded about his day as he gazed into the fire. Zeke, having recently polished off the last of Katy's most recent pesto experiment, had flopped down in front of the hearth. His dish lay beside him. Matt was studying at the kitchen table.

The whole scene should have felt cozy and serene. But Luke could not shake a nagging feeling that he had left loose ends dangling somewhere. Or perhaps it was simply Atwood's last words that were getting to him: *At least I didn't sleep with her before I moved on.*

Everyone seemed to agree that Katy was not his type, Luke reflected.

He glanced up as she came out of the kitchen carrying two small glasses of brandy. She smiled softly as she handed one to him and sat down beside him.

"You've been awfully quiet this evening," Katy said.

"I'm thinking."

"Ah. Never interrupt a Gilchrist when he's in a contemplative mood, I always say." Katy took a sip of brandy. "Are you ready to tell me how it went today?"

"I think Eden can forget about Atwood."

Katy put her hand in his. "Thank you, Luke. This is going to mean a great deal to Eden."

"I don't really give a damn how much it

means to Eden. I didn't do it for her. I did it for you. And this had better be the last time, Katy."

She turned her head on the cushion to look at him with searching eyes. "What's wrong? Why does it bother you so much to help the members of your family?"

"They don't deserve any help. They resent me, they're suspicious of me, and they think I'm only here to get revenge for what happened to my parents."

Katy raised a brow. "Well, you haven't gone out of your way to reassure them otherwise, have you?"

"Why should I bother? I won't be around long enough to worry about what they think."

"You are in a bad mood tonight, aren't you?"

"What do you expect from a Gilchrist?" Luke put down his brandy glass. "Let's take a walk."

"All right." Katy got to her feet and put her head around the kitchen door. "I'll be back in a little while, Matt."

"Okay," Matt said.

Zeke picked up his bowl and followed Luke and Katy outside.

Luke walked in silence for a while, conscious of Katy's soothing presence. She had a calming effect on him even when he was

368

in a surly mood, as he was tonight. He realized he was beginning to look forward to this strange sense of contentment that he experienced around her.

He had never known this kind of deep certainty before with any other woman, not even Ariel. It occurred to him now that one of the attractions with Ariel had been the very lack of certainty he had known when he was with her.

The wildness in her had been exciting, but tonight Luke questioned again how long the relationship would have lasted if Ariel had lived. How long before the jealousy and the passion and the never-ending roller coaster of emotional uncertainty would have combined into a bitter tonic that poisoned the marriage? he wondered.

With startling clarity Luke realized he did not want a lifetime of chills and thrills. He wanted some peace. He wanted some softness in his world. He wanted happiness.

Now that Katy had forced him to start thinking about his future, he was finding it impossible to stop. It was as though a small leak had been opened in a dike that had been holding back a great river. The hole was widening daily.

Luke tightened his hold on Katy's hand as if she could somehow keep him afloat.

"How did you persuade Nate to leave Eden alone?" Katy asked.

"I dug up some information on him. Some false financial statements he prepared a few years ago. Figured where there was smoke there must be fire. Convinced his latest backers that he was a high risk. They folded and left him with a deal that's dead in the water. I told Atwood there was more where that came from if he kept hounding Eden."

Katy looked up at him in amazement. "My God. You make it sound so easy."

Luke shrugged. "It wasn't hard."

"Maybe not for you. For anyone else it would have been impossible. You're incredible, Luke."

"Rescuing idiots is not as incredible as it looks on the surface."

Katy smiled wryly. "You don't have to be so hard about it, you know. It really was very nice of you to rescue Darren and Eden. And they're not idiots. They're just impulsive. And melodramatic. And naturally inclined to desperate measures. It's in the blood."

"Katy, I'm warning you right now, I'm not in the mood to listen to any nasty generalizations about Gilchrists tonight."

Katy giggled. "I can't help it. I love the way you rise to the bait."

He came to a halt, pulled her into his arms, and kissed her into silence. When her laughter had faded and soft little moans had taken its place Luke was satisfied. He lifted his mouth from hers and framed her face between his hands.

"How much did hc mean to you?" he asked softly.

"Who?" Her eyes were dreamy in the moonlight.

"Atwood."

"Oh, him. It hurt at the time, but I got over it quickly. I don't feel a thing now."

"You never slept with him." It was a statement, not a question. Luke was certain of the answer.

She wrinkled her nose. "Well, no. It never felt right somehow. I kept waiting until things clicked. It didn't quite happen. And then Eden came along, and Nate was gone, and that was the end of it."

"You're sleeping with me, Katy."

She touched his mouth with a gentle fingertip. Her eyes gleamed with amusement. "Only occasionally. Very occasionally."

He was irritated by her attempt at humor. "Doesn't matter how often. The point is, you're sleeping with me. Does that mean it feels right? That things have clicked?"

"You tell me," she whispered. She stood

on tiptoe and brushed her mouth against his.

"Katy . . ."

"When I'm with you, Luke, I try not to think about that part of my future. It's easier that way. And you've already made it clear you're only looking six months ahead yourself. Maybe less if you clean up the problems at Gilchrist before that date. So let's not talk about the future."

A slow anger rose inside Luke, chilling his insides. "Everyone, including you, says I'm not your type."

"Yes, well, it works both ways, doesn't it? I'm not exactly your type either. So please don't play games with me, Luke. Let's at least keep what we have honest."

"Shows how much you know," Luke muttered. "Take it from me, honesty is not always the best policy."

"I think it is in the long run," she said, looking serious.

"I'm not so sure of that. But I guess that's one of the problems with angels. They put too high a value on some of the lesser virtues."

He pulled her back into his arms before she could argue. Some of the cold anger in him dissolved beneath the warmth of her kiss.

Not until much later that night, when Luke

was lying alone in his bed, did he admit to himself it might not have been anger he had been feeling earlier.

It might have been fear. Fear of a future without Katy.

That realization was too much to handle. Luke went back to being angry. It was easier.

Three days later Luke strode down the hall to his mansion office. He was feeling good. He did not have to go into Seattle today, which meant that he and Katy could have lunch together. He was looking forward to it. He had already planned a tantalizing menu that did not include food.

Liz glanced up from some notes she was making as he paused in her doorway.

"Any messages?" Luke asked.

"Mrs. Igorson just phoned. She says Mrs. Gilchrist wants to see you and Katy downstairs at ten. She wants another update on the company's status."

"I'll just bet she does. Tell her we'll be there." Luke glanced over his shoulder at the sound of footsteps in the hall.

Katy walked toward him looking bright and cheerful in a sunny yellow jacket and royal blue skirt. She had her hair clipped back behind her ears in an unusually polished style, and she was carrying an expensive-looking leather briefcase. She looked as if she was leaving for Seattle.

Luke frowned, remembering how she had slipped out the other day to see Eden. "Going somewhere?"

She raised her brows at his peremptory tone. "I have an appointment after lunch with a real estate agent."

"What the hell for?"

"We're going to look at some location possibilities for Pesto Presto."

It was becoming clear to Luke that Pesto Presto was his chief rival for Katy's affections. He reacted accordingly. "Don't you have work to do this afternoon?"

"Nothing that won't keep." She slipped past him and went into the office. "Any messages, Liz?"

Liz glanced speculatively at Luke, and then she smiled at Katy. "I was just telling the boss that Justine wants to see both of you in her quarters at ten for an update."

"All right." Katy tossed a smile over her shoulder as she headed for the inner office. "See you at ten downstairs, Luke."

Luke scowled at her door as she closed it for all intents and purposes in his face. He realized he had just been dismissed.

"Don't worry about it," Liz advised confidentially. "She ran things around here for so long on her own that she kind of got in the habit of acting like the boss."

"I'll try to keep that in mind." Luke stalked out of Katy's office and into his own.

He sat down behind his desk, switched on the computer, and leaned back in his chair. The mystery of who had been skimming money from the restaurants had been solved, but that still left the problems at Gilchrist Gourmet. He gazed moodily at the screenful of data. Roger Danvers, the computer investigator, was closing in on the troubles that had been plaguing the operation, but Luke was not interested in reviewing the latest information.

All he really felt like doing was brooding over the love affair Katy was having with Pesto Presto.

At ten o'clock Luke reluctantly got to his feet again and went out into the hall to join Katy. She was waiting for him, brows drawn together in a quelling little frown. Luke's spirits brightened somewhat. He knew he was about to get another lecture. At least that meant Katy was concentrating on him rather than on her future for a while.

"You will be tactful this time, won't you?" Katy trotted down the stairs beside him.

"You know me, Katy. I'm the very soul of tact."

She glowered anxiously. "I'm serious, Luke. You won't say anything that might give her a hint about Eden's little problem, will you?"

"It wasn't exactly a little problem, Katy." Luke reached the bottom of the stairs and crossed the hall toward Justine's suite. Katy hurried to catch up with him. "Eden skimmed thousands of dollars out of the two restaurants."

"Yes, I know, but we mustn't let Justine know about it. I mean, that was the whole point, if you will recall."

Luke summoned up a suitably thoughtful expression. "Are you by any chance asking me to participate in another cover-up?"

"No, of course not. Just be diplomatic, that's all. The problem is under control, so there's no need to bother her with the details."

"Is this my honest little angel talking?" Luke knocked on the door of Justine's suite.

"Luke, stop teasing me. I want you to promise me you won't say or do anything to make Justine think Eden might have been involved in the problems the two restaurants were having."

"No sweat. Honey, unlike you, I can lie through my teeth without even blinking. It's in the blood."

Mrs. Igorson opened the door just as Katy opened her mouth. The housekeeper glared accusingly at Luke as Katy hastily closed her mouth. "Oh, it's you."

"Who were you expecting?" Luke took Katy's arm and propelled her gently through the entrance. "A door-to-door salesman? Excuse us, Mrs. Igorson. I'm sure Justine is waiting."

"She's waiting, all right," Mrs. Igorson muttered. She switched her accusatory glance to Katy. "She wants a few explanations, and I reckon she's entitled."

Katy flushed but managed to maintain her serene smile. "Yes, of course. Excuse us, Mrs. Igorson."

Luke watched Katy hurry on ahead. Then he turned to the housekeeper. He deliberately allowed a hint of menace to creep into his voice. "Was there something you wanted to say to me, Mrs. Igorson?"

"Not hardly."

"Are you quite certain? Because if you're going to say something — anything at all — about what you witnessed the other evening in the conservatory, it had better be to me and not to Katy. Or anyone else. Understood?"

Mrs. Igorson's look of scathing condemnation faded slightly. It was replaced with an expression that reminded Luke of a trapped rat. "I know my duty, and it ain't to you, Luke Gilchrist. I work for Mrs. Gilchrist, in case you've forgotten."

Luke smiled without any warmth. "You might want to bear in mind that as long as I'm saving Gilchrist, Inc. I can do just about anything I want around here. It shouldn't be too hard to make life hell for one nosy housekeeper. Mind your manners, Mrs. Igorson."

Without waiting for a response he strode down the hall toward the living room.

"She's too good for you," Mrs. Igorson hissed behind him, her tone filled with brave defiance. "Too good by half. You're not her sort at all."

Luke set his teeth, but he did not pause or turn around. He walked straight ahead into the living room, where Katy and Justine were already seated. A silver tea service gleamed on a small side table.

Justine eyed him coolly. "About time you got here. I certainly hope you have more information for me than you did last time. I do not like being kept in the dark about events in my own company."

"Gilchrist is going to survive, Justine. Stop worrying about it." Luke went to stand at the window. "These things take a little time.

I warned you about that."

"I understand, but I want to know exactly what's going on. Let's begin with the trouble we've been having at the two restaurants that are losing money. Any progress there?"

"Yes," Luke said.

Katy shot him a warning glance.

"Well?" Justine demanded. "What progress? I want facts. Why have they been losing money when they've been functioning at full capacity?"

Apparently not trusting Luke to handle the pointed question, Katy made an effort to step into the breach. "We think there might have been a few problems in the accounting department."

Justine turned on her with the shrewd instincts of a woman who had survived in a cutthroat business for nearly sixty years. "Embezzlement?"

Katy instantly went pale and started to stutter frantically. "Heavens no, Justine. Nothing like that. I mean it was just an accident. One of those things. Bookkeeping problems. Luke has taken care of everything."

Luke sighed inwardly as he listened to her flustered rambling. The problem with angels was that they always had a tough time when they tried to play out of their league. It took one Gilchrist to lie to another Gilchrist. He stepped in to handle the situation before Katy screwed it up completely.

"The losses were being caused by an error in the computer program that handled supplier accounts," Luke told Justine. "It was no big deal. The glitch has been found and fixed. There won't be any more problems."

Justine eyed him narrowly. "Are you quite certain of that?"

"You can bet on it," Luke said.

"Well, then. That's one thing out of the way." Justine sipped tea. "What about Gilchrist Gourmet? Are you going to be able to repair the damage there?"

Luke thought about the information he and Danvers had put together. "Yes."

"What is your verdict on the problems there?" Justine persisted. "Do you feel we're in the wrong market, as Fraser Stanfield insists we are?"

"We can compete in that market if we want to continue doing so," Luke said. "But it's a tough one, and I'm not sure it's worth our time and effort."

"I want to see this company diversify," Justine reminded him. "I would feel better if I knew that the next generation of Gilchrists will have more than just the restaurants to sustain them. Restaurants are too dependent on the state of the local economy."

Luke kept his gaze on the sea. "I'll clean up the problems at Gilchrist Gourmet, and then we can talk about its future."

"Very well." Justine looked at Katy. "Would you mind very much leaving us, my dear? I have a few things I want to discuss with Luke."

Katy flushed and stood up at once. "No, of course not." She glanced uneasily from Justine to Luke, obviously not trusting them alone together. "I have some things to do upstairs."

"I'll be up in a few minutes," Luke said.

"Good-bye, Justine." Katy leaned down and gave her a quick, affectionate little hug. "See you later."

"Good-bye, my dear."

Justine watched Katy leave the room. Luke mentally braced himself. He was fairly certain he knew what was coming next.

Justine did not hesitate. She rounded on Luke as soon as the door closed behind Katy. "What is going on between the two of you, Luke? Mrs. Igorson was very upset by a scene she apparently witnessed the other night in the pool."

"I'm sorry to hear that."

"Don't you dare take that tone of voice

with me. I told you the day you arrived that I did not want you playing games with Katy. I meant it, Luke."

"I'm not playing games with her."

"You have seduced her, according to Mrs. Igorson. What do you call that?"

"I call it nobody else's business." Luke turned around to face her. "My relationship with Katy is personal and private, and it stays that way."

Justine's hand clenched on the arm of the chair. "Damn you, Luke, I will not have that young woman hurt."

Luke smiled faintly as he started toward the door. "What about me, Justine? Or don't you care if I get hurt?"

"*Luke.*"

Luke did not stop. He kept going, past a triumphantly scowling Mrs. Igorson and out into the main hall. There he stood alone for a couple of minutes.

The cold feeling inside him was starting to twist and curl into something that bore an unpleasant resemblance to fear. Once again he summoned up his anger to repress the other emotion.

When he was ready he went back upstairs and halted in the doorway of Katy's office. Katy was leaning over Liz's desk. The two women were poring over a map that showed the area north of Seattle all the way to Edmonds.

"We're going to concentrate on the least expensive locations first," Katy said. She circled a spot on the map with a yellow marker. "The agent is going to show me some space that will be available in a couple of new, small outdoor malls."

Luke walked forward to stand in front of the desk. "I'll come with you this afternoon."

Katy looked up, surprised. "There's no need for that. I'm sure you have tons of things to do."

"So do you," he reminded her.

"I've arranged to take this afternoon off. Everything's under control here."

"The last time you arranged to take a day off we discovered all kinds of computer problems in Payroll and Accounting, if you will recall."

Katy turned red. "That was a different matter entirely."

"Is that right?" Luke glanced down at the map. "Look at it this way. I'm doing you a favor by coming with you and the real estate agent this afternoon."

"How do you figure that?" Katy grumbled.

Luke smiled his most saintly smile. "Selecting successful restaurant locations is one of my areas of expertise, Katy. No one's better at it than I am. You need me, and you're getting a terrific bargain. Normally I charge an astronomical fee for this kind of advice."

"Why do I get the feeling I'll wind up paying dearly for any free advice I get from you?"

"Katy, for a guardian angel you have a very suspicious mind."

Katy smiled grimly. "It comes from hanging around Gilchrists all these years."

CHAPTER
SIXTEEN

Katy had suspected from the start that it was going to be a mistake to take Luke along on the tour of potential restaurant locations. Her suspicions were well founded.

The entire afternoon was a disaster.

At six o'clock that evening she stormed through the front door of the cottage, Luke at her heels. Matt was sprawled in front of the television watching MTV. Zeke was stretched out beside him, his nose inches from his dish.

The dog got to his feet to greet Luke.

"I was wondering when you guys were going to get home," Matt said. He used the remote to switch off the music video he had been watching. "How did the tour go?"

"It was a complete fiasco." Katy dropped her briefcase onto a chair and cast a fulminating look at Luke. "A total waste of time. Furthermore, I have never been so embarrassed in my entire life."

"Take it easy." Luke rubbed Zeke's ears.

"It wasn't that bad. I gave you my honest opinions of the locations the agent showed you, that's all."

"Some opinions," she fumed. "You didn't like any of them."

"They were all bad. What did you want me to do? Lie?"

"They were not all bad, and you know it. You were in a terrible mood. You made rude comments about every single location."

"I was not rude. All my comments were of a professional nature."

"You were rude," she snapped. "Rude and obnoxious."

Luke shrugged. "I'm sorry you didn't like what I had to say, but I was giving good advice."

"Is that so? What about that new mall location? What was wrong with that?"

"I told you what was wrong with it. It's the wrong neighborhood for the kind of take-out place you're planning to open. That neighborhood can sustain pizza and burger joints, but a trendy operation like Pesto Presto will wither and die there."

"The agent said it was a neighborhood in transition. She said it was starting to attract upwardly mobile young couples."

"She's guessing," Luke said. "And even if she's right, it could take years before it's changed enough to support a place like Pesto Presto."

"All right, what about that little place near Edmonds?"

"Too far out of town."

"And the location near the interstate?"

"It was all right for a gas station," Luke admitted, "but not for a place like Pesto Presto. Take it from me, Katy, the agent didn't show you one decent location. They were all second rate."

"She was showing me locations in my price range."

"Then you'd better think twice about opening up Pesto Presto anytime soon. Wait until you can afford a decent location."

"I'm not going to wait one second longer than I absolutely have to wait," Katy ground out.

"Don't let your irritation with Gilchrists in general drive you into doing something stupid."

"I don't believe this." Katy threw up her hands and turned to Matt. "You see? It was like that all afternoon. He just sat there in the backseat and made nasty comments about every single location the agent showed me. It was a miserable experience."

Matt looked distinctly uncomfortable. He glanced quickly from one to the other. "Uh, yeah. Well, I guess there's no big rush, is there? I mean, you've got time to find something."

Luke smiled approvingly. "Good point, Matt. There's no rush at all. Katy's got plenty of time to find a location."

Katy gave him a smoldering look. "Fortunately, I do have some time. But I will undoubtedly have to find another real estate agent before I can go out looking again. That poor woman who took us around today will never want to see me again. I still cannot believe some of the things you said."

"Business comments." Luke ambled into the kitchen and opened the refrigerator. "You should have been grateful."

"Business comments my foot." Katy trailed after him, still scolding. "You were deliberately trying to make things difficult, Luke Gilchrist. And I will never, ever take you out on another location search. What are you doing?"

"Pouring myself a glass of wine. I'm pouring one for you, too. Something tells me you need it even more than I do."

"If you think I'm going to invite you to stay for dinner after the way you behaved this afternoon, you can think again."

Luke gave her a reproachful look. "I don't

have anything to eat back at my cottage."

"Tough."

"Think of Zeke. You know how much he looks forward to trying out your pesto creations."

"I am not cooking for your dog."

Zeke appeared in the doorway, looking hopeful. Luke smiled sadly at him. "It's not looking good, boy. I'm trying to talk her into a meal, but she's in one of her moods. Probably that time of the month."

Katy's outrage jumped another notch. "Don't you dare make stupid, idiotic, macho comments like that."

Luke smiled grimly. "I'm just evening the score a bit. Or don't you think I get a little tired of all those Gilchrist mood remarks? I swear, if you tell me one more time that I'm sulking or being difficult or melodramatic because it's in the blood, I'm going to do something drastic."

"Yeah?" She lifted her chin in challenge. "Like what?"

"I don't know. Try it and see."

Katy took a deep, calming breath and went to the refrigerator to take out a plastic sack full of fresh basil. Zeke whined happily.

Matt came to stand in the doorway. "Have you two stopped arguing?" he asked.

"I have," Luke assured him. "I don't know

what your sister's plans are for the evening."

Katy realized she would sound extremely petty and childish if she continued to berate him for his actions that afternoon. She adopted an air of lofty disdain as she rinsed the basil leaves. "Don't worry. I don't intend to discuss this matter any further. Suffice it to say I have learned my lesson. I will never hire you for professional advice, Luke."

"Your loss," he said cheerfully. "By the way, I'm going into Seattle to talk to some people at headquarters tomorrow. I want you to come with me. We'll be staying over, so bring a bag."

Katy smiled brightly. "Sorry. I'm going to be busy tomorrow afternoon. Got to catch up on some of the things I had to put aside today."

"You work for me, Katy, remember? I want you with me tomorrow."

She eyed him warily, not trusting the bland tone of his voice. "In that case, I'll take my own car. There's no need for me to stay overnight."

"Yes, there is. We're having dinner at the Pacific Rim. I'm going to sample the menu and check out the service."

Katy scowled at him. "Fat lot of good it will do for you to show up for dinner. The staff will jump through hoops trying to please you. That won't give you a good indication of the service or the quality of the food."

Luke took a swallow of his wine, unconcerned. "I'll be able to tell a lot by watching the customers."

Dinner at the restaurant was an excuse. Katy was certain of it. Luke wanted to spend the night with her, so he was using his clout as her boss to arrange it. She was still annoyed enough with him to be perverse. "I'm not sure I can get away."

Matt spoke up from the doorway. "Don't worry about me, Katy. I can take care of myself. And I'll have Zeke here."

"I'll think about it," Katy temporized as she dumped the fresh basil into the food processor.

"You do that," Luke said. "And pack your bag while you do your thinking."

At ten o'clock Luke reluctantly took himself off. Zeke padded through the doorway after him. Katy stood watching from the window as dog and man vanished into the night. Matt came to stand beside her.

"He's making this a regular habit, isn't he?" Matt observed.

"You mean eating my food and stuffing his dog full of my best pesto sauce? Yes, he certainly is."

"I think he likes you," Matt said. "How come you were so mad at him this afternoon? He said he was only trying to help."

"You know as well as I do that when a Gilchrist offers you a rose you've got to check for thorns."

Matt considered that briefly. "Sometimes I think you're too hard on him. Luke's okay."

Katy glanced at her brother. "You really think so?"

Matt nodded. "He's not like the others. Did you know the guy has a black belt?"

"What other color belt would a Gilchrist own?"

Matt rolled his eyes. "Geez, Katy. I'm talking about the kind of black belt they give out in the martial arts."

"Oh."

"Yeah, Luke's all right. I like him."

"So do I," Katy admitted softly. It was a lot worse than that, Katy thought. She knew full well she was in love with him.

She could not bear to look ahead to what was going to happen when the six months were over. She had to keep her wits about her. Concentrate on the present.

But Katy knew deep in her heart that if she had intended to remain sensible and pragmatic, she should never have started sleeping with Luke.

Matt shot her a quick, searching look. "What did he do this afternoon that was so bad?"

"It's hard to explain." Katy's jaw tightened. Luke's behavior had been extreme, even for a Gilchrist. "He was just so incredibly negative about everything."

"Because he didn't think any of the locations were suitable?"

"It was more than just that. He had no positive comments at all. No helpful ideas. He just kept making everything sound impossible and hopeless. It was as if he thought the whole idea of opening Pesto Presto was a stupid waste of time. As if it didn't stand a prayer of being successful. It was as if he was trying to discourage me for some reason."

Matt grinned. "Hey, if he thought that, he doesn't know you all that well, does he? You always find a way to make things work."

Roger Danvers and the final report he had prepared were both waiting for Luke the next morning when he and Katy arrived at the Seattle offices of Gilchrist, Inc. He glanced at Katy.

"I want to talk to Danvers. Why don't you go see Eden? Make sure we're not having any more computer problems in Payroll and Accounting."

Katy gave him a chilling look. "There's no need to be sarcastic." She went on down the hall, greeting several members of the staff along the way. Luke noticed that one of the people who stepped out of his office to speak to her was Fraser Stanfield.

Luke watched the two of them disappear around the corner together. Then he walked into his own office and sat down.

"Okay, Danvers. What have you got?"

"No proof." Danvers tapped a foot restlessly and tugged at his earlobe. "But a definite pattern. The guy's clever. I'm not going to be able to nail him with hard evidence, though."

"So there's no point in going to the authorities?" Luke switched on the computer and summoned up the coded file he and Danvers had been using.

Danvers shrugged and waggled his toes. "It's the usual story. You know how it is with this white-collar crime stuff."

"Yeah, I know. Most of the time you count yourself lucky if you can figure out who's probably screwing you, and then you just fire the son of a bitch. Not much else you can do. The kind of proof that would stand up in court is too damn hard to get."

"You got it."

"And in this case," Luke continued

394

thoughtfully, "we're not even dealing with a clear-cut embezzlement scheme or cash-skimming operation. Just a lot of little things that have been going wrong in the past six months."

"Yeah. No real obvious crime. When you get right down to it, the only thing you could really accuse the guy of is bad judgment. He had some managers do business with some suppliers who were financially shaky. Got burned. He encouraged Gilchrist Gourmet to expand too far, too fast. Got a little overextended."

"And had to retrench," Luke concluded. "Had some trouble with the bank and lost a financing commitment. A definite pattern over and over again." Luke turned off the screen and sat back in his chair. "Okay, Danvers. You did a good job. I'll take it from here. Thanks."

Danvers nodded and got to his feet. His left eye twitched. "Sorry I couldn't give you something you could use in court."

"What the hell. It costs money to go to court anyway. I can fire the bastard for free. And at his level in upper management, I don't even need to think of an excuse."

Danvers grinned. "You've got a point."

Luke waited until the door had closed behind Danvers, and then he sat quietly for a few minutes considering his options. The tricky part was going to be handling this without letting Katy know what was happening.

She was fond of Fraser Stanfield.

Hell, she felt grateful to him for helping her hold things together during the past few months.

She would never believe him guilty of a deliberate pattern of corporate sabotage.

Luke fiddled impatiently with a pen as he thought about Katy. She was too softhearted, that was her problem. She would go to bat for Stanfield without hesitation, just as she would for a member of the Gilchrist clan. She would look for excuses to explain Stanfield's behavior. She would find mitigating circumstances and ask for clemency.

Luke knew the last thing he wanted to do was debate this matter with her. He always seemed to lose arguments such as this when he got involved in them with Katy. He would handle this problem quietly, cleanly, and without any fuss.

Luke got up, picked up the file, and went down the hall to Fraser Stanfield's office.

Stanfield looked up from a printout he was studying. He smiled quizzically, his gaze watchful. "Morning, boss. Heard you were in today. Saw Katy in the hall a few minutes ago."

Luke tossed the file down onto the desk. "The names Lawtry, Gibson, and Ragsdale mean anything to you?"

Stanfield leaned back in his chair. "Should they?"

"Yeah. They're three of the reasons you're going to be out on the street within thirty minutes."

Stanfield straightened abruptly in shock. "What the hell are you talking about?"

"I'm talking about your deliberate attempt to drag Gilchrist Gourmet into a sea of red ink. Not enough to drown it, just enough to lower its value."

"If this is some kind of joke, Gilchrist, I don't get it."

Luke smiled thinly. "You don't have to get it. All you have to do is get out of here by ten-thirty." He glanced at the clock. "That's twenty-nine minutes from now. Clean out your desk. I'll escort you downstairs personally."

Stanfield got to his feet, his eyes never leaving Luke. "Jesus. Are you crazy? Does Katy know about this?"

"No. And she's not going to know. As far as Katy is concerned, you got a better offer. And now that Gilchrist, Inc. is in good hands again, you're going to ride off into your own rosy future."

"You're not going to get rid of me that easily, Gilchrist. I've worked in the inner circles of Gilchrist, Inc. long enough to know that Katy holds a lot of power. She'll go straight to Justine and tell her I'm being fired without cause. She'll tell Justine that Gilchrist, Inc. needs me, and Justine will believe her."

"Justine isn't running the company any longer, Stanfield." Luke smiled again. "And neither is Katy. I am. And there's nothing you can say that will convince me I need you around."

Stanfield shoved his hands into the front pockets of his trousers. His face was tight with fury. "Mind telling me just what I'm being condemned for?"

"The investigator says the nicest thing I can call it is bad judgment. The contracts you had with Lawtry, Gibson, and Ragsdale are good examples of your extremely poor judgment, aren't they, Stanfield?"

"You can't blame those contracts on me."

"I can and I will. And then there's the little problem Gilchrist Gourmet is having with the bank. Another example of really bad judgment."

"Cash flow problems," Stanfield said quickly.

"Caused by overextension and poor planning," Luke said. "I could go on, but I'm sure you know the rest. Sure, I suppose we could call it six months of bad judgment on your part. That's probably what Katy would call it. Me, I'm calling it deliberate sabotage, and I'm handing you your walking papers."

Stanfield took a step back from the desk. "You won't get away with this."

"Who's going to stop me?"

Stanfield smiled coldly. "Katy will."

"No, Stanfield. That's not the way it's going to be this time. Katy works for me. She does what I say."

"Well, I'll be damned." Stanfield's gaze filled with speculation. "The gossip is true, isn't it? You're sleeping with her."

"Shut up, Stanfield. And clear out your desk. You've got twenty-five minutes left. I'm not leaving here until I walk you out the door." Luke leaned one shoulder against the wall and waited.

Stanfield shrugged and opened a drawer. "You're the boss. But before you congratulate yourself on having gotten rid of me, you'd better think about who helped me make all those bad judgment calls."

"Are you telling me you weren't working alone?"

"Yeah, that's what I'm telling you, all right."

"I'm not buying that. There's no indication there was anyone else involved."

"That's because my partner was a little smarter than I was about covering up her tracks." Stanfield jerked files out of the desk drawers and stuffed them into his briefcase. "Hell, she was smarter than I gave her credit for, that's for damn sure. Got to hand it to her. She set me up to take the fall on this one."

Luke smiled faintly. "You did it all on your own, Stanfield. We both know that."

"If you want to believe that, it's your funeral. But don't blame me when six months from now you realize you've still got trouble. I wonder how long it will take you to figure out that you're sleeping with the one person in the company who will stop at nothing to see the whole Gilchrist empire brought down."

Fury roared through Luke. "Katy? Why, you son of a bitch."

He propelled himself away from the wall in a swift movement, glided around the desk, and grabbed a handful of Stanfield's shirtfront.

"Take your hands off me, Gilchrist."

Luke slammed Stanfield down into the chair and leaned over him. "I've had enough of you, Stanfield. I've changed my mind. You don't have any time left. I'm taking you out of here right now. One of the secretaries can pack up your desk."

"Use your head, Gilchrist," Stanfield said urgently. "I'm telling you the goddamned truth. Katy hates all Gilchrists."

"Why would she hate us?" Luke demanded.

"She figures you all owe her. The sabotage was her way of getting even before she quit her job."

"You're lying."

"Am I? Think about it. What do you think it's been like for her all these years? How do you think she's felt knowing that by rights she should have had a chunk of Gilchrist, Inc.?"

"What are you talking about?"

"Don't you know?" Stanfield smiled grimly. "Justine made a deal with Katy's grandfather, Richard Quinnell, to merge her company with his."

"What's that old merger deal got to do with this?"

"She and Quinnell agreed to join the two restaurant chains on the day your father married Katy's mother."

"Hell, everyone knows that."

"There was no marriage," Stanfield said, "so there was no merger."

"What are you trying to say?"

"All these years that Katy's been forced to work for Justine she's been stewing over the fact that Justine didn't keep her part of the bargain thirty-seven years ago."

"Stanfield, you're crazy."

Stanfield grinned without any real humor. "Am I? The Quinnells kept their part. They were all at the church. If Justine had honored her end of the deal, Katy and her brother would now own a chunk of Gilchrist. They would be heirs to a fortune."

"You think I'm going to believe Katy's been plotting revenge all these years? You're out of your mind."

"Hell, a Gilchrist, of all people, should be able to understand revenge. Your family wrote the book on holding grudges. How would you feel if you were in Katy's place?"

Luke turned cold inside. Stanfield had a point. If the situation had been reversed, a Gilchrist would never have forgiven or forgotten. "Katy's different."

"If you think that, you're a fool. As Justine's personal assistant, Katy's been part of the inner circle for years, but not really a part of it, if you know what I mean."

"No, damn it, I don't."

Stanfield met Luke's eyes. "She's been almost like family, but not quite family. Not when it counts. She's had to take orders from Gilchrists rather than be in a position to give orders. She's had to put up with Gilchrist moods and whims and dramatics. And all the while she's known that by rights she should have owned part of the damned company."

Luke hauled Stanfield up out of the chair. "You're leaving. Now. If you go quietly, I'll bury the evidence that the investigator dug up. Make a scene or cause trouble and I'll smear your reputation with so much mud you'll never work in this town again. Your choice."

"You know what I think has eaten at her the most?" Stanfield asked softly. "The fact that her precious brother was screwed out of his inheritance. Matt's the most important person in Katy's life. You should know that by now. I think Katy would do just about anything to get even for what the Gilchrists did to her brother. Think about that the next time you're in bed with her."

Luke picked up Stanfield's briefcase and shoved it into his hand. He yanked Stanfield's jacket off the wall hook and tossed it to him. Then he jerked open the office door and shoved Stanfield out into the hall.

They nearly collided with Katy, who was walking down the hall toward Luke's office.

Her eyes widened in surprise as she glanced first at Luke's grim face and then saw Stanfield's derisive smile.

"Is something wrong?" she asked anxiously.

"Nothing's wrong, Katy." Luke clasped Stanfield's shoulder in what he hoped appeared to be a comradely fashion. The truth was, he was squeezing hard enough to paralyze nerve endings. He smiled with false regret. "Except that we're losing our right-hand man here. Stanfield's had a better offer. He's leaving today."

"Leaving?" Katy was startled. "Fraser, you didn't tell me you were looking for another position. I knew you were concerned about your future with Gilchrist, but I had no idea you were thinking of leaving."

Luke responded before Stanfield could say anything. "You know how it is in the fast lane of the business world, Katy. An up-and-coming executive type like Stanfield here has to grab his opportunities when he sees them. Isn't that right, Stanfield?"

"Sure. Right. Got to grab your opportunities." Stanfield's eyes were mocking now. "Katy understands that. She's been waiting for her big chance for years."

"And it's almost here. Just as yours is." Katy smiled warmly. She stepped forward and gave Stanfield a quick, impulsive hug. "I'll miss you, Fraser. I don't know what I would have done without your help. I can't thank you enough for your support."

Luke's stomach knotted. "Sorry. Can't hang around for any long good-byes. Stanfield tells me he has a plane to catch. I promised I'd cut some red tape for him in Personnel." He yanked Stanfield out of Katy's light grasp and steered him down the hall.

"Good-bye, Fraser," Katy called.

Stanfield raised a hand in farewell as Luke practically shoved him into the elevator. "What about Personnel?" Stanfield asked dryly as Luke punched the button that took the elevator to the lobby.

"Forget Personnel. I'll have them send you the necessary paperwork."

Stanfield laughed softly. "It was a good deal, you know?"

"What was? The sabotage? I assume it must have been to make it worth your while. Who was paying you to make Gilchrist Gourmet look sick?"

"A consortium that wanted to buy it cheap. I was going to hand it to them on a silver platter at a cut-rate price after Justine finally realized she had to sell."

"How much was the consortium going to pay you for arranging things?"

"I was going to get a piece of the action. I would have been CEO of Gilchrist Gourmet once it was under new management."

Luke nodded. "It might have worked. Except that I don't think Justine would ever have sold Gilchrist Gourmet."

"She'd have sold. Eventually."

"I doubt it."

"You'll never be able to prove a thing. We both know it."

Luke shrugged. "I know. But I don't have to be able to prove anything to keep you from getting a decent job anywhere in the restaurant industry in the entire Northwest. One call from me and any future employer is going to think twice about hiring you. Keep that in mind, Stanfield."

"I'll do that. And while I'm thinking about that, you think about the fact that the reason I got as far as I did in the scheme was that I had plenty of help from Katy."

Luke restrained himself from hurling Stanfield through the plate glass windows in the lobby, but it wasn't easy. It required a considerable amount of self-discipline, the kind that took years of training.

After Fraser had left the building Luke took the elevator back upstairs and went down the hall to his office.

"Hold my calls," he ordered as he went

past his secretary's desk.

He closed his office door, sprawled in his chair, and sat staring out the window for a long while. Katy would probably have accused him of brooding.

Stanfield was wrong, he thought. Sure, a Gilchrist might have plotted revenge for what had happened between the Gilchrists and the Quinnells thirty-seven years ago. But Katy? No way. Katy was the self-appointed guardian angel of the Gilchrist clan. She would never deliberately try to destroy the family business.

But she would do just about anything for her brother Matt, Luke reminded himself. If she honestly believed that Matt had been deprived of his inheritance by the Gilchrists, there was no telling what she would do in retaliation.

A Gilchrist in that sort of situation might conceivably conclude that because Justine had reneged on the merger thirty-seven years ago, someone was owed something.

Any self-respecting Gilchrist would have had no qualms about bringing down an entire company for the sake of a brother who had gotten the shaft on his inheritance.

Luke felt a cold chill go through him as he contemplated whether or not Katy had the same taste for vengeance.

CHAPTER SEVENTEEN

"Hello, my name is Bill, and I'll be your waiter for this evening."

Luke looked up slowly from the wine list. He regarded the earnest young man in front of him with a basilisk gaze. "My name is Luke Gilchrist. And if I ever hear you announce yourself like that again in a Gilchrist restaurant, you'll be looking for another job. Wait staff in Gilchrist restaurants do not form a personal relationship with the patrons."

Bill, the waiter, flinched and turned a painful shade of red. "I'm sorry, sir. Mr. Gilchrist, I mean. I didn't . . . that is, I'm new here, and at the other place where I worked we — "

"Forget it. Give us the menus and leave."

"Yes, sir." Bill's hand trembled as he handed the menu to Katy.

She smiled at him warmly. "Thank you."

"Yes, ma'am. I'll, uh, be back in a few minutes to explain the specials." Bill cast another nervous look at Luke, who was ignoring him, and departed hastily.

Katy glowered at Luke as soon as the waiter was out of earshot. "There was no call to snap at the poor man. He was just trying to do his job. Can't you tell he's nervous? You should make allowances."

Luke scowled at the back of the retreating waiter. "I hate wait staff who introduce themselves as if they were your new best friends."

"Try not to take it personally," Katy murmured dryly. "I'm sure he doesn't consider himself your good buddy. Not now, at any rate."

Luke sighed inwardly. Things were not starting off well. He glanced around, trying for professional detachment.

The Pacific Rim was the premier establishment in the Gilchrist chain. It was a true Seattle-style restaurant featuring an eclectic menu of seafood and meat entrées served in a casually chic atmosphere. The menu showed evidence of Asian and Italian influences blended in the unique and sometimes eccentric manner created by Northwest chefs.

The restaurant was also a cash cow.

In addition to catering to local residents, the Pacific Rim enjoyed a highly profitable long-standing relationship with the concierges of most of the major downtown hotels. That relationship guaranteed it a never-ending stream of out-of-town visitors and conventioneers.

Luke started to open a neutral discussion with Katy on the subject of the Pacific Rim's success. But before he could even say a word the bus person hurried over to fill the water glasses. The wine steward appeared at the young man's elbow. The bus person was startled and jumped. Water spilled on the white tablecloth.

Luke muttered in disgust and brushed water droplets off the sleeve of his jacket.

The bus person looked shell-shocked.

"Sorry, sir." The wine steward nobly tried to take charge. "I'll get a towel."

"Forget it." Luke gave him the name of the wine he wanted served with the meal.

The wine steward and the bus person escaped as swiftly as possible.

Katy laughed softly. "I told you we'd get impeccable service."

"Service? We haven't been left alone for more than three minutes." Luke was beginning to realize he had made a mistake bringing Katy to a Gilchrist restaurant. Unfortunately, having used the unannounced test as an excuse to force Katy to spend the night with him, he had felt obliged to go through with it.

He was about ready to walk out. All he

wanted was to be alone with Katy. He had to talk to her. He had questions he wanted to ask, but he was not certain he wanted to hear the answers. The conflicting emotions were driving him deeper into his already foul mood.

The questions were simple. Luke wanted to ask Katy if she was plotting revenge against the Gilchrist clan.

He also wanted to ask her if she would stay with him after the six months were up.

How did a man ask a woman if she was as angelic as she seemed? Luke wondered. How did he ask her if she secretly hated his guts and had conspired against him and his entire family?

So many questions.

Luke eyed Katy with brooding fascination. She looked like a dawn sky tonight. She had on a vivid yellow and turquoise dress that floated around her like a gossamer veil. The weightless fabric seemed to glide over her soft breasts and sweetly curved hips, never clinging close enough to satisfy Luke, but following the outline of her body just enough to tantalize him.

Luke could not quite see through the delicate fabric, although he had certainly been trying to do so since she had emerged from her hotel room. From the hints he had gotten so far he thought there might be a sort of yellow silk slip underneath the airy dress.

He was intensely aware of the sensual hunger in his guts. He told himself she surely could not smile at him like that if she were secretly plotting to destroy the Gilchrist clan.

Could she?

"You can't possibly conduct a true unannounced test of one of your own restaurants," Katy said chattily. "I told you that. They knew who you were the minute you walked in the door, even if you did make the reservations under another name."

"I've given up trying to test the operation," Luke grumbled. "I'd settle for some privacy."

"In that case, it was an even bigger mistake to choose a Gilchrist restaurant." Katy glanced up and smiled at someone moving toward them through the cluster of crowded tables. "Here comes the new manager. He'll want to know if you're happy with what you've experienced so far. Be nice to him, Luke. His name is George McCoy, and he's a good man. You're lucky to have him working for you."

"You don't have to play personal assistant tonight. I can remember the man's name, and I know what kind of job he's been doing here." Luke put down his fork as a tall, lanky man with thinning hair stopped beside the table. "Hello, McCoy."

"Sir. Good to have you with us." McCoy smiled at Katy. "Good evening, Ms. Wade. Glad to see you here tonight. Just thought I'd drop by and make sure everything was satisfactory."

"It's wonderful, George." Katy smiled brilliantly. "As always. Isn't that right, Mr. Gilchrist?"

"We could do with a little less attention from the wait staff," Luke said.

McCoy was instantly alarmed. "Of course. I'll speak to them immediately. I hadn't realized. You know how it is when the boss is around."

Katy shot Luke a warning glance and then gave McCoy another reassuring smile. "Mr. Gilchrist and I were just noticing the addition of a couple of interesting vegetarian entrées to the menu. He commented that it was a terrific idea, because the Northwest has become something of a haven for vegetarians." She looked straight at Luke. "Isn't that right, Mr. Gilchrist?"

Luke drummed his fingers on the tablecloth and studied her from beneath half-closed lashes. "From your lips to heaven's ears, Ms. Wade. If you heard me say that, then I must have said it."

McCoy turned a dull red, pleased at having

found favor with the boss. But it was the bright color in Katy's cheeks that amused Luke. Angels had a hard time with lies, even white lies.

"The new chef and I decided to try the vegetarian entrées as an experiment," McCoy confided proudly. "So far they've gone over surprisingly well. It's amazing how many of our regular restaurant patrons have stopped eating meat. Not that we'll be abandoning the traditional menu any time soon. Tourists and conventioneers still want their steaks and chops, of course."

"Of course," Katy said, still pink-cheeked. "Benedict Dalton is the new chef, isn't he?"

"Yes. Great credentials. The man is truly brilliant in the kitchen. We're lucky to have him with us." McCoy turned to Luke. "I'll rein in the wait staff. Sorry about that. They're a good bunch. Just a little overeager at times."

"Right." Luke nodded in dismissal, and McCoy hurried off toward the kitchen.

"Honestly, Luke, you have been in an absolutely rotten mood lately, and it's getting worse." Katy frowned in concern. "Is something wrong?"

"No."

"Are you sure? Are you worried about how we'll manage without Fraser? Is that what's bothering you?"

"Trust me, we're going to get along just fine without Stanfield." Luke picked up his menu. "McCoy had better not let his new chef get carried away with this vegetarian kick. Most of the population still wants meat."

"I'm sure he won't get carried away," Katy said soothingly. "Gilchrist has always given the individual chefs and restaurant managers a lot of freedom to create their own menus."

"Everyone knows you can't turn a chef completely loose in the kitchen. They're temperamental prima donnas. You've got to control them, or they get all kinds of crazy ideas."

Katy grabbed her napkin and used it to muffle the sound of her laughter.

"What's so funny?" Luke looked up from the menu.

"A Gilchrist complaining about someone else's temperamental nature." She managed to still the laughter, squashing it to the point where she was only giggling. She put down the napkin. "Talk about the pot calling the kettle black."

"I'm glad you're amused."

"When one hangs out with Gilchrists one has to get one's jollies where one can. By the way, where is Fraser going?"

Luke blinked slowly. "Why?"

"Because he's a friend, and I've been working with him closely for the past six months, and I thought it was odd that he left with so little notice. That's why."

"Beats me. He just told me that now that everything was under control at Gilchrist he was going to accept a long-standing offer from another firm." Unlike Katy, Luke reflected, he could lie without blushing.

Katy looked thoughtful. "Are you certain that was the reason he left?"

"You think there might have been another reason?" Luke asked smoothly.

"Well, no, I suppose not. It's just that he kept asking me what your plans were. He wanted me to keep him fully informed."

"The hell he did." Luke closed his menu and folded his arms on the white tablecloth. "He asked you for inside information?"

Katy's brows drew together in a tiny frown. "I wouldn't put it quite like that. After all, he was an insider himself."

"No," Luke stated, "he was not. He was an employee. Nothing more. What did you tell him? Did you mention the investigation I was doing?" But he already knew the answer to that, Luke thought. Katy had obviously not warned Stanfield of the computer investigation. Stanfield would have either tried to cover his tracks or resigned before being discovered.

"You told me not to say anything about it," Katy said equably, "so I didn't. But if you want my opinion, Luke, I think you're inclined to be much too secretive."

"Katy, I think it's time we had a talk," Luke began determinedly. But before he could complete the statement he spotted a familiar couple advancing through the crowded restaurant. "Damn."

"Now what's wrong?" Katy followed his gaze. "It's Maureen and Hayden. They must be here for dinner."

"You were right," Luke muttered. "Coming here tonight was a mistake." He resigned himself to the inevitable as his aunt and uncle approached the table.

Maureen and Hayden, both dressed in their customary black, sauntered like royalty through the restaurant. They walked straight toward Luke and Katy, pulled out the two extra chairs at the table, and sat down.

"We were told you were dining here tonight," Hayden said without preamble.

"Is that right?" Luke arched a brow. "Who told you that?"

"Your secretary at the corporate office."

"That's the last time I ask her to make reservations for me," Luke said. "Maybe it will be the last time she does anything for me."

"Now, Luke," Katy murmured.

"I need a secretary who can keep her mouth shut."

Katy gave him an exasperated look and turned to Hayden. "Was there something you wanted to talk to Luke about?"

Hayden looked at Luke. "Yes, as a matter of fact, there was."

"Can't this wait?" Luke asked impatiently.

"No. Darren came to see me yesterday. He told me you had helped him out of a rather unpleasant situation."

Luke shrugged. "He got himself out."

"Under your guidance," Maureen said. She flicked a quick glance at Katy and then looked back at Luke. "I also understand from my daughter that you had a long talk with her ex-husband."

"It was a short talk, not a long one, and I really don't want to discuss any of this tonight," Luke said.

Maureen did not even flinch. "You did her a great favor, Luke. I knew that terrible man was pestering her again. I was afraid he wouldn't go away quietly after Justine's lawyers got through with him. Eden said he was demanding money from her."

"Blackmail," Hayden said in sepulchral

tones. "Outright blackmail."

Luke glanced at Katy, who was looking surprised. Then he frowned at Hayden. "Eden told you?"

"Yes." Hayden shook his head sadly. "The whole story came out when Maureen confronted her about the fact that she was seeing Nate Atwood again. I think Eden was so relieved that he was off her back, she broke down and told her everything."

"My poor, brave daughter had been keeping that awful secret to herself all these months." Maureen shuddered. "When I think of what she must have been going through I could just weep. Her growing fear, her sense of desperation, her anxiety must have been nearly unbearable."

"It wasn't doing much good for the bottom line of either of the two restaurants involved, either," Luke said dryly.

Katy frowned at him. "Eden was desperate, Luke. You know that."

Maureen sighed. "She had no choice. She did what she thought she had to do to protect me. If only she had come to me in the beginning, I could have helped her."

"Yeah?" Luke gave her a skeptical glance. "How?"

"For one thing, Hayden and I could have assured her that those clippings about my conviction were extremely misleading."

Hayden patted Maureen's hand. "Maureen was the victim of another unscrupulous gallery owner who took advantage of her trusting nature."

"I lived in New York at the time," Maureen explained. "I was young and naïve and new in the business. It was Hayden who helped me get myself out of that terrible mess."

"I had just met her," Hayden said. "I'd gone to New York to find myself as an artist, and I found Maureen instead. We were both wildly in love. I knew she wasn't guilty of deliberately selling the forged works. She had been set up."

Maureen's eyes glittered briefly with tears. "Hayden believed in me. Unfortunately, no one else did. My career was in shreds. Hayden suggested I come out west with him. The rest is history."

"Couldn't possibly explain all that to Justine, of course," Hayden muttered. "She would never have understood. She was already furious because I wasn't showing any signs of business acumen, and she hated the whole notion of my having a career in the art world."

"The idea that Hayden was marrying someone who had once been embroiled in criminal charges would have sent her through the roof," Maureen said grimly.

"You know Justine," Hayden continued with a rueful shake of his distinguished head. "Later, after Thornton ran off with Cleo, I knew we had to keep quiet forever about Maureen's past. I saw what Justine did to Cleo. I couldn't allow her to treat my wife like that. I thought everything was safely buried." He frowned. "I wonder how Atwood discovered those old press clippings."

"Probably just went looking through some newspaper indexes," Luke said. "Atwood is no fool. He knows the value of information, and like me, he survives by being able to gather it. He knew enough family history to figure out where to start digging."

"So he went looking for some old scandal material that might be useful," Hayden concluded.

"And found me," Maureen said tightly. "While he was married to Eden he learned a lot about us. He knew what Justine was like. He knew it wouldn't take much to upset her."

Bill the waiter appeared at the table. He looked extremely nervous. "Uh, I thought I'd see if Mr. and Mrs. Gilchrist would care for anything."

Maureen looked up. "Why, yes. My husband and I will be joining this party. I'll start with a martini, please."

"You can bring me a manhattan," Hayden said pleasantly.

Luke swore silently, aware that he had lost whatever privacy he might have had left in which to talk to Katy. When he looked at her he saw the laughter in her eyes and knew she was once again being amused by the overbearing Gilchrist clan.

It occurred to him that if she found them so humorous, she could not possibly hate them.

Or could she?

Hayden settled back and assumed a thoughtful expression. "Maureen and I have decided it's time to get a few things out on the table, Luke. It's obvious from what you've done for Darren and Eden that you aren't out for revenge against the entire family. But I must insist on knowing what your plans are for the company."

Katy spoke up quickly. "He's told you what he's going to do for Gilchrist, Inc. He's going to put it back on its feet."

Hayden frowned. "Yes, but are you still intending to take the Pacific Rim as your fee? That's what I want to know."

"Sure," Luke said. "Why not?" He glanced around the interior of the restaurant again. "I think this is going to be a damn good investment, although I may have to get rid of the chef."

Maureen gathered herself for an impassioned speech. Hayden looked funereal.

Katy tapped her knife crisply against the edge of her plate and gave Luke a quelling glance. "I think it would be best if we all avoided that topic of discussion tonight. Luke's plans have not been finalized."

Luke's brows rose. "They haven't?"

"No," she said firmly. "And I think we should all wait until the end of the six-month period before making any rash statements."

Maureen gave Katy a shrewd glance and then nodded. "Very well. Perhaps it would be best to wait."

Hayden started to argue and then appeared to change his mind after exchanging looks with his wife. He sighed heavily as he turned back to Luke. "You know, my boy, I wouldn't blame you if you did bring the whole damn company down. I'm hoping you won't, of course. It's my children's inheritance, and I have a vested interest in protecting it. But I would understand."

Katy wrinkled her nose. "Only a Gilchrist would."

Hayden shrugged. "Perhaps. The thing is, what Justine did thirty-seven years ago was unforgivable."

"And sure enough, Luke's side of the family never forgave her." Katy shook her head in amazement. "Typical."

"That's enough, Katy," Luke warned. He was not in the mood for any of her Gilchrist generalizations.

"You know," she continued, paying no attention to him, "I've always wondered about something. Since we're getting all this juicy old gossip out in the open tonight, maybe this is a good time to ask."

"What's that?" Maureen asked.

"I understand why Thornton Gilchrist ran off with Cleo. He was wildly in love, and Gilchrists do dramatic things, especially in dramatic circumstances. But why do you suppose he never bothered to at least send a note to my mother so that she wouldn't have to endure the humiliation of being left at the altar?"

Luke stared at her, aware that Hayden and Maureen were also staring. No one had an answer. For the first time in his life Luke felt some of his unquestioning loyalty to his parents waver. Katy was right. His father could at least have let poor Deborah Quinnell know she was going to be abandoned.

"I don't know why he didn't contact your mother," Maureen finally said. "Probably didn't even think about it. He was undoubt-

424

edly more concerned with marrying Cleo and protecting her from Justine's wrath than anything else."

Hayden squeezed Maureen's hand gently. "It was unfortunate, but I can see how it would have come about. Thornton was probably afraid Justine would try to get rid of Cleo if she had any warning of his intentions. And if Deborah Quinnell had learned of the elopement in advance, she would have naturally said something to her father."

"Who would have gone straight to Justine to find out what was going on," Maureen concluded. "You have to understand just how powerful Justine was in those days. The whole family shivered when she so much as sneezed. Thornton was right to be afraid of what she might try to do to Cleo."

Katy looked at her. "What could she have done?"

"Who knows?" Hayden said. "Tried to buy her off, perhaps. Or threatened her in some fashion. Maybe even convinced her she would ruin Thornton's life by marrying him."

Maureen nodded. "The point is, Thornton obviously knew his primary task was to protect Cleo."

"And Deborah Quinnell came in second on his list of priorities," Katy murmured. "Just another Gilchrist road kill."

Luke went cold with anger. "What's that supposed to mean?"

"Nothing." Katy smiled wryly. "Shall we order? I'm going to try one of the chef's new vegetarian entrées."

Road kill. Luke gazed unseeing down at the menu. He had never felt less like eating in his life. *Road kill.* Was that how Katy saw her mother? An innocent victim of Gilchrist passions? A mere thump under the wheels of a Gilchrist warrior's chariot?

Every time he looked at the situation the way a Gilchrist would look at it he was forced to realize that Katy had grounds for revenge.

"I'll try a damn vegetarian entrée, too," Luke muttered. The last thing he wanted to do was get something on his plate that might even remotely resemble dead meat.

"Fate plays odd tricks," Maureen observed philosophically. "Just think, Katy, if Justine had gone through with the merger thirty-seven years ago in spite of the wedding being called off, you and Matt would be part owners of Gilchrist, Inc. today."

"It boggles the mind," Katy agreed with suspicious blandness.

Hayden dismissed the whole idea with an elegant wave of his hand. "There was never any chance of Justine going through with

426

the merger after Thornton ran off with Cleo. The merger between Gilchrist and Quinnell was contingent on marriage between the two families as far as she was concerned. Justine would die before she would hand over part of Gilchrist to outsiders."

Luke's insides dropped another notch below zero. Stanfield had been right. It was easy to come to the conclusion that Katy's family had lost badly thirty-seven years ago. The question was whether or not Katy saw it that way.

The uncertainty he was experiencing tonight about Katy's true feelings was going to drive him mad, Luke thought.

"Well, that's all water under the bridge," Katy said with an odd smile. She sat back in her chair and gazed thoughtfully around the busy restaurant. "I've been thinking. One of these days Gilchrist is going to have to redo some of the restaurant lobbies. This one, for example, is very pleasant but starting to look a trifle dated."

"Restaurant decor gets old, just like anything else." Luke was more interested in his own roiling thoughts than in the subject of interior design.

Katy smiled brightly. "I've got a suggestion to make."

"What's that?"

"I think we should redo all five of the restaurant lobbies to take advantage of the company's connection with a famous artist. We should display some of Hayden's pieces. Maureen could supervise the interior designer to make certain the art was shown off to its best advantage."

Maureen gasped. Her eyes gleamed with excitement. "Katy, are you serious?"

"Certainly. I've been thinking about it for some time. We could even underline the impact of the display by simultaneously creating an endowment for the arts. It would generate some terrific public relations. Great image stuff for Gilchrist."

A gleam of enthusiasm shone briefly in Hayden's eyes. Then it died. "Forget it. Justine would never go for it."

"Justine isn't running things around here now," Katy reminded him gently. "Luke is. And I'll bet Luke loves the idea, don't you, Luke?"

Luke gazed into her crystal-clear eyes and wondered how he could have ever imagined that she had conspired with Fraser Stanfield. No one who hated all Gilchrists would have schemed to undo some of the effects of the rejection that Hayden and Maureen had suffered.

Guardian angels did not sit around and

428

plot revenge, Luke realized with sudden insight. They had other priorities. They got on with life.

His spirits abruptly felt lighter and more exuberant than they had all day. He brought his attention back to the matter at hand, aware of Maureen and Hayden watching him with intent gazes.

"Well . . ." Luke said slowly. He broke off, wincing as Katy kicked him under the table. He looked at her and saw the warning expression in her gaze. He almost grinned. "Well, sure. What the hell. Why not? Put Hayden's glass in all the lobbies."

Something relaxed in Maureen's face. "Thank you, Luke," she said softly.

Hayden appeared stunned, but he started to smile slowly. "Didn't know you appreciated my work, Luke."

"It's a relatively new interest of mine," Luke admitted.

Luke pulled Katy into his arms as soon as he had closed the hotel suite door.

"I thought I'd never get you alone," he muttered as he covered her mouth with his own. The sense of urgency that was driving his emotions tonight had created an aching hunger in him that only Katy could assuage.

Katy parted her lips for him without protest. Her arms went around his neck, and she leaned into him.

The wispy silk of her yellow and turquoise dress was as thin and insubstantial as it looked. Touching her through the gossamer stuff was almost the same as touching her without anything at all in the way.

Almost, but not quite.

Luke stripped the dawn-colored dress from her and dropped it onto the floor. Katy's eyes were clear and warm and welcoming as he carried her to the bed.

He wanted to take his time with her, but his need was overpowering. He left a trail of discarded clothing on the rug, his own as well as Katy's. She made a soft little sound when he put her down on the white sheets, and then she reached for him.

His hands were shaking with need a few minutes later when he parted her thighs and lowered himself over her. He entered her slowly, pushing carefully against the natural resistance of her tight passage. When he was safely inside he drove deep, seeking release and reassurance and the comfort of knowing she wanted him as much as he wanted her.

Katy closed around him, hot and wet and clinging. He felt the dampness of his own sweat on his shoulders and the exciting bite of her nails as she clutched at him.

When her small, sharp little teeth bit into the muscle of his shoulder all the questions that had made the day a maelstrom of uncertainty for Luke vanished. His body surged toward climax. He heard Katy call his name, and he shuddered. And then he was lost in the free-falling dive that would tear him apart and put him back together once more, a whole man.

How could he have thought for one single minute that Katy had been plotting vengeance? he wondered.

"So why have you been in such a rotten mood for the past couple of days?" Katy asked conversationally.

Luke lounged against the pillows. Katy was lying on her stomach, her arms folded on top of his bare chest. One of her legs was bent at the knee and she was swinging it idly back and forth above the rumpled bed.

"I have not been in a rotten mood for two days." Luke threaded his fingers through her hair.

"Yes, you have." She grinned. "Even by Gilchrist standards."

He gave her a playful swat on her nude rear. "I resent that. You can't judge my moods by Gilchrist standards. You have to

431

judge them by my own personal standards. And you don't know me well enough yet to make judgments like that."

"You're evading the issue." She plucked at his curling chest hair.

"Ouch." He grabbed her tormenting fingers. "Whatever my mood has been, I can assure you I am feeling terrific at the moment. Or at least I was until you started torturing me."

She eyed him narrowly. "Are you sure you're no longer in a foul mood?"

"Positive. Look, I'm smiling."

"Gilchrists can smile even when they — "

Luke closed her mouth with his fingers. "Don't say it." He took his hand away.

"Okay. If you're sure your mood has vastly improved since yesterday," she murmured slowly, "I've got a question for you."

"What's that?"

"What did you really think about the locations the real estate agent showed us yesterday afternoon?" Katy asked eagerly.

Luke considered the terrible possibility that Pesto Presto was ultimately going to be more important in Katy's life than he was, and some of his good mood started to fade.

"They all sucked," he said.

Katy grabbed a pillow and began bashing him with it. Luke laughed until he felt his body growing hard again, and then the laughter turned to passion, and he was lost once more in the sweet heaven of Katy's warmth.

CHAPTER
EIGHTEEN

Two days later Luke responded to the knock on the cottage door, a cup of coffee in one hand, his mind on some figures he had been crunching on his computer. He knew by the way Zeke flicked his ears that whoever was on the other side of the door was a friend. That limited the possibilities to two: Katy and her brother.

Luke hoped it was Katy.

It turned out to be Matt. His hands were bunched into fists at his sides, and his face was rigid with anger. There was sharp accusation in his eyes.

"You're sleeping with my sister," Matt said.

Luke stepped back and held the door open. "Come on in, Matt."

Matt took one step into the tiny hall. His shoulders were stiff with the tension of issuing a challenge. "You're sleeping with her."

"Did she tell you that?" Luke led the way into the kitchen. Matt followed reluctantly.

"She didn't have to tell me. I figured it out for myself after you two got back from Seattle. Jesus. What do you think I am? Stupid?" Matt slammed his hand against the refrigerator door. "You think because I'm only seventeen I don't know what's going on?"

"No. I just figured it wasn't any of your business." Luke sat down at the table and pushed aside some notes he had made.

"She's my sister. I gotta look out for her. She's real smart about a lot of stuff, but she doesn't know much about guys. Not guys like you, at any rate."

"What's wrong with me?"

Matt ran his fingers wildly through his hair and flung himself down onto the other chair. "I told you once, you're not exactly her type."

"And I told you I'd take care of her."

"I know, but I saw how she was yesterday after the two of you got back." Matt broke off, glowering. "Are you going to tell me you're not sleeping with her?"

"No. I was just reminding you that I gave you my word I'd take care of her, and I will." Luke studied Matt's impassioned expression. "What was wrong with your sister yesterday? What got you so concerned all of a sudden?"

"She cried, dammit. Katy almost never cries. But I saw her. She was in her room." Matt shoved his hands into the front pockets of his jeans. "She doesn't know I saw her."

"You think Katy was crying because of me? Because of something I did?"

"Yes."

"What makes you think that?"

"She's my sister," Matt ground out. "I know her better than anyone. The last time she cried like that, all by herself in her room, was when that dumb Nate Atwood ditched her and started dating Eden."

Luke's mouth tightened. The comparison with Atwood was an unpleasant one. "Matt, I promise you I am not going to treat her the way Atwood did."

"No, you're going to treat her worse than he did. She's going to be more torn up about you. At least Atwood didn't seduce her. She told me that when I asked her."

"You're kind of a nosy younger brother, aren't you? What the hell gave you the right to ask her a question like that?"

"Because I was gonna do something if he had," Matt declared.

"Like what?"

"I dunno." Matt looked sullen. "Something. Katy said I wouldn't have to do anything to him regardless of whether or not he had seduced her because Atwood was going to be punished enough as it was."

Luke slanted Matt a wary glance. "Yeah? How?"

"She said he would get everything he deserved when he married a Gilchrist."

Luke drummed his fingers in irritation on the table. "That sounds like something Katy would say, all right."

There was silence in the kitchen for a while. Zeke padded in with his dish. He surveyed the tableau of the two males glowering at each other across the width of the kitchen table. He put down his dish and rested his head on Matt's knee, offering silent sympathy. Matt absently stroked his ears.

"Why did you come here, Matt?" Luke asked quietly.

"To tell you not to hurt Katy."

"How do you suggest I avoid that now?"

Matt looked briefly uncertain. Then he scowled again. "You should at least ask her to marry you. Then she wouldn't feel like you were taking advantage of her."

Luke absorbed that. "You want me to ask her to marry me?"

Matt straightened in the chair, looking newly determined. "Yeah. Yeah, I think you should."

Luke felt oddly lightheaded. "All right. I will."

Matt eyed him with vast skepticism in his young eyes. "You will?"

"Yes." A deep certainty filled Luke as he met Matt's gaze. "As her brother I guess you have a right to know what my intentions are. I give you my word they're honorable."

"Yeah?" Matt was clearly taken aback by Luke's readiness to do the right thing.

"Word of honor," Luke said solemnly. "But you had better know up front that the problem here is not my intentions. It's your sister's intentions."

"Huh?"

"I'm not at all sure Katy's intentions toward me are honorable," Luke said softly. "I'm not sure she wants to marry me."

"Oh, yeah, I know." Matt looked relieved. "I just think you should ask her, that's all. She probably won't actually want to marry you. You're a Gilchrist, after all."

Luke set his back teeth. "It's not easy, you know."

"Being a Gilchrist? Yeah, I can understand that." Matt brightened. "So you'll ask her?"

"Yes."

"Okay." Matt nodded, satisfied. "All right." He apparently considered his mission accomplished. "Hey, you want to go down to the gym and work out? You could help me practice some of my throws."

"Sure, why not?" It was as good a way as any to relieve the tension seething in his gut, Luke thought.

Katy saw Zeke watching her from inside Luke's cottage when she went past on her way to the beach. The big dog had his face pressed against the kitchen window, a somewhat awkward position given the fact that he had his dish clamped in his mouth. Zeke tracked her with an intent gaze, ears half cocked.

Katy hesitated, aware that the dog was alone. Matt and Luke had left for the Dragon Bay Athletic Club an hour ago. She told herself the dog was not really lonely and that he would be just fine by himself for a while.

Zeke continued to stare hopefully at her through the glass. He probably knew she was on her way down to the beach, she thought. Zeke loved to go down to the beach.

"Okay, okay," Katy muttered. She used the key Luke had given her and opened the cottage door.

Zeke trotted out with his dish and headed straight for the cliff path.

The dog hit the beach several yards ahead

of Katy and dashed off to explore the exciting scents left behind in the wake of the outgoing tide. Katy followed slowly.

She was in a strange mood today, she realized. Actually, she had been that way since returning from Seattle with Luke. Last night she had actually cried quietly in her bedroom. Thank heaven Matt had not heard her. He would have been concerned and would have asked her what was wrong.

Katy knew she could not have supplied a clear answer. She could hardly tell Matt that she was in love with Luke and that there was very little future in loving him.

Loving Luke was a monumentally stupid thing to do. But she had known from the first time she went to bed with him what the probable outcome was. If she was honest with herself, she had to admit she had sensed that outcome the first time she had met him.

The best thing she could do was not look beyond the next few months. Take what was offered for as long as Luke was in Dragon Bay. Be prepared to have him walk away at the end of six months.

Katy sighed. It was going to be hard. She was accustomed to long-term plans and commitments. She was accustomed to looking into the future.

Luke was still recycling his own past.

"Katy."

Katy turned in surprise at the sound of her name being called above the roar of the surf. Zeke glanced up from where he had his nose in the sand farther down the beach.

"Fraser." Katy smiled as Fraser Stanfield loped down the cliff path. "What on earth are you doing here?"

"I came to say good-bye." Fraser reached the beach and strode quickly toward her. "Didn't get much of a chance yesterday."

"I thought you were on your way to the airport."

Fraser gave her a grim smile. "Didn't you realize what was happening? Gilchrist was hustling me out of the building. He had just fired me."

Katy was speechless. "Fired you? I don't believe it. Why would he do such a thing?"

"It was business." Fraser's mouth twisted. "No hard feelings, you know?"

"No, I don't know. What is this all about?"

"Gilchrist was afraid I was too close to the inner circle of Gilchrist power. He saw me as a threat and decided to get rid of me."

"But the only reason you were close to the inner circle was because Justine asked you to help us hold things together."

441

"Hey, don't worry about it, Katy. I'm a big boy. I know how these games are played."

"But if what you say is true, it's horribly unfair." Katy was stricken. "This is terrible. I'll speak to Luke right away. I won't allow him to fire you just because you were helping me keep tabs on things for Justine."

"Forget it, Katy. It's done. You'll never change Gilchrist's mind. We've both worked with Gilchrists long enough to know that they always get their own way when they want it badly enough."

"But it's not right."

Fraser laughed sourly. "You always were a little naïve about business ethics. Stop worrying about it. I'll land on my feet. I always do."

"This is awful. I feel terrible. This is partly my fault. You were helping me do my job."

Fraser's eyes darkened. "Personally, the only reason I feel terrible is that you and I never had an opportunity to get close. But I figure that situation can be changed."

He grabbed her arm before Katy realized his intention. She tried to jerk herself free. When that failed she drew herself up and fixed him with a stern calm.

"Let me go, Fraser."

"No. Not yet." Fraser's fingers bit through the sleeve of her sweatshirt and into her arm. "You're right about one thing, Katy. You owe me."

"I told you, I'll talk to Luke."

"Talking to Gilchrist is a waste of time." He gave her a shake. "I invested a lot in this operation. I stand to lose a bundle because you screwed things up for me."

"What was I supposed to do? I didn't realize Luke was going to fire you."

Fraser loomed over her. "You were supposed to keep me informed of his plans, remember? You never told me about the goddamned investigation he was running."

Katy sucked in her breath. "I wasn't free to talk about it."

"Yeah? I thought I was your friend. You're not very loyal to your friends, are you? All your loyalty goes to those damned Gilchrists."

"What do you want from me, Fraser?" Katy asked quietly.

"Access to the Gilchrist computers for the next couple of months. You can do it, Katy. You can get me the new entry codes and the information I'll need to get into the computers and manipulate some data."

Katy stared at him. "Why?"

"Because I've set some plans in motion that will work if they're given a chance. I'm too close to the finish, Katy. I can't quit now. Help me and I'll cut you in on the deal."

"What deal?" she snapped. "What have you been doing, Fraser?"

"I had a real sweet arrangement going. All I had to do was make Gilchrist Gourmet look like it couldn't compete. Things were working out just fine, thanks to the fact that I was close to the inner circle."

Outrage blossomed in Katy. "You were sabotaging the corporation, weren't you? Luke was right all along. The culprit was an insider."

"He can't prove a damn thing, and he knows it. All he has are a lot of suspicions. That's why he fired me yesterday instead of bringing charges. But you're going to help me finish this thing, Katy."

"No."

"Yes. I'm going to get my own back. Gilchrist can't treat me the way he did and get away with it. I'm going to force him to sell Gilchrist Gourmet."

"How?"

"With your help, of course. And a computer. I can do it."

"Don't be an idiot. I would never help you do that."

"Sure you will. If you don't, I'm going to make it look like everything that went

444

wrong at Gilchrist Gourmet during the past few months was your fault, not mine. I'll send the proof straight to Justine."

Katy was horrified. "What proof? There is no proof. I've never done anything to hurt the company."

"There will be plenty of proof when I get finished. I can manufacture the evidence in the computers and provide documentation. And the Gilchrists will believe every bit of it. You know what they're like."

"That's a lie. Justine, at least, trusts me. And Luke."

"No Gilchrist ever trusts anyone completely. You know that. Especially not Justine. She'll be quick enough to believe the worst. After all, she doesn't need you anymore. She's got her precious grandson back."

"Damn you, Fraser, I thought you were my friend." Katy pushed her wind-whipped hair out of her face. "How could you do such a thing?"

"It's just business, honey."

"You should be ashamed of yourself. This is wrong."

"Skip the lecture. I'm not in the mood. You're going to help me, or I'll send Justine an anonymous printout that will make it look like you were the one who tried to undermine

Gilchrist Gourmet. That's it, Katy. No alternatives."

"Go to hell," Katy answered. She tried again to jerk her arm free of his grasp.

Fraser yanked hard in retaliation. Katy stumbled and fell to the beach. Fraser reached for her, his eyes in slits.

"You little bitch, you're going to do what I say. There's too much money riding on this."

Katy screamed as Fraser's hands closed around her shoulders.

Zeke dropped his dish in the sand and charged.

"What the hell?" Fraser straightened abruptly as he caught sight of Zeke racing toward him in a silent, ferocious rush. "For Christ's sake, call him off." He backed up quickly, stumbling over a length of seaweed. *"Call him off."*

Fraser caught his balance, whirled, and started to run.

Katy rolled to her feet just as Zeke flashed past. She saw the dog launch himself at Fraser's fleeing backside. Zeke's massive jaws opened wide. He caught a mouthful of Fraser's windbreaker and ripped savagely.

Fraser shrieked and started to struggle out of the torn windbreaker. Zeke jerked hard, tangling Fraser in the jacket. Fraser stumbled and went down, yelling in terror.

"*Zeke*. Stop." Katy gasped as Zeke planted his front paws on Fraser's chest. "That's enough. Stop, Zeke."

Zeke looked at her, wagged his tail, and whined pleadingly, as if asking for permission to go for Fraser's throat.

"Get him off me," Fraser hissed.

"It's okay, Zeke." Katy approached Fraser and the dog warily. "Good boy. Good dog. Take it easy. We don't want him to sue. That's a good boy."

"Get him off." Fraser started to wriggle out from under Zeke's paws.

Zeke snarled softly in warning. Fraser instantly stilled.

"Jesus," Fraser whispered, staring up at Zeke. "The goddamned dog will kill me."

Katy was not precisely certain herself just what Zeke was going to do next. She took another step forward, intending to grab the dog's collar.

At that moment Zeke raised his head and looked toward the cliff path. He barked loudly, summoning assistance.

Katy glanced up and saw Luke and Matt descending the cliff path at a run.

"Luke." Katy dashed forward and threw herself straight into his arms when he reached the beach. "Thank heaven you're here. I

447

wasn't sure what to do next."

Luke's arms closed fiercely around her. He spoke to his dog over the top of Katy's head. "Zeke. Steady, boy. That's it. You can let him up now. I'll take care of things."

Zeke obediently stepped off Fraser's chest and trotted toward Luke.

"Matt, take Katy and Zeke up to the house. I'll handle this."

Matt reacted instantly to the soft tone of command. "Yes, sir. Come on, Katy."

Katy raised her head from Luke's shoulder. "Wait. I have to explain what's going on here."

"I know what's going on." Luke's eyes were on Fraser. "Go with Matt."

Katy realized she was too shaken to argue. It would have been futile in any event. Luke was clearly in charge now. Without a word she stepped away from him and started toward the cliff path with Matt.

Zeke raced back down the beach, grabbed his bowl, and dashed back to join Katy and Matt.

At the top of the cliff path Katy turned to glance down at the scene on the beach. "I do hope there isn't going to be any trouble because of this."

Matt grinned, his confidence in Luke evident. "Believe me, there will be trouble.

But not for you. Luke will handle it."

Katy was feeding parsley and basil into the food processor when Luke walked through the cottage door a short while later. Zeke was sitting in the middle of the floor, his dish parked at the ready. His tail moved in a brief greeting when Luke appeared, but he didn't take his gaze off the food processor.

"What's going on here?" Luke took in the scene in the kitchen with a glance that was probably meant to reflect amusement but somehow failed. There was a cold wildness in his sorcerer's eyes. "Starting dinner already?"

Matt, lounging against the kitchen counter with a can of soda in his hand, looked at Luke. "It's for Zeke. Katy's making him an entire batch of pesto."

"An entire batch all for him?" Luke rubbed the dog's ears. "Zeke's going to think he's died and gone to heaven."

"He deserves it," Katy said softly. She was intensely aware of the subtle tension in Luke. "He was a real hero." She pressed the machine's lever down for a few seconds, grinding up the fresh leaves. While the food processor was running she quickly added the remaining ingredients.

"Yeah," Matt said admiringly. "A real

hero. Good dog, Zeke."

Zeke acknowledged the accolade with another thump of his tail, but his gaze did not waver from the food processor.

Katy risked another glance at Luke. His eyes were dangerously green, his expression unreadable. "Luke, what happened down there? What did you do to Fraser?"

"Not much," Luke said.

"What's that supposed to mean?" Katy switched off the machine and ladled the entire batch into Zeke's bowl. She glanced up anxiously. "You didn't do anything rash, did you?"

"No." Luke's mouth curved faintly as he watched his dog go to work on the pesto. "Is there any more soda, Matt?"

"Sure." Matt waved the can in his hand in the general direction of the refrigerator. "Help yourself."

Katy put the food processor bowl in the sink. "Luke, was Fraser telling me the truth? Did you fire him the other day because you suspected he was behind a scheme to sabotage Gilchrist Gourmet?"

"Uh-huh." Luke opened the refrigerator and selected a can of cola. His movements were those of a prowling jungle cat, fully controlled but radiating a potential for instant violence.

"Why didn't you tell me the truth?" Katy was outraged all over again. "Why did you try to make me believe he was leaving for another job?"

Luke opened the can of soda. His eyes were implacable as he met her annoyed gaze. "Because I didn't want to get into a major argument with you over it. I knew you would defend the guy."

Katy chewed reflectively on her lower lip. "There must have been mitigating circumstances. I can't believe Fraser would do that sort of thing without a very good reason."

"He had a good reason," Luke said succinctly. "He stood to make a lot of money."

"Maybe there was more to it than that. Maybe he was coerced into it or something."

Luke muttered something under his breath. "Stanfield is an opportunist. When Justine started to withdraw from daily supervision of the company a power vacuum developed. When she asked Stanfield to take on more responsibility he saw his chance and took it."

Katy sighed. "I just can't believe it. You should have told me the truth when you fired him, Luke."

Luke shrugged. "Maybe I should have. At the time it seemed simpler not to get you involved."

"But I was involved. Fraser was my friend. Or at least I thought he was. I depended on him during the past few months. He was so helpful."

"He used the power you and Justine gave him to weaken Gilchrist Gourmet," Luke said bluntly. "He was going to turn it over to a consortium of investors for a fraction of its real worth and collect his reward. It was a neat scheme."

Katy frowned slightly. "Perhaps he did it because he knew there was no hope of rising any higher within Gilchrist, Inc. He may have felt that because it was a family-owned firm he would never have an opportunity to go to the top."

"Damn it, Katy, this is exactly why I didn't tell you what was going on the day I fired the son of a bitch. I didn't want to have to listen to you make excuses for him."

"I'm not making excuses. I'm just trying to understand why he did what he did."

"Bull."

Katy was keenly aware of Matt listening to the argument while he drank his soda. Zeke had finished his pesto and was sitting beside his dish. The dog's gaze moved from Katy's face to Luke's and back again.

"You are making excuses," Luke stated, "and I don't intend to listen to them. There's a time and a place for playing guardian angel. This isn't it."

"I suppose you have a point. He was trying to hurt the company, after all." Katy slanted him a sidelong glance. "He came to see me today because he wanted me to help him finish his scheme."

"I know." Luke took a swallow of soda.

"He told you?"

"Yeah."

"Oh." Katy pushed her hair behind her ears. "He said if I didn't help him he would send information to Justine that would make it appear I had been the one sabotaging Gilchrist Gourmet all along."

"Uh-huh."

Katy stared at him. "He told you that, too?"

"Yeah. It was just a meaningless threat, Katy."

She looked out the window. "He might have done it."

"It wouldn't have mattered," Luke said gently. "Even if he had sent the information to Justine and even if she had believed him, it wouldn't have mattered. Justine doesn't run things around here anymore, remember? I do."

Katy smiled tremulously. "Yes. And you wouldn't have believed him?"

"Christ, no." Luke's teeth flashed in a brief grin. "You're the Gilchrist guardian angel. You're the last person on earth who would deliberately hurt the family firm."

"I wish you'd stop calling me an angel," she muttered. But she felt herself warming under the impact of his obvious faith in her integrity. Gilchrists did not trust easily, she knew. The fact that Luke trusted her meant a great deal.

There was silence for a moment in the kitchen. Matt broke it.

"Good thing we got back when we did," he offered conversationally.

"You can say that again," Katy murmured. "I wasn't sure how to make Zeke release Fraser. I had visions of lawsuits and all sorts of problems."

"There won't be any more problems from Stanfield," Luke said.

Something in his too-quiet voice alerted Katy. Her brows snapped together in a worried frown. "Luke, you didn't do anything violent to him, did you?"

Luke looked her straight in the eye. "Hell, no. I know you don't approve of violence. I gave him a stern lecture on business ethics and a very forceful warning."

Matt suddenly choked on a swallow of soda. He gasped, sputtered, and nearly bent over double as he tried to recover himself. Soda sprayed from the can as Matt hastily set it down on the counter. Katy's attention was momentarily diverted.

"Are you all right, Matt?"

"Yeah. Sure." Matt coughed and made a production out of clearing his throat as he reached for a sponge to mop up the soda. His gaze flickered to Luke, who looked politely concerned. "Uh, I think I'll take Zeke for a walk or something. See you later. Come on, Zeke. Let's go, boy."

Zeke obediently scooped up his dish and trotted after Matt. Katy waited until the door closed, and then she turned back to Luke.

"About Fraser," she began deliberately. "I really think you should have kept me informed, Luke."

Luke put down his can of soda and reached for her. He leaned back against the refrigerator door, spread his legs, and pulled her close between his thighs. Katy could feel the heat and the strength in him. She responded to it as she always did, with a heady little rush of excitement.

"Luke?" She raised her head to look up at him. There was an unnerving intensity in his emerald gaze.

"Do you have any idea of how I felt when

I saw you down there on the beach and realized what had happened?" Luke's voice was as rough as the surf hitting the cliffs below the cottage window. "Do you know what could have happened if Zeke hadn't been there?"

The fierce protectiveness in him touched Katy deeply. She gentled Luke's hard jaw with soothing fingers. "It's all right, Luke. I don't think Fraser would have actually hurt me. He was just very upset and angry, and he wanted to make me help him. But I don't think he would have used force."

"Angel, sometimes you scare me to death. How the hell have you survived this long without a guardian of your own?"

Before Katy could reply Luke took her mouth, kissing her with all the controlled ferocity she had seen reflected in his eyes since he had walked into the cottage.

Katy could feel the battle-ready tension in him and instinctively knew that whatever had happened between Luke and Fraser, it had not been entirely civilized.

She also knew there was nothing she could do about it now. Luke would never tell her the whole truth. Perhaps she did not really want to know the details, she thought.

Katy surrendered to the urgent demand in Luke's kiss, using her softness to drain off the remnants of the fury that had blazed in his eyes.

When the tension had eased in him Katy raised her head. "Luke? What are you thinking?"

"I'm thinking of something Stanfield told me before he left a few minutes ago."

"What was that?"

"I asked him for the name of the man who was behind the consortium of investors who were trying to buy Gilchrist Gourmet."

"He told you?" Katy asked, surprised.

"I guess he was feeling cooperative. He said he never actually met him, but the guy's name was Milo Nyle."

"Good heavens," Katy said. "That's the name of the man who tried to con Darren. Mr. Nyle was certainly an active mischief-maker."

"Yes," Luke said, apparently lost in his own thoughts. "He was."

CHAPTER NINETEEN

Two days later Luke sat at his Seattle office desk gazing into the crystal ball that was his computer. He absently tapped a gold pen against the polished wood of his desk.

Displayed on the screen was information on a real estate deal Gilchrist, Inc. had done fifteen years earlier.

The maneuver had involved the purchase of a small, aging building near the Pike Place Market. The structure itself was useless to Gilchrist. It was the property Justine had wanted, and there was no denying it had been a brilliant business decision. It was the site on which she had later built the Pacific Rim. Not only had the restaurant been incredibly successful, but the land itself had skyrocketed in value as Seattle had come into its own in recent years.

Another Gilchrist success.

Luke had found several memos from Justine pertaining to the deal. They made it clear that before the old building could be torn down the handful of small businesses that occupied it had to be removed. Some leases were canceled, others were not renewed. The net result had been the closing of a small restaurant, a cleaning establishment, and a bookstore. The restaurant had been named the Atwood Café.

Luke studied the screen, but a portion of his mind was on Katy. It was fortunate he could do two things at once, he thought, because a part of his mind was always on Katy lately.

She consumed his full attention in his dreams and nibbled at his thoughts all day long, regardless of other distractions. Now that he could start to see a future again he could not envision it without her.

The commotion in the outer office pulled Luke's attention away from the screen. He heard familiar voices issuing orders. His secretary wavered and fell under the Gilchrist charge.

A moment later Luke's door opened. He looked up in resignation as Maureen, Hayden, Darren, and Eden stormed into his office. They took up positions around his desk as if it were a pentagram.

"No wonder Katy thinks of us as a coven," Luke muttered. He leaned back in his chair. "I take it this is not a social call?"

"We've talked this over, Luke, and we've decided you should know our feelings on the matter," Maureen announced.

"What matter is that?" Luke asked politely.

"Katy." Eden drifted toward the window. She settled on the sill and adjusted the hem of her black wool skirt. "You're sleeping with her, Luke. We all know it. You told me yourself that you were involved with her."

"So?"

"So we want you to know our feelings on the subject," Maureen repeated.

"Hell." Luke tossed aside the gold pen. "Don't tell me you're all here to give me a lecture on how to conduct my love life. I'm not in the mood to listen to it."

Maureen glared at him. "This is important. None of us wants Katy hurt."

"She's right," Darren said.

"Since when did any of you start worrying about Katy?" Luke asked.

Hayden frowned. "We've always been very aware of Katy. She's almost a part of the family. No one wants to see her hurt. She went through a bit of a rough patch back when Eden and Atwood were married. Don't want to see her go through something like that again."

"Thoughtful of you," Luke observed.

Eden's eyes flashed. "I never wanted to hurt Katy. But Nate and I — well, it was just one of those things."

"And Katy was just another road kill," Luke said.

Eden gave him a sharp look. "What's that supposed to mean?"

"Forget it." Luke eyed the handsome faces of his family. "If you came here to gang up on me and tell me to stop seeing Katy, you're wasting your time."

"Hell, we know that." Darren moved one shoulder in an elegant shrug. "It's obvious you want her, even if you are all wrong for her."

"Thanks for the vote of confidence," Luke said dryly. Apparently no one considered him right for Katy. If he was honest, he had to admit he had not even considered himself right for her back at the beginning. It was a depressing thought.

"The thing is," Maureen put in, her voice grimly forceful, "we don't think you should lead her on. We don't want you to use her and then cast her aside."

"Is that right?" Luke cocked a brow. "What do you suggest I do?"

"Marry her," Hayden said succinctly.

"What makes you think she'll have me?" Luke asked quietly.

All four of them stared at him in amazement. It rarely occurred to Gilchrists that they could not have what they wanted. Not if they wanted it badly enough. And if they wanted something, they usually wanted it badly. Luke scowled at the thought. He was starting to make the same generalizations Katy made.

"What in the world are you talking about?" Maureen demanded. "If you ask her to marry you, she'll marry you."

"Of course she will," Hayden said. "She wouldn't be sleeping with you if she didn't love you. Katy wouldn't sleep with someone she didn't love."

Eden and Darren both nodded in agreement.

"Ask her," Darren said.

"It's not going to be that easy," Luke murmured.

"Why not?" There was a militant gleam in Maureen's eye.

"I can't cook," Luke explained.

If the four Gilchrists surrounding his desk had been amazed a minute earlier, they were all flabbergasted now.

"What the hell's that supposed to mean?" Darren asked blankly. "What's cooking got to do with it?"

"Katy told me once that the man she marries will have to be able to cook," Luke said. "Have you ever known a Gilchrist who could cook?"

They all looked at one another again.

"Justine said that she would never cook after she got Gilchrist, Inc. to the point where she didn't have to be her own chef." Hayden's gaze was reminiscent. "I remember how hard she worked in those early years. She slaved night and day in the kitchens of that first Gilchrist restaurant. Couldn't afford staff. Every night she fell into bed exhausted. Thornton and I grew up with the notion that cooking was a pretty dreadful thing."

"And you passed that idea on to your children." Eden smiled wryly. "But it's not all that difficult. I've done it on occasion. You just open a box and add stuff and then you stick it in the microwave."

"Salads are easy," Maureen added helpfully. "You just wash off the lettuce and add some bottled dressing. You can get some interesting things like capers to sprinkle on the top. No problem."

"Some of the frozen entrées Gilchrist Gourmet makes are really good," Darren offered. "Take 'em out of the microwave box, put 'em on a plate, and no one would know they aren't homemade."

"Katy would. And I'm not talking about

that kind of cooking," Luke said. "I'm talking about real cooking. Gourmet stuff."

"Unfortunately," Hayden admitted, "none of us has ever had much interest in the subject."

"Katy's interested in it. Passionately interested," Luke said.

"So learn to cook," Darren advised. "It can't be all that difficult. Prove to her you can do it, and then ask her to marry you."

"How do you suggest I go about learning to be a cordon bleu chef in a week?" Luke asked blandly.

Eden frowned. "I don't see any problem. We've got a couple of dozen chefs on the payroll. We'll get one of them to teach you."

There was a general murmur of agreement. Everyone looked relieved.

It was Luke's turn to gaze at the other members of the family in amazement. "You're serious, aren't you?"

"I'll be perfectly frank with you," Hayden said. "It would have been best if you had never started an affair with Katy. She's not your type, and you're definitely not hers. But since it's a fait accompli, we feel you should do the right thing by her."

They all glowered at Luke.

"All right," Luke said.

They eyed him closely, obviously wary of such easy victory.

464

"Soon," Darren stipulated.

"Soon," Luke promised softly. "Very soon."

"I'll line up one of the Gilchrist chefs to give you instructions," Eden said.

Luke got the message summoning him to Justine's suite the next morning. He went downstairs to the first floor of the mansion and presented himself at the door.

"Mrs. Gilchrist is very upset, and it's all your fault," Mrs. Igorson announced as she opened the door.

"Don't worry," Luke said. "By the time I leave she'll probably be even more annoyed."

Justine was waiting for him in her favorite wingback throne. The gray light of a cloudy day dulled the silver in her hair but not the glitter in her green eyes. Justine was in fighting form, Luke noted. As he approached she seemed to stiffen with anger. Her shoulders were rigid beneath her black blouse.

"What is this I hear about you asking Katy to marry you?" Justine snapped.

"False gossip and malicious rumor," Luke said mildly. He sat on the window seat and looked at Justine. "I haven't asked her yet."

"But you intend to ask her?"

"If I can work up the courage."

Justine's mouth tightened. "Don't joke with me, Luke."

"It's no joke. There's a good chance she'll refuse. You know we Gilchrists have a hard time with rejection."

Justine's hand clenched on the arm of the chair. "Damn you, Luke, I told you I did not want her hurt."

"Everyone seems to be very concerned about me hurting Katy. I have to admit I'm a little surprised."

"What did you expect? Katy has been almost a daughter to me. I won't stand by and see you take advantage of her."

Luke studied the toes of his boots for a moment and then glanced up with a quizzical smile. "The reason I'm surprised at all this interest in my relationship with Katy is that Gilchrists don't usually concern themselves with innocent victims."

Justine's eyes flashed with anger. "What a ridiculous thing to say. I have no idea what you're talking about, but I want to make it perfectly clear that you are not to ask Katy to marry you."

"You think I'd make her a lousy husband?"

Justine closed her eyes briefly. When she opened them again her gaze was steady. "Our family has done enough damage to hers. I do not want to see it happen yet again."

"You're referring to the famous incident thirty-seven years ago, I assume?" Luke tapped the file he was holding against his thigh.

"We agreed we would not discuss it," Justine said coldly. "But since you raise the issue, yes. We are talking about the fact that the last time a Gilchrist got involved with someone in Katy's family he left her at the altar. I will not allow it to happen twice."

Luke slanted her an assessing glance. "What makes you think I'll leave Katy at the altar?"

Justine's gaze never wavered. "I am not a fool. Bringing you here to take over Gilchrist, Inc. was a calculated risk on my part. I was well aware that you might use the opportunity to take revenge on me and the family."

Luke suddenly understood. "You think I might set up a replay of what happened thirty-seven years ago just to humiliate you and the others?"

Justine drew a deep breath and looked away. "I think there is a possibility you might see it as a fitting revenge."

Luke nodded thoughtfully. "A true Gilchrist revenge. To make it work I would have to sabotage the company first, of course.

Then I could give you the coup de grace by setting up a scenario that would humiliate you in front of your friends and business associates just as you were humiliated thirty-seven years ago. Not bad. Think how they would all laugh at you, Justine. And those that weren't laughing would pity you."

"Stop it," she snapped. "As I said, bringing you here was a calculated risk."

Luke got to his feet and began to prowl the room. "Has it ever occurred to you that if you had kept your end of the bargain with Quinnell thirty-seven years ago Katy and her brother would be Gilchrist heirs today?"

Justine's gaze was stony now. "Yes."

"That was the real reason you gave Katy the job as your personal assistant after her parents died, wasn't it? Not because of what my father did to her mother, but because you felt guilty about what you had done. You knew Katy and Matt would not have been left penniless if you had gone through with the merger."

"There was nothing left of the Quinnell business after Katy's father died," Justine said softly. "He had driven it into the ground. If the merger had taken place, that would never have happened. I could have run both the Quinnell restaurants and my own. Richard

Quinnell's empire would not have gone under. Katy and her little brother would have been financially secure."

"Quinnell saved you years ago when you found yourself widowed with two small boys to raise, didn't he?"

"Yes."

"You owed him."

"Yes. But I could not go through with that merger." Justine's hand clenched once more. "I could not take the risk of giving away partial control of my company to outsiders. I do not regret what I did, and I have done what I could to make amends. Katy has never blamed me for anything that's happened."

"No, she wouldn't do that. All Katy wants is to be free of Gilchrists once and for all." Luke stopped in front of the window. "I'm going to ask her to marry me, Justine."

"Damn you."

"Look on the bright side. Maybe she'll turn me down."

"And if she accepts?" Justine asked, her eyes hard.

Luke smiled grimly. "If she accepts, you're going to have to sweat out my real intentions until the day of the wedding, aren't you, Justine? You won't know until the last minute whether I'm plotting revenge or if I've actually fallen in love with Katy."

Justine paled. "You aren't in love with her."

The certainty in her voice made Luke curious. "How can you be so sure of that?"

"Because your father told me thirty-seven years ago that no Gilchrist could love a woman like Katy's mother. He said she was sweet but unexciting. There was no passion in her, he said. No drama. He needed a woman like Cleo. Katy is the image of her mother."

"But she's not her mother, and I'm not my father."

"You are more like him than you will ever know. And you are attracted to the same kind of women. I saw the photos of your wife in the papers. Compared to her Katy must seem very plain indeed. Don't try to tell me you're in love with her."

Luke shrugged. "Okay. I won't tell you that."

"And if you're not in love with her," Justine continued relentlessly, "then there is only one reason you would ask her to marry you."

"The final act of my revenge?"

"Yes, damn you." Justine leaned forward, her fingers tight around the arms of her chair. "Luke, I brought you back here to save the company and the family. Katy believes you're going to help us, not destroy us."

"It will be interesting to see what you believe, won't it?" Luke started toward the door. "Will you be in church on the day I marry Katy?"

"There will be no wedding," Justine grated.

"How will you stop it?"

"I shall convince Katy to reject your proposal if it is the last thing I do."

"Poor Katy. Caught in the middle of a Gilchrist duel. Well, may the best Gilchrist win." Luke paused. "By the way, does the name Sam Atwood mean anything to you?"

Justine faltered, clearly thrown off balance by the change of topic. She scowled. "Atwood? Any connection to that dreadful Nate Atwood?"

"His father."

"No. I never knew his father. I understood the man was dead."

"He is," Luke said. "He committed suicide about fifteen years ago. He lost his wife to cancer, and shortly after that he lost his business. Apparently it was too much for him. He put a bullet in his brain."

Justine gave him a sharp look. "What has that got to do with anything?"

"Nothing, I guess," Luke said softly. "Just another Gilchrist road kill."

The following afternoon Luke stood in front of one of the large stainless steel sinks in the gleaming kitchen of the Pacific Rim. He silently cursed all temperamental chefs.

"No, no, no, Mr. Gilchrist." Benedict Dalton, resplendent in pristine white from head to toe, frowned at the bunch of green leaves Luke clutched in his fist. "One must handle spinach very carefully. One does not wish to bruise it."

"How the hell am I supposed to get the stem off if I don't hang on to the leaf?"

Benedict sighed. "With great care, Mr. Gilchrist. And a proper respect for the freshness of the produce. Once again. Hold the leaf gently in your left hand, and take the stem between thumb and forefinger. Remove it gently."

Luke jerked the stem. The leaf tore apart.

Benedict was outraged. "My God, you have no feeling for the spinach at all, Mr. Gilchrist."

"If it's so damn sensitive, maybe I should forget using it in the salad."

Benedict's lips pursed. "This is to be a practice session, if you will recall. And you were the one who chose the spinach salad for your menu, so it makes perfect sense to practice with spinach."

"It's a hell of a nuisance, if you ask me."

"If you do not wish to learn how to clean spinach properly, you are, naturally, free to prepare your salad with the sand left in it."

Luke slanted the chef a surly glance. "No, thanks."

Benedict smiled beatifically, obviously secure in the knowledge that he held the upper hand. "If you wish to select other greens, you may, of course, do so. There is romaine, curly endive, arugula, watercress. All, however, are even more fragile than spinach."

"Never mind." Luke eyed the leaves floating in the water. "I've started with the damned spinach, and I'll stick to it. Is it really necessary to wash each leaf by hand?"

"I'm afraid so." Benedict's tone did not sound particularly sympathetic.

"You're enjoying this, aren't you?"

"It is not often one has a chance to give orders to a Gilchrist," Benedict said cheerfully. "Now then, have you decided which dressing you will want to prepare?"

"The lemon vinaigrette."

"Excellent choice. Have you ever made a vinaigrette dressing?"

"No."

"It will be an interesting experience, I'm sure. Are you a patient man?"

"Not when it comes to cooking." Luke painstakingly rinsed off another spinach leaf.

"Perhaps you will learn patience as we go on."

"I doubt it." Luke ripped off another stem.

"Then it is unfortunate that you have chosen to do a soufflé for your dessert course."

"I chose it because I think the lady I'm inviting to dinner will be impressed by a soufflé," Luke said through his teeth. He ripped off another stem with a savage movement.

Benedict tut-tutted disapprovingly. "My, we are wasting a great deal of spinach, aren't we?"

"I can afford it," Luke muttered.

He grabbed another leaf out of the water and held it under the faucet. This was stupid, he told himself. Really stupid. He did not stand a chance of impressing Katy with one home-cooked gourmet meal. She would probably find his efforts hilarious. She found it so damn easy to laugh at Gilchrists most of the time.

The plan to cook and serve a spectacular meal to her and then ask her to marry him was no doubt doomed before it even got off the ground.

She would never marry a Gilchrist.

On the other hand, his instincts told him

she would not sleep with a man she did not love.

She was sleeping with him. That had to mean she loved him.

But she'd never said anything about love, he reminded himself.

Luke set his teeth and rinsed another spinach leaf. This terrible sense of uncertainty was new to him. He didn't like it.

Katy raised her brows when Liz told her she was wanted downstairs in Justine's suite.

"She wants to see me alone? Without Luke?"

"Uh-huh." Liz narrowed her eyes with an air of clinical assessment. "If you ask me, she is in a state of anxiety. I wouldn't be surprised if she's on the verge of a panic attack."

"She called up here herself? It wasn't Mrs. Igorson?"

"Nope. It was Mrs. Gilchrist. Sounds like she needs a dose of vitamin V."

"I beg your pardon?"

"Valium." Liz chuckled. "A little professional joke."

"When do you start your new classes at college, Liz?"

"In about six weeks," Liz said. "Until then I'm your resident shrink."

"I was afraid of that."

Katy glanced at her watch. It was nearly four-thirty. She was looking forward to her five o'clock swim tonight. Luke would be coming over for dinner this evening, as usual, and she intended to try out another recipe on him and his dog. She needed to wash a lot of spinach leaves for her latest pesto creation.

She hurried downstairs.

The sight of Justine's drawn face was a shock. Katy frowned in concern as she walked into the living room.

"Justine, are you all right?"

"Calm yourself." Justine smiled wearily. "There is nothing physically wrong with me. Sit down, Katy. I want to talk to you."

Katy sat. "What's the problem?"

"My grandson, of course. When I think about it, he has been the problem one way or another for some time now. Some days I wish I had never taken the risk of turning Gilchrist, Inc. over to him. Other days I tell myself he is the only hope this company and this family have. But today is one of the days when I think I may have made a grave mistake."

Katy relaxed a little. Justine was always grumbling about Luke. It meant nothing. "What's he done to upset you now?"

"He intends to ask you to marry him."

Katy opened her mouth, found no words, and closed it. She waited a couple of seconds and tried it again. "He *what?*"

"You heard me. He apparently plans to ask you to marry him."

"I don't believe it." Katy surged to her feet. She felt shell-shocked and giddy. A part of her was soaring free with happiness. But another, more realistic part was sure there was some terrible mistake. Somewhere another shoe was about to drop.

"It's true, all right," Justine said. "The question is, how do you feel about it?"

"I'm not sure," Katy admitted.

Justine's eyes turned bleak. "You're in love with him, aren't you?"

"Yes."

"I was afraid of that. I knew you wouldn't have become so intimately involved with him if you didn't love him. Have you told him?"

"No."

"My advice is that you refrain from doing so. Katy, he's different from you. You're honest, straightforward, and open. But Luke is . . . well, very deep."

"I know that. He's a Gilchrist." Katy turned to face Justine. "You're trying to warn me that he may be pursuing some objective of his own, right? That even if he asks me

477

to marry him, he may not be serious about it?"

"We must face reality, Katy. My grandson is still an unknown quantity to all of us. We knew at the beginning that his motive for assuming control of Gilchrist might be vengeance."

"How would marrying me fit into any revenge plan he might have concocted?" Katy asked.

"It is entirely conceivable that his agenda is to destroy the company and, as a final act of vengeance, restage the humiliating debacle that took place thirty-seven years ago. Only this time it would be you, not your mother, who was left at the altar."

Katy was stunned. "You can't be serious. Luke would never do that to me. He doesn't hate me."

"Of course he doesn't hate you." Justine shook her head sadly. "It's me he would be trying to humiliate and crush. And I think he has guessed that leaving you at the altar would hurt me more than anyone could possibly realize. Luke is very, very clever. He knows the truth."

"What truth?"

Justine stared at her. "I believe Luke realizes that although I have tried to pretend otherwise, there is nothing I would like better than to see you married to him."

Katy sat down again. Hard. "You *want* me to marry him?"

"I was not merely indebted to your grandfather for all the help he gave me during my early years in the restaurant business. God help me, I was in love with him."

"Justine, I had no idea."

"Neither did he. Or if he did, he was too kind to say anything." Justine sighed. "He was happily married to your grandmother. I knew I could never give him the sunshine and joy that she gave him. So I called myself a friend of the family and pretended that was enough. Some friend. In the end I was no friend at all."

"That's not true, Justine. You were my friend when I needed one."

"Thank you, Katy. That means a lot to me. Thirty-seven years ago I thought I would be content if I could unite the families through the marriage of my son and your mother. I wanted that marriage to take place with all my heart. It was almost as important to me as Gilchrist, Inc."

"Almost." Katy smiled wryly. "But not quite?"

"No. Not quite. The company meant everything to me. It was my children's and grandchildren's inheritance. The future of the family was tied up with the restaurants. I had no right to surrender that future unless I knew for certain I would be surrendering it to family."

"And as much as you loved my grandfather, the Quinnells were not family."

"No. And I lost my chance to make them family when my eldest son ran off with his little slut of a secretary."

"You mean when he ran off with Luke's mother," Katy corrected her firmly.

"Whatever. But I have never completely forgotten my dream of uniting the families. For a while I rather hoped that you and Darren might get together."

Katy smiled. "Not a chance. Darren and I could never be anything more than friends."

"I soon realized that. But I did not give up. When I learned Luke was widowed it occurred to me that one day there might still be a chance to bring the Quinnells and the Gilchrists together through marriage."

"Justine, you are unbelievable. Devious, clever, and dangerous."

"Desperate, my dear. Not dangerous. But now that my fondest wish appears to have come true, I realize I am very much afraid."

"Because you think Luke has guessed your secret and has deliberately set out to build up your hopes and then bring them crashing down."

"Just as his father did. And, being Luke, he will no doubt bring Gilchrist, Inc. down along with all my other secret dreams."

Katy smiled slowly. "You know what your problem is, Justine?"

"What?"

"You're too much of a Gilchrist. You're always looking for the dark, melodramatic side to everything. You've got to have more faith in your own family."

"I know this family far better than you do," Justine muttered. "I assure you there is a great risk that we are all doomed if you agree to marry Luke."

CHAPTER TWENTY

"Are you sure I can't help?" Katy lounged against the counter in Luke's kitchen and surveyed the chaotic scene. She was impressed.

Plates, pans, wire whisks and long-handled spoons lay everywhere. There was a massive pile of freshly washed, still-dripping spinach in a bowl. The makings for a vinaigrette dressing were set out nearby. Water was boiling on the stove for pasta. A round of sourdough bread waited on the cutting board. Judging from the amount of egg white in one bowl, Luke was going to attempt a soufflé.

"No, thanks." Luke's fierce features were set in lines of deep concentration as he minced capers, olives, parsley, and anchovies. "Everything's under control."

"I didn't know you enjoyed cooking," Katy said.

"What did you expect? I was raised in the restaurant business." He swore softly as an olive skittered out from under the knife. It rolled off the cutting board and onto the floor. Zeke ambled forward to eat it.

"This is a real treat for me," Katy continued. She hid a smile as another olive rolled off onto the floor. Zeke quickly devoured the evidence. "I can't remember the last time someone cooked a meal for me. Matt's idea of cooking is to stick a frozen pizza in the oven."

"Kids," Luke said indulgently. "Victims of the fast food mentality. You gotta feel sorry for 'em. Wonder who's going to do the cooking for the next generation."

Katy grinned. "Maybe everyone will eat out more often. That'll be good for Gilchrist, Inc. and Pesto Presto."

"Good point. Damn." Luke dropped the knife and went to the stove.

"What's wrong?"

"Nothing. The water's already boiling. I'm not ready to cook the pasta."

"So turn the water off. Luke, I had a long talk with Justine today."

"Yeah? So did I." Luke switched off the pasta water and picked up a notebook that was lying on the counter. He frowned over it intently.

"She seemed somewhat upset."

"She's always upset. It's in the blood."

Katy blinked. "I beg your pardon?"

"Forget it. Hand me that pan, will you?"

Katy picked up the skillet and gave it to him. She watched as Luke put it on the stove and coated the bottom with olive oil. A great deal of olive oil, she noticed.

"The thing is, Luke, she doesn't seem to feel she can trust you completely. She wants to believe you're going to save Gilchrist, but a part of her is still afraid you're only here to take revenge."

"That's her problem." Luke went back to the notebook, scowling darkly. His scowl deepened as he glanced back over his shoulder at the oil in the skillet.

"Have you told her that you've solved the problems at Gilchrist Gourmet?"

"No. I didn't get around to it. When I saw her yesterday she wanted to talk about another matter." Luke dumped the minced capers, olives, and anchovies into the skillet.

"So what it boils down to is that you never gave her a logical explanation for what was wrong in the case of the two restaurants that were losing money, and she has no idea you've stopped the sabotage of Gilchrist Gourmet."

"Computer problems, remember?"

"I don't think she bought that."

"Too bad. There *is* no logical explanation

for what was happening at the two restaurants except the truth. You said I couldn't tell her that her granddaughter was skimming cash to pay off a blackmailer, so that was that."

"Of course you couldn't tell her about Eden. But what about the troubles at Gilchrist Gourmet?"

"As far as Gilchrist Gourmet is concerned, I just haven't had a chance to tell her about Stanfield's sabotage." Luke eyed the vinaigrette fixings as if they were components for a batch of nuclear fuel. He gingerly picked up the whisk. "Would you mind if we discussed this some other time? I'm kind of busy at the moment."

"No, but I think this explains why Justine is worried about your intentions toward Gilchrist, Inc. Luke, if you would just try to communicate with her and let her know that you're not out for revenge, it would relieve a lot of her anxiety."

"Who says I'm not out for revenge?" He held a bottle of olive oil in one hand and tried to drip the oil into the lemon mixture. He was whisking madly with his right hand. Oil and lemon juice spattered the countertop. "You know something? I'd like to throttle a certain chef right now."

Katy smiled. "I know you're not out for revenge, Luke."

485

"Is that right?" He shot her a surly glance. "How do you know that?"

"Because of what you did for Eden and Darren, among other things."

"Don't bet on it. Saving Eden's and Darren's rears might have been part of a much larger plan. Hell, I might be plotting to bring all of Gilchrist crashing down."

"Come on, Luke. Stop making a joke out of it."

"No joke. I'm serious. Even if I told Justine the truth, she probably wouldn't believe me. It's possible the only reason I pulled my cousins' bacon out of the fire was to buy myself time to carry out my own schemes." Luke broke off abruptly. He inhaled sharply. "Damn."

He leapt for the stove and yanked the skillet off the burner. The smell of singed capers, olives, and anchovies rose from the pan. Luke glared at the smoking mixture.

Zeke watched hopefully as Luke carried the skillet over to the sink.

"It's too hot for you, Zeke," Katy said softly. "Give it a chance to cool."

Luke set about mincing more capers and olives with an ominous expression. Katy decided not to try to continue the conversation. She sipped a glass of wine in silence and watched Luke grow increasingly darker of brow.

He made repeated trips back to the note-book, muttering softly. Katy winced when he began whipping egg whites for the soufflé. Disaster loomed, she was sure, but she dared not say anything. For some reason Luke was trying to pretend he was a master chef.

By the time they sat down at the table Luke's jaw was rigid. His eyes were very green as he passed the salad to Katy.

"Wonderful," Katy murmured as she helped herself. She noticed the dressing had not adhered to the leaves. Luke had forgotten to dry the spinach after washing it.

Luke took a bite and swore. "It's watery."

"Just a bit damp. Wonderful flavors in the dressing."

Luke tentatively tasted the main dish. His face darkened. "The pasta's mushy."

"Nonsense. It's terrific." Katy munched enthusiastically on the soggy pasta.

"Don't bother trying to lie about it," Luke growled. "It's mushy."

"Perhaps it was boiled just a wee bit too long. But it's no big deal, Luke. I didn't even notice it until you mentioned it." There was no point adding that the pasta was also stone cold. Luke could figure that out for himself.

"I know five-star cuisine when I taste it,"

Luke said. "And so do you. This isn't it."

"Don't worry about it."

"I'm not going to worry about it. I'm going to fire that son of a bitch."

"Who?"

"Benedict Dalton."

Katy stared at him in astonishment. "The chef at the Pacific Rim? Why on earth would you want to fire him?"

"He set me up."

"Good heavens, Luke. What a ridiculous thing to say. How on earth could he do that?"

"Never mind." Luke eyed her plate. "Are you sure it all tastes okay?"

Katy recognized the desperate appeal of the cook who knows things have gone terribly wrong. "It's wonderful, Luke."

"Yeah?"

"Yes."

He looked doubtful but clearly did not want to argue the point. There was silence at the table for several minutes.

"Is something wrong, Luke?" Katy finally asked.

"No."

"You seem preoccupied tonight. Maybe this wasn't a good evening to try to get together."

"Matt's working, and he won't be home

until midnight. I figured this was my best shot."

"At what?"

Luke looked uncharacteristically tense, even uncertain. It occurred to Katy that in all the time she had known him she had never seen him with quite that expression in his gleaming eyes. It was as if he were dealing with something that was out of his control. The experience was obviously an unusual one for him.

"Did Justine say anything else to you today?" Luke asked bluntly. "I mean besides the fact that she doesn't trust me?"

Katy concentrated on collecting a forkful of the mushy pasta. It was not easy to get the stuff to curl around the fork. "No. Not really. Mostly she just talked about how concerned she is. She wonders if she did the right thing in asking you to come here."

"Katy, look at me."

Reluctantly Katy raised her eyes and found him watching her with shattering intensity. "Well . . ."

"Tell me the truth. You're no good at lies, not even white ones. What else did she say to you?"

Katy flushed furiously. She picked up her water glass. "She said something about being careful. She's afraid I'm getting too involved with you."

"What else?"

"Luke, please, this is getting awkward."

"She told you I was going to ask you to marry me, didn't she?"

Katy felt herself going red from head to toe. She tried to swallow a sip of water and wound up choking on it. She began to sputter and cough.

"I knew it." Luke put down his fork, stood up, and slapped her between the shoulder blades. "That old witch is really beginning to annoy me."

"She's not an old witch," Katy gasped. She managed to catch her breath. "She's just concerned, that's all."

"She's an interfering busybody who thinks she can run everyone else's life. Hell, nothing is going right tonight. I knew this was going to be a disaster." Luke pounded her on the back one last time and sat down. "So what's your answer?"

"I beg your pardon?"

"You heard me." He gave her a ferocious scowl. "What's your answer?"

Katy realized this was his proposal of marriage. Her eyes widened in outrage. "I haven't heard the question."

"You know damn well what the question

is. Are you going to marry me or not?"

Katy tossed down her napkin. "Luke Gilchrist, that is a disgraceful way to ask a woman to marry you. You should be ashamed of yourself. I expected more from a Gilchrist."

"Yeah? What did you expect?"

"Roses and champagne. Maybe a moonlight stroll on the beach — heck, I don't know. I'm not the dramatic one around here." Katy glowered at him. "I'll tell you something else. I resent the implication that I don't deserve a full-dress proposal. Where are the hearts and flowers? Why aren't you on your knees? You think I'm not worth the effort?"

"Effort?" Luke was incensed. "You don't think I put any effort into this?" He indicated the mushy pasta and the bowl of wet spinach with a sweeping gesture of his hand. "I slaved for hours under that tyrant Dalton. He was supposed to teach me how to make a gourmet meal. Today I spent all afternoon in the kitchen busting my ass to produce this dinner. And this is the thanks I get?"

Katy was intrigued. "You really don't know how to cook, do you?"

"I don't know any Gilchrists who can cook. At least not the kind of cooking you mean. But I sure as hell made an effort. And I want some credit for it."

491

"You did a wonderful job, Luke."

"Don't pat me on the head. Just tell me whether or not you're going to marry me so we can get on to the soufflé."

"Okay. I'll marry you."

Luke looked stunned. "You mean it?"

"Yes. But I would like to point out for the record that you have no right to accuse the Gilchrist chefs of being temperamental. You're worse than any of them."

"Say it again."

"I'll marry you."

The frustration and uncertainty vanished from Luke's eyes in an instant. "My God, I don't believe it. I'm going to give Benedict Dalton a raise."

He surged out of his chair, reached down, and pulled Katy to her feet. He swung her around in a triumphant circle and carried her over to the couch.

Katy was torn between laughter and desire as he put her down on the cushions. Luke sprawled on top of her, green fire blazing in his eyes.

"You won't be sorry, Katy." Luke framed her face between his palms. "I swear it. I know you think we don't have anything in common, and I know you think Gilchrists are severely dysfunctional, but we can make our marriage work."

Katy smiled. She was aware of a deep sense of happiness welling up inside her. "I never said Gilchrists were severely dysfunctional."

"Good. Because we do have a few strong points, you know."

She wrapped her arms around his neck. Her smile curved into a teasing grin. "Such as?"

"We're faithful, for one thing."

Katy stopped laughing at him. She searched his eyes for a moment. "You've got a point. You Gilchrists are as intense and passionate about your marriages as you are about everything else."

"Damn right. My mother and father were committed to each other until the day they died. I never once cheated on Ariel. And look at Maureen and Hayden. They're still together, too. The only divorce in the crowd has been Eden's, and I think it's safe to say there were a few extenuating circumstances."

"And your grandmother never remarried."

Luke's mouth twisted. "Justine was married to Gilchrist, Inc. And she's definitely been faithful to the company."

"She had another passion, too," Katy said slowly. "She told me this afternoon that she secretly loved my grandfather."

Luke frowned. "She said that?"

"Yes."

"If she had a secret passion for Quinnell, he definitely came in number two on her list. But it would explain a few things."

"Such as her desire to see your father marry my mother?"

Luke nodded. His gaze turned reflective for a few seconds, as if he were analyzing something or putting the pieces of a puzzle together in his mind. Then he smiled his slow, beguiling smile. "Katy, I don't want to talk about the past tonight."

"What do you want to talk about?"

"The future." He bent his head and kissed her throat. "I've spent the last three years living in no-man's-land. The worst of it was that I didn't even feel any desire to escape. And then you landed on my doorstep and started lecturing me about my responsibilities. You forced me out into the future again."

Katy giggled softly. "You were extremely annoyed, and I thought your dog was going to eat me alive."

Luke's eyes gleamed. "You're confused, Katy. I'm the one who's going to eat you alive." His hand moved down over her thigh, and his leg slid between her knees.

"Speaking of eating . . ." Katy murmured.

"Umm?" Luke was nibbling on her earlobe now.

"Did you leave something in the oven?"

Luke's head came up with a jerk. Something akin to panic flashed in his eyes. "Holy shit. The soufflé."

Katy collapsed in laughter as Luke leapt to his feet and raced into the kitchen. Zeke bounded after him, carrying his dish on the off chance that some other culinary disaster might end up in it.

Katy got up, still laughing, and straightened her clothes. Then she went into the kitchen. Luke, hands sheathed in plump black hot pads, was cautiously lifting the soufflé out of the oven.

"Don't even breathe," he whispered as he set it on top of the stove.

"Too late," Katy said. "It's already collapsing. Look, there it goes."

Luke gazed in outraged frustration as the golden dome of the soufflé began to sink. "Dalton swore that if I followed directions it wouldn't collapse. Look at that sucker. It's going to turn into a pancake."

"The good thing about soufflés, Luke, is that they taste the same whether or not they collapse."

"Bullshit. That does it. I'm going to fire Dalton first thing in the morning."

"You are not going to fire poor Benedict Dalton, so stop making threats and serve your dessert course." Katy smiled. "And while you're at it, you can tell me you love me."

Luke jerked his attention away from the collapsed soufflé long enough to meet her gaze. "I've really made a hash of this, haven't I? I love you, Katy."

"Good. I love you, too. Let's eat."

A long while later Luke felt Katy stir languidly beside him. They were lying in front of the fire, curled up on a quilt. Zeke had retired with dignity and his bowl to the kitchen, bored with human sexual conduct.

Katy's dress, bra, and pantyhose were hanging haphazardly over the back of a chair. All she had on was the black cotton shirt Luke had been wearing earlier. Luke thought she looked incredibly sexy in it.

Luke was wearing nothing at all. He savored the feel of Katy's leg sliding alongside his own. She was so soft, he thought. Sweet and gentle and soft. And she loved him. She was going to marry him.

He could hardly believe his luck.

He dared not believe his luck.

With an instinct that had been born in him three years ago when he stood staring at the smoking remains of a downed jet, he started looking for the dark side of his good fortune.

Katy yawned. "I suppose I should think about getting back to my own cottage. Matt will be home soon."

Luke glanced at his black steel watch. "You've got another hour or so. Katy, I want us to be married as soon as possible."

She turned in his arms. Her hair, backlit by the fire, glowed like the sun. "Oh, no, you don't. This is going to be my one and only wedding, and I'm going to do it up right."

"I don't care how you do it up so long as you do it up fast." He tangled his fingers in her fiery hair. "I mean it, Katy. I want to know you're mine as soon as possible."

She propped herself up on one elbow and looked down at him. The black shirt fell open, revealing the curve of one milk-white breast. Luke could just barely see the outline of her pink nipple.

"What's wrong, Luke?"

"Nothing." He reached inside the shirt and found the tantalizing nipple. It grew firm instantly at his touch. "I just don't want to wait any longer than absolutely necessary."

"I was thinking sometime in the fall, after Matt goes off to college," she said slowly.

"I was thinking sometime next week."

She tilted her head. "Luke, are you serious?"

"Yes."

"I can't possibly be ready that soon. There are so many things that have to be taken care of."

"Such as?"

"Where we'll live, for one thing. There isn't room for you to move in with Matt and me."

"Yes, there is. Matt has his room. We'll use yours. After he leaves we'll find a place of our own. I don't intend to live next door to Justine for the rest of my life."

She absorbed that. "Well, I suppose that might work. All the same, I feel strange rushing into marriage like this. I'm sure there are all sorts of other things that have to be considered."

"Name one."

"Pesto Presto," she said.

Luke caught her face urgently between his hands. "Marriage won't stop you from opening Pesto Presto."

"I know. It's just that there are so many things I have to do to get it up and running."

"You can do them after we're married, can't you?" Luke asked tightly.

Katy smiled. "Yes, I suppose I can." She

kissed him lightly.

Luke relaxed. Once he had her securely bound to him Pesto Presto would no longer seem like a rival. "Trust me." He eased her down onto her back. "I'll handle everything."

She smiled tremulously, her eyes glowing with love and laughter. "You're sure?"

"I'm sure. Just leave everything to me."

He moved his leg over hers, pinning her gently on the quilt. Then he bent his head to taste her again. He remembered how it had been that first night he had brought her back here after the dinner at Justine's.

He had blamed his sense of urgency on the fact that it had been a long time since he had held a woman in his arms. But he had known then, just as he knew now, that the need he felt to make himself a part of Katy went beyond the desire for sex.

He had once been convinced that Ariel was his natural mate. Perhaps she had been, in the sense that she had been the closest thing to a female version of himself he had ever encountered.

But Luke realized tonight that what he had found in Katy was something infinitely more precious. She was not a reflection of him, but his natural opposite. Day to his night, sunlight to his shadow, equal and opposite. Both necessary to form a complete whole.

That was how she made him feel, Luke thought. Complete and whole. With Katy he felt he could be more than just himself.

He reached down and found her softness. "You're getting wet already," he whispered against her breast. He moved his fingers on her, and she arched herself against his hand.

"Luke, I can't believe what you do to me. I feel so free when you hold me."

"You're the one who's unbelievable." He moved down her body until he was lying between her thighs. The exotic fragrance of her stirred all his senses. When he cupped her buttocks in his hands and tasted the essence of her, Katy cried out softly. Her fingers clenched in his hair.

Luke was hard with his own need. More than hard. His muscles were knotted and bunched with the effort it was taking to control himself. But he could not resist the temptation to watch Katy climax from this intimate vantage point. He bent her knees and pushed her thighs more widely apart. Deliberately he slid his thumbs into her, opening her gently.

Katy sucked in her breath. "Luke."

An electrical charge went through Luke. His name was a siren's call on her lips. He was her captive, and he did not care if she knew it. After all, she belonged to him just as surely as he belonged to her.

He kissed the swollen nubbin of female flesh nestled in the red curls. He rasped it lightly with his tongue until Katy was breathless and clinging to him. Her responsiveness made him feel both deeply awed and at the same time gloriously proud.

He would cherish her always, Luke promised himself. He would do his best to keep her safe. She was giving herself to him, and he would treasure the gift.

She was, after all, giving him a future.

When his hands were slick with her and she was clutching at him as if she would never let go, he opened her a little wider with his thumbs. Her tight passage contracted, and her wetness glistened on his fingers.

"Oh, God, Luke. *Luke.*"

He stretched her gently again, felt her tighten convulsively around his fingers. She twisted and cried out. And then she was shivering with her release.

Luke watched the passion in her face as long as he could, and then, unable to hold back any longer, he moved up the length of her body. He drove himself deep inside her pulsating warmth, drowning in her sweet fire until he was lost.

Until he was free.

Until he had found the other half of himself.

Luke waited until he had walked Katy home before he asked the question that hovered like a shadow in his mind. He took her in his arms on the front steps and studied her face in the porch light. She looked up at him, her eyes filled with sensual contentment. He wished he could take her back to his bed.

"Katy, you've spent the past few years looking out for Gilchrists."

"I've spent the past few years working for Justine," she corrected with a smile.

"It's been a lot more than a job, and you know it. There's something I've got to know." Luke took a firm grip on his courage. "You're not marrying me because you feel sorry for me or anything like that, are you?"

Her laughter was soft and sweet, and it touched his soul. "Good grief, no. I don't know where you got the idea that I'm some sort of guardian angel, but I can assure you I would never marry anyone just to keep my halo and wings."

He rested his forehead against hers. "I love you, you know."

"I know. And I love you," she whispered.

"Even though you are difficult, temperamental, and stubborn."

He smiled. "You love me even though I'm all those things?"

"Uh-huh. You see, I knew almost from the beginning that you were educable."

The sound of a car coming down the road put an end to any thoughts Luke might have had about seducing Katy again. Zeke wagged his tail, recognizing the familiar vehicle. Car lights flashed as Matt turned into the drive and parked in front of the cottage. A few seconds later the car door opened and closed.

Matt, dressed in jeans and a denim jacket, ambled toward the porch. "Hey, what are you two doing out here?" His eyes went from his sister's flushed face to Luke's steady gaze as he bent down to pat Zeke.

"I've just asked your sister to marry me," Luke said quietly. He realized he was suddenly coiled and ready for battle. Matt had been so certain Katy would turn him down. Luke was not sure how the boy would react when he found out she had accepted.

"Yeah? Well, great. That's great." Matt looked at Katy. "So what did you say?"

Katy smiled serenely. "I said yes."

Matt stared at her, obviously surprised. "You did?"

"Yes."

"But Katy, he's a Gilchrist," Matt said softly, his gaze flicking uneasily to Luke.

"Yes, I know. But he can cook."

Matt stared. Then he grinned. And then he was laughing. Katy joined him. She laughed so hard she had to wipe her eyes with the back of her hand.

Luke watched them both, aware that he was starting to grin, too. And suddenly he was laughing with them. The night was filled with the sound of their laughter. The world and his future seemed very bright and fresh and untarnished.

He had seized the happiness Katy was offering, Luke thought. He would never let go.

CHAPTER
TWENTY-ONE

Justine was waiting for Katy at the edge of the pool. Katy finished her lap and looked up, startled to see her standing there. Justine stood gazing down with bleak resignation in her green eyes.

"He is going to have his final vengeance after all," Justine said. Her voice rang with the hollow gloom of the prediction. "I know he is. He's just like his father. He will finish destroying my company, and then he'll leave you at the altar the same way his father left your mother."

"I don't think so, Justine."

Justine looked down at her. "Poor child. You have your grandfather's unrealistic approach to life. So optimistic. So naïve."

"I'm not a child," Katy said gently.

"I tried to save you," Justine whispered. "God knows I tried. It's fate. You are doomed to be the instrument of my final humiliation. I only wish you didn't have to suffer along with me."

"You aren't going to be humiliated at the church, Justine."

Justine paid no attention. "I suppose I have no right to chastise you for your naïveté. Lord knows I was filled with foolish hope myself when you finally persuaded Luke to take over the company. I, too, had my silly dreams."

"Your dreams weren't silly," Katy said. "Have some faith in them."

"I wish I could," Justine said, "but I dare not. I fear that Luke is only using you to punish me."

Katy hid a smile. "We won't really know for certain until we see if he shows up for the wedding, will we?"

"You think my fears are amusing now. But wait and see how you feel when you find yourself abandoned at the altar. I was there when it happened to your mother. I saw the grief and the shame in her eyes. I shall never forget it. Nor shall I ever forget the look on your grandfather's face when he turned to me that day."

Katy was horrified to see the tears start down Justine's cheeks. She hauled herself out of the pool and grabbed her robe. She quickly wrapped it around herself and then hugged Justine, offering what comfort she could.

It was difficult to console a Gilchrist bent on embracing the depths of melodrama, Katy reflected ruefully. But she did her best. After all, while Gilchrist emotions sometimes seemed overstated, there was no denying they were genuine. It was one of the reasons Katy had always found herself able to be sympathetic to the members of the coven.

"Calm yourself, Justine. It all happened a long time ago."

"I betrayed your grandfather that day," Justine said brokenly. "Not once, but twice. Not only was the wedding called off, but I was forced to call off the merger. In the end I gave him nothing. After all he had done for me I gave him nothing. *And I loved him.* How could I have betrayed him?"

"It's all right," Katy soothed. "Let the past go."

"How can I let it go? Thanks to my grandson, I am going to be forced to relive every minute of that awful day."

Eden and her mother took charge of the wedding preparations right from the start. After a few useless attempts to regain control of the situation, Katy surrendered. She soon found herself swept up into a frenzy of activity that included everything from ad-

507

dressing invitations to choosing a menu for the reception.

Liz gave her a book to read on the subject of the intricacies of the male brain.

"Every woman should read it before she gets married," Liz said.

"I need a book on the intricacies of the Gilchrist male brain, not just any old male brain," Katy complained.

"You already understand Gilchrists better than anyone else on the face of the earth," Liz assured her.

A few days after she had tried to comfort Justine in the conservatory Katy walked into her office and found Eden and Maureen hovering over Liz. Both Gilchrists were issuing orders in typical rapid-fire style. Liz, looking distinctly harried, was dutifully taking notes.

"We'll hold the wedding in Seattle, of course. That way it will be convenient for members of Gilchrist management and staff to attend. And Justine has a host of business acquaintances in the city that must be invited," Maureen said.

Eden nodded. "Yes, definitely Seattle. It also makes sense to hold the reception there. We'll use one of the restaurants."

"The Pacific Rim has banquet facilities," Maureen reminded her. "Make a note, Liz, to talk to the manager and chef there."

"Yes, Mrs. Gilchrist." Liz shot a beseeching glance at Katy.

"Good morning everyone," Katy said brightly, trying to break into the barrage of instructions.

Eden glanced over her shoulder, brows drawing together in concentration. "Oh, there you are, Katy. We're going to shop for a gown today. I've told Liz you'll be out of the office every day this week until we find the right one."

"I was just about to suggest they put you in black rather than the traditional white," Liz murmured. "So appropriate to a Gilchrist wedding, don't you think?"

In standard Gilchrist style, Maureen took the remark seriously. She eyed Katy critically. "No, I don't think black would suit Katy."

"Mother's right," Eden said. "I have nothing against the idea of going against tradition, of course, but black just isn't Katy's color."

Luke materialized in the doorway. "Whoever tries to put Katy in black will answer to me."

Liz sighed. "It was just a thought."

Katy grinned. "Don't worry. The groom will be wearing black."

Two days before the wedding Matt wandered into the living room, where Katy was poring over a new cookbook. She was examining an interesting recipe for a pasta salad featuring a pesto flavored with sun-dried tomatoes.

"You're sure you want to go through with this?" he asked quietly.

Katy did not look up from the list of ingredients she was studying. "I think it will work out very nicely for the Pesto Presto lineup. The sun-dried tomato flavor will add variety to the menu."

"Earth to Katy. I am not talking about a new recipe for Pesto Presto. I'm talking about your wedding. You really love the guy?"

Katy looked up and saw the concern in Matt's eyes. "Yes, Matt. I really love him."

Matt hesitated. "You don't think there's any chance Justine's right, do you? He wouldn't stand you up, would he?"

"No."

Matt looked relieved. "I don't think he would either. He's okay, you know?"

"I know."

"I like him. Even if he is a Gilchrist."

Katy smiled. "I'm glad."

"He said he'll take care of you. It's kind of a relief to know that he'll be around here after I leave for college. I was worrying about you being all alone. I knew you'd be busy with Pesto Presto and everything, but still . . ."

Katy put down the cookbook and got to her feet. She wrapped her arms around Matt and hugged him close. "I'm going to miss you very much, Matt."

"It's just college," he reminded her gruffly. "It's not like I'm going halfway around the world or anything."

Katy's eyes misted. "Yes, it is. And that's the way it should be. I want you to promise me you'll enjoy every minute of it."

Luke was up at dawn on the day of his wedding. He automatically glanced out the kitchen window as he made coffee. Katy's cottage was eerily quiet. Eden and Maureen had dragged her and her brother off to Seattle last night.

Hayden had driven Justine and Mrs. Igorson into the city also. They were all ensconced in a hotel that was convenient to the church and to the Pacific Rim.

Luke had stayed behind with Zeke. He was planning to leave for Seattle around eight. That would give him plenty of time to dress at Darren's apartment and drive to the church for the eleven o'clock service.

By noon Katy would be his. Luke felt a rush of satisfaction that filled him with a simmering energy. Nothing had ever felt so right in his life.

At seven-thirty Luke was too restless to hang around the cottage any longer. He tossed his black formal clothes into the backseat of the Jaguar and turned to Zeke.

"Come on, pal. You get one more run on the beach, and then I'm on my way. Matt will be here this evening to feed you."

Zeke picked up his dish and dashed ahead to the cliff path. He bounded eagerly down to the beach, leaving Luke to follow.

A few minutes later Luke came to a halt at the water's edge. A deep sense of uneasiness descended on him, wiping away the anticipation that had been flowing through his veins. He glanced down the beach and saw Zeke at the far end nosing around a tide pool.

Something was wrong.

Luke looked up at the cliff and saw nothing. There was no one around. No reason to be concerned. Everyone was safely in Seattle. He had talked to Katy just last night.

But Luke could not shake the feeling of impending doom. If Katy were here, he thought, she would laugh and tell him he was simply falling prey to another Gilchrist mood.

This feeling of wrongness was more than

just a mood, Luke realized. He had a sudden, urgent need to talk to Katy.

Determined to call her at the hotel before he started the drive to Seattle, Luke whistled for Zeke.

Zeke reluctantly picked up his dish and started trotting toward him from the far end of the beach. Luke did not wait. Zeke knew his way back to the cottage.

Luke climbed the cliff path, the sense of urgency stronger now. He started to walk toward the cottage and then broke into a loping run.

The man in the stocking mask was waiting just inside the front door of the cottage. He had a gun in his fist.

"Close the door," the man said in a rough, rasping voice. "I don't want to have to deal with the dog."

Luke ignored the gun as he slowly closed the door. He kept his gaze on the man's eyes. "What's this all about?"

"Relax, Gilchrist. You might as well sit down. We're both going to be here for a while."

"Is there a point to this?"

"The point is that you're going to miss your wedding."

"Why?" Luke asked softly.

"Isn't it obvious? When you fail to show

up at the church this morning your family is going to assume the worst. They'll figure you've finally had your revenge. Justine will never forgive you. The others will never trust you again. No one's going to give you a second chance. With any luck Gilchrist, Inc. will go down the tubes without you at the helm."

"What about Katy?" Luke asked. "Or don't you care about her feelings in all this, Atwood?"

The intruder went still for a moment. Then, with a shrug, he reached up and jerked off the stocking mask. "It doesn't matter if you know who I am," Atwood said. "You'll never be able to prove a thing. I'll see to it that there's no evidence I was here today. Who would believe you were kept away from your wedding by me?"

"I'll find you, Atwood. And when I do I'll crush you."

Atwood smiled wearily. "Maybe. Then again, maybe not. I've made arrangements. I'm going to disappear this afternoon. When I reappear it will be with a new name in a new city a long, long way from Seattle."

"It won't be the first time, will it? You've had practice using other identities, haven't you? Milo Nyle, for example."

Atwood's brows rose in mocking admiration. "Not bad. How did you figure that out?"

"It fit. You're out to punish Gilchrists, you're a born salesman, and you know your way around the investment business. Once I got to thinking about it I realized that con job you pulled on Darren had your finger-prints all over it. So did that deal you cooked up with Fraser Stanfield."

"I realized you were on to Stanfield when you fired him." Atwood's eyes slitted. "You're the one who cued Darren that he was being conned, aren't you?"

"Katy asked me to help him out of a jam," Luke said, watching Atwood intently, "so I did."

"Katy always was too soft for her own good. You probably won't believe it, but the truth is, I felt sorry for her back at the beginning."

"But what the hell, you had your plans, didn't you, Atwood? You were roaring ahead with your schemes to destroy Gilchrist, and Katy was just another road kill on the high-way that led toward your goal."

"I needed her as a way into the family circle," Atwood admitted. "I used her, but not nearly as badly as you did."

"What the hell's that supposed to mean?"

Atwood smiled coldly. "At least I didn't

drag her into an affair and then abandon her at the altar the way you're going to."

"Katy knows I wouldn't use her to punish Justine and the others."

"I doubt it. She's a woman. Any woman who's been left at the altar would be a fool to trust the man who abandoned her there. But it doesn't really matter what Katy thinks. The only thing that counts is what Justine believes. She'll never trust you with control of Gilchrist again. And without you the company will die."

"You're very sure of that."

"I know you Gilchrists. I know how you think." Atwood motioned with the gun. "Into the living room. We're going to sit down. I don't feel like spending the next couple of hours standing here in the hall."

There was a scratching sound at the front door. Zeke whined urgently.

"If that dog gets inside, I'll kill him," Atwood said. "Give me too much trouble and I might just put a bullet in you, too. It wouldn't bother me to cripple a Gilchrist."

Luke walked down the hall ahead of Atwood. The clock on the mantel read eight. By now he should have been in the car on his way to Seattle. He still had time, Luke reminded himself.

Not much, however.

★ ★ ★

Eden was fastening the tiny row of pearl buttons on the back of Katy's wedding dress when the door of the church anteroom opened without any warning. Darren stuck his head inside. He looked dark and dashing in his black tux and black bow tie. He also looked upset.

"You're not supposed to be in here." Liz waved him out of the room. "Go on, get out of here. It's bad luck or something."

"It's bad luck for the groom," Katy murmured. "And since when is a semiprofessional shrink worried about luck anyway?"

"You can't be too careful," Liz sniffed.

Eden glowered at Darren. "Go take care of Luke."

"That's just it. I can't," Darren said. "Luke isn't here."

"What on earth?" Maureen put down the bouquet she had been fussing with and stared at him. "Where is he?"

"That's the problem. I don't know. When he didn't show up at my apartment an hour ago I figured there had been a miscommunication. I thought maybe he'd driven straight here to the church. But I've checked. No one's seen him. There's no sign of his car."

"Did you call his cottage in Dragon Bay?" Eden demanded.

"Yeah. No answer." Darren looked at Katy. "Christ, you don't think he'd really do it, do you?"

"Abandon me at the altar?" Katy smiled reassuringly. "No. Don't worry, Darren, he'll show. Maybe he ran into traffic on the interstate."

Darren ran his fingers through his black hair and scowled. "He allowed for traffic problems. Luke always allows for that kind of thing."

"Oh, my God," Maureen whispered. "Don't tell Justine. Not yet, at any rate."

Eden looked stricken. "What are we going to do?"

"Finish getting me dressed," Katy said calmly. "I refuse to walk down the aisle with the back of this gown hanging open." She met Eden's stark gaze in the mirror. "Relax, Eden. He'll be here."

"Oh, my God," Maureen said again. "He's going to do it. Justine was right after all. He's set this whole thing up to punish the family. There's no telling what he's been doing to the company. He's probably made certain it's on the edge of bankruptcy."

"He'll be here," Katy said again. "Would someone please help me with this dress?"

The three Gilchrists looked at each other,

doom and disaster mirrored in their witchy eyes.

"Why do I have the feeling I'm about to diagnose my first case of mass hysteria?" Liz asked.

Zeke stood on the other side of the living room window and stared at Atwood through the glass. His gaze never wavered.

"Does he always carry that stupid dish around in his mouth?" Atwood asked irritably.

"Zeke never goes anywhere without his dish." Luke sprawled on the sofa and watched his captor.

Atwood had said he wanted to sit down, but he had been prowling the room, gun in hand, for the past thirty minutes. He was restless and clearly nervous. When Zeke had shown up on the other side of the window Atwood had nearly jumped out of his skin. He might have been at ease plotting blackmail or a clever financial trap in which to catch his victims, but schemes requiring guns were apparently new to him.

Atwood glanced at the clock. "Another hour and a half and it will all be over. How long do you think Justine will wait at the church hoping you'll show?"

"You really hate her, don't you?"

"I hate your whole frigging family, Gilchrist."

"Yeah, that figures. I know about your father."

Atwood paused in his pacing and swung around. The gun trembled in his hand. "What do you know about my father?"

"I looked up the records of the deal in which he lost his restaurant. I know he shot himself. You blame my family for his death, don't you?"

"Damn right." Atwood's eyes were filled with a corrosive bitterness. "Justine killed him when she closed down his restaurant. She might as well have pulled the trigger herself. And you know the worst of it?"

"Yes. I know the worst of it. She never even knew what had happened or who had suffered because of that deal," Luke said softly.

"He tried to get an appointment with her. Tried to talk to her. He couldn't get past her damn secretary." Atwood started pacing again. "She wouldn't even see him."

"I know."

"I was only twenty. I couldn't do anything at the time, but I swore I'd pay you Gilchrists back one day if it took me the rest of my life."

"You know something, Atwood? You're

not going to believe this, but I understand."

"Bullshit. You Gilchrists don't give a damn about anything except what you want. You don't care who gets in the way or who gets hurt."

"You're not any different, are you?"

Atwood's face contorted with fury. "I'm nothing like you. Do you hear me?"

"What about Katy? You used her a year ago to get at Eden, and today you're setting her up so that she'll get hurt right along with the others."

"Look, I'm sorry about Katy, okay? I had to use her last year. And it's a shame she's going to have to go through what's happening today. But that's the way it goes. I had no choice."

The rationale sounded all too familiar, Luke reflected. "Maybe that's what Justine would have said fifteen years ago if your father had asked her not to close down his restaurant. No choice. Just good business. You know how it is. These things happen."

"Stop it," Atwood snarled. He brought the nose of the gun up with a threatening motion. "You're all going to pay. One way or another, you're going to pay."

"Nothing will bring back your father."

"I know that, damn you. But at least I'll know that he was avenged. The only thing

Gilchrists care about is money, so that's how I'm going to hurt you. Financially. It's sort of a symbolic thing, you know?"

"I see."

Zeke whined and edged forward.

"Why is that dog watching us like that?" Atwood demanded.

"Who knows?" Luke answered softly.

At that instant Zeke tried to put his nose right up against the glass. His dish banged on the window.

The sound was like a gunshot in the small room. Atwood, already shivering with nerves and rage, whirled toward the window.

Luke came up off the sofa in a single motion. Atwood jerked back toward him, but it was too late. Luke kicked the gun out of his hand. It flew across the room, hit the wall, and skittered on the hardwood floor.

With an anguished yell of frustration and fury Atwood threw himself at Luke.

Luke sidestepped the charge and brought his hand down in a short, slashing chop that sent Atwood to the floor.

It was all over in an instant. Atwood groaned, tried to rise, and collapsed in a defeated heap.

Luke stood over him for a moment. Then he went across the room to pick up the gun. He took out the clip and saw that it was empty. Whatever else he was, Atwood was no killer.

Just a man trying to avenge a road kill.

Luke glanced at the clock on the mantel. He had a little time left. He went over to Atwood and hauled him to his feet. Atwood was dazed but not seriously hurt. Luke dropped him into a chair.

"Katy is always after me to deal with confrontations in a sensitive, nonviolent manner," Luke said. "I'm a slow learner, but I do try."

"Shit. What is this all about? Why don't you call the cops and get it over with?" Atwood leaned his head back in the chair and closed his eyes with an expression of final weariness.

"I haven't got time to call the cops," Luke said. "I've got to get to a wedding."

Atwood opened his eyes. "So?"

"So I've got maybe fifteen minutes before I run out of time altogether. Instead of you and me slugging this out like the tough, macho, hard-assed dudes we both know we are, why don't we just do what we do best?"

"What's that?"

"Let's make a deal," Luke said.

★ ★ ★

523

The bride's anteroom was filled with Gilchrists sunk in doom and gloom. With Liz's help, Katy was trying to put on the lacy little garter she was supposed to throw later, but it was difficult. There was very little space left in the room.

Hayden, looking like a depressed vampire, was taking up most of the area in front of the mirror. Maureen was sitting on the stool, twisting a black hankie in her hands in silent despair. Eden was moving restlessly back and forth across the tiny room. Darren was propping up a wall with his shoulder. He looked grim. The only one who was not present was Justine. She was in the family pew at the front of the church.

"Who's going to tell Justine?" Hayden asked in his darkest funereal tones.

"God, this is just like last time," Maureen whispered, her gaze anguished. "I can't believe Luke is doing this. You know, I had actually come to trust him. I bought the whole story. He had convinced me he meant to be part of this family. That he cared about us."

Eden shot Katy a sidelong glance. "I can't believe he'd do this to Katy."

"I'll kill him," Darren muttered for about the twentieth time. "He won't get away with this. Maybe he thinks he has a right to humiliate Justine, but he has no right to hurt Katy."

"He hasn't done anything yet. He's just a little late, that's all." Katy snapped the garter into place and lowered the voluminous skirts of her white gown. She straightened and faced the room full of black-clad Gilchrists. "The whole bunch of you look as if you're about to attend a funeral instead of a wedding."

Hayden gave her a pitying look. "He's not going to show, Katy."

"He'll show," she said softly. "And if he doesn't, he'll have a very good reason. One that doesn't involve his secretary." The thought of what that excuse might be was what was disturbing Katy. For an instant she had visions of Luke lying injured somewhere on the interstate. With a sick feeling in her stomach she wondered if she should start calling hospital emergency rooms.

Katy met Liz's eyes in the mirror. For once Liz was not enjoying the latest Gilchrist antics. Her thoughts were obviously running along the same lines as Katy's. "Shall I get the phone book?"

Katy hesitated. "No," she said quietly. "I'd know if something dreadful had happened to him. I'd feel it. He's all right. He's just late."

"Something dreadful *has* happened," Hayden muttered. "We're all financially doomed, and Lord only knows how Justine will take this."

"Has anyone told Matt yet?" Maureen asked. "That poor boy is going to be so hurt by this. He trusted Luke, too."

Darren ran a hand through his tousled hair. "I told Matt to wait out in front of the church. He's supposed to be watching for Luke."

"Oh, God, this is terrible. I just hope the shock doesn't make Justine collapse," Maureen said. "What are we going to tell her?"

Katy adjusted her veil one last time. "I'll handle Justine."

Hayden straightened his shoulders. "You've been handling her for the past nine years, Katy. You don't have to handle this. I'll do whatever needs to be done this time."

Katy smiled gently. "That's very kind of you, Hayden. But I'm afraid that if something has gone wrong, it's a whole lot more serious than Luke deciding to abandon me at the altar."

Eden scowled. "What are you saying? What could be more serious?"

"I'm saying that if Luke isn't here, it's because something terrible has happened to him. Nothing short of disaster would keep him away today. But frankly, I think he's just fine. He'll be here any minute. You'll see." She lowered the veil in front of her eyes.

A knock sounded on the anteroom door. "Hey, Katy," Matt called out. "It's time. Are you ready?"

"I'm ready." Katy plowed a way through the tangle of Gilchrists cluttering up her dressing room. She opened the door and found Matt on the other side. He was fussing anxiously with his bow tie.

"How do I look?" he asked. Then his eyes widened at the sight of his sister in her gown and veil. "Geez. Katy, you look like a princess or something."

"Thank you, Matt. You look pretty terrific, yourself."

Matt grinned. "Wait until you see Luke. He said there wasn't time to change."

There was a concerted gasp of astonishment from the crowd behind Katy.

"Luke is here?" Hayden demanded.

"Sure." Matt glanced at the rest of the Gilchrists. "Why aren't you guys where you're supposed to be? Darren, you're best man. You'd better hurry. The music is starting."

The Gilchrists looked at one another. And then an all-too-rare gleam of relief and happiness appeared in their emerald eyes.

Maureen led the way out the door, pausing to give Katy a brief, surprisingly affectionate little hug. Her eyes glittered with emotion. "You look lovely, Katy. Just lovely."

The others followed, each one stopping briefly to give Katy a quick embrace. When they were gone Matt held out his arm.

"Ready?" he asked.

"I'm ready." Katy glanced at Liz. "Ready?"

"Wouldn't miss it for the world. I've always wanted to be a bridesmaid." Liz picked up her bouquet.

"You're not gonna believe this," Matt said, his eyes full of laughter. "The photographer is having a fit."

"Gilchrists never do anything quietly or routinely," Katy said in cheerful resignation. "How bad is it?"

"Not bad. Just funny. You should have seen the look on Justine's face when she saw Luke. Boy, is she pissed. But I think she's also real happy."

"Let's get this over with." Katy took her brother's arm and started down the aisle.

Luke was waiting at the front of the crowded church, right where he was supposed to be. Katy blinked in astonishment at the sight of him. And then she nearly dissolved in laughter.

Luke was as disheveled as it was possible for any Gilchrist to appear. He had obviously used his fingers rather than a comb to rake his ebony hair into some semblance of order. Instead of his formal clothes he was wearing a pair of black jeans, a black pullover sweater, and low black boots that had not even been polished for the occasion. His sorcerer's eyes gleamed with green fire at the sight of Katy coming down the aisle.

Luke did not wait alone at the altar. Zeke, dish clamped between his jaws, sat proudly beside him. The dog's tail thumped happily when he saw Matt and Katy.

Most of the audience was grinning. The minister looked resolute. Justine was clearly annoyed, but her eyes, when they met Katy's, glowed with a deep joy.

The remainder of the Gilchrists were clearly too relieved that the whole thing was going to go off to express any displeasure over Luke's appearance or the presence of his dog.

Luke smiled as he took Katy's hand firmly in his own. "Sorry I'm a little late," he whispered. "I was unavoidably delayed by some unfinished business."

Justine finally cornered Luke an hour later,

just as he was about to lead Katy out onto the dance floor.

"I assume you have an excuse for showing up for your own wedding in a pair of jeans?" she said imperiously.

"Yes, ma'am." Luke's fingers tightened around Katy's.

"Well, then . . ." Justine lifted her chin. "What is it?"

"I don't know if you really want to hear it now," Luke said.

"I am not budging until I get the full story out of you."

Luke shrugged. "I had some business I had to finish up. I sold the Pacific Rim to Nate Atwood for one dollar."

"You *what?*" Justine stared at him in stunned disbelief.

"Don't worry. I bought it back again."

"For a dollar?"

"Not quite." He looked at Katy, aware of a deep sense of tender possessiveness. She was his at last. He could hardly wait to take her into his arms. "We settled on a price that was close to fair market value."

"Good heavens." Justine looked dazed. "I don't believe this. That would be in the neighborhood of several hundred thousand dollars. Why on earth would you do a thing like that?"

"Let's just say I was cleaning up after an old Gilchrist road kill."

Comprehension dawned in Justine's eyes. "You did this because of what happened fifteen years ago when I bought that property? Because we kicked Atwood's father out of the old building?"

"You've got it, Justine. From now on we don't do business that way. The Gilchrist guardian angel does not approve." Luke saw the love and laughter in Katy's eyes. He was the most fortunate of men, he thought. Life and the future had never looked more promising than they did at this moment.

"I don't believe this," Justine fumed. "It's insane. What an idiotic way to do business. You'll run Gilchrist, Inc. into bankruptcy with that approach."

"Not likely." Luke grinned at her. "I've got your talent for business, remember? Making money is the easy part. The last thing Gilchrist, Inc. is going to do is go broke. Don't worry, Justine. The next generation of Gilchrists won't have to learn how to cook either."

Justine eyed him closely. "You'll be staying on at the helm, then," she said with satisfaction.

"Looks like it." Luke smiled at her.

Justine seemed startled by his smile. Then

she, too, smiled. Tears glittered in her eyes for an instant, and then she started to laugh. The sound was so rare that everyone in the room turned around to look.

Katy looked up at Luke, her face radiant with love. "Welcome to the family, Luke."

Luke grinned. "Welcome to the family, angel."

He swung her into the first waltz and the brilliant, love-filled future that awaited them.